ASTROLABE

ASTROLABE

A NOVEL
BY
ELIAS RAHIMI

Copyright 2020 © Elias Rahimi

Published by Kontor Press LLC

All rights reserved. No part of this publication may be reproduced, distributed, or transmitted in any form or by any means, including photocopying, recording, or other electronic or mechanical methods, without the prior written permission of the publisher, except in the case of brief quotations embodied in critical reviews and certain other noncommercial uses permitted by copyright law.

Print ISBN: 978-1-7355169-1-2

Hardcover ISBN: 978-1-7355169-0-5

Ebook ISBN: 978-1-7355169-2-9

Any references to historical events, real people, or real places are used fictitiously. Names, characters, and places are products of the author's imagination.

Front Cover and Layout Design by Damonza.com

ACKNOWLEDGMENTS

My greatest gratitude goes to my editor, Valarie Valentine, who used her awesome skills to make my words shine. You did an incredible job Val! I appreciated your wisdom and encouragement all along the way.

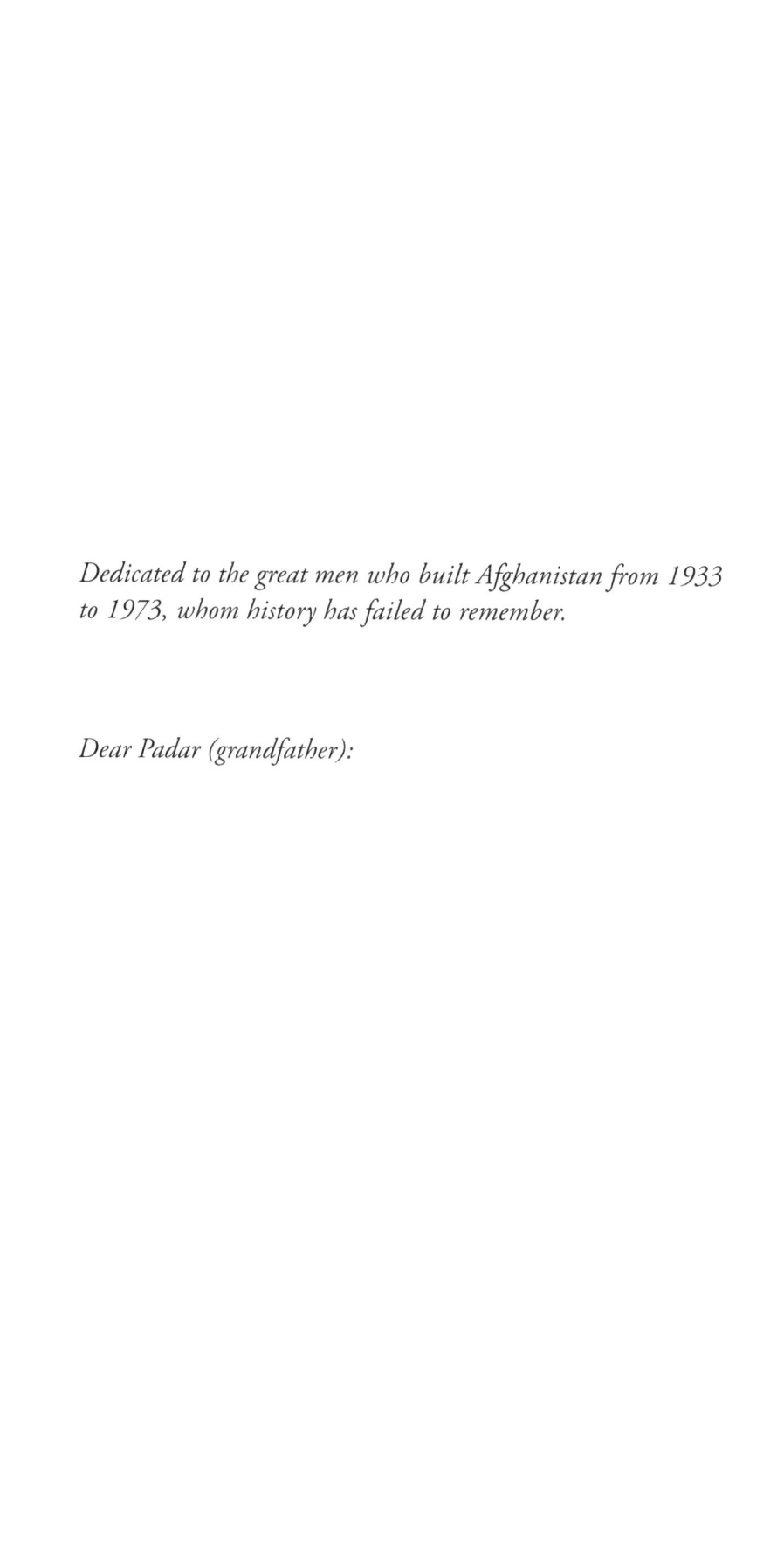

Dedicated to the great men who built Afghanistan from 1933 to 1973, whom history has failed to remember.

Dear Padar (grandfather):

CHAPTER ONE

Can this be his new creation? Hamza Awad wondered as he gazed around the auditorium. His nose picked up a delicate scent, a faint combination of rose and jasmine. He hadn't smelled it before, but remembered him talking about the aphrodisiac, ylang ylang, "The flower of the flowers," a scent meant to sexually arouse the female body. The fragrance blew through ducts ventilating the immense room like a mild, circular aromatic wind.

His gaze fell to the walls where the row of life-size erotic paintings of women anchored above queen-size beds on the outer perimeter. Every portrait was unlike the one before it. The acrylic paint amplified the essence of female beauty beyond anything he had seen before. The subjects were of different skin hues, from brown to white, olive to black, yellow-tan to chocolate, and they were all nude in variety of poses. He pondered the few commonalities that tied every subject to one another: every face was veiled, they all wore a cartwheel hat, round with a flat, wide brim, and they were all numbered.

The artist's paintbrush had repetitively stroke a linen drape from the brim of the painted cartwheel hat to hide the face and continued down to the shoulders. The paintings appeared the same theme from the neck up, but bodies painted on the canvas revealed the true intricacy of the artwork. Every curve, down to the veins and the light shimmering on the women's bodies, was captured by the artist. They reflected faceless modern day Renaissance paintings of nude women. Hamza's eyes trace the numbers, inked crisp on the bottom right of each canvas—one through thirty-three—a conundrum that he could not decipher.

This is far too elaborate for just sex. He lowered his gaze to the row of beds, stationed side by side underneath every portrait. The colors of the duvet were meticulously chosen to flow with the skin tone of the woman in the painting above the bed. It contrasted her body if she were to lie in it. The process was repeated for every portrait—all reflecting a flow of color coordination between canvas and the bed. The beds were also joined with two mahogany veneer nightstands, matching the backboard and the portrait frame.

His attention to detail seems to never fail.

At the center of the auditorium, the limestone floor dropped down to a marble Roman bath. Dark angel statue fountains placed on pedestals arose from water pointing their chiseled marble fingers skyward to the reddish mosaic ceiling. The array of directional spotlights illuminated the red gems, which were suspended from the ceiling and cast reflection of red spots over the pool. He redirected his eyes to the pointing direction of the angels. His gaze came to a standstill once he saw the bronze downward-pointing pentagram. It hung from four chains and faced every direction, like a three-dimensional star floating in midair.

As his gaze lingered on the pentagram, the echo of his words from a long time ago rang in his mind.

An angel advocating for empowerment of mankind through knowledge.

The ambience leaves him perplexed yet again, as it often is when it comes to understanding *his* work at first sight, but he knows he will have a thorough answer very soon. He knows him too well by now… and knows behind obscurities awaits a path that leads to his mastery.

"His Eminence is expecting you," said the butler, "this way, please."

Hamza followed the Butler down the corridor. The dark brown Breccia marble floor curved around the rear end of the building until it emerged in front of a chestnut door. The Butler gently opened the door to a private steamroom.

"Well, I presume you saw it on your way in."

Hamza fixed his vision across the steam that hovered like gray fog over the upper end of the in-ground granite pool where he sat, neck deep in hot water. His reddish, pale skin and shaved scalp had the glow tonight, as it often did whenever he saw him.

"I did, and I'm baffled."

"That, my dear… is the new Garden of Eden. One that will spring our life's work."

The new Garden of Eden, Hamza recalled the revelation, *he actually did it.*

"You've been gone so long," said Mabus, his expression was full of passion, one that bestowed certainty of his admiration.

Hamza took a few steps towards the pool. Now he could see his sharp blue eyes that shone like crystals in his red face. He was right. He had been gone for a long time, four years to the day. He took a second; he wanted to say what pleased him most.

"All the pieces have fallen into place… it will start soon!"

"Yes, it has…" he too had waited four years, yearning for this news, and his return. "Come…" he motioned to the space on his right.

Hamza reached over his head and began to unwind the black turban layer by layer until the long garment was fully unwrapped. He then took the white cap off his shaved scalp, folded it in half, and placed it on the top shelf of the wooden cabinet by the door. He followed by removing his tunic and trousers until his flesh was bare.

"I don't know if I could ever forgive myself for having you wear that outfit."

"I can…" Hamza shot back. "It's merely for a cause far greater than what man has seen."

"Yes, we are one step closer today. Soon the manmade religions will come under fire. At last, the human mind will be at ease."

Hamza couldn't help forming an obedient smile. He took one step into the in-ground pool. He then closed his eyes and opened his arms wide horizontally like Christ the Redeemer and muttered under his breath.

"I submit myself to my desires, my attributes; my natural abilities that has evolved through years of progressive consciousness in human race. I am my own God!"

He then opened his eyes, leaned forward and brought two hands full of water and splashed his face, seemingly his hands followed down around his long black beard penetrating it with warm water.

I am my own God!

He then walked across the shallow water and sat next to him. He felt rejuvenated when his body soaked. At last, the dust of the dry mountains seemed a distant past.

I haven't had this experience in a long time.

He had missed this lifestyle, of course. He'd been sleeping on the dirt floor of the mountains of Afghanistan for the last four years. At times, he lay restless in cold nights, wondering why. But then he always reassured himself with his task and the significance of his role.

"You've done a great service for the cause," said Mabus.

Hamza closed his eyes and leaned his head back, resting it on the pool's rim.

"You know…" Mabus continued, "I was thinking the other day."

Hamza's relishing moment was short-lived. He lifted his head and gave him his full attention.

"I thought of the advancements in the world militaries. Their satellites, planes, ships, machines, surveillance, tactics, and so on… yet they're still behind, in a way."

Hamza cocked his head, curious to hear what his mentor would say next.

"You see, despite all the money they spend enhancing their militaries, they still have not conquered the most essential weapon—the human mind. Surely, they have lots of weapons that could fire from miles away, but still, theirs could never be as efficient as ours."

Hamza understood what he was intending here. He cordially nodded. He knew his mentor was paying him deserving compliments.

"Our weapons," he continued, "can think for themselves, and go to the places commanded, no matter how long it takes or how far the journey. They could blend among any group of people, live in any country, and target anyone."

"That's extraordinary" Hamza chimed in agreement.

"Indeed. Now that's a true advancement! Seven billion people living on this planet, yet the world's elite thinks they could control masses and implement world order with their technology. I come to find that very wrong. And I believe sooner or later, they'll come to the same conclusion."

Hamza learned long ago not to interrupt Mabus whenever he became passionate about a certain subject. By far it was better to let him finish before saying something.

"You can't control masses from the outside. The control has to come from within!"

"I agree," Hamza chimed in.

"I read the other day," he went on, "that the U.S. military is attempting to build a robotic soldier; in fact, they already have a few prototypes, but they are full of glitches. In reality, they're a long ways from accomplishing such."

"And we're already there," said Hamza.

"Yes, all we do is tweak a few things in the religion and we get our robotic soldiers—ready to kill and blow themselves up!" he chuckled.

"So I presume you'll tell me about tonight?"

"Yes," Mabus revealed a proud expression. "As you were making progress on your end over in Afghanistan, I made quite a few here on this side."

Hamza fixed his eyes keenly on his smooth red face; he had an idea, but lacked the details. "Were you able to?"

Mabus's proud expression grew.

CHAPTER TWO

It's been over thirty years since the day when Hamza was among the attendees in Al-Azhar University's *Sahn*. It was there, under the blazing sun, in the university's courtyard, where a voice resounded through the thousand-year-old arching columns that surrounded the Sahn.

He still recalled that sense of admiration when his eyes first fell upon the young French speaker. It wasn't like looking at someone and admiring their courage for standing center stage, but rather, more like a fondness that grew inside him—one that magnetically pulled him towards the young speaker without a thorough understanding. A few moments later, he had found himself mesmerized in the front row, listening to the baritone voice speaking French. And it wasn't long until Hamza heard murmurs in the audience of such that were typical of this crowd: rejecting anything that defied their religious beliefs, which they'd held for over a century in this institution. A few minutes later, sounds of a scuffle came behind him, then thumping feet marching away from the assembly.

To his dismay, after seeing some of the crowd leaving, the young French scientist played oblivious to their notion and continued his presentation—patiently describing the evolution of organisms and how time changed their habitual traits. By that point, the French academic was versed in the odd behavior of his spectators, because it repeated whenever he was at the podium in this part of the world.

For the past couple of months, the scholar had traveled around North Africa for the mere purpose of bringing the idea of evolutional science to an area heavily saturated by strong Islamic beliefs. Intrigued by that revelation, he purposely had set his course on giving lectures to some of the most conservative Islamic institutions, Al-Azhar University among them. It was not uncommon for students and scholars to leave in the midst of his presentation as their personal religious beliefs pulled them away. Many years later, he would discover that his talk at this University would be one of his most fruitful lectures.

Hamza stole a few lingering gazes of the French academic when he stood in the center stage. He vividly remembers his tall figure towering over the podium as his hands gently rested on the wooden sideboards. His auburn hair was combed straight from right to the left, long enough where the strands covered his ear. But what enticed him the most were his bright-blue eyes, which accented his reddish face—a divergent. For the most part, in his life he had only seen men of his own origin—dark-brown complexion with dark eyes—that on its own made the Frenchman more appealing, almost exactly like the men Hamza saw in the films when he went to theaters in Cairo.

Those few lingering gazes propelled Hamza to believe that at any moment he would stop his presentation and point to him for his own thoughts about the matter he spoke of, a subject of which he knew little.

His admiration for the speaker was tarnished once his eyes fell on the round figure of Imam Nasser, the headmaster of the Islamic studies at Al-Azhar University. He stood on the far left of the stage, eyeing Hamza directly. Imam Nasser's reputation and influence was as large as his figure himself that orbited around the university and beyond. His stance and piercing eyes fixed on Hamza conveyed a demand: he was leaving this assembly and wanted Hamza, his protégé, to join him.

As Hamza rose from his seat, he caught a glimpse of the Frenchman's blue eyes connecting to his, but then they suddenly shifted away, along with his posture, now arching over the podium facing right, showing his back towards where Hamza was standing.

Ideals are far more superior than affection. The thought swirled in Hamza's mind.

A couple of hours later, Hamza found himself in the university's study hall. There, under the hall's high ceiling, arching columns supported by long posts, he was reminiscing about the scholar, and his words, the content of which had infuriated the audience to dissipate like a flock of ducks at the sound of a shotgun.

He remembered a year ago when an Arabic translation of Darwin's *On the Origin of Species* was found in possession of a student. As the story went, the faculty taunted the student for being an atheist and a lost soul. The harrassment ultimately resulted in departure of that student from the university. What happened at the Sahn was another illustration of that: the university prohibited science that was not parallel with the Islamic belief.

"You must've not liked my presentation."

Hamza looked up to the blue eyes peering down on him. They radiated a sense of calm as they perfectly contrasted his reddish skin.

"No… it's not that. I had to leave," he answered with agility.

"Did you leave on your own will?" he pressed with a mild grin.

"I left because it was time for me to leave."

His tall slender figure towered over Hamza, who sat stationary on a chair facing the dark old mahogany table. He started scribbling on a piece of paper.

"I came here to learn something," he said.

Hamza arched his eyebrows, waiting for him to say more.

"Oppression."

"Oppression," Hamza repeated.

"Yes… oppression in the context of human mind."

Hamza felt as if he had already spoken to the voice inside his head, one that advocated merit and questioned the hypocrisy of his daily life, a voice he ignored. He found the man's blue eyes connecting to his, as if he too was hearing the echo of that voice. Even in those few spoken words, Hamza felt himself being drawn to the Frenchman as if he was a floating object and *him* the gravitational pull.

He handed him the piece of paper and said, "If your curiosity exceeds beyond these walls, you can find me at this address." And with that, he turned around and walked away.

Hamza looked down at the piece of paper. It was the address to the Shepheard's Hotel in Cairo.

Hamza's life was predetermined. It was all decided when he was a boy. He was to become a man like his father, a man with unblemished faith in Islam, a man of honor. He too would become an *Ulama* by any means necessary. Then his mission would be: traveling the western countries to bring the message of Islam to the non-Muslim people, the *infidels*. Although, Hamza was reluctant deep down, on the surface he was following a map carved by his father. He was at the Al-Azhar University for one reason: to become his father.

"Someday, you too will achieve the gratification of elite Muslim clerics for your work," his father had said.

He dreamed of having the spine to stray from father's command, but such dreams appeared farfetched. He mostly needed it two weeks ago on that evening when his father walked into his room.

"You are going to marry Aabidah!" he demanded.

Hamza couldn't muster his courage under the stern look of his father's shrewd eyes. And just like with all the demands before, he was submissive, again.

Aabidah was the daughter of his father's friend and fellow alumni, Yosuf Tawab, who lived in Madinaty, a suburb of Cairo to the northeast. His father had already made the arrangement behind the curtain. Hamza was to marry her once he was a proper age. She was a woman that he came to know for the first time on their wedding night. Aside from having the right lineage to be a perfect wife, there was not much more he could see. On that night, for the first time in his life, he was in the presence of a woman, alone. Her gaze, one he couldn't fathom, was studying him as he locked the bedroom door. She waited on the edge of the bed, still in her white wedding gown.

Hamza had casually heard stories of such moments before. A few times from a loudmouth classmate who offered his demented fantasies, other times, from dirty street vendors shouting obscenities about what he'd do if he could get his hands on the other person's wife. Hearsay words about sex in the most derogatory fashion: that's all the sheltered twenty-two-year-old Hamza knew about intimacy. However, there were those visual aspects, and those were the times when he snuck away from his confined world to a movie theater in Cairo that played European romance movies.

At times, he was flabbergasted as he sat alone in the dark movie theater wondering about the actor and the actress being engaged in something that seemed so natural. But somehow, he managed to reassure himself of his good faith in Islam, and how adultery, even if presented in a film, didn't lure him. He thought of it as triumph over the desires of committing sinful acts—a mere pat on his own back.

Tonight, a woman who he only shared a few words with, was waiting for him. He felt numbness through his body when the thought of having sex with her appeared in his mind—an impartial feeling to the urges and sensation of sex—that's all he felt. He flicked the light switch and the room became pitch black.

Aabidah was anxious about the moment. She noticed in the gloom the sound of his footsteps walking around the bottom edge of the bed as he made his way to the other side. Then she heard the flap of bed sheets as they lifted up, and then the cracking of plywood beneath the bed when he lied down. He pulled the quilt over him.

He must be as nervous as I am, she thought.

She remembered her younger aunt Majida's words from a couple of days before. Majida was a married woman closest to her age. Aabidah's mother had tasked her younger sister to speak to her about the most taboo subject in a Muslim household.

"Remember: you don't have any desires of your own at this time." Majida had said under the sunlight when she was manicuring her nails. "Also… you shouldn't welcome his touch. Respond unfavorably!"

"Why not?" Aabidah had asked playfully.

Majida's eyes change from calm to stern.

"Because that's not the norm for a good Muslim girl!"

"Then what is the norm for a good Muslim girl?"

"You'd show tension and illustrate dissatisfaction, but yet allow him do as he must." Majida had said, "the portraying message: make him feel like even as pitiful as this act might be for you, you're going through it for him… do as you must! That should be his takeaway! You are going through it for him!"

She was not to relish any pleasure; if so, she'd be deemed unworthy and of a kind that wants or would enjoy sex with other men. That was the core message. With her aunt's words still echoing crisp in her mind, she gingerly lay down on the right side of the bed.

On the left side, Hamza was restless. His eyes were wide open in the stillness of the dark focused on the ceiling above. He sensed the motion of the bed as his bride shifted her weight beside him. He felt mist on his brow as his heartbeat started to pick up.

Does this feel natural? he thought.

He wanted to shake off the numbness. He knew somehow he had to become aroused. He needed something alluring to stimulate his mind. He brought himself to the scene of a French movie he saw a few weeks earlier. He pictured himself as the male actor hovering over the actress, their lips scarcely touching, her responding to his touch erratically. Then he pictured Aabidah in her place, and himself on top of her, the cornea on her brown eyes reflecting his face, her semi-round face reacting to his movement.

A repugnant feeling gushed through his nerves. He ignored it. He kept his mind set on picturing Aabidah in that scene: her breath cooling the sweat on his brow, the expressions of her face revealing uneasiness but calm, her breathing getting heavier with each movement. He felt himself aroused. This was the first time he encountered such feelings. He pressed on further to the memory of that scene in the film, the sensation overtaking him now.

And then it happened. Shame clawed its way in his mind and jolted him back to present. As he toned down his imagination, he was hit with a new fantasy. His mind had shifted his pleasure upside down. He found himself lying down on his back in the place of Aabidah. The French actor was on top. He was staring at his blue eyes and white face. He was aroused.

On the right side of the bed, Aabidah lay awake. It had been awhile now. The feeling of being rejected had dimly started to project. She felt pity because her aunt didn't prepare her for this. Her words only described a wife performing her duties to a husband in the noblest way. But there seemed nothing noble about her tonight. She would wake up the next morning untouched. She was not going to have those moments that her female cousins had, when they playfully shied away upon receiving instigating looks from other girls the day after their wedding nights. Aabidah knew that she would stand in disgrace, not having anything to reveal other than plain rejection on her face. Then arose the question of honor—her father's honor—that could only be mended if she betrayed her husband.

They will be looking for my blood tomorrow.

She could endure the rejection and might even hide it through her silence. But not having the bloodstain on the white bed sheets presented to the mother of her husband would ruin her father's name by proclaiming her not a virgin.

There was the dilemma. She pondered it: she does not posess her own identity. Not after tonight. She was either someone's daughter or someone's wife. She lay awake in the juncture between the two. After tonight, she was no longer titled the daughter of her father or wife to her husband, should he choose not to touch her. She was teetering in the dark, envisioning the worst thing that could happen to her: being disowned by her family, husbandless, ushering men to a room in the darkest alleys of the old town. That could be her fate if he decided to betray her to save his own honor—his impotence.

She felt her gaze upward in the dark, getting hazy as tears rolled from the corners of her eyes down to her earlobes. She was eighteen years old, and her life hung in the balance—scaled by the man next to her—a man she did not know.

Hamza heard the sniffle of his weeping wife beside him. He could not fathom the consequences of her telling the truth in the morning. He envisioned her sobbing, telling everyone that her husband prefers his own kind over her. Then the image of his father's Colt revolver loomed in his mind. He could even picture the gold-plated grip shining around his father's fingers as he stared at the barrel. That would be the prize for his infidelity and lust for men. The powerful Ulama, the man of faith and iron principle, was not going to be shaken. He would shoot his own son for the mere display of his own principles.

Aabidah heard him rolling to his left, facing her directly for the first time that night. Her earlier thoughts evaporated along with the tears. She was not rejected after all. It wasn't long after when she felt his right hand on top of her abdomen. His fingers felt long and masculine. This was the first time she had ever been touched by a man. She felt the sensation, but then her aunt's words rang in her mind again. This time the words came rightfully, so she played her dutiful part as instructed two days earlier.

He pushed his hand down until a knot around her trousers met his fingers.

"Take it down!" his deep voice hushed.

Her right hand touched the back of his hand as she moved to untie the knot. She fought the urge to rest her hand on top of his just for a touch. As she untied the knot, she grew confident that she'd have plenty of his touch. Again, dutifully she fell back to her aunt's words.

She brought herself to an upright position. Then with her two thumbs hooked around her trousers, she slid them down to her knees. She laid down anticipating what would happen next. She had done everything as commanded, and for that she was overjoyed, but played dissatisfaction.

Hamza knew this had to be done. It was for the good of his own survival, saving him from his father's wrath. He concentrated very hard in an attempt to find courage. A few seconds later, courage finally emerged. He slid his right hand further down between her thighs. Then with a good amount of force, he pushed two fingers inside her.

Aabidah wailed drastically. Instantly, the pain had paralyzed her for a few seconds. When she regained consciousness, she was gasping for air through her nostrils. In that moment all she could see was his large silhouette hunched over her. He had his left palm pressed against her mouth and the other hand penetrated inside her.

Hamza felt liquid gushing out and dripping down from his right palm. He became satisfied when his nose made the smell of blood.

"You are to tell everyone that everything between us is fine!" he commanded as he hovered over her. His tone was stern and his eyes keen in the dark staring at her face.

Aabidah held still, motionless. He extracted his fingers and took his large hand away from her mouth. Still, she remained motionless with the exception of gasping for breath. Shortly after, she gained full coherence. This event was beyond the borders of her young mind. As she lay there in a pool of blood and agonizing pain, her mind eased. The bed sheet would reflect her duty and maintain her father's honor. They'd act like a blanket covering her against all elements of indignity.

For the last couple of weeks, Aabidah had done exactly as she was instructed. *You are to tell everyone that everything between us is fine!*

❦

Hamza watched the image of the young Frenchman descend the stairs until he disappeared behind the study hall's dark wooden door.

Later that day he found himself walking the streets of Cairo, from the dirt alleyways to the crowded bazaars. The loud voices of shopkeepers haggling over cotton, the braying donkeys, the fumes from the vehicles—none of them caught his attention. He was somewhere in his own mind. He was mingled with the events that took place in the last couple weeks of his life. He walked immune to the commotion of the city, not heeding anything that was happening in his surroundings. All he heard were those words, still echoing in his mind.

If your curiosity exceeds beyond these walls, you can find me here.

A few hours after strolling through the busy streets, he found himself standing in front of a chestnut door on the fourth floor of the Shepheard's Hotel.

When the door swung open, he saw the young Frenchman appear with a towel wrapped around his waist. There were traces of water still running down his torso dripping on the floor. His reddish, pale face was shimmering under the light from the room's window.

"Come in," he said.

His blue eyes still radiated the calm he remembered earlier, and his face bore a cordial inward smile. Hamza hypnotically took a step forward into the room. This was the first time he experienced a dazed feeling of this magnitude. He seemed possessed by something he could not fathom.

"It's quite natural," the Frenchman declared after studying Hamza's body language. "We were born this way."

Hamza shot him a glance and then shied away, fixing his gaze to the window.

"You should've stayed longer in my presentation. I spoke of the gay genes on the X chromosomes."

Hamza seemed oblivious to his words. He has never heard nor had read anything so compromising. The only imminent thing was the mesmerizing feeling that rushed through his body when the Frenchman stepped behind him and placed his hands around his hips.

"Genetically, we are an exception to the rule of natural selection. I call it: special selection. You shall see someday."

With the warmth of his body behind him, Hamza searched for qualms pulling him away from the moment, but there was none. Everything seemed like pieces falling into place, ones that he searched for but never found. At that moment, all the missing pieces of his life were found and they fit perfectly to their preordained place within the mosaic.

He closed his eyes and submitted to the rushing desire. Then he leaned back, partially distributing his weight on his newfound lover.

Aabidah lay awake that night. She was pondering the whereabouts of her husband who was missing from her bed. A husband would be an embellishment. He was merely a platonic bedmate for the last couple of weeks. Platonic was satisfactory for now, but then a time would come when she'd be expected to produce offspring. If this trend continued, she'd have to conjure a way to avoid those certain questions. For now, she knows time is on her side. But three months from now, that would not be the case, when prying eyes would fall on her flat belly, then rise up to scrutinize her face for answers.

"You are a scientist with profound knowledge in human genetics, yet you are interested in learning about oppression. They seem too far apart from one another, if you ask me."

He reached his arm over Hamza's body and grabbed his forearm. Then he placed himself directly behind him. They were both laying nude on their left side, their flesh pressed and tied to one another.

"Yes, maybe…" he rested his left cheek on Hamza's right temple, "you see… human genetics is substantive, thus it could be changed. Someday we will have the power to alter our own genetic destiny."

"So, how does that correlate with oppression? You said you came here to learn." Hamza asked in a solemn tone.

"It doesn't. They're two different entities," he gave a long sigh as if there was more to say. Hamza waited. He continued, "you see, I've been traveling the world in the past couple of years as a scientist. I'm merely bringing new proven ideas that negate human life as it stands today. Somehow, everywhere in a different fashion of course, people shut the door in my face. There is absolutely no room to even nudge their centuries-old ideals."

"And what would be so scary to people where they wouldn't listen to a scientist?"

He tightened his grip around Hamza and said, "Evolution."

Hamza loosened his grip and shifted his body to face him directly.

"Yes, it defies religious beliefs that has kept people in order for centuries. The aquatic ape was never mentioned in any of the their books!"

After hearing the word "religion," Hamza jolted from his ecstatic state back to grim reality. The image of this act loomed in his mind. For an instant, he pictured his peers knowing about this infidelity he had just committed. *Engaged in a homosexual act with a foreign man.*

Fear cooled Hamza's flesh. He could not even fathom the consequences if anyone was to find out. He felt aggravated with himself for not thinking about this thoroughly before arriving in this hotel room. He had given in to his curiosity, which later led to urging desires. And there he was, in that moment, lying down next to this foreign man and embracing his touch that brought him the ultimate pleasure—one he never felt in the presence of Aabidah.

"You seem distressed," the Frenchman said as he studied Hamza's face.

Hamza shifted his eyes away from him and focused on the ceiling. He was searching for words but none came easy. He thought about his life going forward from here on out, but no future was clear in that moment. He was in a spiral, a haze, spinning, and couldn't see what he was going to do; he simply did not know. Then it dawned on him.

"There is no place for me here. Not anymore," he felt his eyes welling up with tears.

"There never was a place for you here to begin with." The Frenchman said as he gently kissed Hamza's forehead, then soothingly ran his fingers over his face—feeling his square jawline, his dimpled chin—then he flipped his hand and felt his cheek. He noticed the outline of a full beard, his straight nose, and his deep set of brown eyes. He thought Hamza's features flowed perfectly with his light brown skin.

The young Frenchman did not believe in love. Whenever the subject of love arose, he thought of it as conditioning over time. He had convinced himself to hold a scientist's position on such matters and reject any emotional notions affiliated with love. But in that moment, gazing at this young Arab man's face, something lured him to go forward.

His ecstatic demeanor became stern, and with a tone filled with excitement, he said, "I want you to come with me in this journey."

※

For the past couple of weeks, Aabidah saw her husband less than a few hours. She pondered questioning him on his whereabouts. But then she felt relief when he told her that he was out seeking guidance in the ways of becoming a proper husband and needed the time to implement the changes that he wanted to bring upon himself. He told her that he sought the counsel of an Imam who was widely known for helping men in their marriages. She refused to question the content of his statement, because after all, it offered the promise that she so desperately wanted.

She took her place next him on their bed. Astonished by renewed hope, she felt her heartbeat rising.

Soon he will perform the husbandly duties, she thought.

It has been more than a month now since the night of her wedding.

Her aunt's words had faded through the agony of lingering days considering her circumstances.

To hell with what she said. I cannot push him away... not when he is so fragile like this. I must keep him wanting it and coming back for more!

She felt the adrenaline pumping through her veins. She wanted to please him. *It's a good feeling.* She thought about the apples that she shared with him earlier.

"The Imam blessed these for us," he had told her.

The yellow one was for him, and the red one for her. She devoured the red apple and he had the yellow one as they sat side by side on the edge of the bed, gazing in each other's eyes. She was struck with hope to the extent that she chose not to question the bitter taste of almond in the apple.

Why damper the moment, she thought. This was the first time they passionately shared something. She turned her thoughts to savor the moment rather than the bitter apple.

Soon after, she was lying down. As she closed her eyes for a second, in a glimpse, she saw Hamza wearing a long tunic with matching white trousers, sitting on the steps of their courtyard stairs. He was calling for the mischief to stop. He seemed older. In the center of the yard—a boy, school age—was running around the well's cement ring. His tunic was half wet and his trousers glazed in mud around the knees. There was also a little girl, a toddler, frantically chasing the boy with a watering can. Her face, a mirror reflection of her young self, revealed agitation as her short strides couldn't keep up to her older brother. The girl saw Aabidah and received the most assuring look, one that's only bestowed by a mother's love. Her face became calm, and her strides became faster.

It's a vision of the future. She felt the jolt of pain in her stomach. She felt sleepy, but yet not ready to let go of what she was seeing.

I want to see their faces again; they're coming around the well now.

She honed her mind on the appearance of the little girl as she made her way around. This time, her face was a blur. A long second later, the blur cleared. Now she was gazing at a child's face tormented by horror.

Aabidah snapped from the vision. She pinned her elbows and forearms flat on the bed and hoisted herself up.

This is not a vision... I'm hallucinating!

Then, she felt her throat burning as if it was torched. *Water.* She tried to speak, but she couldn't. Her nervous system was already shut down and blocked muscle movement. She plummeted from her hoisted position when her elbows went numb. And then, in the last seconds of her consciousness, she was drawn into history repeating itself from her wedding night. She saw the monster's large silhouette as he had his large palm under her chin—pushing her jaw upward—and the other palm pressed at the back of her head. His hands acted like a vise, pressing her mouth shut.

Aabidah saw deceit and treachery in her last gasp of this world. Then everything went pitch black.

༄

Earlier that day, Hamza stood in the corner of the hotel suite that housed their love affair for the last couple of weeks. He went to his house for short periods of time whenever he needed a change of clothes and other personal items, but then swiftly he was back. They predominantly ordered room service and feasted inside the room. As they sat in the room in the long nights and lingering days, the Frenchman told Hamza about the course of his life and everything he had done up to that point. Most importantly, he spoke of his cause, where he sought to end the imprisonment of the mind.

Humans should be free of imposing beliefs that have plagued the mind. The time has emerged for a new beginning, where man will thrive through science and facts.

"Make sure you close the mouth shut after she takes her last breaths. This is crucial, because if the corpse's mouth is left open, traces of potassium cyanide could be visible on the tongue and mouth," The Frenchman said.

"And when would I know she'll be taking the last breath?"

"It's right after the hallucination phase."

Hamza produced a confused look.

"I take it that you haven't heard stories of poison causing hallucination?" he said with a smirk.

"It's been done throughout history. The American Indian tribes of Huichol people consume a poisoning cactus, peyote, to see visions."

Hamza shook his head.

"After eating the peyote buttons," he continued, "they start vomiting, and then the hallucination phase begins, which lead them to see whatever it was. Also, in the tropical areas people used psilocybin mushrooms to achieve the same thing."

Hamza watched him produce a scalpel from the inner pocket of his briefcase. He then walked over to the fruit basket, placed by the hotel's hospitality maid earlier that morning on the room's table, and grabbed a red apple.

"An apple?" Hamza shot out.

"Not just that…" he sharpened his eyes on the apple, "the forbidden fruit!"

"The forbidden fruit?" Hamza repeated in a baffled tone.

He hoisted the apple in midair and started reciting with a loud voice, as if he was a preacher given a sermon to a crowd.

"And the Lord God commanded the man, saying, Of every tree of the garden thou mayest freely eat: But of the tree of the knowledge of good and evil, thou shalt not eat of it: for in the day that thou eatest thereof, thou shalt surely die. Genesis 2:16."

He placed the scalpel on the apple's stem and meticulously started carving, "you know, there is an art in doing this," he shot Hamza a confident look.

From a distance, Hamza saw the inner perimeter of the apple coming out like a coil while the peel and the shape remained intact. Then with his thumb and index finger, he pulled the coiled carving from the end and stretched his arm towards the ceiling. He playfully opened his mouth and slowly lowered the rings in it.

"An apple a day keeps the doctor away!" he said teasingly, taunting Hamza with the cliché.

Hamza waited motionless in anticipation of what he'd do next.

"What heals me destroys another," he said. "If we lived in Abraham's time, when human sacrifice was considered a good omen, this would've been exactly that. But, today in our time, this is 'special selection;' we human beings have progressed in the methods of our sacrifice."

He then placed his right hand into his pocket and produced a poly bag. He sliced the top with the scalpel and carefully dispensed the white powder on the stump. Then with his meticulously skilled hand, he used the scalpel to spread the cyanide around the inside perimeter of the apple. After that, he pushed the stump back to its place.

"Here," he gave the apple to Hamza. "Can you even see this apple was tampered with?"

Hamza tried to grasp what just happened in front of him. He held up the apple for a better view, and he still couldn't tell or see any unnatural blemishes on the fruit. Then across the room, he noticed the Frenchman's calm blue eyes took on a piercing quality. Hamza had noticed the trait revealed when he spoke of something substantial in the last couple of weeks of being with him. So when Hamza met his piercing gaze, he knew that something related to his belief was about to flourish. And then, there it was.

"All Abrahamic religions start with Adam and Eve in the Garden of Eden. And then, as the story goes, they were punished for eating fruit from the tree of knowledge of good and evil. And then they were expelled from the garden so they couldn't eat from the second tree: the tree of eternal life. What the religions fail to admit to this day is that there was an angel advocating for the empowerment of mankind through knowledge. When God returned, he asked Adam why he ate from the tree of knowledge of good and evil. His voice must've been shatteringly loud. Adam finally came out of hiding and pointed to his wife, Eve, for making him eat the apple. Now, God was mad, so he kicked Adam and Eve out of the garden, because he sure as hell does not want the two of them to be eating off the other tree, the tree of eternal life, and sticking around forever. As a bonus, God kicked out the angel, too, and deemed him evil—all for crushing God's ego!

"Now, there it is, ladies and gentleman! That is the basis of humanity. A story of such among a whole bunch of others has a snowball effect throughout history and brought us to the present moment. Stories such as this have prohibited the thrive of human achievement here on earth. They have punished men, women, and children on ideological beliefs based on which book or which story they subscribe to. They have murdered and alienated people for more than two centuries! And this will continue until someone stands up to say, enough! And by making a statement of enough, that person needs to form and build a movement to abolish the scripture and the believers who have tormented this world for two thousand years!"

Up until two weeks ago, Hamza had lived his twenty-two years of life behind a mask of social obedience. He was obliged to accept his displacement because of fear. The fear of being taunted or put to shame for going against the grain of his society for being gay, in that society he would be deemed the work of devil. And of course, his father would gladly serve him an imminent death. Even if he didn't do it himself, he would most likely have one of his devoted students do it for him once he found out from Aabidah about his homosexual lover, which Hamza thought would be inevitable.

The Frenchman had convinced Hamza that being gay was merely a genetic trait rather than a personal preference. He said, "Had those self-righteous bigots accepted science instead of their scripture, it would have made their societies accept all human beings. But why would they? The gay population is less than three percent. Why blemish religion for such a small amount of people? Oppression would be more suitable."

"There is that word again," said Hamza. "Oppression."

"Yes, I saw that in your eyes on first glance, when you were sitting on the front row." His blond-haired and blue-eyed lover wrapped his arms around him and placed a gentle kiss on his right cheek. "I knew the resonance of that word would bring you to me. You are free now… we are free! Together, we will abolish the oppressors."

One thing was clear to Hamza. He found a place in his company. He didn't feel shame nor fear when he was with him. In a life where he had no stake of his own, the Frenchman showed him purpose. He took Hamza in through the depth of his ideals and the calling of his cause. He said, "It was most prudent to humanity," and within that cause, he had given him a purpose. Hamza had accepted, willingly knowing that he was going to follow this man wherever he went. After weeks of mental thriving and lust, their bond was concrete.

"This apple resembles the dawning of our cause," said the Frenchman.

Hamza left the hotel room that evening carrying the first plot of the cause. He had two apples, one red with potassium cyanide, and a regular yellow for his own consumption.

On the way to his house, he thought of Genesis 2:16.

The abolishment of scripture starts with the same fruit. An apple. Poetic justice.

CHAPTER THREE

PRESENT DAY: Earlier in the day, a Gulfstream G550 landed in Islamabad International Airport, Pakistan. The privet jet arrived there to pick up an Arab businessman who came to Pakistan three days earlier to purchase dry goods.

The man is a major purchaser. He arrives in Pakistan on a regular basis, two to three times a year. He normally travels from Islamabad to Peshawar—which is the hub for dry goods in Pakistan—by car to keep a low profile during his business encounters. He has advised the Pakistani authorities that he feels comfortable conducting business in Peshawar in an incognito fashion. Peshawar, a Pashtun providence of Pakistan, has been known for kidnapping and murders of foreign businessmen in the past. That among the other reasons compels him to tone down his extravagant appearance so he could blend into the impoverished city. Mr. Awad was a prominent purchaser; therefore, the Pakistani authorities cooperated with his demands and granted him certain special privileges as a token of their hospitality. One of those privileges was complete sovereignty from Pakistani customs.

Normally, when his plane lands in Islamabad, a customs superior officer is waiting on the tarmac. There, he stood and watched the private jet's door drop open from its sealed position. As Mr. Awad emerged from the plane, the officer would open his right hand, strike it flat against his chest, and bow.

"*As-salaam Alaikum*, Sheikh Hamza," he would say in a submissive tone. After a few moments of small talk about the Sheikh's flight, the officer would reach out and open the rear door of an awaiting vehicle. The vehicle would then approach the airport gate, where a guard would swiftly start pulling on a chain. The chain would spin a metal pulley causing the massive fence-gate to move from the path of the Sheikh's Toyota Land Cruiser. In return for the kindness, the airport officers received a decent amount of bribes in the form of gifts, which they happily accepted and looked forward to celebrate his next arrival.

Today, the guard had received the command from his superior officer about the Sheikh's departure, and he was instructed in the usual protocol. "Let his vehicle pass without inspection!"

The white Land Cruiser arrived at the gate. As instructed, the guard opened the gate without looking intently inside the vehicle. As the vehicle drove off towards the private jet, the guard caught a glimpse of the Sheikh through the tinted windows—a man with a long black beard in the backseat. The guard saw the Land Cruiser going and making a circle around the lone plane on the tarmac, and then coming to a halt on the other side where the plane's fuselage door was, away from the guard's view.

Unusual, thought the guard.

Normally, the fuselage door faced the guards, but today the nose of the plane was facing north, so the left side was not in view. It wasn't long until the Land Cruiser returned to the gate. The guard automatically opened the gate for the departure of the Sheikh's driver.

The guard saw the Land Cruiser re-enter at the gate; it had been fifteen minutes since it left. The rear passenger window rolled down.

"I forgot your gift, my brother," the grinning face of Sheikh Hamza appeared in the backseat. "I had to go back to get it for you."

He held out a box in his right hand. On top of the box rested his passport. The guard smiled and bowed. The puzzle of seeing the Sheikh twice in a matter of fifteen minutes vanished when he came to know what would be in the box. He had already received the rubber customs exit-stamp that day from his superior officer. He gladly used it to stamp the Sheikh's passport and handed it back. The guard opened the box. He was stunned to see three crisp hundred-dollar bills lurking in a pile of green raisins. As the Land Cruiser drove off to the private jet, he was thrilled to know the Sheikh had paid him the equivalent of his one-year's salary.

Inside the plane, Hamza reclined the seat. His back felt sore from sleeping on the uneven floor. His skin was sunburned and dry. But he was glad to know that he wouldn't be back to this forsaken place again. He closed his eyes and relished the moment.

Hamza opened his eyes and saw himself walking into the cabin and then taking the seat on the otherside of the aisle. He looked much better than *him*. His skin was not sun-struck like his. It was moist and tan, with far fewer creases around the corner of the eyes. His long black beard was nicely trimmed. His trousers and tunic lacked any specks of dirt and were perfectly pressed. His hands resembled his face, nice and smooth without any calluses, as they were vividly present in *his* hands.

He recalled what his mentor had said: *"The deception has to be flawless."* A slight inward smile formed around his lips as the Rolls-Royce BR710 turbofan engines came to life outside the cabin.

The captain radioed the tower and declared the flight plan to Abu Dhabi International Airport. A few minutes later, the G550 was ascending in the air.

⁂

Hamza never got remarried after the unfortunate death of his wife Aabidah, who he dearly loved and was heartbroken over her sudden departure from this world at a very young age. He went hysterical after the burial services and ended up locking himself in a room for forty days, mourning her in solitude. It was then in his confinement when he received a calling from God. He commanded him to follow the true path of Islam and enlighten all the souls he encountered. That was his portrayal. As for his true intent, he kept that a secret.

He finished Al-Azhar University and became an Ulama—emphasis on Islamic law. A couple of years after his graduation, his father used his connections to secure him a position in Al-Azhar University teaching Islamic law.

A few years into his teaching, Hamza changed his course's curriculum to the extreme views of radical Islam. That instantly drew skepticism from his peers in the university, who saw him as pushing his own hard-line interpretation of the religion. His father protested his extreme views as well and pleaded with him to reconsider, but that did not alter his views. In September of 1990, the university panel took a unanimous vote and expelled him. Their concession was that Hamza's views tainted the image of Islam as the religion of peace, and therefore he should not be allowed to teach in Al-Azhar University or any other scholarly institutes of Egypt.

He acted baffled by that decision, yet he embraced it as a pivotal move for himself. Deep down, he knew that this was all part of the plan, from the poisoning of his wife all the way to changing to radical views.

The Soviet invasion of Afghanistan had ended the year before. Now, there were thousands of remaining Afghan-Arabs returning from the war in Afghanistan, making their way back to their homes within the Gulf States. He sought sanctuary among them, knowing that among them he could rise to his destined place. His conclusion remained: *if they have the faith and the determining will to travel to a foreign land to fight in what they deem a holy war, then they are ready to go to the ends of the earth for that faith. One could adjust their faith and claim their power.*

He remembered his mentor telling him in that hotel room in Cairo some years back, "God's will becomes man's power on earth."

Shortly after his expulsion, he left Cairo and went to Khartoum, Sudan. There, in a country torn by a civil war, he established his place, and above all, his plan. He remained in the shadows of other extremist movements. Unlike the conventional funding of other terrorist organizations that cascaded from Saudi Arabia, his funding came from a French billionaire in the form of diamonds, which he liquidated in the Jebel Ali Free Zone of the United Arab Emirates. Then, with the untraceable cash in hand, he started building a coalition on the principles of his own ideologies, which held as the centerpiece hate towards any *Kafir*, a non-Muslim person or state.

He was artfully meticulous about his leadership role, with a natural way of conquering one's hesitations. He was extremely tall in comparison to an average Arab, towering over six-foot-three inches, with a well-built upper body and slender waist. He spoke with a deep voice, soft and cordial. His sharp brown eyes sent a soothing ray of hope to the observer whenever he spoke. His most potent characteristic was his words, which came crisp and convincing. He saw an interesting time ahead. Thousands of returning Afghan-Arabs needed a new purpose now.

They are worriers, he thought. *And every worrier must be given a purpose to carry out the rage in his blood.*

He used his resources, including his superb intellect, to court the leaders of the extremist movements for the mere amplification of their cause, the proclaimed jihad against the infidels. Soon after, his ideals were implemented within the extremist movements, like water penetrating the dirt and turning it into mud.

Although he was massively engaged in politics of extremists, the irony of it remained, to all their dismay. He was never part of any organizations, nor did he ever want to be credited for any of his work. He was the modern day phantom, emerged from the shadow and dissolved within the same shadow, but yet he left the terrorist movements with enlightenment—the darkest of all—with hate at its nucleus. Unlike the other leaders of terrorist movements who rose to stardom amongst their believers and followers, he never existed.

To his peers and family members in Cairo, he remained a businessman living in Abu Dhabi. He had remarried a woman name Jinna and had three children: two teenage boys, and an eight-year-old daughter. Through his postcards, letters, and phone calls to his extended family members, Hamza convinced everyone from his past that he had left his bold views of radical Islam from the days of the Al-Azhar University behind. Now he was a family man only looking out for the best interests of his children and living lavishly.

After his expulsion from the Al-Azhar University, which in theory left him devastated, he made a vow to never return to Egypt. In 1990, he moved to Abu Dhabi and soonafter started an import and export business. The bulk of his business was the importing of dry fruits and nuts from Pakistan to the Gulf countries. Later he managed to expand to the European and U.S. markets of dry goods as well. Within the span of twenty years, Hamza Awad became a major player in the dry goods industry. His enterprise won numerous praises by various organizations that rank global companies. And behind the scenes, he was cherished for his libertarian views. He was one of the few Middle Eastern tycoons who actively donated to the most progressive causes in Europe as well as the United States. He traveled the world extensively in a private jet. He would set out to North Africa, South Africa, Europe, North America, and Asia to check on his company and his satellite offices. He was known to have a very hands-on approach in his business role.

&

The air traffic controller in Abu Dhabi International airport saw the G550 taxiing off the runway to its designated drop-off point where a two-tone silver and black Rolls-Royce Phantom waited on the tarmac. The captain had requested a refuel truck to be ready upon their arrival. The charter plane was going to deplane its only passenger, then refuel and take off immediately.

A few moments later, the fuel truck operator saw the G550 parked on the tarmac and next to it the two-tone Rolls. Although there are plenty of G550 private jets that come and go from this airport, what sets Sheikh Hamza Awad's plane apart is the two-tone Rolls-Royce Phantom, which the operator instantly recognized.

Inside the cabin, Hamza saw himself, the presumed Sheikh Awad, a businessman, standing to leave the plane. They never share any words. He simply smiled at him and then walked down to the tarmac to his awaiting car.

The creation of a decoy took place in September of 1990 as Hamza was making his way to Khartoum while Iman Efhad was undergoing plastic surgery. Efhad was a lone blacksmith who moved to Cairo from the countryside a couple of months earlier. He had Hamza's features, and his exact unusual height—close enough to pass for a biological twin. He was given a choice. And that choice was: destroy his own identity and become someone else. In return, he would receive an immense amount of money and counsel to become a successful businessman. And he would live that life without any legal or social blemish. The only condition: he was to be present whenever he was demanded.

Efhad did not know anything beyond that… it was a vital precaution for a future lie-detector test. Efhad accepted the offer, and proceeded with surgery. They changed some minute details around his cheeks and jawbone, and with it, on September of 1990, all proof of his existence were burned and erased. After the surgery, he emerged as Sheikh Hamza Awad. He was sent to Abu Dhabi, where he was funded to start an import and export business, which was the perfect line of work for a traveling decoy. He made the real Hamza Awad become invisible in the world. A phantom. But yet, if it was necessary for him to travel somewhere, he could travel as himself—a legitimate businessman, and have proper identification and proof for all the ports. The most important factor of all, he had an all-time flawless alibi in Efhad that obscured him from any incriminating acts.

The G550 was ascending for the second time. The plane had dropped off its passenger, Sheikh Awad, and it was now bound for the charter company's hub, a five-and-a-half-hour flight to the Republic of Mauritius, a small island nation one thousand two hundred miles from the southeast coast of the African continent. The charter company based in Mauritius had three registered planes in its fleet, a Boeing 737-200, a Bombardier Q400, and the Gulfstream 550. The fleet was owned by an investment group in Switzerland and operated mainly around the African continent as well as the Middle East.

Hamza looked outside the plane's window to the west as the sun sank low, almost parallel to his eyesight from fifty-one thousand feet. He sees the red glare of the atmosphere.

It will be dark when I arrive. Perfect timing.

Tonight was going to be a great night for their cause, his mentor had said. He did not give details in the encrypted message but said enough to pique Hamza's curiosity.

Five-and-a-half-hours later, the G550 touched down on the runway in Sir Seewoosagur Ramgoolam International Airport in Mauritius. The pilot radioed the tower in the landing approach to declare the return of the jet after a completed charter. The presumed empty plane taxied past the terminal and the five jet-ways, two of which had commercial planes standing in front of them, to a lone hangar on the east side of the airport.

On the plane's arrival, the hangar door rolled open, like a moving wall, and the Gulfstream proceeded inside the building.

The Native Island pilots and the plane were not subject to customs inspection—if the plane was declared empty of passengers. The Swiss investment group also happened to be a shareholder of the airport, which was owned jointly by the Mauritius government and private investment.

Hamza was well aware of the U.S. military's surveillance and was frequently updated on the technological advancements that rapidly occurred. In Afghanistan, he traveled only at night. He avoided days because of the U.S. military's facial imaging capabilities from drone surveillance. He knew it could be taken beyond the line of sight, where the person would never hear nor see the drone. Also, he was well versed in covering his body with *Gill-e-sar-shoiy,* a sticky plaster mud found in the banks of the rivers in southern Afghanistan. This type of mud was adhesive to the human body and prevented the extraction of body heat, which deceived the thermal sensors that were equipped in drones. These extreme measures were necessary on his part in order to maintain the flawless image of his decoy. It wouldn't be in their best interest if Hamza Awad, the business tycoon's picture, was captured in rural Afghan deserts and mountains alongside the Taliban.

By now the sun had sunk completely and night had fallen. Hamza saw the pushback tractor parked inside the hanger. Once the plane came to a halt, the captain put blue overalls over his pilot uniform. He then swiftly exited the plane and sat behind the wheel of the tractor. Hamza followed and sat on the jumpseat beside him. They drove off to the southside of the airport where he boarded an awaiting speedboat. Soon after, the boat was moving over the waves of Indian Ocean to another Island thirty miles south.

As the boat neared the shore, from the distance he saw shining lights in the middle of the island.

A paradise even at night, he thought.

He'd been away for a long time. He had completed his mission and soon everything would become in order—exactly as they had planned for all those years.

The speedboat came to a stop on the side of a cedar dock. The view of illuminated lights above the cliff aroused him. He stepped off and walked over the dock onto the narrow pavement to a shed, the docking station of an elevator mounted on the face of the cliff. He stepped inside and the elevator started to ascend. Once the elevator reached the top, the rear door slid open. Hamza turned around and saw the enormous mansion with its arching columns, the surrounding garden and fountains—all lit up.

An awaiting butler, wearing a black tuxedo, greeted him by the elevator. He ushered him through the weaves of limestone walkway. This was his first time here. They had purchased this Island five years ago. The construction took nearly all that time as materials were brought from all over the world to complete their lasting paradise. He had seen the blueprint a few years back and thought it looked marvelous, but that was an understatement—it was far beyond what he imagined.

CHAPTER FOUR

The name was chosen to reflect their cause. The scripture talks about the Garden of Eden as the cradle where life flourished. And that's exactly what they wanted, a cradle where a new breed of human life would emerge—one guided by science to perfection. And this island is where they would take form—the new Garden of Eden.

As Hamza was occupied with gaining ground for radicalism in the Middle East, Mabus had been busy with his own endeavors. For the past ten years, a team of scientists in one of his biogenetic laboratories was experimenting with alteration of the human genome. The initial goal was to patent the discoveries and sell them for the purpose of advancing human health, as he had done with numerous other genetic discoveries that arose from his laboratories. The MH66 DNA coding was an alteration in the human reproductive process, where through next-gen sequencing, it could substitute a parent's genome. In essence, it allowed people to make a decision whether they wanted to prevent passing on bad genes such as hereditary diseases, psychological problems, and a long list of other human deformities to their offspring. The formula consisted of exons, the instructing DNA pieces of an individual DNA that made protein, to be engineered rather than taking the course of natural mutation. This was the fundamental base of genetically engineering a human being. He had built his platform on the roots of cloning. That technology had been available for quite some time now, but he had taken his process a few steps further, to where he could engineer a genome and pass it through a male and female reproductive process at the time of conception. The result: MH66 DNA coding would erase the natural genome of the parents and lay its own genetically engineered foundation in the embryo. This was his latest discovery, which he did not intend to sell, but rather kept very confidential.

"Tonight we shall witness another triumph," said Mabus, "the code is in place."

Hamza arched his eyebrows. He remembered hearing voices of men in the corridor earlier when he was making his way to steam room.

"The men," he asked, "who are they?"

"They're believers in our cause… and the carriers of code."

"Are they fully aware of everything?"

He shook his head. "That's the deception." Mabus smiled mildly and continued, "They were given a vaccine when they first arrived on the island a months ago. Then they underwent a series of health checkups where we monitored the MH66 presence to where it needed to be."

"What will happen to them afterwards?"

"Nothing. When they're done, they'll just get the rest of their money and be flown out."

"And the women?"

"They'll stay longer. But then… they will leave, too."

"I'm more concerned about women not wanting to part from…"

"Don't be," Mabus reassured him, "we have this form of anesthetic that causes permanent amnesia. It's straight U.S. military textbook for PTSD. They won't remember a thing. Of course, that's used as a last resort if they don't cooperate with us."

Hamza learned long ago to never doubt him. Somehow, in the most promising way, he had always managed to stay ahead of the game when it came to tactical planning. He calculated every move ten steps in advance, like the greatest chess players.

"Are you ready to see it?"

Mabus allowed him time to comprehend what he'd just told him. He understood that he had been away for long and needed time to ease his mind before being overwhelmed with information. But, it had to be done. It was crucial for him to understand what was bound to happen that night.

Hamza opened his eyes, lifted his head from the rim of the tub and nodded.

Mabus extended his left arm to the rim and pressed a button. In less than thirty seconds, the side door to the steam room opened and two tall figures entered. Hamza noticed that they both appeared to be in their mid-twenties, slender, with muscular upper torsos. One of them had brown hair and the other was bleached blond. He noticed their square jaw structure, which was the origin of their dimpled smiles. And above all, he was struck by their deep blue eyes. Mabus knew his soft spot.

He turned his gaze away from them to Mabus, who cordially bowed his head and said in a reluctant voice, "I have gotten older, my dear idealist. What I cannot give in physical manner, I provide."

Hamza eyed the two young men again as they stood attentively.

"They are my gift to you."

Hamza closed his eyes and bowed in acceptance.

He had told Hamza long ago that he chose not to believe in human emotions—he perceived it as a burdening cast over the conscious mind. He was adamant that emotions set perimeters around the mind, preventing it from further expansion. He gave morality as an example: "A set of norms inflicted upon human minds by perpetrators who held their own agenda." He had dissected life into three essential segments: facts, drive, and animalism. *Fact* was what was known through scientific proof. *Drive* was the goals that he wanted to achieve. *Animalism* was the body's physical desires.

Mabus hoisted himself up. "Come," he motioned to Hamza. They both stepped out of the tub, and then wrapped themselves in silk bathrobes.

"This way," he gestured towards the side door.

One of the men swung the door open for them. They set off from the marble chamber heading towards the west side of the building.

As they approached a solid brown door at the end of the chamber, Hamza's senses alerted him of the aroma again.

"Here is that scent again…"

"Ah, yes…the flower of the flowers,'" said Mabus. "It's been said to help with fertility… but of course no scientific proof… the women seem to like it," he shot him a wink.

The door opened to another massive room. This room was designed like a wing in a hospital. There were gray cubicles aligned with one another on the outer perimeter. In the center of the room sat a monitoring station in the shape of an octagon that housed various medical machines and computers. There were also four people wearing white lab coats, standing in front of some equipment. Hamza recognized one of them as Dr. Bach. He was a scientist who had been with Mabus for a long time. Mabus noted Bach as a brilliant man, but also recognized him as a person of emotional tendencies and needs. Upon noticing their entrance to the room, Bach's five-foot-three-inch frame started to make his way towards them. Hamza remembered him having a full head of silver hair, long enough that it draped down over his ears, partially covering his round face, which he thought was the quintessential scientist look—short frame, chubby face, and frantic hair that proclaimed him as someone who just didn't care about his appearance. But now, his head was shaved, and his glasses had a modern square frame. The thing that still proclaimed him as *frantic scientist* was his black bushy eyebrows that he hadn't trimmed in a while.

"They are almost ready!" he said in a most excited tone, which could only be a testament to his own triumphal achievement.

Hamza fixed his gaze to a biotech refrigerator standing at six-feet in the center of the room. He could see clear tube canisters stacked on the top shelf. Then he saw some of the emptied ones on top of the lab table resting directly behind the refrigerator.

"Oh, those are strong doses of Clomiphene," Bach said, following his gaze.

He eyed the canisters some more and revealed a perplexed demeanor. Bach looked at Mabus for further explanation, which he was always eager to offer. Mabus nodded in approval then smiled, knowing that this was a moment of indulgence for his head scientist—explaining his accomplishments.

"Clomiphene is needed to release extra hormones in the female body to enhance fertility. Our group of females have to be extra fertile because we have lower sperm count than the normal rate."

Hamza kept his gaze on the short man, still trying to grasp what he was trying to explain to him. He was startled by the only thing that he understood from the scientist's statement.

"Did you say low sperm count?"

"Oh yes… the MH66 is programmed to eliminate the female sperm in the male testicles… the X chromosome, to be precise."

Hamza anxiously turned to Mabus. "Does that mean…"

"Yes," Mabus nodded, "all of our offspring will be males."

"Our offspring," the news drove a surge through Hamza's flesh. At that moment, he could not fashion a proper reaction. For a few seconds, he imagined himself as a father. The only image painted in his mind was the portrait of his own father ringing his religious cause. But then he brought himself back to the present moment and realized that he was not his father. He was his own man with his own cause.

Mabus grabbed Hamza's hand and gave it a gentle squeeze.

"My dear idealist, the MH66 is constructed from both of our DNA."

"So that means that they will be our children?" Hamza uttered quietly.

"Yes," Bach chimed in, "but not hundred percent."

Hamza shot him a sudden glance.

"You see, the MH66 consists of both of your intellects and the mix of physical traits. But certain components of your genes were taken out. The hereditary diseases. Instead, other compromising genes were added to complete the genome."

Hamza raised his eyebrows and emitted a confused look.

"Where were those components obtained?"

Bach rolled his eyes up to the left, a motion of accessing his memory.

"They came from blood banks. We meticulously chose athletes and people of long life cycles."

Hamza recalled the very first time he spent with Mabus. He had spoken the words *special selection*. "Someday I will show you." And here it was.

"So the offspring would have our intellect with exceptional athleticism… and live a long time?"

"Yes… but not quite," Bach added. "We need the second X chromosome that comes from the female as well. That carries usually between twenty to twenty-five thousand genes. Unfortunately, we don't have the technology to alter the female egg as we can the male sperm with MH66 right now, maybe someday..." He trailed off to a daydream-like expression as he contemplated the possibilities of *someday*.

"We wouldn't want that, either," Mabus chimed in, "because we want the evolution to still progress. If we did a hundred percent cloning, then evolution would stop! And we don't want that. We still want to keep evolving, always!"

"Also," Bach added, "we need the female genome as well. But rest assured, all the male genes are dominant compared to the female who were chosen to have recessive traits in the area where we are implementing changes in the natural process. So, if we missed something regarding the technological aspect, the female genome would complete the process through the natural course as a redundancy."

Hamza shifted his gaze to his left, towards the outer perimeter of the room. He could see the row of cubicles stationed next to one another against the wall. He fixed his eyes on the closest three, where a person from the center of the room could view the occupants inside as they lay down on the beds. There was the sound of mild laughter and giggling coming from some of the cubes. He then, intently eyed one occupant. She had a tan complexion, was slim around the waist, wrapped in a silk burgundy bathrobe that covered the top part of her torso, but revealed her long, tan slender legs glowing under the white neon light from the ceiling. The most astonishing factor came when his eyes shifted passed her neck in search of her face, where then he became perplexed once more.

"Her face... why is it covered?" he asked as he saw the black veil.

Mabus eyed Hamza, and then took a short pause to process the answer. He wanted to phrase it in the most delicate manner.

"Their faces are covered because we want to keep the emotional aspect of the process out."

Hamza looked around to the other cubicles in the surrounding and saw the same thing.

"We want to abolish favoritism in this process," he added.

Hamza's face reflected bewilderment again.

"It is imperative for the process to be identical or as close as we could get. We could not have attraction or repulsion dictate the process, because then, the outcome would take a natural course, where some women will receive more of MH66 from men and some not as much."

Hamza remembered the beds placed on the outer layer of the auditorium. He had wondered about it, but then knew that a proper explanation would come later, and at last it did. The thought of thirty-three people having intercourse loomed in his mind, where he couldn't help letting out slight laughter.

Mabus' instinct followed his thought train. "Yes, my idealist. We are having what they call an orgy tonight!" And he let out slight laughter, too.

"Is it really necessary?" Hamza added, "I have read about artificial insemination. Why is that not being done here?"

"Artificial insemination is possible, but it's not the best solution in our process. They have to go through natural insemination." Bach responded. "We have to rely on the natural process to give us the strongest possible embryos. Although the MH66 is engineered with chosen genetic traits, it still relies on the biological donor to complete other compartments. The natural process would validate the embryos' conception from the strongest sperm with the better genetic traits passed from the biological donor."

"The irony here," said Mabus, "is that we are trying to establish what we want, and the best possible way to achieve it is through the natural process, where nature would select the strongest bi-genes needed to complete our engineered genome. So if we artificially inseminate females, we might miss out on some strengthening bi-genes that nature could provide for us through the natural course. Or we might even screw up the bi-genes and get different results. Evolution is the alteration of substance over time through a natural course. And that's what we are doing here: altering the substance and implementing it back to the natural course."

Hamza tried to digest what was being explained to him by Mabus and Bach. He clearly knew that this was not his field of expertise. He knew that he was masterful with manipulation of the mind and turning it to any direction he commanded. But when it came to scientific matters, he had to take refuge in trusting Mabus to make any sense of it.

"What about the men?" Hamza asked quizzically.

"They would have their masks on as well," Bach replied.

"And how long would this cycle continue?"

"Six days, on and off, between recess… and then we would start the testing phase."

Mabus turned to Hamza. "You seem exhausted from your trip. Perhaps you should rest for a while. I will send for you later."

He motioned towards the room's large brown door. Hamza turned his head in that direction and found his gifts waiting for him attentively. He took his leave. As he approached closer, the blond one stepped outside the room, holding the door open for him. The other one followed after him as he made his passage. He was bound to his lustful desires, which he too had been apart from for a long time.

CHAPTER FIVE

"Mr. Higgins, can you take a call?" the woman's voice on the phone was tense. The FBI director knew at this hour in the evening whenever that question arose something outlandish was about to unravel. He fetched his encrypted phone out of his blazer and eyed it. The indicator light showed full charge.

"Yes, I can."

"Okay, you'll receive the call on your other line momentarily."

There were only two people who called the director on the encrypted phone at this hour. Higgins scanned across his living room over to the kitchen where his wife was preparing dinner.

"Honey, I've got to take a call from my office. It might take a few minutes."

"Okay!" he heard his wife's voice over the sound of the juicer coming from the kitchen as he ascended the stairs.

Upstairs in his home office, Higgins stood peering out the window at the pouring rain. His eyes turned keen on droplets running down the window. His mind swirled around one question.

What the hell is this call for?

The encrypted phone buzzed to life.

"Bill, we need to have an early morning meeting tomorrow."

He could instantly recognize the baritone voice of Steve Williams, Director of National Intelligence, one of the two men who called this phone.

"Sorry to have called you at this hour, but NSA's got something… we are told to check it out."

"Yeah, that's fine. I can clear a couple of hours. What's going on?"

"You know how this new president is paranoid about cybersecurity…"

Higgins echoed that sentiment, pointing to the fact that NSA agents were now swarming FBI with dead-end leads. It was all part of the new collaboration of all federal agencies to beef up cybersecurity, a notion Higgins thought was a waste of time, and even more so, money.

"Yes, I kind of sense that about your boss," said Higgins.

"Well, I tell you Bill, this one is a little different, or should I say… unconventional."

Higgins had a good sense that earlier in the evening, as Steve Williams was briefing the president on his weekly debriefing, the president ordered him to call Higgins and set up the meeting on this new arising issue. But what left him startled was the *unconventional* part.

"NSA cryptology," Williams's voiced reappeared, "actually, this Dr. Bernard has a theory about the next breach, and she sent it up the ladder. Now the president wants it examined."

Another wild goose chase, thought Higgins.

"And what's this theory?"

"Well, she believes the terrorists are either still searching or have already discovered an astrological codebook."

"A what?" asked the startled Higgins.

"It's a fifteenth century book that teaches communication based on astrology."

"And how is that significant?"

"She says it will enable any group to communicate over the Internet completely undetected because of the immense amount of astrological keywords that enters the web everyday."

"Oh Christ, Steve! We'll be chasing every goddamn palm-reader gypsy with a computer."

"Exactly! That's what she says, too!"

Higgins pondered the idea. It seemed vague and unrealistic, but then he recalled a documentary he had seen a few years back, which highlighted Nazis using astrology in WWII. *Could this be something like that?* He was intrigued.

"You know the president's mantra."

"Yes. 'Leave no stone unturned.'"

"Well, Bill… this is one of those stones that we have to turn."

"Okay," sighed Higgins. "We'll hear Dr. Bernard tomorrow."

"Also, I would like to have the members of the Kabul attaché in the meeting as well. She says part of this stuff is in Afghanistan."

"Afghanistan? Does this have anything to do with the war?"

"No. She said this is not tied to the war. It has its own course."

J Edgar Hoover Building 935 Pennsylvania Ave NW Washington, DC. April 27th 2005 7:55 a.m.

Jack Rivers walked into his office. He took his coat off and hung it on the hanger near the office secretary Joyce's desk.

"Rough morning?" she said as she eyed him over the rim of her glasses.

"Yeah. It's pouring out there!"

He gazed around the office and found the cubicles empty.

"Where is everybody?"

"They've all gone to the west conference room," Joyce shot back.

"What the hell is going on?"

"Don't know. It's not like anyone ever tells me anything."

"Oh yeah, me too," Jack gave her a curious look.

"They told me to tell you to be there exactly at eight a.m., and not to be late!"

"Now you tell me?" Jack said, a bit annoyed.

"Better hurry, Jack!"

The west conference room in the J. Edgar Hoover building is generally used when other government agencies arrive for collaboration with the FBI. It is one of the few places within the building that general government security clearance levels will be honored. Although there is no classified information in the vicinity of the west conference room, FBI still required visiting officials to have a clearance level III.

Jack Rivers joined the FBI's counterterrorism tactical group in 2003 after he ended his Navy SEALs career. Before joining the bureau he pondered a few options in terms of a career path: the NAVY, doing a desk job, but he didn't have the desire to push papers. The other was becoming a trainer for the SEALs group. He thought that was not his forte either, for the lack of good pay. There was one lucrative opportunity in the private sector: his friend Charles Young's security company, which offered services to corporate executives. The idea and the money of the private sector had enticed him, but he wasn't ready to take the slow train, and he didn't see himself fit to be babysitting a bunch of overpaid executives, not when he still thought he could be a good asset for the government.

Down deep, he was a patriot and saw himself as too young and too sharp to be missing out on the action, especially after 9/11, when he profoundly wanted to do more to avenge those lives lost and prevent another attack from happening. So, at the age of thirty, FBI's counterterrorism had become his sanctuary.

In the past three years, the job served his adventurous aptitude, however, there were drawbacks. One of them was his abrupt departures for long periods of time, taking a toll on relationships he acquired.

"City girls don't wait around for a guy!" a friend told him once. "You ought to try the small-town girls!"

In the past three years, he has been deployed six times to Afghanistan, and three times to Iraq, performing reconnaissance. Jack could recall a couple of those departures that lost him a relationship during that particular time, which did prove his friend to be somewhat correct.

He stood six-foot-two-inches tall with a well-built upper torso and modestly broad shoulders proportionate with the rest of his body, which proclaimed him to be in excellent shape. His hazel eyes fitted nicely in his square face. He was told by his parents that somewhere in his gene pool he had Italian ancestry, which did explain his dark brown hair, now with a few strands of gray on his sideburns, a trait that women found attractive, fitting the clichéd mantra, tall, dark and handsome.

Jack didn't care much about that or any other mantra. He had a tendency to be obscured from any element that did not pertain to him on a deeper level. The thing that hindered his life from being satisfactory were the times when he was bound to come home from an overseas deployment where he knew that he was coming back to an empty apartment in Georgetown. And those were the times when he most wanted that woman. One who would wait for him. One who fulfilled the void and promised him children. He knew time was arching away from him as he entered his thirties now, but the hope still remained the same. "*Someday…*" He hoped in those quiet moments.

He picked up his pace through the hall that connected the east to the west side of the building, and as he made his way over, all he could do was wonder about this abrupt meeting not in the schedule.

The Critical Incident Response Group, which oversaw counterterrorism, was located on the west wing of the building. There were no windows on this side. Agents required an internal security clearance, one directly issued by the director himself to access CIRG. He knew the director was going to be present in this meeting; he usually was whenever a meeting was held on this side. But what left him perplexed was the other attendees; they too could be prominent people, *bigwigs* as they were called.

When he walked into the room, he found six people sitting around the long conference table. He quickly recognized his team members from counterterrorism who were all huddled together towards the bottom-end of the table—sitting a distance away from the other three. On the far end of the table was Bill Higgins, director of the FBI, on his right, an older man with silver slick-back hair whom he did not recognize, and directly in front of him, a woman with midlength brown hair, whom he had also never seen before. She appeared to be in her early thirties, having brown eyes with long eyelashes, and flawless skin that glossed over her cheekbones and around her square jaw. Her full lips painted with pink lipstick contrasted her full allure that drew the observer magnetically to her. On the first instance, Jack could tell that she was not a field agent.

The director fixed his eyes on Jack over his reading glasses and made the introduction.

"Jack: this is Steve Williams, Director of National Intelligence," motioning to the man with the slick-back hair. "and this is, Suzanne Bernard. She's with the NSA, cryptology."

She looked up and slightly nodded in recognition. Her gaze lingered for a brief second, but then she fixed her eyes back on the paper that she held in front of her.

"Folks, this is Jack Rivers, one of our counterterrorism team leaders."

The mood around the room was somber. It echoed on the stern faces of his teammates. This was not too unorthodox. He knew this was the environment that orbited the FBI director. Whenever he was around, everyone had their poker face on. But he couldn't help but wonder about the beautiful NSA agent as he took the seat on the lower end of the table next to his team members.

"Well, now that we are all here, Dr. Bernard, please begin."

Doctor, Jack thought.

Suzanne Bernard rolled her chair back and then turned to her right, towards the white projection screen.

"Can we get the lights, please?" her voice chimed like the sound of an anchorwoman, crisp and confident.

In a millisecond, the lights went out and the projection buzzed to life, revealing a slide on the white screen. It was a satellite image of a few buildings in dry terrain. Jack could instantly identify the image as a compound in Waziristan, a mountainous tribal region northwest of Pakistan bordering Afghanistan.

On his last deployment to Afghanistan, he led a covert reconnaissance mission to this region. The intelligence suggested that this area was used for a new terrorist training ground, but after excessive monitoring and fieldwork, the conclusion was drawn that these buildings were simply a school. There was no further evidence to prove this site to have the status of a terrorist camp, like the ones observed previously in other areas between Afghanistan and Pakistan. Due to the conclusion that negated this facility a terrorist camp, the military was not commanded to perform tactical action.

The next three slides were also images from the satellite, showing the compound from above in the mountainous region. The fourth slide, however, was a more elaborate photo of the compound taken from the mountain peak on the south by Jack's team during their 2004 operation. The photo revealed twelve men sitting in a circle on the ground of a courtyard, and at the center stood a man in a dark outfit—very likely an instructor. Each of the twelve men had an open book laid flat on the ground in front of them. Some were hunched over, and others sat sideways, but all the faces seemed to be focusing on what was in front of them.

The photo also suggested fatigue in some men, which indicated they had been sitting in this position for a long time.

Jack fixed his eyes on Tim Stewart, one of his colleagues sitting directly in front of him at the lower end of the conference table. Upon noticing Jack's gaze, Tim shook his head, concurring his curiosity.

"I believe this photograph was taken by your team in 2004?" she asked, looking at him dead ahead from the other end of the table.

"Yes ma'am." Jack answered with a mild grin. "Oh, and there are other ones, too… pretty much all of them showing this group of guys studying in a schoolyard."

"And what do you think they are studying, Special Agent Rivers?" she carried a bit of a condescending tone.

"They're studying the Koran, as they do in the other madrasas in Peshawar, Islamabad, and Kandahar, or just about any other place that we've got surveillance."

"That maybe true in the *other* madrasas, but we in the NSA believe not in this one."

There was a dumbfounded look shared among some of the occupants of the room. She pointed the red laser to the slide.

"These books are placed on the ground in front of them. Well, Muslims are prohibited from placing the Koran on the ground so it's not parallel to their feet, which would be in this case."

"So, if I am understanding this correctly, the NSA is making the determination of these buildings not being a school, which we have concluded throughout our extensive surveillance and fieldwork, all based on where Muslims place the Koran?" said Jack, raising his eyebrows.

"Actually, Special Agent Rivers, you are right. This location *is* a school… but their curriculum is a little more complex than the other madrasas."

The following slide showed one of the participants sitting in the perimeter of the circle dressed in a beige *Perahan Tunban*. He was looking at a piece of paper he held in his hand. The photo was taken from his back, revealing the paper over his left shoulder.

"Can this be of a ritual of some sort?" Tim Stewart suggested. "If it is, this would be the first of these madrasas that would've had such thing. The previous ones that were observed had little boys sitting crosslegged, rocking back and fourth, and the audio was coming as if the whole place was a beehive."

"We are not one hundred percent on what this gathering is… all we know is this symbol," she said as she reached to change the slide.

The next slide was the zoomed image of the paper the man held in his hand. It appeared to be a sign that none of the counterterrorism team members in the room could recognize. The symbol was stamped top-center on the paper with words that followed underneath. The wording was hazy because a high-definition camera was not used to take this photo, which in most cases would have capture the clarity of a document when it was shot from a mile radius. In this case, the team's intent was to gather intelligence on the grounds of the area and physical activity, not the content of a document.

Suzanne pointed the laser to the image.

"This symbol right here is called an astrolabe." The leaser beam flickered on the faint image of an elaborate compass-like object.

"In western society, an astrolabe has the meaning of an astrological compass. It was used throughout history for locating and predicting the position of the sun, moon, planets, and stars, determining local time through local latitude. In eastern society, it was used for similar purposes, but was taken a step further by calculating the movement of the moon, which is the basis of the Islamic lunar calendar."

She stood up and walked towards the screen, and then turned around to face everyone.

"Gentlemen. We believe this symbol in this rugged area holds a much different meaning." Her facial expression was stern now. "This is the new breed of terrorism!"

Everyone's eyes were fixated on Suzanne Bernard, as her words had escalated their curiosity with one question whirling in their minds: *how can a symbol be the new breed of terrorism?*

Jack cocked his head; he wanted to say something, an afterthought, but he hesitated when the door swung open. A thin man made his way into the room. His square button-up shirt was tucked unevenly inside his khaki pants, with his red and blue tie hanging past his belt buckle. He appeared in his midtwenties. His sense of style reflected a college kid who tries hard to set himself apart from others in the classroom to pass as someone with a sense of originality.

"This is Skip Curtin with NSA cybersecurity. Skip is one of our talented recruits from MIT. He currently heads cybersecurity and has been hailed by NSA as one of our brightest talents." Suzanne Bernard made the introduction.

The kid pulled up a chair next to Suzanne and slouched. Jack could never imagine any FBI agent ever mustering the courage to slouch in a chair in the presence of the director. He made the assumption that the kid's odd behavior and attire was a testament to his uneasy self-confidence yet was trying hard to convey otherwise.

"I believe we are ready for you, Skip. Oh, but one second please… Special Agent Rivers, were you going to say something before Skip walked in?"

Jack was astounded by her sharpness. He had only entertained the thought of saying something, but yet she had already caught on to his anticipation. In previous briefings, the visitors usually became oddly nervous and they fumbled through words or lost their sense of self in the FBI headquarters. It was mainly due to the design of the building and all the psychological research that was embedded in the blueprint of the architecture, wherein the sole purpose would cause the occupants of the building to always be on edge, an overbearing burden to any visitor. This was implemented based on a theory presented by J. Edgar Hoover himself: "If you broke someone's psychological and habitual behavior, you may get the answers you never knew were there." Jack thought none of that held any relevance to Suzanne Bernard. Unlike the kid, she held herself clear and confident.

"Yes ma'am. I did have some technical questions, but I'm sure Skip will answer them for me as he goes along."

"Agent Curtin!" the kid shot back.

"Apologies, Agent Curtin. I have no questions at this time," said Jack, but underneath he was forming a slight dislike towards the young NSA agent.

CHAPTER SIX

Skip Curtin brought himself to an upright position. He then reached for the remote control and flipped the slide.

The next screen was the main Google page with the words: *Zodiac*, *Astrology*, and *Horoscope* typed in the search box.

"I am going to start with the basics. Just to make sure everyone understands what's at stake here." He then passed his gaze around the table, connecting with everyone. Now, his confident level was high and his voice crisp. He was in his own element. He continued.

"After 911, one of our strategic counterterrorism measures was to disrupt the terrorists' communications, so they could not communicate freely. Having put a lot of time and emphasis on that notion throughout the years, our counterintelligence agencies were able to make advances in finding the bad guys. The National Intelligence Program (NIP) spends eighty billion dollars a year funding sixteen agencies to obtain information on any terrorism activity. And because of it, we haven't had a domestic homeland attack in the United States ever since. Now, imagine if we no longer could disrupt their communication. Where would that leave us? The combined Internet search list for the words Zodiac, Astrology, Horoscope, and more, exceed millions of different sites. In the past and also our present time, our cybersecurity approach is to target only materials directly linked with IP addresses of certain regions or countries. A little background: The United States assigns a Regional Internet Registry throughout the world by five different regional segments. The RIR has a mandate to govern distribution of the Internet Protocol addresses and domain registration. The architecture of the Internet requires every computer accessing the Internet to have a unique IP address, which instantly gets assigned to that computer when the computer logs onto the web. We at the NSA consistently monitor the RIR group African Network Information Center, which is the regional gateway to all the IP addresses assigned in Africa and the Middle East, for unusual activity against our normal protocol context."

"Isn't there something of a legal ramification that would prevent the U.S. government from prying on people's computers in the Middle East?" Jack asked.

"No, Agent Rivers," Skip shot him a mild grin. "That would have been the case, if the Middle East owned their own IP addresses. But they don't. We own all of that. You see: no country or entity could own an IP address. They could only be assigned to them. We had our legal departments fighting this behind the scenes in Switzerland courts from 1985 through 1987. And I tell you, it was a hard battle to win a U.S. government mandate in a Swiss court. But, after some behind-the-door threats against the Swiss banking system, they were compelled to honor our implantation over the Internet; otherwise we would have taken their banking system to the toilet. In August 6, 1991, once all the technological logistic mandates were in place, CERN publicized the new World Wide Web project, which today we know as WWW."

How could all this be connected to a picture in the rural part of Afghanistan? They don't even have electricity there or running water, for that matter, let alone computers. Savages and savagery are the hidden general concession that nobody wants to admit. Those were among the streams of thoughts lurking in Jack's mind.

"This is how it all comes into play," Skip continued. "We have lists of leads that are presented to us in the NSA by other counterterrorism agencies. Our job is to gather and find more information about these individuals in the cyberworld. We follow a set of criteria to obtain some general information from these leads before we classify them as a threat to the national security, which we call a *Mark*. As we go through our process, we look for activity online, sent and received e-mails, and most importantly if they had any interaction with any other individual whom we had declared as a Mark previously. We also generate further leads ourselves based on the affiliation of our own Marks. In those cases, we will then send those leads to the National Security staff for their review and further assessment."

Jack remembered a mission where his team was asked to provide surveillance on an address in Cairo, where the results of the material gathered were sent to NSA without the FBI's evaluation. He spent four days in disguise, sitting in a nonventilated room above a bakery in a dusty Egyptian bazaar peering at a building across the street. His only task in that dreadful time was to turn a handheld device on and off. The little gray screen, the size of a calculator, only showed encrypted symbols, a new kind of encryption that he hadn't seen before. It sent the information—whatever that may have been—directly via satellite to a classified location. Despite the summer heat and the bakery's wood-burning clay oven below, which became a contributing factor to his misery by generating extra heat below him, as he consistently listen to the screaming merchants chanting in the street below as they tended to their business, he was burdened with another irritation. He was commanded to turn the device on and off every fifteen minutes. There were a few times when he had to tend to his personal needs and missed the beeping sound of the device's timer. Within a minute at every time, he received a reminder SMS on his satellite phone. The message read, "Wakey Wakey. Hop Hop." On his third day, in the midst of all that commotion, he became irritated by those reminder messages, as he was exhausted from heat and all the other sources of discomfort that had taken its course.

"What is the meaning of all this?" Jack replied back.

"Wakey Wakey = Stay focused. Hop Hop = my name. The rest is Higher Shelf. You only worry about Wakey Wakey." The sender responded back.

Jack knew the term "Higher Shelf." It stood for the material being beyond a person's security clearance level. That part of the message was perfectly sound to him. However, he remained disoriented about Hop Hop, as to why that would be an agent's name or call sign. *Hardly any agent ever used call signs*. He dismissed the Wakey Wakey part as an act of an ill-mannered person.

The National Security Agency does not have field agents to conduct covert operations directly. Prior to 1997, they frequently used CIA agents to gather information regarding any individuals or entities that were at question. After 1997, as advancements were made in the FBI TecOps, NSA requested that the FBI conduct the fieldwork necessary for NSA to obtain information to perform its cyber counterintelligence duties. At all events, the information was never passed between the employees of the two agencies. The gathered data was channeled through the National Security Counsel (NSC), and from there it trickled down to the proper department within each agency.

FBI agents were often disgruntled when they were asked to do surveillance or fieldwork for NSA. They find the assignments to be out of their realm of operations and boring. It's due to that sentiment that they pass the NSA assignments onto one another without willingly striving for it.

Jack's Cairo experience topped the worst occasions that any of his team members had encountered performing missions for the NSA. He was one of very few agents in the TecOps team, out of the seventy agents, who had the qualifications to travel abroad in the danger zone territories, such as the Middle East and Afghanistan. As a former Navy SEAL and graduate from the top of his class at the FBI Academy when he was a new recruit, he had proven his survival skills time and again to his superiors. Therefore, they made the determination that he would be one of their more qualified agents to conduct covert operations outside the United States and was chosen for this role.

Alongside all his qualifications, he was a man with a profound appetite for perilous work. No matter what his assignments were, as long as they were not repetitive, Jack Rivers always found a way to justify it as an adventure to himself. He had never been verbal about his personal sentiments regarding his job to his superiors and peers. They all perceived Jack as a very patriotic person who dedicated himself immensely to his country and the bureau. However, there were a few times where Jack himself had questioned the effectiveness of his job and his role in the FBI from a moral standpoint, but he had found ways to convince himself that the job he was doing was for the greater good of the country, despite the immoralities.

Skip continued his presentation.

"Throughout the years, we were able to breach the alleged terrorists' computers by remotely logging into them. Earlier in the previous decade, we single-handedly went and changed the status of a dynamic IP address to static without the user even noticing on their end. We also frequently changed those assigned static IP addresses as it would randomly happen if it were dynamic so the user could see the change if they checked, and wouldn't detect something wrong. We assigned and rotated over a hundred static IP addresses per computer. We had also encrypted their computers to ask for that specific batch of IP addresses whenever it logged on to the Internet, no matter where that computer or laptop traveled. If a Mark used a laptop in Sana'a, Yemen, and then a few weeks later he used it in Cairo, Egypt, we would know the whereabouts of his location and his travel route—had he used it somewhere in between and so on. We are able to receive vital information as well as their location through these methods. Now we have advanced to track every IP address that is assigned in the RIR AfriNIC regional hub for Africa, as well RIPE NCC, which is the regional hub for central Asia."

Jack gazed around the lower end of the table at the blank expressions of his team members and then to Skip.

"Agent Rivers, is there a question?" he asked.

"Yes… forty percent of the world population lives in this region. And most of them doesn't like us or totally hate us. There ought to be millions of blogs, chat rooms, and websites on which these people are expressing hate towards us… the point I'm trying to make: it's not just a few individuals, but everyone! How could NSA or any other agency determine which one of those loudmouths expressing hate towards us online would actually be the one who would forge action?"

Skip looked down for a second as he gathered his thoughts. "Our largest contributors to information so far has been the Marks. Which category they fall under based on the data determines whether they have sought action. Those are the individuals we follow. Usually, the Marks are more cautious than regular people. We see them going and reading up on a lot of things, but rarely they leave any comments. For example: they would go in a chat room or an anti-American blog and read up on stuff, but they would not leave any verbiage expressing any of their own thoughts. Some low-category ones do, occasionally, but the higher-category Marks don't. They tend to follow the al-Qaeda protocol 101, 'How to blend in.' Sometimes, these types of behavior patterns are the gateway to categorizing the Marks at the level of the threats that they pose."

"And how does NSA take action against these guys?" Jack asked.

Skip looked at Steve Williams as though seeking his approval to answer the question. The man with the silver hair slightly gave him a nod.

"We send information to NIC to determine the course of action."

"And, has NIC ever taken action on those matters?" he pressed on.

Steve Williams took his reading glasses off and placed them on top of the document in front of him.

"Agent Rivers. The actions that NIC takes is beyond your clearance level. Not to say that they are extraordinary, but that is how they're categorized. You have to understand that the majority of the NIC decisions have political ramifications due to being the president's subcabinet."

Jack found the director's eyes fixed on him in a disapproving manner. That is something that Jack has become accustomed to because of his bold questions. In this case, the question was intended for Skip, but when the DNI stepped in, it reaffirmed that whatever their objective was here, it was already corroborated by NSA and NIC together.

"Agent Curtin," the Director said, "Please continue."

Skip put his forearms on the conference table and hoisted himself up to a solid upright position again.

"I want to conclude with the note that two weeks ago all of the perceived high-profile Marks went radio-silent. We have not seen any of their personal computers come online. However, we have detected some low-profile individuals to be visiting sites and materials on the Internet that have affiliations with these words."

He pointed the laser to the projection screen inside the Google search box. It read: *Zodiac, Astrology, and Horoscope.* And underneath the Google search box, in a light gray font it read, "About 2,960,000 results."

CHAPTER SEVEN

Suzanne Bernard fetched a small folder and laid it flat on the conference table in front of her.

"We recently went through the interrogation folders of the detainees in Guantanamo. This particular guy... Hassan Farooq seemed a little unconventional."

"Unconventional, how so?" Jack shot back.

Suzanne's powerful brown eyes lifted from the document straight towards Jack.

"Meaning that he is not exactly like the other detainees... Well, first of all, he wasn't from Afghanistan or Pakistan. He was picked up in Yemen from his place of business."

"Aren't there a few other ones that we've picked up from other places, too?" asked Stewart.

"Yes, and those guys were either militant or had affiliations with Al-Qaeda. But not this guy."

"Then what is he being held for?" Jack asked. And again, he instantly received the disapproving glance of his director for asking the controversial question that arose in the media every day—deeming Guantanamo prison camp as unethical and unconstitutional for detaining innocent people without a trial.

"This guy is a demolition expert. He's being held under the suspicion of having ties to September 11th from the building's structural standpoint. In essence, we are trying to determine whether this guy had any role in the architecture of the attacks, given his demolition expertise."

"How does this guy correlate to our meeting today?" Stewart asked.

"Well, he spent three months in Afghanistan in 2001. He was hired to take part in the demolition of the giant Buddha statues in Bamiyan. According to his testimony, he was paid to place explosives in the base of the statue where it would crumble down. He said that they didn't want explosives in the center of the statue where they *didn't* want the middle parts of rock to be damage with dynamite."

"Why would they not want to damage the middle part? Wasn't their intent to destroy the whole thing? This doesn't make sense," said Jack.

"Apparently not," Suzanne answered, "he said they were looking for something."

There was a startled look on some members of the group. Some of them remembered the headlines from the day when Taliban destroyed the statues despite the pleading of other nations opposing that act and condemning them for obliterating a world's historical artifact.

"So, Dr. Bernard," Jack said, "the NSA believes the statues were destroyed because of another reason? Meaning the Taliban justification of the statues being un-Islamic was just a sham?"

"No, Agent Rivers, this is not what the NSA believes. This is only a theory for now, going in accordance to what the detainee had declared. I have concluded some key points from his testimony. May I…"

She eyed the director for his approval to take extra time.

"Please…" the director said as he gestured for her to go on, "continue, Dr. Bernard."

Suzanne started reciting from the piece of paper in front of her.

The demolition had to be done in a precise measure.
I was forbidden to place explosives in the shafts.
Some of those shafts were barricaded with rock-filled
concrete, which made it impossible to drill through, given
the limited supply of drilling equipment they
had. The conclusion was to bring down the statues
so they could examine the materials hidden inside
those concrete barricaded shafts. Once the

demolition was complete, I noticed people canvassing the remnants of the statues at night, looking for something. I was not told what they were looking for.

She placed the piece of paper back on top of other pieces in the folder and said,

"His testimony in regards to this matter was deemed as a non-threat to the U.S., that's why it was rated level two in terms of priority. Level-two info is almost like archives, and there are thousands of electronic files that no one ever looks at."

"It is logical to think," said Tim Stewart, "if the Taliban were looking for something within the statues, it would be easier for them to demolish the whole thing than to start an excavation process. The whole world could take an interest in their archeological quest. This way, the world sees and accepts that they're a bunch of bearded idiots, and that's their obstruction from revealing the true intent."

"That's a very good observation, Agent Stewart. But it was not the Taliban."

"*It was not the Taliban.*" Jack witnessed the attendees' faces looking intently to Suzanne, as if they'd just woken up for the second time today in this conference room.

"Have you ever seen any early episodes of *Planet of the Apes*?" she asked Stewart.

"Excuse me?" the anxious Stewart shot back.

Suzanne took her eyes off Stewart and rolled them up thoughtfully as though searching for something creative.

"The Taliban are like the gorillas. Al-Qaeda is the chimpanzee, and the orangutans are the ones who propel these menaces. But there is one problem here. We don't know *who* or *what* the orangutan *is*."

The director cleared his throat, projecting the notion of order in the meeting.

"Dr. Bernard," he spoke, "assuming this detainee's statement is correct. What is it that you believe they were looking for, and furthermore, how is it significant?"

Suzanne fixed her posture and brought herself up to a position as if she was teaching a class in cryptology, which she sometimes did at Georgetown University in the evenings. But unlike the eager students in her class who thrived to learn anything that the professor throwed at them, this group of men was all professionals. Some of them had credentials and experiences far greater than her. On the other hand, they could challenge her tremendously, and her theory could be dismissed in a most embarrassing fashion. She had to deliver it flawlessly. If these men perceived her theory authentic, then her career would take a great leap. She was going to have one shot at this, which she knew coming into this meeting.

"I have to give you folks a little history lesson about this, because this is rather complicated and would require some background in order to thoroughly understand it. I hope you don't mind."

The director canvassed the faces around the table in a flash and said, "Please continue, Dr. Bernard."

She began.

"In the sixteenth century, an eastern astrologist, Ulugh Beg, created what he called an astrolabe. A bit of history about this guy: he was the grandson of Tamerlane, the conqueror of west, south, and central Asia. Tamerlane was known to be the founder of Timurid dynasty that ruled the region for hundred-fifty years. Ultimately, after the death of Tamerlane and his son, his grandson Ulugh Beg was crowned as the ruler. To provide a reference, these were the ancestors of the later Mughul Emperor Shah Jahan, who built the Taj Mahal."

She paused and searched some faces for the level of interest. Upon absorbing their body language, she was reassured that they were interested in hearing what she was saying. She continued.

"Now this guy Ulugh Beg was a ruler and a genius. He was a mathematician, as well as an astrologist. With respect to astrology, he had built the first astronomic observatory in Samarkand, in today's Tajikistan. There, in the span of five years, he completed his invention—an astrological codebook that gave him enormous advantage over his enemies. The book consisted of actual astrological language, which could manifest into codes. It allowed those who were versed in the language to decipher the content of a phrase, quadrant and so on."

"With astrology being a guideline in many people's lives in their time, they could broadcast an astrological forecast into a hostile territory. It may have seemed like normal astrological talk to most people, but to their agents it had a specific meaning. In essence, the astrolabe is a coded language that piggybacks over the astrological forecasts. And the only people who could decipher those codes were the ones who had studied them in the original astrolabe text."

She turned to face Skip Curtin. The young agent shot her a nod.

"Agent Curtin will now tell you what this means to our modern day cybersecurity."

Skip Curtin placed his elbows on the conference table and hoisted himself upright in his chair again. Then he reached to the middle of the table and turned the projector on. The white screen showed the previous snapshot of the Google website with *Zodiac, Astrology, Horoscope* in the search box with the search results of 2,960,000.

"As you see on the screen," said Skip, pointing the laser, "the number of the search results is over two million references for those words. It means if we were to look for something, we would have to skim through two million references each day to find what we are looking for. We do have systems in place to observe the immense amount of references, but that's not all. In this case, we wouldn't even know what to look for. We'll be looking for an invisible needle in a haystack. We have codebreakers in the NSA who could decipher just about any code, but this is something else. I mean, the problem here is: they will be using an existing large-hit platform to send their messages over. And their messages would be embedded in the wordings of the same platform. We need to have the specific coded meaning to each word in that book. In other words, a full-on copy of it.

"The cybersecurity team in the NSA has deciphered codes ever since its formation. The general technique is intercepting exchange messages that contain red-flag contents. The system searches the web and finds references to the NSA's pre-programmed algorithms. Once that's obtained by the system, then the next phase begins, which is filtration—authenticating a phrase to be a coded message. The NSA has not witnessed coding over a vast platform with over two million hits. In essence, the NSA needs to develop algorithms that matches words in the astrolabe text, because the system only looks into matching phrases and words. Granted, if the system doesn't have anything to match, then it just spirals, and most importantly, messages will be undetected."

The FBI director knew that this was another task that the NSA wanted to hand over to the FBI. He knew if the substance of what was presented was accurate, the FBI was their first stop. He knew this was on a different scale for the CIA to get involved. This task needed collaboration between different agencies beyond the NSA and FBI. But he wanted to be sure that this was real.

"Dr. Bernard," the director spoke, "what solid evidence do you have that supports the theory of this book existing in the first place?"

"We have a few key elements that suggests the existence of the astrolabe," Suzanne offered. "Lieutenant-General George Molesworth of the British Army who served in British India wrote about the Third Anglo-Afghan War. He stated in a few official letters that an array of astrological forecasts started appearing in the press prior to the war in British India. He said that the British Army's intelligence tried to make sense of it, but came up short. In essence, they couldn't decipher what those messages meant. And when they traced the source, they found that they came from Kabul. So, they immediately resorted to the censorship of the press in British India by precluding any printing of astrology. A general synopsis of his letters claimed that those astrological forecasts set in motion the rise of insurgency in the tribal region of British India, which led to the Third Anglo War in 1919, where Afghanistan ultimately claimed their full independence from the British. That date is still being celebrated in Afghanistan today."

"Is there any other evidence?" the director asked. As it appeared, he wasn't entirely sold on an idea that was supported by a set of letters close to a hundred years old.

"The other evidence would be…" Suzanne continued, "the Taliban raid of the Kabul Museum in early March 2001, right after the destruction of the Buddha statues. Another key point: the Kabul Museum was established in 1919, right after the Third Anglo War. Research suggests that the Taliban were looking for the same object as they were destroying the artifacts as well as the walls of the museum in their search."

"Dr. Bernard," Jack intervened, "you suggested earlier that you believed that it wasn't really the Taliban who destroyed the Buddhas, but now you are saying they destroyed the museum. I guess I'm confused about how Buddhas and the Kabul Museum are connected."

"You raise a very good point, Agent Rivers. My research convinces me that they are connected. Also, it suggests that the Taliban are the mere front to this. The real players are obscured somewhere in the back. And I say that because this astrolabe thing is very sophisticated, far above the mindset of the zealot Taliban."

The room's vibe gave Suzanne another cue that more convincing was needed. For a brief moment, there was a silence that suggested all occupants were contemplating what they just heard. The new idea: *Taliban are the forefront to a larger conspiracy.*

Suzanne had two more pieces of evidence up her sleeve. She thought this was the moment to unleash them in hopes of turning the room in her favor.

"Can we roll back to those photographs again?" she asked.

Skip Curtin hit a few buttons on the projector and the picture of the men sitting in a circle reappeared on the white screen.

"In this picture," she continued, "you see twelve men sitting in a circle. They're strategically positioned to reflect the astrological calendar. We don't have the precise information on how this really works, but we have gathered some information that suggest some of their teaching techniques. This photo implies each man is representing one of the astrological houses, perpendicular to the astrological months. So from a scholarly perspective, it is permissive to believe that they're learning astrology. This theory is supported by the next slide."

She turned to Skip Curtin to move the slide. The next slide revealed the close-up picture of a document taken over a man's shoulder. It showed the seal of the astrolabe.

"Can we definitively say that we've seen anything of this sort in any of our other research conducted in the last ten years from this part of the world?"

She then scanned her gaze around the table to study the reaction. But there was still that ring of silence from earlier.

"Oh, and there is also the evidence of the Marks going radio silent and the low-profile ones snooping around astrological websites on the Internet, as Agent Curtin pointed out in his presentation earlier," said Suzanne in her crisp clear tone.

The director heard enough of the NSA agent's theories. He was a man who respected things being more tangible, and that's what he had based most of his career upon—hard evidence, not theories that suggested that something having a potential of happening. This scenario placed him in a unique predicament. He had the Director of National Intelligence present in this meeting, who was sent by the president. The moment had come for him to tilt one way or the other. But before making up his mind, he needed to hear what the NSA wanted to do about this.

"Dr. Bernard," he spoke, "what would you suggest for a course of action?"

Suzanne received the confirmation that she was hoping to get. This indicated the start of the next phase. She knew that she had to start small and then work her way up step by step. She needed to gather more information in relation to her theory, but she could not ask for a lot. She had to start small and work her way up by feeding the system.

"For starters," Suzanne spoke, "I would like to visit the detainee."

The director was aware of the fact that the Joint Task Force did not like any internal agencies to interfere with their processes, especially visiting one of the detainees. In the past they had taken all measures necessary to block inquiries made by the FBI. In those times, they frequently pointed the FBI to the general data that they had sent to all agencies. GTMO remained an island that was barricaded by red tape.

"Dr. Bernard," the director spoke, "I don't think a meeting with a detainee would be authorized. They have sent his testimony via interrogation, and that's what they'd want us to go by."

Suzanne eyed the director, who looked serious.

"I believe there is more he could offer. The interrogation dialogue was aimed towards obtaining information from a military perspective, which he clearly could've been oblivious to because he wasn't a militant. That's why they placed him in a low category."

"Dr. Bernard, earlier, your presentation suggested this guy's observation about the statues was unrelated to the military. Logic leads me to believe that the interrogation process was thorough, and they tried to obtain information about this guy as a whole."

Suzanne listened to the director countering her argument. She got the sense of the director not having complete knowledge of this particular detainee, which she knew wasn't part of his job. But what she didn't understand was why he would offer resistance.

"If we were to read the interrogation dialogue," she said, "we'd see that the detainee shares the information about the demolition of the statues as a plea to justify his innocence with respect to combative terrorism. I believe we have to project the questioning from a different spectrum to see what he knows about the content of what they were looking for on that day when they demolished the statues."

Jack was fascinated by the way Suzanne handled his director. Normally the stage was set in these meetings for the director to command authority and deliver what he deems the adequate solution to each situation. But in spite of all the stage-setting that aimed in that direction, the young NSA agent took charge and schooled the FBI director on what he was missing. And she did it in such an attractive manner that Jack formed a fondness for her.

"Well, Dr. Bernard," the director said, "there is still the authorization matter, which could raise a few eyebrows in the Joint Task Force."

"I will authorize it," said the DNI.

The Director of National Intelligence was attentively sitting quietly throughout the meeting up until now. Jack had a hunch that this could have been preplanned prior their arrival today. This appeared to be another one of those NSA leads that sent the FBI on a wild goose chase. But the only question that startled him from the beginning of the meeting was: *what is the DNI doing here?*

The DNI is the president's personal adviser. *And why are they willing to cut the red tape?* This whole thing was preordained by the higher-ups, and the FBI happened to be the last leg of the plot.

Steve Williams took off his reading glasses and placed them on the conference table in front of him. He lifted his head and then fixed his gaze on Jack. "I believe Agent Rivers is well qualified regarding the matters in Afghanistan."

"Yes, Agent Rivers have been deployed there many times," said the director.

"Very well then. Can we ask the agent to accompany Dr. Bernard to Guantanamo?"

The director eyed Jack for a brief second and then shot him a nod.

"Yes, of course," he said, as he authoritatively reserved the right to speak on behalf of Jack as his superior.

"Alright then… this concludes our meeting today. Please arrange all logistics necessary for their trip ASAP." He then gazed around the table with a stern face and said, "We will treat this matter as a potential breach to our cybersecurity and will act on preventing it immediately, unless Dr. Bernard tell us otherwise."

"Dr. Bernard," the director said, "the Bureau's plane will be waiting to take you and Agent River to Gitmo in twenty minutes."

"Thank you, sir," she warmly said to the director.

Jack sat stationed in his seat as the room emptied. He caught a glimpse of Suzanne as she was leaving. Their eyes met for a brief second and then she shot him a cordial professional smile and turned her eyes away. For a second he tried to read her face, but then grasped that in the same time she was probably thinking about him, too—and the task that would have them both together.

He noticed her high-heeled shoes, her smoothly shaven long legs, and her beige skirt tightly hugging her below the waist. Her midlength brown hair flowed down slightly past her shoulders, and her white blouse obscured her tan skin underneath.

"Looks like you'll have a good time," said a smiling Tim Stewart, noticing Jack's gaze.

"You wanna trade places?" Jack shot back.

"Can I?" Stewart asked, knowing that he'd be spending a great amount of time with the attractive NSA agent.

"Sure, I'll just call Thelma to let her know that you've taken on an assignment with a most attractive woman."

"Please do… she'll be more excited than I'd be… knowing that she'll be collecting the fruits of my excitement."

"What?" asked Jack in a confused manner. "The fruits of your excitement?"

"You don't understand marriages… do you? Sometimes she even encourages me to go to titty bars, just so I can come home excited."

Jack shook his head in disbelief of his teammate and friend's twisted sense of humor.

"Let's go," he said.

"You better not screw this up, Jack!" barked Bob LeMay, the Executive Assistant Director for the national security branch, Jack's direct superior and the person he reported to.

Jack stood in his office offering a blank look as to why he would say that. On noticing his demeanor, LeMay shot back, "Oh, I haven't forgotten the apology letter that I had to write the NSA because of your last bullshit."

"Oh yeah," Jack countered, "I think I figured it out! I can tell that it was this little punk from today! Skip."

"I don't care who it was." LeMay said in an irritated voice, "do not insult another NSA agent. Period."

"Oh trust me, I would never insult Dr. Bernard. Unless she is being a really bad girl, then I'll turn her around and spank her… not very hard… gently."

"Jack, listen to me," said LeMay, his voice calm and serious now, "this shit is putting all of us under the microscope. That guy Steve Williams, for God's sake, he sits in meetings with the president. Director Higgins had me walk him to his office, and he reminded me twice along the way not to screw this up. Everybody is shitting bricks because of this, including the director."

"Is it because of Steve Williams being in our meeting or because NSA really thinks that there is something to this wild goose chase?"

LeMay fixed his eyes sharply at Jack. "It's because the president wants this! That's why!"

Jack arched his eyebrows and nodded. *They really believe this shit.*

"How can we be so sure that the president even knows about this? Clearly, this guy Steve Williams didn't say anything about it."

"He doesn't have to," LeMay fired back. "Here is how it works: the NSA sends whatever they deem serious enough to the NIC. The contents of that information are disclosed to the president during their regular meetings. And if he sees that a course of action is necessary, then he sends someone like Steve Williams to the proper place to go get it done!"

"Okay…"

"Oh… and just so you know… whatever the sexy doctor writes in her report will go straight to Steve Williams. So, try to keep it in your pants."

"Okay, my shop is closed… at least for—"

"Your what?"

"Afghans, they refer to your zipper as *the shop*. My translator taught me that in Bagram last time I was there," said Jack.

"I'm sure he did."

"You wanna know about the shopkeeper?"

"No, I don't wanna know! Now get the hell outta here!"

CHAPTER EIGHT

Jack arrived in the Andrews Air Force Base around ten-thirty in the morning. The rain had not stopped. It was pouring all throughout the morning.

At least it'll be nice and sunny in Cuba. He thought.

The black Chevy Suburban made a left turn on the tarmac and drove inside the hanger. Jack stepped out of the backseat and walked towards the awaiting FBI private jet.

The director is lending us his jet.

In 2003, FBI had petitioned congress for the purchase of two luxury Gulfstream V jets to be used for counterterrorism, but instead, the jets were mostly used for executive travels of the FBI director and the attorney general, including some personal trips that no one seemed to care about. Jack never had the pleasure of traveling in the Bureau's luxury jet, but as he often thought: *every dog has his day.* And today was his day.

As he stepped inside the cabin, he noticed Dr. Bernard had already taken her seat in a full-on camouflage U.S. military uniform.

"Wow, Doctor, I didn't know that you and I were going to a war."

Suzanne studied Jack's grinning face for a brief second and then shook her head. She was still confused about him. Her impression of him so far was of a cute Boy Scout with sparkles of arrogance.

"I was not going to indulge our detainee friend with an image of an American woman," she shot back.

Suzanne already knew what she needed to know about Jack. She read his file on the fifteen-minute drive over to Andrews Air Force Base. NSA trained their agents in speed-reading so they could read three-thousand words per minute. With such skills, she read the fifty-seven-page profile, which included all his missions along with some personal attributes, in less than ten minutes.

"So, what's all this?" he said, still startled by the fact that they were traveling in the director's jet.

"Looks like you've gotten used to traveling in the military C-130 too much, Agent Rivers."

"Oh, please. Call me Jack. And yes, that's how we travel when we do OPS overseas. This is very new. I could get used to it, though."

Suzanne wasn't quite convinced the FBI saw any value in her presentation this morning. In the past couple of weeks, she had been working tirelessly trying to gather the data they received in regards to the Marks going radio silent and low-profile ones trying to educate themselves in astrology. She knew she could've come to the FBI on her own, but then her theory could be thrown out the window very easily. So, she needed Steve Williams to be present there as well, and for that to happen, she pressed every button that sounded like *cybersecurity in danger*. As she peered out the window of the ascending jet on the way to Guantanomo, she knew that she was on the right track. The only issue was proving that her theory is correct. The most essential thing in this moment was to convince the skeptical FBI agent who accompanied her, for she knew that a dismissal notion from him would jeopardize or could negate this theory as false, and that would be the end of all her hard work.

"How do you feel about this mission, Jack?"

For a second he pondered how nice it sounded when she called him by his first name as opposed to Agent Rivers. But then he jolted himself back to think of an answer.

"Well, Suzanne, if I may…" he raised his eyebrows in seeking her approval to call her by her first name as well.

"Yes, please…" she said as she revealed her perfect smile, "you can say Suzanne, but not Sue." She chuckled.

He took a second to absorb what she just told him.

I like Suzanne better than Sue myself, too.

"Here is what I think, Suzanne." He shifted his body to face her directly. "This is really not a mission yet. As far as I know, we are just going to see what this detainee has to say, that is, if he even has something else to say other than what he already told the Joint Task Force."

"But, do you think that our national security could be in danger, from what you heard this morning?"

He took a deeper breath and fixed his eyes to the right, away from her in an afterthought.

"I think what you concluded in the meeting is far beyond the regional intellect. And I say that conclusively after going there numerous times. Ninety percent of Afghanistan is illiterate. How can this be?"

She thought that Jack did have a point there. But he seemed to not be convinced about the theory's other clause. *It's not the Taliban who is seeking the astrolabe.*

"I concur with the notion of the illiteracy," she said, "but I am firm in believing that there is another source propelling the Taliban to obtain the astrolabe."

"And who could that be?" Jack asked.

"Not too sure. But the source has to be above the militant grade."

Jack revealed a perplexed expression. He was trained to lean on solid facts whenever a situation arose. What he heard all throughout the morning was inconclusive to the data that was accumulated from Afghanistan in the past ten years. But if this seemed that important where the president was anchoring the weight of the executive branch, then there surely was more information obscured from the FBI. He found himself in one of those instances where it was best for him to just go along.

"What's your plan on interrogation?" he asked.

"Well, I hear you FBI guys are really good at that," she said in an eager tone. "I was hoping for you to lead that process."

"Okay... but what type of information are we looking for?"

"For the most part, we'll be looking for anything out of the ordinary from their normal protocol and our assessment of their protocols. Pretty much anything that stands out."

"I'll put a plan together, then. Let's see what we come up with."

CHAPTER NINE

The Gulfstream touched down on the runway of Guantanamo Bay, Cuba. As the plane came to a halt on the tarmac, a military Humvee appeared by the left wing. An officer got out of the driver's side and made his way to Jack and Suzanne.

"Agents Rivers and Bernard, I'm Lieutenant Misgen. Welcome to Guantanamo!"

Misgen had a stern demeanor about him. He stood five feet in front of them as he spoke and made no indication of being interested in shaking hands.

"We're glad to be here, thank you Lieutenant," said Suzanne.

The officer eyed them skeptically and said, "Please follow me," and started walking towards the Humvee.

During the ten-minute drive, the trio remained quiet inside the vehicle. Evidently Lieutenant Misgen had set the tone by his body language, gesturing he had no interest in talking to them. During his tenure in Camp X-ray, he had seen plenty of panels coming and going. But what disgruntled him and the rest of the Joint Task Forces in Gitmo were the times when those visitors went back and called foul on the treatment of the detainees. That was one of the prime reasons why they resisted outsiders visiting the camp.

The vehicle came to a stop in front of a fence. On the other side of the fence, Suzanne watched a mob of scattered men in orange jumpsuits, the kind worn by inmates in a prison.

"This way, please." Misgen ushered them through a walkway inside a building, then onto a room already set up for them. "You can take these seats," he motioned his hand to the two chairs sitting side by side in front of a square table.

"Are you ready for this?" Jack asked Suzanne after Misgen left the room.

"Yes," she shot him a confident look.

A minute later, two guards in military uniform entered the room. Following them was a man in an orange jumpsuit, his hands and feet tied in shackles, followed by another soldier and a translator. The detainee eyed the two agents quizzically and then went to take the seat where one of the guards was pointing.

Suzanne turned to Jack and gave him a nod.

"Hassan Farooq, my name is Agent Rivers and this is Dr. Bernard. We want to ask you a few questions about March 21st 2001, the day when the Buddha statues in Bamiyan, Afghanistan were destroyed."

The translator started speaking in Arabic while the prisoner sat looking at Jack and Suzanne. After the translator was done, the man showed no reaction. He just sat still, his gaze lingering. Jack sharpened his eyes at the prisoner, studying his face more intently. He noticed his deep-set brown eyes were agile as he studied these two new faces. Jack had seen a fair share of the captured militants in Begram, Afghanistan as well as in Kandahar. He knew that there was a pattern of expression among those men, for instance, their eyes radiated the uttermost hate and agony, fiercely glaring at any American during an encounter. He had regarded them as those who had nothing to lose, hence being ready to blow themselves up at any moment. In that brief moment within this room in the presence of Hassan Farooq, he didn't receive those vibes. Also, earlier in the plane, he was able to skim through some of the previous interrogation logs conducted in the last eight years since Farooq had been captured. After reading those, he realized that Suzanne was right. The dialogue was projected from the protocol of interrogating an Al-Qaeda combative, but this man didn't strike Jack as one of those. Jack contemplated his interrogation process. He needed it to be different from the conventional ones that had been conducted in the last eight years in order for him to get a different result.

"Why did you blow up the statues?" Jack asked.

The translator turned to the detainee and started speaking in Arabic.

Shortly after, the detainee revealed confusion and he frantically started speaking back in Arabic.

"It's because they paid me to do a job," the translator spoke.

"Is that all it was… a job?"

"Yes," he answered.

"Well, you destroyed a two-thousand-year-old artifact. And that's why we are here. We want to know who is responsible for destroying the ancient Buddha statues."

The man looked him quizzically, almost in disbelief.

"I have told them everything," the translator echoed the man's words. "I am not affiliated with Al-Qaeda. I was hired only to do a job."

"Yes, you did," Jack shot back. "You destroyed a country's historical monument. And you'll stay in this jail for a long time."

"How can you say I destroyed something if the government of that country helped me with my demolition?"

"Are you referring to the Taliban as the government?"

"Yes!" the man barked.

"The Taliban were never the government of Afghanistan. They were not recognized by most of the nations as a solid government, other than the terrorist-supporting nations of Pakistan, Saudi Arabia, and the UAE. The official head of the Afghan government was this guy, Burhanuddin Rabbani, and he did not want those statues destroyed. You were a terrorist in his country."

The man took a few seconds and eyed his surrounding. He was baffled by a new confusion today. No one in the previous interrogations had brought up the subject of him being charged for the destruction of the statues.

"And you said that they were looking for something? We don't think that's true. We believe you are making that up."

"No I'm not," the detainee shot back. "There were a group of people who gave me instructions on where to place the detonators. They even had a blueprint of the statues."

Jack turned to Suzanne. Neither of them had read anything about a blueprint on this guy's testimony on the previous interrogation logs.

"Where did you receive these instructions?" asked Jack.

"In Peshawar, Pakistan. It was on the third day after I had arrived there."

"I presume it was a meeting… tell us who was in that meeting."

"I already have," the detainee said. "There was two Pakistanis, three Taliban, and one Arab man."

Jack and Suzanne had seen this part of his testimony in the log before. The two Pakistanis were declared as hired engineers in Pakistan by the Taliban to advise on the demolition, which the Taliban had declared was being done because of the religious aspect of the statues deemed as not suitable in an Islamic land. The Pakistani government confirmed the two men to be irrelevant to the September 11th events, therefore, they were never detained. The two Taliban were of the Pashtun descent, and they later were dispersed amongst other Taliban and their whereabouts were unknown. The crucial part of this group was the Arab national named Mohammad Saleem, who died during the coalition air strikes of Tora Bora in December of 2001. Jack and Suzanne had already been through this information on the log. The only piece that was not on the log was what the detainee said about the blueprint of the statues, which would have not had any vital significance to the Joint Task's investigation.

"Tell him that this is nothing new," Jack said to the translator. "He will still be held responsible for the destruction."

Jack motioned for Suzanne to step outside. He got up and went for the door. Suzanne followed.

"What's going on?" she asked, as they were outside the room in the concrete barrack's hallway.

"The Arab… we have to follow him." Suzanne still remained disoriented. "The Arab who was in that meeting with him in Pakistan," he reminded her.

"Jack, that guy is dead," she declared.

"I know that. But does *he* know that?"

"I don't know," she shrugged.

They both reentered the room. Jack went on to take his seat directly in front of the detainee. He remembered reading on the log about Mohammad Saleem being a Saudi Arabian national.

Jack fixed his gaze dead ahead at the detainee's eyes again.

"We capture Mohammad Saleem three months ago." He paused to study the detainee's face to see whether he would show any sudden surprise. He didn't. That indicated that this detainee didn't know that the man he was with in Pakistan was already dead.

"He tells us that he had nothing to do with the destruction of the statues. It was all you."

"That's not true," the detainee shouted. "He is lying!"

For a second, Jack was glad to see the interrogation protocol had been followed correctly. Sometimes it wouldn't go like that. The objective of the whole process is to extract as much information without giving any back. He was happy to see that the Joint Task Force hadn't given this detainee any information in regards to Saleem dying in the bombing raid of Tora Bora.

"Well, he says you were the mastermind behind it, and certainly the person who placed the detonators."

"Mastermind?" the detainee repeated. "Saleem was the one who organized the whole thing." His eyes beamed on the table as if he was recalling that instance in Pakistan four years earlier. "There was another man there, too, but he wasn't in the room with us."

Suzanne felt a jolt of disbelief streaming through her. *Another man?* She looked at Jack.

Jacked kept his face calm, still revealing apprehension about the detainee's statement.

"I think you are making this up," he said to the detainee. He wanted to see how fast he could describe the man. If he could do it fast, then there was validity in his statement from the interrogation perspective.

"No, I'm telling the truth," he pleaded. "Saleem took the blueprint to him after I made markings to pinpoint the places where explosives were to be inserted."

"Did you know who he was?"

"No."

"You said that one of those Taliban served as a translator to you and Saleem, because you two only spoke Arabic. Is that correct?"

"Yes, his name was Abdul Sammay."

"And did Abdul Sammay accompany Saleem when he took the blueprint to that man?"

"No," the detainee shot back instantly, "he stayed in the room with us."

Jack turned to Suzanne. He fought the urge of blurting out what he wanted to say: *Sweetheart, I just found your orangutan!* But, instead he had to settle for boring professionalism.

"Dr. Bernard," addressing her in the presence of the military personnel, "the person that Saleem went to see appears to be of an Arab decent, presumably someone high up the chain, and most certainly someone who orchestrated the destruction of the statues."

Suzanne took a moment to absorb everything that just happened. Her mind recited the words of an astrologist, Martin Kemp, who had written an essay on the destruction of the Bamiyan Statues. He described it as 'the beginning of the clashes of civilizations.' He argued that it was meticulously planned, giving references to March 21st 2001 being the first day of the first year of the new millennium in an astrological calendar.

Jack turned to the detainee and said, "If you could help us convict Mohammad Saleem and the other guy, then we could motion for your exoneration."

The detainee nodded in agreement.

"We'll send someone in to make a sketch of that man."

Suzanne and Jack stepped outside the room for the second time. There in the barracks hall, they saw Lieutenant Misgen approaching them. The man's face echoed his anger as he took steps towards them in his stiff military posture. Suzanne could instantly tell that the man was not happy about what he had heard in the interrogation recording of their segment.

Jack shot her a mild grin. "Don't worry about it."

"Lieutenant Misgen," said Jack, "can you send a forensic artist to sketch a new lead for us?"

Misgen ignored Jack's question. "You are not authorized to make promises to a detainee here!" he barked.

"We are authorized to do or say anything to obtain new information!" Jack returned with his own loud voice.

"Oh, so you think you can just show up here and dismiss our system and start your own? We've busted our asses for the last four years interrogating these terrorists accordingly to the protocol."

"Your protocol?" Jack fired back. "Looks like the goddamn waterboarding hasn't produced shit for results! My way just brought you a new suspect! Are you going to give us a sketch or should I call one in?"

"Gentlemen!" yelled Suzanne.

"Look," Misgen responded, "if you don't follow through with what you said to this detainee, then that's going to jeopardize our future interrogations with the other ones. Because they see us as The United States of America, if you lose credibility, that means we lose credibility!"

"How am I losing credibility here?" asked Jack.

"You just told the detainee you would exonerate him if he cooperates. Tell me, are you in a position to exonerate a detained terrorist?"

Jack turned to him with a calm expression and said, "First of all, I didn't say that I will set him free. I said, 'we could motion for your exoneration.' And, yes. You are right, Lieutenant Misgen. I don't have the authority to exonerate him, but the Director of National Intelligence has, and I think he would read my motion for that man's release if I filed one."

Misgen was reminded of the phone call the base had received earlier that day from the office of DNI, commanding them to provide all means necessary for the two arriving agents. He contemplated for a second and decided that it was best to put his personal distaste aside and go along with what this FBI agent was saying. He thought if there was to be any kind of a backlash, he would certainly be cleared of it.

"I'll get you the sketch."

"Thank you Lieutenant," said Suzanne.

From the other end of the hall, a younger sergeant made her way towards them. As she neared, she called out to Jack.

"Agent Rivers: Agent LeMay is on the phone. He wants to speak to you. He says it's urgent."

Jack skeptically eyed Misgen. His first intuition was, perhaps Misgen and his team had called his superior to make a complaint, but then he remembered that he had turned his phone off when he entered the interrogation room.

What could be so urgent that he is tracking me down here?

"This way, please." She motioned the way. "You too, ma'am. He said he needed to speak to both of you."

CHAPTER TEN

Suzanne and Jack followed the young sergeant to another office where she led them past a few desks into a conference room to a waiting agent, Bob LeMay, who was holding the line.

"We're here, Bob," said Jack as he hunched over the speakerphone. Then he turned to Suzanne who shut the door, confining them in solitude inside the room.

"What's going on down there?" said the monotone voice of LeMay over the speakerphone.

Jack eyed Suzanne for a second to read her demeanor. He thought his first intuition was correct. Misgen may have phoned LeMay to convey his complaint before coming to get them.

Suzanne stood without motion, eager to know why the FBI Executive Assistant Director for national security had summoned her with his own agent to take a phone call.

"We got a new lead," answered Jack, "and this guy was not in the Joint Task's interrogation log."

"Who is he?" asked LeMay.

"We don't know yet. One of their composite artists is working on a sketch right now."

"Did you get a name?"

"No. The detainee didn't know his name. But he said he saw his face."

"That's a long shot, Jack."

"I know. But this man was there in a meeting a few days prior to the destruction of the statues. Oh, and check this out. The detainee said that they had a blueprint of the statues in Pakistan, and that's where he made the markings for the insertion of the explosives. Then the blueprint with the markings was taken to another man, very likely of Arab descent, for his approval."

The line went quiet for a brief moment as LeMay took in the information.

"Okay," LeMay's voice reappeared, "so you are saying that the Joint Task Force didn't have this info in their logs?"

"Nope, they did not," said Jack swiftly in his proud tone.

"Well, good job. Let's see what we can do with it."

"Thank you, sir," said Jack, "we'll send the sketch for analysis once we have it."

"Jack, I've actually called about another matter."

Jack eyed Suzanne and then shook his head, thinking of Misgen. *Oh shit, here it comes.*

"The U.S. Embassy in Kabul wired us about an abducted American citizen about an hour ago," said LeMay.

Jack arched his eyebrows and exuded disorientation. Clearly, this was not something that he thought he was going to hear from LeMay. As it turned out, he was wrong about Misgen.

"Okay," said Jack, baffled by this news. Generally the hostage negotiation team of the Bureau received news of this stature. The question remained as to why this was given to LeMay and, more importantly, why *they* are being briefed on it.

"Have the abductors made any demands?" Jack asked, locking eyes with Suzanne.

"Not yet," said LeMay, "in fact, that's where it gets kinda hazy. They didn't follow the forty-eight-hour wait protocol."

Jack didn't seem surprised when he heard that. Generally, in the U.S. the FBI has a seventy-two-hour wait time before they declare someone missing after the arrival of the first initial report. However, Jack knew that in the War Zone areas, seventy-two hours had been condensed to forty-eight.

"How is the embassy so sure of this being an abduction?" asked Jack.

"The Interior Minister of Afghanistan made the phone call and said that there was a witness who saw the whole thing. He asked for an escalation."

The Interior Minister of Afghanistan called this in?

"Who is this guy?"

"He was the hired American translator to the Minister. But here's where it gets odd. He had just arrived in Kabul the day before his abduction."

"Sounds like someone was waiting for this guy."

"Yeah, that's what it looks like," said LeMay.

"Who was the witness?"

"The Minister's thirteen-year-old boy saw a man hitting Omar Hafizi, the victim, over the head with a metal pipe and then dragging him to the backseat of a white Toyota Land Cruiser. That's what's written in the report. Once the Minister was alerted about his abduction, he found the man's belongings, and as he went through them, he saw his American passport. So, it means: wherever Omar Hafizi is, he did not leave the country."

Jack knew that Afghanistan was probably the worst place in the world when it came to border security. The country borders six other countries where people could venture in and out without anyone seeing them. That was the first blow to the coalition forces in 2001, when the fleeing Taliban remnants were running to Pakistan without any resistance from the Pakistani border patrol. Jack could dismiss his passport not being in his possession; it would certainly not have any implications. The most tangible aspect framing this as an abduction was the fact that this man was an American citizen, which the FBI had come to know as the first sign of terrorists' retaliation. But what truly was swirling in his mind was why he and Suzanne were being briefed on this. There had to be more, which he anticipated LeMay would tell them.

"What do we know about this guy, Omar?" asked Jack.

"He is clean. No file. Works as a security guard, lives in Seattle."

No FBI file, so no affiliation to any of the terrorist groups.

"Oh, and there's more," said LeMay. "It was thought that this guy Omar might be connected to Dr. Bernard's theory from this morning. Not for sure, but he just might."

Suzanne's eyes sharpened. Earlier that morning, she didn't think that she had the FBI on her side of the court, but now all of a sudden they were shifting to her side with a theory of their own. This came as a surprise to her. She focused her gaze on Jake, as he sat there eagerly awaiting the same thing that she wanted to know: *How?*

"We traced Omar Hafizi's phone records for the last three months. One of the called numbers belonged to a British art dealer, Peter Wilson. Two weeks ago, he placed three calls to Wilson's office."

Jack looked to Suzanne to gauge her thoughts about this. She just shrugged, remaining oblivious.

"Dr. Bernard," LeMay's voice came to life again, "do you think there is any correlation here between what you said this morning and this American, Omar?"

"Not exactly," she answered. "Obviously we don't have a whole a lot of information on this guy."

"I guess we are trying to see why he made calls to an art dealer before going to Afghanistan. Logic points us to the direction of this guy looking to sell something. If he were… now, would that be something relating to your theory? Because, if I remember correctly in the meeting, you mentioned art and artifacts a few times."

Suzanne took a few seconds to contemplate what she was hearing. Clearly, there was no direct correlation between what she was saying that morning and the current situation.

"No, not really," she answered.

"So let's put it this way: do you think this astrolabe would have a monetary value?" LeMay asked.

"Yes! It will be worth millions upon millions to a collector, and a lot more to someone who would actually attempt to use those codes."

"Dr. Bernard," LeMay continued, "Agent Curtin concluded in his report that the Marks went radio silent on April 12th. Is that correct?"

"Yes, that's the correct date."

"Well, the last phone call from Omar Hafizi was made April 11th to Peter Wilson."

"So, if we were to go by this revelation," said Jack, "this means that Peter Wilson alerted the Marks to go radio silent?"

"No!" exclaimed Suzanne. "It means whoever Peter Wilson was intending to sell the astrolabe to signaled the Marks to go radio silent."

"Then why the abduction? If they were going to have it anyway?" asked Jack.

"Not sure, but we need to rely on one of the first things we've learned in the Bureau. Follow the money!" said LeMay.

Jack tilted his head and shot Suzanne a quizzical expression.

"Dr. Bernard," said LeMay, "I think we could authorize the next step to confirming your theory."

"I'm sorry Agent LeMay, I don't quite understand." She gently shook her head at Jack in bewilderment.

"Well, if we are on to something, then this is just the tip of the iceberg; if not, then the kidnapping of Omar Hafizi is a totally different matter. Now, you two still have the director's jet, correct?"

"Yes, I believe it's still parked out on the tarmac," said Jack.

"Alright then, fly it to London and go see this Peter Wilson. I'll call the CID to let them know you're coming."

CHAPTER ELEVEN

"Did you receive the sketch?" Suzanne asked as she had her phone pressed to her left ear. "Okay, good. You can send the results to the plane's onboard station."

She turned to the front right of the fuselage and fixed her gaze on the communication equipment that was set up exclusively for the FBI director. *The director could run the Bureau from forty thousand feet*, she thought.

Jack sat on her right, he was going through the Joint Tasks' interrogation log for the second time as the plane taxied towards the runway.

"Looks like we'll be Mr. Wilson's first customers tomorrow."

"That's right," she agreed, "we'll be in his office bright and early."

"Maybe after we are done with him, we can fly to Paris and go have lunch," he said, baring his boyish smile. "We could bill the NSA."

"Hold that thought," she said, and then stood up and walked towards the end of the plane.

This was a first for Jack. There had been other days when he locked up his two-bedroom flat in Georgetown to come to work only to find out that he was catching the next military plane full of cargo and military personnel on a sudden mission. But this instant, at this moment, flying in the director's private jet in the presence of an attractive NSA agent did seem surreal. This surely could've been the dream of every aspiring young man who wanted to work for the government. Except those dreams resulted in a happy ending when the mission was done. There were a few instances where he had found himself drifting into a blank stare, naturally admiring Suzanne's beauty, but then he was jolted back to reality when she caught him—the first and the most obvious time happened in the meeting this morning—where afterwards an inward smile showed on her face. *This girl is sharp,* he thought as he sat there, embarrassed.

Suzanne appeared from the plane's lavatory in her beige skirt and white blouse, the outfit that she had on earlier that morning. She gave Jack, who seemed disoriented, a smile when she took her seat.

"Now, what were you saying about Paris?" she asked, presenting a toying look.

He could tell that she was capitalizing from that morning when he slipped a couple of times, revealing his admiration. Also, the earlier comment about lunch in Paris was being used by this extremely intelligent woman to amuse herself at his expense. He had to say something, knowing that silence could have many meanings.

"This guy, Wilson—we cannot have him alert the abductors."

Suzanne changed her playful expression. For a moment she considered the possibility of having lunch with him as she stood behind the mirror, putting on her lipstick. But it appeared that they had to get back to the serious matter at hand, the job.

"Well, we don't even know if he does have a role in it in the first place."

"This is how I think we should approach this," said Jack. "We'll leave out the abduction part."

"If we left that out, then what would be the premise of our meeting with him? He would demand to know why we came to his office."

"We can incriminate him."

Suzanne arched her eyebrows, looking at him skeptically.

"You mean to tell me that we'll falsely incriminate an American citizen?"

"No, we are creating a diversion in the interest of our national security."

"But our legal statutes still stand when it comes to American citizens."

"That's true… but those statutes don't stand for other nationals and terrorist suspects, thanks to the Patriot Act."

"So, what would you suggest we say to Wilson?"

Jack took a few seconds to skim through some of the scenarios that he had in his mind. He thought he shouldn't say anything fraudulent, because he could lose credibility in terms of selling something to Wilson. Tax evasion would not work either, he thought. That would portray him as a cheater, and that could call into question the authenticity of his offering to Wilson.

"Okay, I think I know," he said.

"What?" she asked eagerly.

"Murder."

"Did you say murder?"

"Yes," he widened his eyes a tad. "He is wanted for the murder of an anti Islamic Christian pastor from, name a small city in Washington state, oh… Bellingham."

She shot him an irritated look, one that echoed her voice: *"Are you out of your mind!"*

"Look, if Wilson conveys that message to his captives, in that part of the world, it will most likely buy this guy Omar some time, that is, if he is still alive. The other thing it will do is negate the notion of us being onto these guys, that is, if your theory is correct, it will make our appearance unrelated to the astrolabe."

"I'm impressed," she eyed him, astonished. "So you will make Omar a hero among the radical fundamentalists, and at the same time you're showing them that we are a bunch of idiots for not knowing what they are up to."

"Well, sometimes we have to do a little good ol' bluffing… but there is one problem here."

"What?" asked Suzanne as she slightly tilted her head.

"Wilson is a British citizen, so he is under no obligation to speak to us if he doesn't want to. And we don't have any paperwork to make him talk, either. So, we might have to decorate our murdered pastor a little to see if we hit his compassionate side to give us more info about our escaped villain."

CHAPTER TWELVE

Their attention was drawn to the beeping printer in front of them as it came to life, spitting out a page. Jack stretched his hand and fetched the printed paper from the tray. He then held it where both of their eyes could see the content. They saw the black-and-white sketch of a man on the top left, and across from it on the right side of the page the color snapshot. They were looking at a Middle-Eastern man's face with a long beard, straight nose, and a deep set of brown eyes. Below the image it was written in bold black, "Ninety-two percent match to the sketch."

Suzanne and Jack shared a silent look for a brief second.

After looking at the man's image a tad longer, Suzanne felt a jolt streaming through her, one that made her heartbeat rise. *Looks like I'm going to be proven right.* Then she pondered the consequences of what this could mean to the country's cybersecurity. And that terrified her.

The machine buzzed again, and another piece of paper appeared in the tray. This document had a few paragraphs of printed words. Jack fetched it and started to read it out loud.

"Hamza Awad, age fifty-two, lives in Abu Dhabi, is married and has three children. Says he is the owner of Awad Enterprise, specializing in import and export of dry goods. No criminal records or suspicions."

He handed the piece of paper to Suzanne. She skimmed through the full length of information in less than ten seconds. She then focused her eyes on Jack as he held his chin up in midair.

"I don't know," he sighed. "I want to believe the detainee lied to us, but that's not convincing."

Suzanne wondered if Jack was able to read the whole document in that brief second, especially the part at the bottom about Awad being present in the U.S. from March 14th to March 22nd 2001. He was one of the keynote speakers at the Williams Corp—a U.S. partner of Awad Enterprise. His company's name had been mentioned over two thousand times in the Internet in various places, all relating to his global business.

Jack turned to Suzanne. For the first time, since he saw her that morning, her face lacked that spark that she'd carried throughout the day. It was a blank calm as her eyes kept still on the piece of paper she held in her hand.

"This happens frequently, you know," said Jack.

She lifted her gaze from the piece of paper and looked at him quizzically.

"The detainees," he said, "they desperately say anything in hopes of getting out of the prison. I mean, there were Afghan detainees that we picked up on the basis of other Afghans proclaiming them as high-level Taliban. Later we found out that they have nothing to do with the Taliban, and those people who told on them did it because of a personal feud. We came to know that after we brought them here for no reason."

"You think that's what this is?" she asked.

"I'm afraid so… the truth is: only a minute amount of information obtained from those detainees realistically has made a difference. And those came from the high-level Al Qaeda, the likes of Khalid Sheikh Mohammad and his nephew Ramzi Yousef. But truly, the small-scale ones haven't provided us with anything substantial."

"What do you think will happen now?" she asked.

Jack sighed again. He was about to tell her the same thing had happened to him in the past where he was pulled out of a mission because of bad intel, which came after he had been deployed.

"We have no solid leads, Suzanne. Right now, they most likely have declared all of this detainee's statement in regards to the destruction of the statues insignificant. And that unfortunately negates part of your theory, too."

"How would this negate my theory?" Suzanne said in a stern tone.

"Well, the detainee is not credible, therefore, the Taliban were never looking for anything inside the statues."

"That's absurd!" she exclaimed.

"Maybe," Jack said in a delicate voice, "but that's what they're gonna go with."

"Jack, we have to go through with this, we have to find a way!" she said, eagerly trying to sway him to her side.

"We really don't have much to go by, Suzanne."

"We still have the kidnapped American citizen," she reminded him.

"Yeah, but that could totally be something unrelated."

"How can you be so sure?"

"I'm not." He looked at her intently. "But that's what they're going to tell us."

The phone stationed on top of the red veneer table buzzed to life. Jack turned to Suzanne and gave her a nod, implying *here is what I was just telling you.*

"I presume you two got the info." The crisp voice of Bob LeMay reappeared on the plane's speakerphone.

"Yes, we looked at it," answered Jack.

"Well, there you have it."

For a brief moment there was a pause on the line as if LeMay was in an uncharted swirl within his own mind.

"Dr. Bernard," LeMay said, "do you have any other reason that would justify you pursuing this further?" he asked, taking the time to choose his words.

There it is, Jack thought. LeMay had a habit of articulating his words carefully before making a conclusion.

"The other justification would be the Marks going radio silent," she answered.

"Dr. Bernard, that notion in the current scenario was supported by the theory of the astrolabe, which ran parallel to the destruction of the Buddha statues supported based on the testimony of a detainee. Well, now the detainee's testimony is deemed inauthentic and has gone off the record. So, if you still want to go further, what evidence are you basing that on?"

Suzanne couldn't help being disgruntled about her theory being rejected, all based on a composite artist's sketch. She was contemplating to see if she could find any flaws in that process. But then, she knew that the sketch was a ninety-two percent match. The other eight percent was fed to a computer where it calculated the possibilities of margin-of-error and produce ten more sketches from the conjuring of the two numbers. Those ten sketches then were given to the detainee to pick the best one from his memory, which he had. Suzanne knew that this system had captured an immense amount of suspects, and it was vowed a plausible part of the process. Now that this process is deemed a false description, she finds herself in a corner.

"We still have a missing American citizen," she said.

"Actually Dr. Bernard, that's now unrelated to this as well. I'm going to send that to a hostage negotiation segment of the Bureau."

They must think my whole presentation was just a crapshoot, thought Suzanne.

"Bob," Jack's voice rang, "let's go see this Wilson guy at least."

"I can't, Jack! You know the drill. Hostage Negotiation is going to have their own analysis and will put together their own plan."

"Come on, we can't change the flight plan right now. The plane is halfway over the Atlantic and it will land in London to refuel anyway." He gave Suzanne a look after he said that.

"Jack, we can't have the ownership of a kidnapping on our hands," LeMay's voice came stern.

"And what about Steve Williams? How is he taking this?" asked Jack.

"Well, they received a copy of the analysis after the elimination of the detainee from the record, and they echoed our decision that there is nothing further here."

Jack fixed his eyes on Suzanne, who remained disappointed, still wondering what went wrong in what she thought could've been the biggest discovery of her career and, most importantly, preventing a cybersecurity breach that she believed was imminent.

"Bob, at least allow us to see Peter Wilson. We'll only have our emphasis on the pretense of seeing if there is something that points to Dr. Bernard's theory. After all, sounds like it has been rejected anyway, so what would be the damage?"

LeMay took a brief moment to articulate his answer.

"The damage would be significant; you could derail the Hostage Rescue Team's investigation. Considering the Kabul embassy is breathing down our necks asking for escalation; oh, and let's not forget the media, which will get ahold of this very shortly. This could be a tornado going through the FBI."

"I get that Bob," said Jack, "but you have to understand if Dr. Bernard is correct, and if this astrolabe falls into the wrong hands, it will be the end of our cybersecurity, unless we can shut down the World Wide Web."

LeMay brought his thoughts back to the meeting from that morning. He didn't fully grasp every intricate part of the young NSA agent's presentation about a cybersecurity breach, but he did remember the bold statement.

"Okay Jack," he said. "I'm only allowing this under the pretense of Dr. Bernard's theory, which I've come to reckon, 'what if she is right?'" And with that, he was off the line.

Jack was astounded that he didn't hear his boss's general announcement at the end of his conclusion sentence: *"Don't screw this up!"* He thought it was most definitely because of the presence of Suzanne, which saved him from receiving LeMay's usual last bark.

Suzanne remained on the bitter side. What she thought was solid earlier this morning had now turned into a dust in the wind; it slowly fragmented, and soon most likely would get lost. She needed another clue, tangible evidence to keep the wheels in motion. *I have to convince them again*, she thought.

She glimpsed at Jack; his seat was reclined and his eyes were closed. She wondered if he truly believed in what she had said, or if he was just advocating because he had a crush on her. She thought about his sporadic lingering gazes. *If he were to open his eyes right now, he'd see that I'm doing the same thing.*

CHAPTER THIRTEEN

The man outside the Heathrow terminal introduced himself as Inspector Sean Gladstone. He was sent by the CID to escort the two American agents to a friendly chat with a British citizen. Inspector Gladstone cordially ushered them to a gray unmark sedan and started driving.

From the backseat of the sedan, Suzanne saw the commotion of London in this dark gloomy morning. She never thought her first encounter with this city would be under such circumstances. She had pictured herself as a mere tourist pacing the streets and absorbing everything this magnificent city has to offer. She felt fairly envious as she heard Jack making small talk in the front seat with the English inspector about the times he had spent here.

She brought the contours of her thought train back to the matter at hand. Inspector Gladstone mentioned earlier that he had *phoned* Wilson earlier and had asked him if he could see two American agents who had some questions in regards to an international case, which the inspector didn't know the details of, either. Wilson was baffled, but still agreed to meet with them in his office.

The vehicle came to a halt in front of a three-story brick building that sat on the banks of the River Thames. The trio exited the vehicle and headed into the building. Inside the building, Suzanne picked up a whiff of the oak floors that added to the character of this old architecture.

"No elevators in these old buildings," said Inspector Gladstone. They took the stairs and began their ascent. Once the flight of stairs ended on the third floor, they walked through the dark narrow hallway, passing chestnut doors on both sides until they arrived to a door at the end of the hall.

"Come in," said Wilson as he held the door open to his office. As they walked into the room, Suzanne couldn't help admiring some of the artwork that hung from the walls. One in particular made her gaze linger, a Matisse that she had seen before.

"Oh, that's a replica," said Wilson in a mild tone.

Jack followed Suzanne's gaze to the Matisse and then onto some of the other portraits that hung from the walls. He had thought of a few scenarios on how to go about approaching Wilson. As it appeared, now he had to negate the ones that pointed out Wilson as having a direct affiliation with a terrorist network. For Wilson's reputation had preceded him as a credible art enthusiast and a dealer for the last thirty years. He pondered on Suzanne's assessment, that the person who is going to buy from Wilson was the one who could have called the Marks to go radio silent. So far that seemed plausible. But before that, the main question remained. *What was Omar selling?* He knew that it was prudent for Wilson to stay oblivious in matters of their investigation, because going by that revelation, he could accidentally gave information to the terrorist network.

"Mr. Wilson," said Jack, "thank you for meeting us. We understand that you are under no obligation to speak to us, but we hope for you to answer a few of our questions about a person who contacted your office two weeks ago."

Wilson gave Jack a puzzling look. For brief second he thought about the amount of calls that he had received in the last couple of weeks. He tried to remember any of them being out of the ordinary, and then it dawned on him. *It has to be him.*

"This is really a domestic matter," said Jack, "but we were wondering if you could tell us a little about Omar Hafizi."

"I don't really know much about him," said Wilson, "I've only spoken to him a few times, if that. Is he alright?"

"Yes," said Jack, "he is alright, he is just in trouble in the U.S. and we believe he has fled to Afghanistan, the country of his origin."

Wilson brought himself to his last conversation with Omar. He recalled Omar oddly reminding him to keep their conversation concealed. *Was he saying that because he wanted to evade the law?*

"He said that his family had the possession of a Vallecillo portrait," said Wilson.

"A Vallecillo portrait!" said Suzanne, her voice carrying a disappointing tone. Jack shot her a glance, nonverbally cueing her to remain calm.

"Yes," Wilson offered, "he said he'll go there to find it."

Suzanne studied Wilson's face that now seemed a little disoriented. She thought she maybe had surprised him with her earlier comment exuding disappointment. But at the end, that's how she felt. First it was the detainee's testimony, which turned out to be a complete sham, and now this… where it points the abduction of Omar Hafizi to a different direction. A Vallecillo portrait fits nowhere in that puzzle—clearly not something that she wanted to hear.

"Was that all, Mr. Wilson?" Jack asked, "Do you remember him saying something else? Did he mention anything further?" Jack shot Suzanne a quick glance.

"No," Wilson said, then he let his eyes roam around as if recalling from memory. "He just said that he was going to find it and then let me know."

Bob LeMay's words reverberated in Jack's mind. *We cannot have a kidnapping on our hands.* He knew that now this belonged to HRT, because it was clearly not related to Suzanne's theory. HRT would go through Omar's phone log and contact Wilson with their own set of questions. And if Wilson resisted or hinted that he already had been through this with them, then it'd be a major conflict between the two departments for tampering with the HRT's investigation. The plausible thing to do was to let themselves out of Wilson's office and call this a dead end, and have HRT start their investigation on the kidnapping. He turned to Suzanne and shot her a look, indicating that it was time to leave.

"Mr. Wilson," said Suzanne, "thank you very much for your time."

"You are very welcome," replied Wilson.

As Jack was getting ready to say his farewells to Wilson, his eyes fell on another portrait on the wall behind where he stood earlier.

"Mr. Wilson, if I may…" he pointed to the portrait.

"Yes, of course."

"This is a Vallecillo, correct?" Jack asked.

"Oh, yes… it's called 'The Dancing Woman.'"

"How much would this cost nowadays?"

"The original… anywhere from fifty to seventy million. Depends on the buyer, really."

Jack looked puzzled and said, "I'm curious how the Hafizi family could afford something like this in the ravaged Afghanistan."

Hafizi: that would be his last name. Wilson remembered Omar not giving him his last name, which he thought was odd, too.

"Well," Wilson continued, "he told an intriguing story. Apparently, his grandfather was a friend of Pablo Vallecillo, and he gifted him the portrait."

"I wish my grandfather was friends with him, too," said Jack with a smile.

"Yeah, I wish that myself as well," said Wilson, echoing Jack. "Speaking of grandfathers, I reckon this lad Omar's great-grandfather may have fought against my grandfather in a war."

Jack turned to Suzanne, who also seemed curious. She was attentively smiling at Wilson as he showed his excitement.

"What can I say, I fancy history a little too much," said Wilson with a slight laugh. He then took off his glasses and wiped his eyes dry.

Wilson appeared to be in his early sixties. He stood five feet six inches tall and had donated all his hair to the years that he had been alive. To their surprise, he had a sense of humor that could go on amusing himself.

Jack shot Suzanne a look that meant, *bear with me here.*

"Hopefully you don't mean your grandfather and his great-grandfather fighting in the war that's going on there right now," said Jack.

Wilson let out another laugh. "Oh no, they may have fought in the Third Anglo-Afghan War in 1919. My grandfather was a soldier in the British Army stationed in British India at that time."

Third Anglo-Afghan War in 1919, why does that sound familiar, thought Suzanne. Then it suddenly dawned on her. *Lieutenant-General George Molesworth of the British Army who served in British India wrote about the Third Anglo-Afghan War.* That was part of her astrolabe research. Her eyes widened in astonishment. With a slight glance, she motioned Jack to keep going.

"In fact," Wilson continued, "I didn't tell him this because his great-grandfather died in that war."

"Oh wow, that *is* intriguing," Jack offered. "Here I thought us Americans and the Russians, of course, are the only two that have gone to war against Afghanistan. I guess that goes to show we Americans should read more history." He chuckled.

"No, we British were certainly the first to start wars in that region," said Wilson, as his voice took more of a serious tone. Jack read it as an indication that the conversation was winding down. He swiftly jumped to his next question but still remained baffled as to why Suzanne wanted him to continue this dialogue.

"Did you say his grandfather was friends with Vallecillo or his great-grandfather?" then he glanced at Suzanne to see if he was on the right track. She slightly parted her lips: *keep him talking*.

"He said his *grandfather* was friends with him," Wilson said.

He had forgotten that he already said that, and was unaware that he was being asked because they wanted to see if they missed something earlier.

"What I thought extraordinary was the part where Vallecillo spontaneously decided to paint his grandfather's gardener when he was a guest in their house in Afghanistan." Wilson fixed his eyes on the hanging canvas as an afterthought. "What I thought was strange was he said they couldn't find a canvas in the local market for him, so his grandfather gave him an existing canvas that happened to be blank in the back. And that's what he painted the peasant on, hence referring to the gardener as the peasant."

Suzanne noticed Jack following Wilson's gaze of bewilderment to the copy of *The Dancing Woman* that hung on the wall, staring back at them. She was almost certain that Jack had missed something here.

"Mr. Wilson," said Suzanne, "did you say that Vallecillo painted on the back of something?"

Wilson was surprised to hear the beautiful young lady speak, who had kept quiet up until now.

"Oh yes, he said that Vallecillo painted the back of a map that was already inked on the old canvas, which was left to his grandfather by his father from the War of 1919."

"I'm amazed that Vallecillo would have used an already inked canvas," said Suzanne.

"Oh, my dear," Wilson countered, "Vallecillo was known to paint over previous paintings. In fact, a few artists did that, especially at the start of their careers when they couldn't afford to buy canvasses."

As they left Wilson's office, Jack saw Suzanne with her phone pressed against her left ear again. He heard her say, "It's a map! They are looking for a map that will point them to the location of the astrolabe."

CHAPTER FOURTEEN

Jack and Suzanne waited inside the Gulfstream's cabin as it sat idling on the tarmac. They were waiting for the phone call, which was about to arrive at any given moment. Suzanne had taken the liberty of calling Steve Williams earlier at his private residence, 10:30 PM on the east coast. He had instructed her to stand by as he made some calls to determine the fate of their mission.

Her anxiety eased when the FBI director, Higgins, spoke over the speakerphone. He instructed them to wait for a brief second until all parties joined the conference call.

"Dr. Bernard," the director's voice spoke. "I believe we are all here. Please proceed."

Suzanne glanced at Jack for a second. She could read his perplexed expression; a feeling she shared with him in wanting to know who else was on this call.

"We believe that Omar Hafizi's abduction is linked to the astrolabe," said Suzanne and then eyed Jack to see if he approved her statement. He gave her a nod.

"What evidence do you have that links those two things?" a woman's voice resounded in the speakerphone. Jack shot Suzanne a dumbfounded look.

She moved her lips and whispered, "White House Chief of Staff."

Jack was moved to discover that Williams had brought the weight of the White House on FBI all in a matter of fifteen minutes in this D.C. off-hour.

"They are looking for a map that contains the location of the astrolabe, ma'am." Suzanne answered attentively.

"What is this? A treasure hunt?" her voice rang in an irritated tone.

Suzanne tried hard not to fumble her words because whatever she said in this moment was going to be received by the president in the morning.

"I'm afraid that's what it appears to be, ma'am."

"I did read your report, however, I'm hesitant to believe it is relevant to any terror networks."

Suzanne sensed the familiar tone—one that suggested the U.S. government believed the terror networks lacking credentials to be more sophisticated than the status quo.

I'm in a hard fix here.

"Ma'am," Suzanne tried to articulate her words, "the Taliban have destroyed the statues and have raided the Kabul Museum looking for this. Now the question is, why would they do that?"

"Well, for the same reason that they resort to blowing themselves up. They're fundamental zealots."

"Ma'am, with all due respect," Suzanne's voice became crisp, "Taliban took control of Kabul and most of Afghanistan in the year 1996, so why did they wait until 2001 to destroy the statues and the museum?"

The speakerphone went silent for a brief second, as if the Chief of Staff was going to counter Suzanne's statement. But she didn't.

"Please tell us your assessment, Dr. Bernard."

Suzanne knew that she hadn't read her full hundred-fifty-page report. She wouldn't have. She glanced over to Jack, who was looking at her, grinning and noting the fact that she just checked The White House Chief of Staff.

"If the proclaimed religious reasoning behind the destruction of those entities were true, the Taliban would've done that immediately after they had control of the country. But they didn't, because they didn't have to. In 1996, the promise of the Internet was a mere theory, especially in that part of the world. However, by 2001 the Internet was already the biggest communication source in human history. Someone realized the potential of the astrolabe and what they can accomplish with it—in terms of communication over the Internet—and they've been looking for it ever since."

"Dr. Bernard," her voice reappeared, "that revelation negates all the factual data we have on the Taliban and even Al-Qaeda."

Suzanne took a moment to consider her next answer. But then she was reminded that she had already presented it in the meeting the day before, which the Chief of Staff would have heard about from Steve Williams. *She can hear it again.*

"I believe it's neither the Taliban nor Al-Qaeda who are looking for this."

"Dr. Bernard, do you realize that sounds absurd?"

"Yes, ma'am," Suzanne paused, roaming her eyes around the fuselage as she articulated the next sentence. "I also believe it's plausible that there is an invisible entity that propels the Taliban and Al-Qaeda that we have not discovered yet."

"And who would those be?"

"People who have scholarly sophistication to make use of the codes."

"Dr. Bernard, are you saying that Al-Qaeda and the Taliban are commanded by a third party?"

"That is undetermined as of yet," said Suzanne, "what I am saying is: it's statistically possible for Al-Qaeda to receive uninterrupted communication. However, they could send and receive instructions and commands globally, if they utilized the coding in astrolabe.

"The only thing we could track would be to read and see if a particular astrology horoscope on the Internet that a sixteen-year-old girl just looked at has some other implication than what she read. Oh, and by the way, there will be ten million of *her*, and a hundred million astrological postings on the Internet each day. Now, which one are we going to chase after? That's what I'm saying, ma'am!

"And yes, the level of sophistication needed to accomplish that is beyond what we've witnessed in the past, which points us away from Al-Qaeda and Taliban. And yes, you are correct about the Taliban blowing themselves up, however, I believe they do it because someone tells them to."

Jack watched Suzanne with astonishment as she went on her resilient spiel. He applauded her silently for her courage to speak in the manner that she just did to a person who has one-on-one conversations with the President of the United States.

"Okay Dr. Bernard," her voice now came in a more submissive tone, "what do you suggest we do?"

"Well, for starters we need to rescue this American hostage."

"Director Higgins," said the Chief of Staff, "what's your suggestion here?"

The director had been quiet listening to the Chief of Staff and the NSA agent raving about something that he thought was preposterous since the first time he heard it. But that was not his call to determine what the Chief of Staff and the NSA agent believed. His main concern was the abducted American who the Kabul embassy wanted found immediately.

"We could have the HRT team at Bagram Air Base in less than twenty-four hours to start the process," said the director.

"Director, we want this to remain top secret on the off-chance that Dr. Bernard is right. The HRT team landing in Bagram in the midst of reporters won't be an option."

Looks like the man himself doesn't make all the executive decisions like people think he does. He's got other people making some of those for him, thought Jack.

This is the first time Jack recalled a Chief of Staff calling shots on a FBI hostage situation. What seemed surreal about it was that the Chief of Staff did not have any jurisdiction to command the FBI directly, unless it was already been preconditioned by the president that his assistant would represent the executive branch as if the president himself was speaking directly to the FBI. *She is his will and his word!*

"The other scenario would be," offered the director, "Agent Rivers could lead the investigation, and the military could back him up under the pretense of a covert mission."

"Director Higgins, I think option number two makes the most sense. Agent Rivers, do you have any objections?"

Jack glanced at Suzanne. He knew that from this point on, he was bound to spend quite some time next to her, working side by side.

"No, ma'am," he said as he kept his gaze on her.

"Ms. Wallace," the director added, "Agent Rivers has an overwhelming resume when it comes this mission. He was one of our best recruits, a former Navy SEAL. And he completed a few successful missions in Afghanistan, so he has a good understanding of that country."

Suzanne remained impressed after hearing the director go on about Jack. She suddenly was reminded of her first impression of him: *a cute boy scout.*

After witnessing the dim smile on her face, Jack thought about whispering to her, *You are still not going to be safe with me.* But he held back and resorted to professionalism.

"Dr. Bernard," Wallace's voice said, "please report your findings to Steve Williams directly."

As the conference call ended, Jack and Suzanne took the next minute to sit there and share a moment of silence. Jack heard the Gulfsteam V engines come to life as the pilots received confirmation of a flight plan to Bagram Air Base from the FBI director.

"I think now would be the appropriate time for you to be wearing your military outfit," said Jack in a toying manner.

"Did you bring one, too?" asked Suzanne

"No, I already have a locker in Bagram. That's where mine is, along with my other stuff."

He noticed her facial expression suddenly changing to a bitter grin, one that showed reality dictating a dim hope.

"Do you think we can really save him?" she asked in a bleak tone.

"I don't know," he sighed. "I mean, it's been well over twenty-four hours by now."

She could tell that there was something more he wasn't saying.

"What is it?" she pressed.

"If he is still alive, I'm sure he's pretty banged up."

"What you mean?" she had an idea what he was going to say, but wanted to hear the exact words.

"Suzanne," he said in a composed voice, "you have to understand. The bastards torture hard in this part of the world."

He fixed his eyes on hers, intently watching for her reaction. She could tell that he was looking for reservations where he might doubt her perseverance, but she was not going to allow it.

"We're going to do this," she said in a definitive voice. "We're going to find him!"

"Okay," said Jack.

Their gaze lingered on each other for a short while after the last spoken word. It seemed there was something else that they were looking for where words could only fall secondary.

CHAPTER FIFTEEN

The security office in Bellevue Mall had various monitors surrounding the box-shaped room. Each monitor was stationed to show the mall from a different angle. At this late hour, not much was revelaed except for a few security guards on patrol, leisurely pacing their way up and down the empty aisles.

Omar Hafizi sat on an old squeaky office chair behind a keyboard. He was monitoring the movement of security guards as they did their routine nightly checks. He had his index finger placed on top of a keyboard, moving the gray images from smaller monitors to the bigger ones in front of him for a more intent look in case there were extraordinary activities. This was to be his routine checkup at the beginning of his graveyard shift. His eyes remained keen on the monitor, looking for burglars trying to break in, a store that could have been left open by a careless employee, or possibly some storeowner who happened to stay late to catch up on paperwork—an act that irritated the security guards often. His job as a controller was to detect movement. Other than the patrolling security officers, every other movement was radioed so the nearest security guard could approach the area in question.

The door behind him opened rapidly, he knew it could only be one person. With a mild grin on his face, he turned his head over his shoulder to seek his curiosity, and unsurprisingly, he was right. Tom Garcia's grumpy face hovered above him as he stood behind his chair. Every Monday night, Tom has his grumpy face on, but it was much more tonight, considering he just got back from his New York City vacation.

"You even look better now than you did before you left," said Omar in his usual sarcastic tone.

"Fuck you! You don't know what's it like to come back to this shithole," Tom replied with his uneasy voice—one that Omar was used to by now.

"You know… why is it that you never go anywhere?" asked Tom.

"It's because I've got nowhere to go," he chuckled, but down deep he knew he was telling the truth.

"Yeah right! It's because they don't allow your Afghani ass on airplanes." And then Tom burst into loud laughter.

※

Evidently Tom was somewhat right about the planes. In February 2002, Omar was bound to catch a flight to Atlanta for his cousin's wedding. After clearing security checks and the long walk to the gate, he found himself in the midst of chaos. The previous flight to Atlanta had broken down and the airline was merging two flights into one. The melee of passengers were scattered in the waiting area before the gate like a flock of confused ducks. The airline's offer to all the fuming passengers storming their kiosk was an airline voucher—for any passenger who would take a later flight. The voucher would reward that passenger a flight on the airline to any of their flying destinations, free of charge.

Omar suddenly started thinking about Acapulco, Mexico—a place where he always wanted to go but could never afford a ticket in his dead-end job's salary. The white sand on the beach was finally within his grasp; in his mind, he could stretch his hand out and grab a fistful. He was so close to it that he could almost feel the warm air of the Gulf hitting his face. All that stood between him and Acapulco was a few hours of wait for a later shuttle to Atlanta. Besides, he was in no hurry to get there fast. The only reason he was going in the first place was because his cousin, Ghezal—the bride herself—had sent him the plane ticket.

Family gatherings always brought him back to the realities of his life, especially when he constantly heard the success stories of his cousins. Most of them spoke about their professions, how successful they were financially or what kind of investments they were making at the moment, or even the kind of cars they were driving, subjects Omar could not relate to, because no matter what, in his mind he remained a simple security guard working a dead-end job and living paycheck to paycheck. The visits with his family came down to one thing, their successes and his failure, and he was tired of explaining his graveyard career. At times, he cursed the Afghan immigrant culture that promoted doing whatever it took to obtain wealth, and all for the mere reason of gloating to others who had less.

When they were kids growing up in Afghanistan, everybody favored Omar as the future star of the family one day, but contrary to the prediction, that never came true. It was the four girls who actually made it far in life, two doctors and two lawyers—and the three who were married, their husbands were doctors, too. On the flip side, Omar barely finished high school. What he hated most was the fact that his successful cousins were very sympathetic towards him. They always offered charity by sending him airline tickets for visitations, or expensive gifts during *Eid*—knowing that he could never afford to send them back anything comparable to what he had received.

He didn't see their nice gestures as acts of generosity. He thought of the expensive presents as a tool of humiliation. In the back of his mind, he saw himself to be viewed by his relatives as the bad apple of the family. The real fuck-up. Those thoughts were triggered after a family gathering where one of his cousins jokingly called him "the genetic defect."

His co-workers at the mall had given him the name "Mystery Man" because of his low-profile lifestyle; that, and also because he never really spoke to anyone. Whatever he had to say, he kept it to himself. He didn't have any real friends outside his job, but even in his job he really didn't consider anyone a friend, except for Tom Garcia.

Tom was the only one who was somewhat of a friend to him, mainly because Tom happened to be one of those people who blabbed constantly about everything and anything, and what Tom needed most was someone like Omar who would sit there without saying much and listen to what he had to say. Tom's topics usually ranged from politics to the environment, art, and his wife Jane, who he was planning to divorce—all of which he constantly cursed. On their routine nights, Omar sat and listened to everything Tom told him. Part of it was because he had to; they both work the graveyard shift, and most of the time they were glued to one another like two incongruous figures.

Omar was a person who lived his life in silence, not caring much for what the winds of life brought him. Like a shadow, he passed through joy and happiness without any reaction. Part of it was because of the scars that he endured during his last days of living in Afghanistan—scars that lasted over twenty years. He often wondered, *What happened to that joyful kid?* The answer remained a mystery, even to him. Somewhere in the journey he had lost that edge, and life had taken him on its own course.

From the far end of the line, Omar waved his boarding pass. The airline supervisor, a young blonde woman with a bob cut, noticed him. She instantly knew that he wanted to volunteer his seat. She motioned him to skip the line and come straight to the other side of the counter. Once he was there, she took his boarding pass and handed him the voucher.

"Thank you for doing this, sir. Your new flight leaves at 6:50. You can go hang out in the food court if you like."

"Thank you," he said and walked back to his seat.

The idea of sitting in the restaurant seemed nice, but he knew the airport restaurants were pricey. A draft beer costs nine dollars, way too expansive for his wallet. Instead he just sat in his seat and dreamed of Mexico. He still couldn't believe that he was actually going there after all these years. As he sat in a row of black terminal seats facing the runways, he was envisioning himself lying under the warm sun and being served margarita by the beautiful señoritas. He thought of their skin tone as it shone under the sun, their warm, welcoming smiles, and even their affable lips that he wanted to kiss so dearly.

About thirty minutes later, his dream of Mexico suddenly vanished when he realized that his luggage had already gone on the original flight. He certainly didn't want his bag to arrive before him and get lost—after all, the only suit he owned was in that suitcase. He decided to let the airline know so they could set aside his luggage once the plane landed in Atlanta. He scanned the gate; surprisingly, the mob of passengers had dispersed into the aircraft, which had already left. He noticed an airline personnel—a middle-aged woman with short, light brown hair and a chubby face. She was standing behind the counter and sorting through some documents that she had in her hand. Omar thought that perhaps it was better to find the lady who had given him the voucher earlier. He looked around for her, but she was nowhere to be found. Apparently she was long gone, helping another bumped flight somewhere else, or at least that's what he presumed.

The woman behind the counter had a boorish demeanor about her; her eyes were down, focused on the counter, and her grumpy face was radiating an uneasy look. Omar was hesitant about sharing his problem with her, but after looking around some more, he could not find any other airline personnel in the vicinity. He calmly started walking to the counter. Upon noticing his approach, her eyes rose up like a cobra on the verge of an attack.

"Can I help you?" she said. But he could tell what she really wanted to say was: *what you want?* Her intimidating gesture got him edgy. He slowly started moving his lips.

"Yes… I was wondering if you could check to see if my luggage is in the plane that just went to Atlanta?"

"Why is your luggage in that plane?" her razor sharp eyes gave him a long stare. Before he could answer the question, she cut him off.

"Sir, what is your name?"

Upon receiving his name, she started tapping her fingers hard on the keyboard.

"Sir, you checked in your luggage over two hours ago on Flight 319. You should have been on that plane, too, how come you are not?" she pressed.

Her direct tone and expression had him speechless. And before he could fathom the answer, she spoke again.

"Sir, this is a matter of security, please step aside." And she picked up the receiver and started dialing on the phone pad. A few seconds later she started saying, "Pam, please come to C-19."

Pam must be the lady who I talked to earlier, he thought.

The people in the seating area of the gate were shocked and turning around to see why there were four men in security uniforms running in the terminal. They all had one question. *What is wrong?*

"Sir, you need to come with us!" said one of the guards who seemed out of breath from the dash.

Omar was oblivious to the situation. For a brief second, he was trying to contemplate if he really had done something wrong, or if these people were making a mistake talking to him in the first place. After seeing their rush—zipping through the crowd—even *he* became convinced that there is something wrong in the airport; he wanted to burst out and say, *you got the wrong guy!* But he didn't, he just held back and did what he was told.

The eyes were drawn to a dark-skinned man with a skinny face, a dark set of eyes, and the aquiline nose which proclaimed him Middle Eastern—a brand of terrorist. Two of the security guards walked him side by side, and the other two were in the front like an arrow splitting the scattered crowd in the terminal in half as they moved through them. A minute later, a man's voice came on the PA system.

"Ladies and gentlemen, this is Lieutenant John Carl from Port of Seattle. Due to a security alarm, all flights are delayed for takeoff. Please stand by for further notice."

People were all in awe of what was happening. Once again, all eyes were fixed at Omar. A middle-aged woman made her way in front of the first two security officers and snapped, "What has he done?"

The two front guards casually ignored the question, instead they picked up their pace. From their standpoint, the best way to keep people calm was to get this man off the scene as fast as possible.

The captain in the cockpit of Flight 319 inbound to Atlanta, Georgia came on the plane's PA system and announced that they were turning around and making a landing back in Seattle. To prevent a panic from occurring on the plane, he reassured the passengers that this was a routine security checkup and reminded them, once again, that everything was alright.

The fairly small security room had one table in the middle and two chairs on each side. There was a window on the left side that only reflected the image of the room, a one-way see-through window. Omar was instructed to sit in the chair that faced the window. As he sat in the confined room, he tried to gather his thoughts about what was happening. *Why was I brought here?* He kept wondering. About ten minutes later, a man walked in the room. His frame was large like an NFL lineman, his collar-shirt was firmly fixed around his broad shoulders, and his tie squeezed tight around his large neck. He placed his right hand on the table and used its support to hunch over and look directly into Omar's eyes.

"My name is John Pierce, I'm the head of security here in the airport." Without even asking a question, his eyes were examining Omar's body language.

"Do you know why you were brought here?" he said with a firm tone.

"No," Omar responded casually.

"You checked in your luggage over two hours ago, but you didn't go on the plane yourself. Why?"

Omar reached into his back pocket and brought out the airline voucher.

"I volunteered to give up my seat to get this free voucher." The officer's eyes were now keen on the piece of paper.

"Sir, your luggage must leave with you. What you have done is against the FAA regulations."

"Well, I didn't know that," he offered, "I thought the airline personnel would automatically take my luggage out of the plane upon giving me this voucher."

"What are you taking with you on this trip?" the man asked.

"I'm going to a wedding, so I'm taking a suit along with some other clothes."

"A wedding?"

"Yes… a wedding, my cousin's."

The man nodded absorbedly. "Just wait here, please," and he stepped outside.

Forty-five minutes later, Flight 319 landed back at the SeaTac Airport. After it made its stop at the gate, the plane was greeted by a half-dozen airport security officers. Shortly after, the unattended suitcase was retrieved, and a thorough inspection of it was made. The airport security declared the situation "a false alarm." For the most part, it was the airline's fault. Upon issuing Omar the voucher, the airline supervisor should have called for his suitcase to be removed from the plane, but because of the uproar of angry passengers from the bumped flight, she simply forgot to do that.

The other obstacle that remained was the media. Because of the tense times about airports and security, this was a heyday for the news crews. As it turned out they only needed two things: the closing of a major U.S. airport and a Middle-Eastern person taken in for questioning. One of the networks was even announcing it as the next terrorist attack.

As the news crews stormed around the airport interviewing some passengers and airport staff, Omar just sat in the security office, clearly ignorant of the circus outside.

Finally, John Pierce made his way back to the room; his appearance suggested that he had a handle on the situation.

"Sorry to keep you waiting this long, sir," he said, bearing a sympathetic face.

The uneasy feeling was rolling through Omar's mind, but still he kept his silence. Pierce took a seat on the chair, which was placed at the other end of the table. This time his gesture suggested calmness.

"Sir, we deeply regret having held you here for this long. We owe you our deepest apologies. It was the airline's personnel who made the mistake; we just do our job ensuring safety and security."

Being a security guard himself, Omar knew that John Pierce was being quite frank about his job and duties. In essence, he could relate to the man and knew that everything he was doing was following the protocol.

As Omar stood to leave, Pierce alerted him about the media presence in the airport. For Omar, this was the beginning of the nightmare. All his life he had hidden from the spotlight, but now he was bound to face the biggest spotlight of his life—the accused terrorist.

"Sir, please don't let me out there like this. I have a life you know… I can't face those people."

Pierce nodded in agreement. "We can have a unmarked security vehicle take you home, but that means you cannot fly today."

Omar sighed, thinking about how he was going to miss his cousin's wedding. After all, she even sent him the plane ticket.

"Sir, even if we managed to get you on board the plane, they'd still get you once you've landed in Atlanta."

Pierce was in agreement with Omar about the media, for he did not want his identity to be revealed. Naturally it'd call into question the integrity of SeaTac security, and he certainly didn't want his airport to be known as one that acted based on racial profiling. With that in mind, he did his best to accommodate this man's privacy.

Omar did not fly that day. Instead, he was secretly escorted to an unmarked security Ford Taurus outside the airport and went back to his apartment. Since the situation in the SeaTac Airport was announced as a false alarm, the media had no intention of pursuing it any further. And Omar, the lone sullen man, never made the attempt to make a wrong right. He just receded back to his normal life. The outcome of that humiliation bore one thing out, though—and that was a promise that he made to himself to never fly again.

✑

From the pocket of his jacket, Tom fetched a miniature book, just a tad bigger than the palm of his hand.

"Here, I got this for you from the Met," he said with a mild grin.

Omar took it from him and casually flipped through some of the pages. "What is it?"

"It's a miniature exhibition catalogue that tells you about the most famous paintings and sculptures, something that you ought to consider learning about."

He skimmed through a few more pages. "Thanks."

"Maybe one of these days," said Tom, "you'll go out with a woman, and knowing this stuff, you might be able to impress her a little… maybe she won't think you are not so bad after all. She'd be like, 'At least he knows a little about art.'"

Omar shook his head as he pocketed the miniature catalogue. He knew he was going to have his spewing of words for Tom later.

Omar and Tom were used to each other. Three years of being glued together five nights a week had manifested into a unique friendship. It was like a platonic bad marriage between two men, if one ever existed. The smart-ass comments, the bickering, and the belittling were a common remedy that kept them both entertained with the job and each other.

Omar didn't connect a lot with other guys, but with Tom the bond was indestructible, even though, Tom—a medium-height curly-haired man who wore his pants high above his waist—was well into his fifties, nearly twice his age.

"Sorry Tom, I hear only gay dudes talk about art, real men like me don't! You see: ever since you came out of the closet, you've discovered this artistic side of you. I think that's the real reason why your wife is leaving you." He then burst out laughing, knowing that he just landed a good blow on Tom.

"Well, at least I was married for thirty years before I decided to be gay. Look at you! You jerked off when you were a kid, and you are jerking off now… and most likely, you'll be jerking off when you are at my age."

Omar shook his head in disbelief of the words that just came out of Tom's mouth.

"I'd rather jerk off than turn gay like you!"

"I'm not gay, you dickhead! I've just had it with women. That's all!" Tom barked.

Later that morning after finishing his shift, Omar was lying down on his single bed trying to sleep. This was his routine. When the rest of the world rose to start the day, he slept. Perhaps this was another testament to his lifestyle, always finding himself on the opposite side of the norm.

His apartment sat above Queen Anne Boulevard, one of the congested streets on the north side of downtown Seattle. The street usually came to life at the same time he was trying to go to sleep. When he first started this job, he had the hardest time sleeping during the day with all the noises outside that came into his studio flat through the old single-pane window, but now, three years later, he had become accustomed to them. Not even the sound of the loudest sirens bothered him anymore. But today, there was something that kept him awake. It definitely was not the commotion outside. It was something that Tom had said the night before, which left his eyes open and locked on the white patterns of the old ceiling and his mind swirling around the trajectory of those words.

"One day you'll meet a woman," Tom had said.

Those words shone a ray of hope on his lonely life, but there was a feeling of uneasiness like a cold breeze chilling his body. But still, Tom's words kept echoing in his mind. *How will she be?* he wondered. A lonely person often dreams of companionship, and in Omar's mind those dreams were glorified, creating that perfect woman. But, of course, reality always spoke a different language, one that shot the dream from sky and dropped it to the ground, and one that made him observe himself first before he could hope. And when he observes, he sees that he has very little to hope for. Reality always found a way to break his dreams. *Would she really love me? Would she really accept me? Or she'd be like Masooma.*

Masooma, a girlfriend of his cousin Homa, was another Afghan-born American living in Atlanta. Just like Omar, she emigrated to the U.S. from Afghanistan at a very young age. He met her in at an engagement party on one of those times when he visited his relatives in Atlanta. She had straight, long brown hair, a dark set of eyes, and a curled nose that sat unfittingly on her round face. After staying in touch with her for a period of time, he thought that she might be the person who'd fulfill the emptiness, that she might be someone he thought of marrying, or at least he had hoped.

But that hope was short-lived. After a couple of months into their long-distance relationship, she was gone, and his emptiness remained— only yearning for her absence. Later he heard that Masooma had said, "I am not going to be marrying a poor security guard." Those words came like a rain of arrows, striking every inch and leaving him on the ground, bleeding. It was the end of hope and the end of courtship with a woman.

He crawled out of his bed and walked to his closet. He was looking for something to keep his racing mind off its course, because in the past, thoughts of Masooma had left him in a slump. He reached inside his security jacket and fetched the little catalogue that Tom had given him the night before. Tom had purchased it as a souvenir from the Metropolitan Museum's gift shop. It illustrated portraits done by famous artists; the colorful canvases printed on the three-by-five-inch glossy pages showing the painting and the artist's name underneath.

Slowly, he started flipping through the pages, studying every page intently. About a quarter of the way to end of the booklet, he came across a portrait that he had seen somewhere before. *Where?* He wasn't sure exactly, but he did remember seeing it. His racing mind had a different track now. *Where have I seen this picture?* His eyes were keen on the three-by-five page of the catalogue, and his mind was searching for the resemblance in the portrait. Somewhere in the past, a long time ago, he had seen the real one, but where? He recalled the real portrait being a lot bigger than what he was seeing in this three-by-five page. There was a period of haziness as he tried to connect the two images. He started thinking if he had seen it in a museum, but then he reminded himself that he had never been in a museum before. The next option was on television, but then it dawned on him. He remembered feeling the canvas under his fingers. Then it came back—the fog lifted and everything was clear.

CHAPTER SIXTEEN

On the dark rainy day of April 25th, SeaTac Airport was hectic as ever. Passengers were scattered all over the airport. A prerecorded voice of a man was on the PA system, and it kept repeating a command: "Do not leave your vehicles unattended! You will be ticketed and towed!"

A green Far-West taxi arrived on the curbside of the ticketing deck. Omar slowly opened the rear door and stepped out of the cab. After grabbing his bags from the trunk, he headed for the entrance. *Hopefully, this would be better than the last time.*

This was to be his second attempt to fly after September 11th. The previous time when he'd arrived at this airport he didn't get to fly, instead, he was detained for an hour in the security office. He remembered it like it was yesterday, humiliated and bitter as he fled the media after being interrogated for suspicion of committing a terrorist act. It was enough embarrassment that he ended up promising himself not to fly ever again. But today he had to break that promise, because a car could not travel to where he was bound to go.

The Toner Airways Flight 606 was headed to Heathrow, London at 6:43 PM, in less than three hours. After waiting in the economy line for nearly twenty-five minutes, Omar finally reached the ticketing counter. A middle-aged lady with dyed blonde hair started to assist him.

"May I see your passport, sir?" the lady asked from behind the ticketing counter.

He reached into his jacket pocket and brought out his U.S. passport. "Here ma'am," and handed it to her.

As the lady was checking his passport, another thought streamed through his mind. *This'll be the first time I'll be using my American passport.*

After looking at his passport and matching his name with the ticket, the lady handed him the boarding pass.

"Your plane leaves from gate S-14. Go around the back and take the escalators down the train, then get off on the S satellite."

As he took the escalators down, he noticed the long line of people who stood in front of the security check. Once again, his memory went back to that brutal day about nine years ago when he wanted to get a free airline voucher. Now, years later, the memory of that event still hung over him. In the back of his head he was thinking, what if it happened again today and he couldn't fly?

He was comforted when he saw the TSA lady's smile at the beginning of the line.

"Do you have your boarding pass and ID?" she asked warmly.

He reached inside his brown sports jacket and produced the boarding pass and his passport. Upon seeing the two documents, the lady made a check on his boarding pass and motioned the way for him to enter the line. Comfort eased over him once he was past the metal detector on the other side.

This is it, he thought. If this trip goes in accordance to his plan, then his life would take a tremendous change. He no longer would be a poor security guard working paycheck to paycheck. He had already thought of what he was going to tell everyone about how he made his money, mostly his relatives, who constantly doubted him to be somebody successful or noteworthy. This was going to change all of that. This trip was going to transport him into high society. He just had to stick to his plan and go forward with it, and above all, not be afraid. There was only one person who knew about this opportunity, and he was that person. This was his path to wealth and a life living without scorn.

The cabin of the Boeing 747-400 was overwhelmingly full; almost every seat had an occupant. The feeling of uneasiness was already mounting in Omar Hafizi. He was never a big fan of airplanes, ever since he could remember he had a hard time bringing himself to a confined area, especially one that went up to thirty-five-thousand feet without a connection to the ground. This was much worse than an elevator. In most places he avoided them and took the stairs, unless the building was too high to be managed by foot, and then he found other alternatives, which often resulted in him not going there in the first place.

The flight to Heathrow was a good nine-and-a-half hours. He could never eat or drink anything onboard a plane. The last time he had food in a plane was on his first flight coming from Pakistan to America, where he vomited shortly after eating. That was over twenty-two years ago, when he was a teenage boy. It was okay for a kid to get airsick, but not now. Not when he is a grown man puking in a little vomit bag while all the other passengers were holding their nostrils. That embarrassment persuaded him to keep himself starved eight hours prior to his departures. Generally, his previous flights were much shorter than the one he was intending now, considering they only went from Seattle to Atlanta, but now he was going over this country and the Atlantic Ocean. That still didn't change his pre-departure plan. He still kept himself starved since dinner the night before, and he was bound not to have anything on the plane until he reached his destination.

Bearing that in mind, he struggled in search of something to keep his mind away from the roaring engines, which were now starting to thunder on each side of the cabin. He quickly rose to his feet and reached to the overhead compartment to locate his black duffle bag. He only had a few seconds before one of the flight attendants commanded him to take his seat, for the plane was already taxing towards the runway. He unzipped the zipper and fetched out a book-sized object from the bag, and with it he took his seat.

As the plane thrust forward for takeoff, he slowly started running his fingers over the notebook where the smooth sheepskin leather illustrated the marks of his fingertips and then faded away. This was the last gift from his grandfather on his fifteenth birthday, two weeks before his departure from Afghanistan. The only travesty was that he didn't write anything in it until a couple years back, where he started jotting the earliest of his memories. For some reason he thought reviving the past could ultimately lead him to redemption. Omar had written his whole youth in this notebook, in a desperate quest to reach salvation or have something on paper to make right what was wronged. Those times when he sat in his tiny apartment, deliberately away from the world, he wrote his memories, one way or the other. This was his way of life, sitting in the cramped apartment and writing about his days growing up in Kabul.

CHAPTER SEVENTEEN

Omar never got a chance to write during the flight. Keeping himself awake the night before had paid off. He fell asleep as soon as the plane became airborne, and was still asleep when it touched down on the runway at Heathrow. From there, he made one more connection in Istanbul, and then onto landing in Kabul, Afghanistan.

The image of Kabul International Airport terminal loomed behind a cloud of dust. The building appeared to be exactly the same as he had seen it last time when he took the flight out of this country. The only differences were the bullet holes in the main building and remnants of material scattered all over the airport from expulsions. The two-story building stood battered and tired. In a way it reflected the image of Afghanistan as a whole—it too stood battered and tired, merely the shell of what this country used to be.

As Omar gazed at the building, the question that startled him was not why this all had happened, but rather why hadn't anything happened in the past four years?

Four years and billions of dollars flooding through this place, yet this airport was still ravaged.

This is the first sign of Afghans at work. What a shame. He thought. *And the world thinks that someday Afghans will govern themselves solemnly and contribute to the world community, huh.*

Outside the terminal, he waved down a taxi that was parked under the shade of an oak tree. A cloud of black smoke appeared behind the vehicle as the engine clunked to life, then the vehicle made its way towards him.

The view from the backseat of the taxi tainted all his childhood memories of this city. The dust was ubiquitous in this dry afternoon like a cloud of faint-yellow fog that hovered forever. He fixed his eyes through the windshield of the car and all he could see was about hundred feet in front of them. Then he would see dim images of the buildings from beyond a hundred feet slowly coming to life as the vehicle got closer to them. He also saw piles of rubble scattered along the dirt-filled roads, and then somewhere in the background of the rubble, there were large mansions with arching marble columns and other stone ornaments.

He eyed one in particular where every balcony had bright green, tinted glass between the railings, which did not go with the flow of the expensive stones plastered on the face of the house. *Bad taste*, he thought. He then fixed his eyes to a sign on the roof of the house saying in Arabic, *Praise Allah*, so the house would be protected from the evil eye.

"These are all built from drug money," the driver said upon noticing Omar's gaze in the rearview mirror.

Drug money… and money stolen by the government officials, Omar thought.

The image of treachery and selfishness was hidden behind the clouds of dust in this country. Clearly this country did not have the economic power to sustain wealth of this magnitude by honest ways of business or invention. He knew that behind every flash of wealth apparent to the eye, there was an immoral justification hidden somewhere in the story.

The car took a left on the Sheerpoor intersection and headed straight to Shar-e-Now. Shortly after, the sound of screeching brakes reverberated when the car made the final stop in front of a gray wooden gate. Omar instantly recognized this gate, although it seemed a lot smaller than the painted image carved in his memory.

A school-aged boy opened the passageway, a smaller door within the large gray gate.

"Yes?"

"I'm here for the translating job, I called from abroad a few days ago," said Omar.

The boy perused Omar's face and body. "I'll call my father. You can wait here." He ushered him inside the yard.

As he stood there waiting, he turned and eyed the gate for another look. This was the first time that he set foot in this house after twenty-three years. He remembered he was able to pass seamlessly through the passage door when he was a boy, but now at five-foot-eleven inches, he had to hunch his back and lower his head as he moved through the small frame within the gate.

The yard stood in the same commonality as the gate. It seemed a lot smaller than what he remembered. The cement pathway where he used to ride his bicycle, day and night, was much narrower than he remembered, as well. There were no rose gardens to be seen, the yard was a field of dirt with hardened mud on its outer edges. He thought of this house as another testimonial to this country—a sheared battleground that served no purpose. All the manicured gardens that once beautified this place were turned to dirt and mud, mimicking Afghanistan—only destruction with no resolve.

From a distance, he saw the figure of a man making his way to him. He was wearing the traditional loose-fitting Afghan attire, *Perahan Tunban*, tunic and trousers. Omar could tell from his walk that the man emitted command. His head sat on his bulky shoulders, only revealing a tad of his neck. He was heavy around the waist. He walked with his chest forward and eyes keenly studying Omar from the far. Omar was instantly reassured that this was a military man. As he neared, Omar could see his dark brown eyes, thick eyebrows, and his flat nose. But the most noticeable aspect on the man's round face was his thick mustache, which revealed his military position.

"My name is Commander Khaled." The man stretched his hand to Omar, "you're the one who called from America?"

"Yes," Omar answered as he took the man's hand.

Omar had heard that his grandfather's estate was confiscated by a northern alliance commander in December of 2001 after the fall of Taliban in Kabul. The commander had claimed the estate as his own prize, and had resided there for the last four years. That was a normal protocol in Kabul. The warlords claim the prestige properties as their own, especially ones where the owners had evacuated the country during times of war. Omar never hinted over the phone that this place once belonged to his grandfather—the house that he was born and lived in during his childhood years. That could have made his circumstances more difficult in terms of getting a job, because the commander, who also happened to be the interior Minister of Afghanistan, could have been wary of losing his prized residence to the rightful inherent.

"I find it rather odd that you come here from America to find a job," said the commander as he eyed Omar anxiously.

"Well, I don't like living in America. I really have nobody there anymore. I also wanted to see if I could contribute to the country I call home."

He noticed the commander's face eased after those words were heard.

"That sounds like a politically correct answer. Wouldn't you think?"

"It does," Omar chuckled. "I do have aspirations of possibly working in the interior ministry someday."

The commander nodded in understanding this young man's ambitions. He had heard from his assistant about this man calling relentlessly for the last couple of weeks, which invoked enough interest on his part to set up a phone interview with him, which ultimately resulted in hiring Omar as his Afghan-American translator. Although the commander remained skeptical of the hiring, when he weighed the pros and cons, he did find it rather beneficial.

"Well then, we are happy to have you here," he said

Omar knew the importance of his role and the prestige it provided Commander Khaled. His role as a translator would give Khaled a rise among his peers, due to the fact that an American citizen was working for him, unlike most of his counterparts who had to rely on their local Afghan translator to help them communicate with the Americans and the American troops. He also knew that his presence could potentially win Khaled a better perception among the Americans as well. And he was confident that Khaled knew the same thing.

"Please come," Commander Khaled guided him through the cement pathway towards the main house.

As they neared the main compound, where the cement pathway came to a fork, the commander took a left turn. Omar had said over the phone after he was hired, that he would need temporary accommodation until he was able to find a place for himself. He had asked if there was a vacant room within the commander's house where he could reside for a short period of time. That request drew the customary Afghan hospitality, where the commander was compelled to provide housing for his new arriving employee who did not have any other place of his own.

"You could stay here for some time until you have a place of your own," said the commander as he opened the door to a one-bedroom maid's quarters across the main compound. "I will send for you at dinnertime."

Omar walked inside the room and placed his duffle bag on top of the bed. Then he started eying the walls around the room. He noticed shards of plaster missing from the face of the walls. His nose also picked up the damp smell of the room, which was very familiar to him. He peered out the wood-frame window across the yard to the main house, and suddenly it happened. He was drifting in his own memory, and the waves were taking him twenty-three years back. This was a sight where he was on the receiving end during those countless nights when she sat by this window, looking to the same direction all for a mere hope of seeing another glimpse of him. He had thought about her a lot. Sometimes, on his nights off, he sat by the window in his Queen Anne apartment only to look outside. He was propelled by the sheer hope of maybe understanding how she really felt, but that never came to him. But here he was now in the same room, looking out from the same window, trying to understand what happened to her. He was seeing the field of dirt in the place of the rose garden. Roses turned into dirt, another sign of this house losing its mighty glory.

As his eyes remained keen through the old window, the image of his past started to loom in his mind. It took him to one of his most memorable days.

CHAPTER EIGHTEEN

APRIL 19TH 1987, KABUL: The rich smell of saffron hovered over the back kitchen, which was detached and located at the rear of the main compound. The head chef of the Khyber restaurant was summoned to supervise other chefs, as they were getting ready to prepare a variety of entrees. Each chef was stationed in his own designated place; some of them were chopping vegetables, some were cutting and tenderizing meat. It was a spectacle of thirteen men dressed in all white with white toques, doing what the head chef had tasked them. The large kitchen was filled with gray smoke coming from the firepit at the back corner. The smoke was not easy for these men to bear, but that's the way it had to be done. The big pot of rice had to simmer over fire, which gave the rice a smoked flavor. Whenever a request like this was made for the chefs, it only meant one thing. There was going to be some prominent people at the party that evening.

Some distinguished families of Kabul had their own signature entrée; this was a tradition that had lasted for over fifty years. The Hafizi family was known for their *Baadjan Palu* by their counterparts. The first step was boiling *Baghlan* rice, then mixing a little sugar with water and oil, and heating it until the color turned dark brown. Once the rice had become soft, then the water was drained and the rice was placed back inside the pot for simmering. At this stage the brown ingredient was added, and that made the color of the rice go from white to brown. It was called Palu, one of the all-time most famous entrees of Afghanistan. The Hafizi family put fried miniature eggplant under the rice, and it was named Baadjan Palu.

That gave the traditional Afghan Palu their own uniqueness. A different terminology for such parties was called "Palau Jangi," which meant the war of Palu. The rich families of Kabul always found a reason to throw a party so they could invite their friends and rivals for an extravagant meal.

Almost any reason would have been good, but today the Hafizes had the biggest reason for the invitation of their guests. Today happened to be their beloved Omar's fourteenth birthday.

From the steps of the main house, Nakebakht called out to Rizwan.

"Have you bathed yet?" she asked in the agitated tone.

"Not yet… I am going to iron my trousers first." She answered in her girly way, completely disregarding the sense of urgency in her mother's voice.

Rizwan felt ashamed whenever her mother asked her about petty things. At the age of fifteen, she saw herself as a grown woman, and little remarks from her mother asking her to do certain things just drove her up the walls.

"Hurry up and get ready! The guests are arriving at sundown!" Nakebakht yelled again across the yard.

Rizwan stood there motionless, pretending that she didn't hear her mother's words. Her serene face was glowing under the evening sun, as her eyes served as a mirror spreading its rays across the manicured yard. Even at this young age, she had the most inconceivable presence, one that even made the richest of elite women to take a second look at this servant girl. Her eyes, unlike most Hazaras, were big and bright, eyes that could make a person stare at them all throughout the day just to see them change color from light green under the sunlight to emerald in the night, and her nose, a little pointy one that fit perfectly in her square face, and her hair, the ornament of her beauty, was like long threads of light-brown silk flowing naturally down her back.

She started making her way around the rose bushes to the other side of the yard towards the maid's quarters. Here, directly in front of the compound wall, rested their one-bedroom hut where she and her mother slept on the two mattresses that lay parallel on each side of the room. On the right side, a camel-color yarn curtain draped over the entrance of a little bathroom.

She took a match out of its pack and lit up the kerosene stove, and then she gingerly placed the big pot of water over it.

For years she has seen her mother clean the four marble bathrooms in the main house, but neither one of them had ever had the chance to bathe in them. She had been using this little bathroom all her life. To her, taking a bath was filling the big aluminum pot full of water, then lighting the stove and placing the pot on the stove for the water to heat. Across the yard in the big house, they just turn the faucet on and hot water flows. Two different lifestyles parted with rose bushes in between.

She grabbed the green dress and walked to the mirror in the room. Then she unfolded it and held it in front of her. She stood there silent, gazing at the reflection.

Green. It matches my eyes, she thought. But more so, she was really wondering if *he* would like it.

Omar was the youngest of all his cousins, and the only boy. The eldest son of Agha Sahib, Namat, had four girls. Mena, Homa, Rawa, and Ghezal, who were all older. Omar was the lonely son of Satar, Agha Sahib's middle son. Since Omar was the only boy among four girls, he always got the most amount of attention from his wealthy grandparents. But for the most part, Omar wasn't the typical spoiled kid, certainly not of the same caliber as his female cousins. He was humble and generous, and decent enough to think of Rizwan as a playmate and friend, unlike his cousins who perceived her as a servant.

Rizwan and Omar grew up in the same yard. As kids they played with each other, and as teenagers they got in trouble together. They were equals during the day, but at night, he slept in his mahogany bed, and she slept on a thin mattress on the floor next to her mother.

Rizwan had always thought of him as a playmate, too. She spent most days with him, either chasing after his bicycle or climbing the walnut tree, or holding his spool when he flew kites. But for the last year or so, as she has reached womanhood, her feelings towards him have taken a different course. He is no longer a playmate. He has become more. She is not quite sure what it is exactly, but she sometimes thinks about him before she falls asleep, or during the times when she can't sleep.

As the sun descended from the sky, the guests were starting to arrive.

Men, women, and their children all dressed in their extravagant clothes were making their way in through the big gray wooden gate. The men were in suits, dark gray, navy blue and brown. Women wore long dresses—suitable for an elegant night, and boys wore jeans, and girls wore short skirts with matching blouses. They made their way through the narrow cement pathway around the rose bushes to the staircase of the entertainment room.

Rizwan happened to be the one who opened the big wooden gate each time someone rang the bell. Rarely did she receive any acknowledgement, or simply a *Salaam*, or someone making eye contact with her. They just walked in as if a machine had opened the door.

Shortly thereafter, the sound of music was echoing throughout the house. All the kids gathered in the living room where the big sound system was playing a tape of a Boney M. song, *Young Free and Single.* In those days, it was fashionable in Kabul to listen to American music, and Boney M. happened to be the prime choice among young people.

From the empty hallway, Rizwan peered inside the room through the open door. She saw girls and boys engaged in the utmost fun. Her eyes kept searching for Omar inside the room. Finally, she spotted him. He was wearing a dark red velvet tuxedo and was standing in the corner of the room, casually watching the other kids. She thought he shined like a little prince, just like from those bedtime stories that her mother used to tell her when she was younger. She stood there still, focusing her eyes on him to see if he'd notice her. She had thought that she looked very pretty with her green dress, even more so today, because her long light-brown hair was combed straight and it was flowing naturally down to her back.

Helai, who was the rich neighbor's granddaughter, spotted Rizwan looking inside the room. She gave her a disgusted look and walked across the room and swung the door shut in her face.

Rizwan started walking to the other end of the hallway. Her head was bowed, and her hands swung slowly with each step towards the little hut on the other side of the rose bushes. Her body uttered defeat. Despite her dreams, this was a battle that she could not win as a servant's daughter. For everywhere in this house, she was just that, and not a tad more.

She was lost in her own thoughts as she sat with her hands wrapped around her legs and her chin resting on her knees. She started contemplating everything to the boundaries of her young mind. She wondered all sorts of questions—ones she could not answer herself. She wanted to be among those rich kids in that room. She too, wanted to dance to that fast music that she was hearing. She wanted to laugh and feel joy as those other kids did. But she couldn't. She was just a "*Muzdoor*" servant. This was not a life that she had chosen, but a life that had chosen her.

Slowly, a tear appeared in her eye, and as it started to roll down across her left cheek, a hand came around her shoulder and wiped it away. She turned to find him kneeling beside her, revealing his white smile.

"See… I caught it," he said with his gentle voice. "Come on now. Let's go!"

He had a way of sneaking up on her. Ever since she could remember, he had a way of catching her off guard. This all started when they were very young, when they played hide and seek. She would go hiding in the big house and wait for him to find her, but he wouldn't come, not until it was late enough where she went out looking for him. And then, out of nowhere, he would sneak up on her for a surprise.

"I am not going to cut my cake unless you're there."

In that moment, every bit of anguish evaporated from her body. Her day brightened, just like how she imagined it. She had her new green dress on and she was going to stand by his side.

The guests were seated on rows of couches in the formal living room. At the center of the room rested a round stainless steel table where a three-layer cake sat on top. All the kids were scattered around the table, awaiting Omar to cut the cake. It had been a few moments since everyone had gathered around in this room, and yet there was still no sign of him. The guests were beginning to scan the room in search of his whereabouts as their patience was being tested. Finally, from the hallway Omar made his way to the room, and trailing him was Rizwan, to the guests' dismay. There was a sudden shock on the observer's faces as they saw him walking in with the servant's daughter. Some guests envied the fact that Agha Sahib Hafizi's grandson would rather spend time with his servant than their kids.

He made his way around the table and stood behind his three-layer cake, which almost was as tall as him. Then the singing of *Happy Birthday* began.

Rizwan sat on the floor near the doorstep, the preordained place where a servant sits. She saw gazes falling on her with the intended question, *Why is she there?* She had not anticipated being there, either, but then he had said, *"I am not going to cut my cake unless you're there."* And that's all she needed to hear to dismiss the indignity. Among all the elevated faces sitting on the couches around the room, she saw one that was genuine, smiling at her, as he stood to cut his birthday cake.

It was a tradition for the birthday kid to share the first piece with his or her favorite person. He wanted to give the first piece to Rizwan, but he couldn't. No aristocrat family serves a servant before their guests. Conveniently, Helai, the neighbor's granddaughter, took her plate and held it in front of him.

"I'll take the first piece, please," she said in a fake charming voice—one that could only be made by a little brat who tried to sound sincere.

Later on that evening, when all the guests were dispersed, Rizwan was helping her mother take away the dirty dishes from the formal dining room to the kitchen. She carried loads through the hallway down to the other end of the house to the kitchen. On her last load, she heard footsteps behind her as if someone was sneaking up on her. This could only be the one person who was a master of sneaking up. As she turned, she saw Omar standing there with his hands hidden behind his back. He had his usual mild grin, not too excited, and not too serious, just genuine. She shot him a mild smile.

"What is it?" she asked.

He brought his left hand from the back and held it in front of her.

"A fork?" she declared sarcastically.

He was holding a silver fork in his left hand. Then he brought his other hand around, and he was holding a plate with a piece of cake on it.

"I saved this for you."

She felt hope in an array of hopelessness. It wasn't the eagerness of having a piece of cake, but to be a piece of his life, where he'd go to such lengths for a small thing for her. It was the acknowledgement, and she wanted to exist more than everything.

He led her back to the dining room, where he pulled up a chair and asked her to sit.

He watched her slowly running the silver fork over the frosting. Then slicing it down to a bite-sized chunk. Then slowly the fork lifted and her lips opened, and the silver fork made its way into her mouth. He sat there looking at her, revealing his inward smile as he witnessed her relishing her moment.

"What?" she demanded as she noticed his unconscious stare.

"Oh nothing," he shook his head.

CHAPTER NINETEEN

The shadow of the large mansion was receding over the rose garden as the sun made its appearance in the early morning. There, on the other side, the tinkling sound of glasses were echoing its way through the narrow hallway into the room.

Nakebakht spent most of the day tending to the main compound. She had very little time to spend doing the chores in her own house, except for early in the mornings when everyone was still asleep at the big house, and then, that was her time to do her own duties.

"Aftowgoo… come watch the flowers."

Aftowgoo was a pet name that she mustered for Rizwan. It meant sunflower in their native Hazara dialog—a language that Rizwan despised and wished that she was not a part of. But Nakebakht, she had accepted it a long time ago. Nakebakht had accepted that she was going to be a servant for the rest of her life, and her daughter would follow on the same path. It wasn't really a path of choice, but a path of fate for a Hazara.

Contrary to her mother's perceptions, Rizwan in her adolescence saw things differently. She wanted to be like Mena, who always had her friends over, and they all listened to music and talked about boys, and which one they thought would make the best suitor. Or at times she wanted to be like Homa, who always kept up with the fashion trends. And then Rawa, who was the most modest of the four sisters, and then it was Ghezal, who she thought had the most beautiful big brown eyes—ones that she even envied at times. That's how she wanted to be, exactly like Agha Sahib's granddaughters. Even as she was confined in her own world, her dreams remained on the other side of the rose bushes.

"Aftowgoo?" Nakebakht's voice rang again. "The sun will be up, and you'll miss your daily ritual."

That only meant one thing. Rizwan's eyes were open now. She definitely didn't want to miss this. If she did, then she would have to wait another eight hours.

Suddenly she jumped up from sleep and made her way to the lone faucet on the other side of the narrow hallway. She turned the faucet and splashed three fistfuls of cold water on her face, and then reached for the toothbrush. In a few minutes, she paced her way to the front of the house where she found her mother sitting on top of the short stool washing the previous night's dishes.

"Isn't it beautiful?" Nakebakht asked, turning her head towards the rose garden, in awe of her sunflower's fulfillment as she fixed her gaze on a garden that was split in half by shade and sunlight. Rizwan told her that it was her favorite time of the day, when the sun appeared a few meters above the main roof, and the edge of the roof cast a straight line in the middle of the rose garden as if light and shadow was separated evenly with a blade. She had demanded to be woken early enough everyday so she could see this occurrence. Saying it was "her favorite time of the day" was a bit dishonest. Shamefully, the truth remained on the other side of the garden, just like every other dream.

On that day, Rizwan sat and watched the battle between light and shade. By morning, the shadow had receded on the grass along the cement pavement, and by mid-morning, the shadow had clawed its way up on the pedestal of the big house, and by noon, the shadow had been fully defeated and light conquered everywhere. Still nothing, and she had seen nothing. Just like the shadow defeated by the light, she had been defeated, too, and receded back to the room on top of her thin mattress, lying on her right side, both palms attached and placed under her right ear, and her eyes wide open in wonder.

Two hours passed and still she was in wonder. Then it all ended when a voice appeared.

"Are you still sleeping?"

She didn't want to turn around right away. A few more seconds would be enough to bury the agony of waiting all day.

"I didn't see you this morning before I went to school. Are you okay?"

She wanted to jump up and shout that she was awake waiting for him when the light was barely touching the rose garden, and she waited until the whole yard was lit, and he still didn't show, but she couldn't. In those few seconds, her hostility from waiting a whole day had evaporated and was replaced by the formation of a smile.

CHAPTER TWENTY

"Do you have the other notebook?" Omar asked.

Rizwan started shuffling some items inside her bag and then produced a thin black notebook.

"You haven't written anything in this?" he asked, "I gave this to you so you can start jotting down your Dari homework in it, not to hang on to it as a souvenir!" His voice turned a bit to the stern side.

Rizwan shot him a sheepish look. She was ashamed for not taking their afternoon studies seriously, considering that he was the only one who wanted her to receive some form of an education, even if it meant sitting under the walnut tree in the midafternoon, teaching her what he had learned in his own class that same day.

Nakebakht never made any attempts to enroll Rizwan in school. She knew the only good thing that would alter her daughter's life was a good husband. She thought that was far more important than education. In a few more years, Rizwan would take on more responsibility around the mansion, ultimately taking over for her in serving Agha Sahib. If Nakebakht had dreams, then that was it. Her daughter would follow in her footsteps. That map was stamped on Rizwan's brow the exact second when she left Nakebakht's womb and entered this world. She was going to be just like her mother.

It only took a few seconds for Rizwan to bury the shamefulness of not taking their study sessions seriously. After all, it was she who waited all day to see him. If she could, she would've blurted out her frustration, but she didn't. She couldn't express how badly she wanted to see him everyday.

And for that, she resorted to silence. She sat there quietly and let the mid-afternoon sun glisten off her eyes in hopes of him noticing something that she could not say. And at last, he did.

"What is wrong, Rizwan?" he shut the Dari book and gave her a concerned look. "Are you okay?"

His soft tone had transformed to mist cooling her body on that hot afternoon. And with it, it brought her the courage to say what she really wanted to say.

"At sunrise, I was waiting to see you."

He lifted his eyes from the Dari book for a quick glance. And then, shyly, he fixed them back.

All this time she was burdened by shame, and never had even considered telling him, but something was overpowering her. It was the thought of him that she held so dearly. She yearned for his presence by her side, but then her heart ached when she saw him across the rose garden, only a few meters in distance but a lifetime apart. Despite the differences between them, she still didn't allow her fate to stand in her way, not in those moments when she was laying on top of her thin mattress and hysterically giving in to the thoughts of them being together. In those moments, every speck of difference was evaporated and she was soothed with an intoxication that could only see him.

"Did you go from the back door?"

"No," he answered. "I went from the same way I go everyday."

"Then how come I didn't see you?" she pressed. "I was up when the sun was hardly touching the roses!"

He chuckled. "Are you still watching the sun to see what time it is?"

He pressed his lips tight. He was trying to hide a laugh that was about to erupt on her account.

"Daylight savings."

"What is that?" she asked abruptly.

"Daylight savings… is the time when they extend the sunlight."

"They can make days longer?"

He let out a mild laugh. "No, they can't make days longer. They just move attendance an hour early in the springtime and then they move it back again in the wintertime."

"Why?" she asked in surprise.

"Well, it's because they can save energy in the wintertime. Also, to make sure everybody works when the sun is out and be home when it's dark."

"Oh… I see what you mean now."

At times, she was really amazed by how smart he was. Sometimes she envied him for it—wishing she could be as bright.

Omar unzipped the front pocket of his school bag and fetched a wristwatch, and then handed it to her.

"Uncle Wali gave me this the other day. Do you like it?"

She brought it closer for a better look. The soft leather band felt smooth under her thumb. The gold-plated face glistened as she tilted it side to side.

"It's very nice."

"See these little arms?"

She nodded.

"See the little one is on three and the bigger one is on twelve. Can you tell what time it is?"

She shook her head.

"See… the little one tells you the hour, and the bigger one tells you the minute. So, if you see the little one on three and the larger one on twelve, it tells you it's three o'clock. You basically start from here and add fifteen minutes on each of these points, "three, six, nine, and twelve."

There was still a look of confusion on her face. For her, it was the first time when she was being told about the concept of time and how to track it. But things started to make sense as he kept persisting in explaining.

She placed her index finger on the faceplate and said, "So you mean to tell me you go to school when the little one is on seven and the bigger one is on six?"

"Yes! See… you got it! That's seven-thirty!"

Her face revealed a proud expression.

"Here… I want you to have it," he gave her the watch. "Now that you know how to read time, you should have a watch."

She placed the golden watch on her palm, and then slowly closed her hand. At any other time, she would have refused a gift such as this, but in this case she really needed to see those two small arms, one on seven and the other on six. In her mind, those two numbers equated seeing him.

Their days were spent in the same order. Evenings, however, were altered. He would remain in his room and she in hers. And for as long as the light from his nightstand was shimmering outside his window, she was watching from across the yard in hopes of another glimpse.

Each night she held to the hope. Often she wondered. She wondered how it was that, up until a year and half ago, all she wanted to do was to sit behind his bicycle, or climb the ladder after him whenever he decided to go on top of the greenhouse. And the times they played hopscotch on the attic floor. Now, those playful days were a scene of the past with bits of those memories seldom flashing in her mind.

Everything transcended into confusion. Her thoughts have twirled on a course of its own. She thought of his eyes, most of the time very calm, but when he was agitated, they were keen. She felt they saw beyond any excuses she presented, straight to the truth. She thought of the times when he bit his fingernails, and how she extended her hand and touched his hand, taking it away from his mouth. She thought about his hand feeling cold in those brief seconds when she touched it. Mostly not at the time when it happened, but later on, when she reflects on their time spent together. She thought of his fragrance, and how she knew he was within her reach when she sensed it. The bewilderment remained with her on nights when she was lying on her back with eyes wide open, staring at the gloom of the room. She thought of the smoothness of his cold hands, his fingers barely touching her hand, and his warmth as he was getting closer to her. At the beginning, she was burdened by shame and always stopped her thoughts from escalating further, but now, many nights later, time has chipped away what used to be shameful. This had become another ritual for her. Every night before going to sleep, she was allowing her mind to take her further. This was sacred. She was the only one who held claim to her mind, and she wanted it to take her far beyond anything she has ever experienced. She wanted to rise up against all the obstacles; she wanted to break all the boundaries. These were her thoughts, and she was not afraid to get lost in them until she felt her heart beating faster, and her body temperature rising and cooling back down, relaxed, and ultimately at ease, falling into sleep.

CHAPTER TWENTY-ONE

Every year in the month of July, the Hafizi family escaped the hot summer of Kabul and went up north to Paghman, to their summer home. Paghman was high in elevation and much cooler than Kabul. This year, the hot weather came to Kabul a bit early, so the family made the migration sooner than their usual time. Schools in Kabul usually took the month of July off, except for this year, due to the government using the newer German-built all-boys school for housing the border militia for two weeks in the month of June, the boys already had two weeks off. Therefore, their summer vacation was cut by two weeks.

Omar and his uncle Wali had to stay behind for two more weeks until their school got off. And because of them, Nakebakht and Rizwan had to stay as well to look after them while everyone else was in Paghman.

Wali was Omar's youngest uncle, just a little more than three years older in age. There was always a rivalry between them. Wali happened to be the youngest of all Agha Sahib's sons, and his wife's favorite, too. On the other hand, Omar was the only grandson, which made them both valued more than the girls in the family. Wali, a discourteous seventeen-year-old, got everything he wanted from his parents. The latest style of clothes, a brand-new bicycle, and everything else that he thought of. His position of being the oldest teenage boy gave him the claim to everything first. He often passed down his possessions to Omar after he grew tired of them, such as by wrapping his old watch as a birthday present for him.

"Oh Come on *bachaim*… it's a Seiko Five! It even has gold plate!" Wali had said.

Omar hated when Wali got all the new things and they became hand-me-downs to him. And the worst part was Wali making it sound like he was sprinkling him with his generosity, though in reality he had already received the replacement for it before it was handed down. In a way, Omar didn't have a whole a lot of room to argue, because traditionally in the Afghan culture that was the norm. The elders got first choice of new things and the younger was destined to take the secondhand items. It wasn't so much about Wali being the heir to all new things, but rather his arragance and entitlement was what got under Omar's skin.

Nakebakht prepared the dinner and placed it on the dining room table. The table usually sat fifteen people. Agha Sahib would sit at the top of the table by the window, and Bebe jaan would sit at the bottom end, facing her husband. In between on each side sat all the sons, their wives and kids. The topics ranged over anything that Agha Sahib wished to talk about, so conversations were broad in subject. Some nights it was the daily news; other times politics, and seldom, how the grandkids were doing in school, Omar's favorite topic. In essence, those were the moments of triumph for him when his grandfather inquired about his grades. He was the top student in his class, an achievement he was not shy about sharing over dinner. Even more than his own triumph, he enjoyed seeing Wali melt in his seat. Unlike Omar, he was not doing well in school, and at some point his grandfather would peer at him, too. And at those moments, seeing his uncle Wali's babyface wince when his father's battered eyes were locked on him in disappointment was the payback for all of Wali's scorns.

"Dinner is ready!" Nakebakht called out in the hallway.

Omar canvassed the empty dining room. The table was usually full by the time he arrived, but today it was only him in the company of the oversized mahogany table. He pulled out his usual chair and sat on the right side, towards the end, away from the window—the spot where he normally sat when the table was full.

A few seconds later, Wali entered the room. He walked by his usual chair, which was directly in front of Omar on the left side, to the top and sat in the place of his father. Omar shot him a disgusted look for taking his grandfather's chair.

"So Omar jaan, how is your Pashto coming along?" Wali asked, mimicking his father. Omar ignored him.

"Now as the top student in your class, do you get to sit directly in front of your teachers?" he continued his sarcastic tone. Omar still didn't want to answer, so he sat still and gave him a blank stare.

"Seriously, the male teachers can come and go… won't matter, but that Pashto teacher… oh god, she is something else."

Robia jaan was a newly graduated teacher. She was a native Pashto speaker of immaculate beauty. She had fair skin, with big brown eyes and long auburn hair over an hourglass body—one that she was not shy about hiding. She wore the most modern clothing, usually miniskirts that draped just above her knees and tight blouses where the tops of her breasts were revealed. At the beginning of the year, she taught older boys up to age of eighteen, but after some mischief related to her modernity, the school administration thought it would be better if she taught younger boys who were too young to marvel at her sex appeal.

"Omar jaan, tell me. Did you ever drop your pencil and kneel under the desk to look at her down there?" Omar noticed the goofy smirk on Wali's face while he waited for his reply.

"No!" he snapped. "Down where?" he yelled in an agitated tone.

"You know… down between her thighs."

Omar's face was blank. But there was a surge of curiosity that he felt. As despicable as Wali may have been, down deep, Omar wanted to hear more.

"You see… I used to do that when she was teaching us at the beginning of the year. Unlike you, I am not a top student, so I didn't have a desk in front of the teacher's desk, but I had learned how to flick my pencil motionlessly from the next row to the row in front of her. Then I would get up and walk over and kneel down to grab my pencil and turn to look."

"If you were caught, you would've been slapped."

"No way, she was pretending to be busy with her papers."

Omar always knew Wali had a special talent when it came to odd mischief. He rarely got caught. He was the family magician. He could make a coin disappear in a second.

"One day, I flicked my pencil. This time it went close, really close…

it landed under the desk in front of hers. And when I crawled under the desk, I saw it!"

"What?" Omar pressed.

Wali's goofy smirk reappeared on his face again, but this time his eyes were closed, recalling it as if it was the only delightful moment of his life.

"What did you see?" Omar pressed.

"It," he answered, "and I know she wanted me to see it, too!"

"What is *it*?"

"Oh you unprivileged donkey. Or should I say… you fool?"

Omar scowled.

"*It* is something you have not seen yet. And something that you won't see for a long time," Wali chuckled.

Later that evening, Omar stood in his room. He was boggled by Wali's story. He felt resentment, because despite his despicable ways, Wali always had the upper hand on him. He was growing tired of him having a proclaimed elevated position over him, and to his own dismay, Wali made sure of it. As the youngest of all his brothers, Wali was granted the cultural acceptance of being spoiled beyond question. But then his throne was threatened when Omar was born, where his parents had to place some of the spotlight on him as well. That drove Wali mad. He did not want the attention to go towards Omar. And to his misfortune, Omar happened to be a kid who everyone praised for being well mannered and smart. That only led Wali to settle matters in his own way. He was going to use his natural talents to destabalize Omar, which resulted in taunting and demeaning him, or messing with his head, as he called it himself.

Omar peered out the window across the yard to the maid's quarters and saw the shimmer of the dime light in the background. It cast the silhouette of Rizwan sitting by the window, looking his way. There she was, someone who would always accept him and stay loyal to him without wavering. She may be ignored as she went about her daily life around the house, picking up the dirty dishes, sweeping the rugs, carrying loads of laundry, and doing so while invisible in the eyes of his wealth-stricken family, but to him, she was perpetually the most visible thing. She shone just too brightly whenever she saw his face.

He waved to her from the window. Shortly after, his eyes created the blue reflection of her under the moonlight, veering around the rose bushes as she made her way to him.

"What is it?" she asked, almost out of breath from her run.

He opened the latch and swung the window open. "Come up," he said.

For a second, Rizwan searched for reservations holding her back, but then she realized that her mother had already fallen asleep and she had turned off the light to their room before she snuck out.

CHAPTER TWENTY-TWO

THREE MONTHS LATER: Omar kept his pace steady as he walked from school. The weather was getting colder as autumn had already approached. He would have his finals next month before the start of the winter break. He anticipated doing well on his finals because his grandfather had wagered a brand new bike if he receives all fives on his report card. He contemplated the possibility of stopping his study sessions with Rizwan so he could fully tend to his own studying. He could continue with her after he was done with the finals. The wind had picked up on that bright October afternoon, so he fastened his pace to the gray wooden gate, which started to loom in a distance. He moved through the passage door into the yard. As he was walking on the cement pathway, he looked to his left for signs of Rizwan.

This is unusual, he thought. *Usually right about now, she waves at me.*

He walked inside the main house. His intuition alerted him that something was very wrong today. There was a quiet feeling throughout the rooms. Everyone's face reflected the dull walls of the house: colorless, lifeless, but present.

He put his school bag in his room and then ventured off across the yard to go see Rizwan. As he neared the maid-quarters, he saw the curtains shut. Ever since he could remember, Nakebakht insisted on having the curtains open during the day in every room. She had said: "The sunlight is a gift from God, we should not drape ourselves from it." And that's exactly what she did. She pulled all the curtains open in the morning, and closed them shut in the evenings. What puzzled Omar was the question of why her drapes were shut in the middle of the afternoon.

He approached the door. It was not locked. He turned the knob and opened it. Omar didn't know that the next thing he saw would leave him perplexed for a very long time.

"Where did they go?" He asked his grandmother after eyeing the empty room.

She ignored him the first time when he asked. He looked to his grandmother, who stood still, her face reflecting fierce anger. He did not hesitate.

"Where?" His tone was stern this time.

"You are not to ever talk about them! Nor to ask any questions!" she shouted those words, "do you understand me?"

He froze like a statue. He had never witnessed his grandmother speaking in that manner before, nor had he even thought the nice gentle lady could be so ferocious.

He nodded.

He left the foyer and made his way down the corridor to the back kitchen. His head was slouched and his arms gently swung around his body when he took each step, wondering what had happened while he was in school.

His ears picked up the tinkling sound of dishes coming from the back kitchen. He knew if he could find any answers, it had to come from a different source. He walked inside the kitchen and shut the door behind him. Upon hearing the door shut, Naim turned to see who had came inside. Naim was the young cook who had been working for his grandfather the last two years. He was slender and tall with a thick black mustache that gave him a very serious demeanor, especially when he arched his eyebrows and looked intently at someone. But contrary to his intimidating appearance, he was a gentle man.

He read the perplexed look on Omar's face instantly. He could see the loss in him as if a part of him had been amputated. He gave a blank look and then turned back to washing the soaked dishes in the sink. Omar made his way next to the counter and stood silently.

"You know, I really need this job," said Naim.

"I know," agreed Omar, "but I need to know what happened."

Naim shook his head in an afterthought, "I do have a family that I provide for, you know…"

"Please tell me," Omar begged.

Naim lifted his chin high and fixed his eyes on the ceiling. Then he brought his head back down and submitted to his reservations.

"I can't," he sighed.

Omar stood there for a moment, silently watching Naim fetching the porcelain teapots from the soapy water and then rinsing them under the faucet. He could tell that Naim did want to tell him what he wanted to know, but then Naim was hesitant because of the consequences, which could alter his fate as well.

"Naim, I promise I won't say or do anything."

Naim eyed him for a brief second.

"I just need to know what happened, Naim."

He turned off the faucet and placed the last teapot on top of the towel, which was there to absorb the water from the clean dishes. Then he turned to Omar.

"Your uncle Wali…"

"What about him," Omar pressed hysterically.

"He is… he's the devil."

"What did he do?" Omar pressed

Naim eyed him. He realized that he was so small compared to his tall, long figure. He hesitated to go on.

"I can't say anything else. I'm sorry, I really am. Please don't ask me, no more…"

Tears started to well up in Omar's eyes. He knew that Wali had done something. He certainly was capable of it as well. In the past, he had his fair share of collisions with the servants. Each time, it ended the same. Wali got his way, and his mother fired those workers—a true shame that only served Wali's ego. The fragile poor became homeless in the snap of his finger.

It was hard for him to imagine that Wali could do something to Nakebakht, who had been working in this house ever since he could remember. And Rizwan, who was born in that little room across the garden on the other side of the yard; but in the end, none of that mattered. The only thing that really did was Wali, and what he deemed right in his self-righteous mind.

"You promised that you won't say anything," Naim reminded him. "If you do, they will throw me out too… and my kids…"

"I promise," Omar cut him off before he finished his sentence.

Omar made his way back to the house, walking through the hollow foyer and the silent halls to his room. He sat by the window. The sun was beginning to sit behind the Asmayee Mountain to the west. The tip of the mountain was casting a shadow in the middle of the yard. He fixed his eyes across the yard to the shade. There rested a room that was empty of life. The curtains were closed, and the door shut as it sat lifeless in the shadow of the mountain. He curled his back and rested his face on his knees as he remembered Rizwan vividly doing in times of hardship. He knew that somewhere in this godforsaken city, Rizwan was doing the same thing. Silently, he began to weep. What he didn't know at that moment was he'd never see her again.

CHAPTER TWENTY-THREE

PRESENT DAY: Night had fallen. He realized he had looked out the window for most of the afternoon, as if it was a window opening into his own past. There were so many other bits and pieces that floated around his memory. Most of it perhaps was conjured as a story by his mind in the absence of truth. He had thought about those missing pieces all the time, but then came to a conclusion that they may not be relevant to the truth. He had spent long years in search of the possibilities—maybe this happened, or what if that had happened—but in the end, his life was an array of maybes and what-ifs in search of closure that never came.

He had hoped for a day that his uncle Wali would come to his senses and speak the truth about what he had done to Nakebakht and Rizwan. But time had elapsed on that revelation, too. Wali, along with his grandfather, had died in a car accident two years after their arrival in the U.S. To his own dismay, Wali had taken his arrogance out on the road one afternoon after he had just received his driver's license. The Atlanta police department's report said the young man was engaged in road-rage with another car on the freeway when he lost control and smashed into a guardrail. It also said neither the young man nor his elderly father were wearing seatbelts. Omar remembered cursing him at the funeral, because his grandfather paid a hefty price for bearing an arrogant son, one who took his own life along with his. A couple of months after their deaths, his grandmother suffered a stroke. She too lived the rest of her days paralyzed, without a word spoken until the day when she didn't wake from her sleep. Some superstitious relatives said that they were cursed. It was a sentiment that Omar resented, but down deep, he agreed. *Karma has a way of balancing injustice.*

Now, with all of them gone from this world, he knew the truth would be obscured forever. Unless somehow the walls in this house could speak and tell the story of what happened on that October afternoon, eighteen years earlier. But he knew that these walls would still remain dull and lifeless, exactly as they were on that day.

Abdullah, the boy who opened the gate for him earlier, appeared by the door. "My father said for you to come for dinner with us."

Omar started following Abdullah as he led him towards the main compound. It was the first sight of this house up close. When he entered the foyer, he felt a chill as his memories were coming to life. Such memories had been plastered in his mind from childhood, but then when he looks around intently, he found the house much changed from what he remembered. Even this house was not unsusceptible to the test of time.

He saw the walls with different colors of paint. Some of the marble tiles were replaced with new ones that didn't quite match the old ones that rested on the floor. But apart from visual aspects, one thing that remained as it did eighteen years ago was the smell of cardamom that came from the kitchen all the way to the foyer.

Abdullah ushered him to the dining room where Commander Khaled awaited his arrival. He was sitting at the top of the table with his back towards the window, exactly the same place where his grandfather used to sit. Upon seeing Omar entering the room, he stood up.

"Please," he motioned to the seat on his left.

"Thank you," said Omar as he took the seat.

Omar looked around the table and saw all the other chairs empty of occupants, an inverse sight from the glory days of this house. He had heard the voices of women when he made his way to the dining room, but then acutely realized that nowadays in Afghanistan, women are not allowed to dine in the presence of an unknown man. *It's another testament to this country moving backwards. They're veiled and locked behind doors.*

"Is the room okay?" the Commander asked.

"Yes, thank you very much. It's fine for now. Hopefully, I'll have a place of my own very soon."

The Commander nodded. "I apologize for having you there, I know it's not the most prestigous place, but unfortunately that's the only suitable place for a male guest."

Omar instantly picked up on what the Commander was implying. A male guest was forbidden to sleep in the same house as the females, no matter how big the house, and how much privacy it offered.

"I completely understand, sir." Omar reassured him.

The Commander's face exuded a sigh of relief. He was happy to understand that Omar knew of the changes that had taken place in this country. He didn't perceive himself as traditional or a religious man, but he still had to go by the norms the culture commanded. He too had hopes for this country to come back to the period of modernization as it once was, prior to the arrival of Soviet Union. But he also knew the coming of such a time was inconceivable right now, given the country's state and it's nourishment of extreme conservatism.

The door swung open. Omar's eyes fell on the girl who entered the room. She had a tray full of dishes in her hands. Her face was half covered by a green nylon scarf, covering her mouth and nose, while allowing her light green eyes to see. She silently started scattering the dishes on top of the table. Omar had considered saying *Salaam* to her, but then noticed that the Commander made no introduction as he sat there silent. After placing the dishes and the utensils in their proper places, she headed towards the door and left the room.

"My American counterparts did a background check on you this afternoon," the Commander broke the silence. "They also went ahead and registered you with the U.S. embassy."

Omar looked at him and nodded attentively.

"It's imperative for every American citizen to register with the U.S. embassy when they are here in Kabul. That way if something happens to them, they can send the Marines for them," and he chuckled.

"And the background check?" Omar asked.

"Oh, actually that's more for them than it is for me."

Omar squinted, confused.

"The Americans have a dim trust with us Afghans. So, they insist on a thorough knowledge of our staff. And of course, you being a U.S. citizen would ease up some of their tensions."

Omar nodded as he listened to the Commander, who he thought was eager to have his presence on his side.

"Oh, and there will come a time when they ask you to advise me on certain matters," he kept his eager expression. "If that happens, then it means that you have fully earned their trust."

Omar wasn't sure whether the Commander had reservations about him surpassing his own tenure among his American counterparts. *That remains to be seen.*

The door swung open again, and the girl walked in. This time she was carrying a larger tray filled with *Palau* and three bowls of steaming entrees. As she placed the tray in the center of the dining room table, the edge of her green scarf came unwrapped over her shoulder and draped down, revealing a full view of her face. Her eyes met Omar's gazing eyes and she quickly fetched the end of her scarf and covered her face again.

After witnessing her embarrassment, the Commander felt the compulsion to say something.

"She's been with us for about four years. She's a brave girl," he said.

"She is not a family member?" Omar asked.

"No," he shook his head, "well, kind of, but not really."

He hoisted the plate of Palau and placed it in front of Omar. "It's a long story," he said.

Down deep, Commander Khaled knew the story of the young brave girl showed a ray of bravery on his part. He knew politically such a true story would attest to his credibility as a genuine person. He knew that he desperately needed his self-portrait to be repainted in the eye of the public. There were times where he had to resort to military force to obtain power, but now those times have changed with the light of democracy. The only thing that mattered to him now was his public image, which would affect his aspirations of power someday if the public were to see his name on a ballot. *But how can I bury my past?* That was a question that puzzled most of the warlords who were assigned high posts in the Afghan government today.

He quizzically looked at Omar's face as he sat still, waiting to hear him speak. He felt soothed, knowing that he was going to tell his triumphant story one more time.

"Very well," he said.

"During the Taliban era, there was a particular Arab who lived in Kandahar. Unlike the rest of Arabs who were affiliated with Al-Qaeda and fought side by side the Taliban against us, this one was not among them. He was here for a different purpose, which was more self-prospering. He was more of a businessman, specializing in human trafficking. He paid really well, and received full immunity from the Taliban. His real name was Qadir, but people came to know him by his round face and overly large body. They called him the Fat Arab. The Fat Arab had distinct requirements, which resulted in bringing him the most amounts of profits. He paid a lot of money for young girls, ages fourteen to fifteen. He paid even more if they had light skin and light-colored eyes. After acquiring such girls, he would then smuggle them to UAE, where he auctioned their chastity to the rich sheikhs. We were told that this guy had converted large mansions into harems where he kept the claimed women for the sheikhs. There was also the unconfirmed rumor of the Fat Arab getting his influential clients in UAE to push forward for the recognition of the Taliban regime in Afghanistan. They ultimately did recognize the Taliban as the official government of this country at the time. If that was correct, then it presumably explains the immunity that they provided to the Fat Arab to go about his business here. The recognition of the Taliban as the official government also helped him fly his chartered airplane with smuggled passengers from here direct to Dubai seamlessly.

"In November 2001, after the consistent bombing campaign of the American forces, we raided Jalalabad. We found very little resistance from the Taliban within the city, they knew that their days were numbered as their operation was amputated by the American bombings and missiles.

"I commanded my troops to push eastwards in pursuit of the remnants of Taliban who were fleeing towards Pakistan. As we reached the outskirts of the city, we came about this deserted compound that was once guarded heavily by the Taliban. The locals told us that they had seen a heavy Arab sheikh come and go to this place from time to time. When we entered the house, we came to find four young girls locked inside the scattered rooms. After the rescue, some of the girls were chanting for Hawa, a girl among the bunch who struck a knife cut across the Fat Arab's right cheek. They said he might have killed her. But then one of the soldiers stumbled on piece of metal that covered a dried-up well. And when we hoisted the metal, we saw her sitting deep inside the well, still alive. One thing that intrigued me about this girl was her sense of calm. It was as though she had already accepted her fate, regardless of what that could have been.

"Shamefully, the four other girls elected to go back to their homes, to the families that sold them in the first place. But Hawa would not go to her parents. She refused to see them after their betrayal. She demanded to be sent to an orphanage. But I refused to do that. Given her bravery and what she had overcome, I managed to find her a home among my own family.

"I see it as her fate was bound with my family. She is here now. She is well, and she does help around here with the chores."

"That's very noble of you for taking her in," Omar said.

The Commander revealed an inward smile and slowly nodded, and then he abruptly changed the subject.

"We have a meeting tomorrow at Bagram with some American officials. They want to talk about reducing their military forces from the outskirts of Kabul, which I think is a bad idea. So brace yourself for translating my long debate."

"Okay, I look forward to it," Omar offered.

"Well, be sure to get a good night's sleep. The meeting is in the afternoon."

The Commander called to Abdullah, who came rushing to escort Omar back to his room.

He thanked the Commander for dinner and followed Abdullah back through the hallway, then to foyer, and ultimately across the yard to his room. A lot had happened today. Before his arrival he held a dislike towards the man who had confiscated his grandfather's estate. But now, he sensed himself growing somewhat fond of him. Commander Khaled didn't appear to be the brute he had anticipated over the phone. He now viewed him as a man trying to reconcile his devious past, one he shared with a lot of other people during the period of lawlessness in Afghanistan.

CHAPTER TWENTY-FOUR

The next morning, Omar took a stroll around the yard. In an unconscious way, he was looking for something to draw him back to his childhood memories where those missing pieces remained. The most important of all, the fate of Rizwan. Her disappearance caused the biggest void in his life.

Where would she be right now? He thought about her restlessly. Maybe he could find some signs of her whereabouts there, but all he saw was a house stripped of everything it once held, and new faces that have no clue about him and the people who once lived there. This house had changed hands a few times during the raids and lawlessness of the nineteen-nineties, and because of that no background check could identify him as a true heir to this house. Therefore, no one knew who the true owners were and no one cared. He had realized that truth in its own grace was paramount to his life going forward. He knew that he could never be at peace with himself until he was set free by it, even if it brought more resentment towards his deceased uncle Wali, who he didn't care for much anyhow.

He found himself walking on the cement pathway. He remembered as a boy he used to watch his grandfather pace on the same cement pathway back and forth early in the mornings. *He was a great man.* He had heard stories of his business endeavors that made him one of Afghanistan's wealthiest men. Omar remembered seeing him pacing back and forth, his eyes looking downwards on the path, and his mind in a wonder that he could not decipher. He spoke very little, but when he spoke he was earnest and sharp as an arrow. With some luck, he too could be a wealthy man like his grandfather. But he wanted it to be right. He didn't want to be overwhelmed with backlashes of guilt presiding over his conscience. He had to see about making everything right. He decided to find Rizwan and Nakebakht, wherever they were.

His reminiscent thoughts were disrupted when he heard Abdullah's voice by the gate. The boy was shouting obscenities at someone outside through the passage door. He turned from his pace and observed for a moment. *A really unpleasant way to speak to someone,* he thought. *But then, this is Afghanistan; they have their own mannerisms here.*

A moment later, Abdullah's grim face appeared as he came walking towards him to the other end of the yard.

"Salaam," he said to the boy.

"Salaam," Abdullah responded, his grim face shifting to excitement when he saw their foreign guest.

"Did you sleep well last night?" the boy asked.

"Yes, I was very comfortable."

"We should go have morning tea. I will bring you some hot water to wash up."

"Oh that's very kind of you. Thank you!" Omar already knew that his place of residence, the old maid's quarters, did not have plumbing for hot water. It had to be either heated on a pot or be brought.

"By the way, who was at the door?" Omar asked.

"A beggar," he said, "we get a lot of them coming to the door."

Beggars appear behind people's houses.

"That is very sad, do they want money?"

"Money and food," the boy said, "but you never give them money in public. Cause if you do, then a flock of them would appear from nowhere, demanding money from you."

"Thanks for the tip," Omar said warmly.

"We usually give them food, which is the best thing someone can do for them."

Omar cordially eyed Abdullah, knowing that he didn't give anything to that person who had came to the door.

"And did you offer something to the person who was just here?" Omar asked with a cordial smile.

"No!" Abdullah's eyes sharpened. "Because that's the crazy old woman!"

"A crazy old woman?" Omar repeated.

"Yeah, and she doesn't want any food or money. She comes here everyday asking for some people."

"Who is she?" Omar asked.

"I don't know," the boy shrugged, "she is this old Hazara woman that asks for someone name Agha Sahib who she says lived here. But we don't know anyone by that name and we keep telling her that, and she still keeps showing up!"

Omar felt his knees going weak. For a second he could see everything that he wanted to know within his grasp, but it was drifting away from him like a log in a fast river. He heard Abdullah's voice behind him calling, "where you going?" but he kept striding forward. He approached the gate and yanked the chain, then swung the door open. He was looking directly across the street, where he could see the wrought iron fence of the Iranian embassy's wall, which spread half a mile north to south.

She's got to be on this side of the road. Think. Which way would she go? He looked at the north side. *That's Wazir Akbar Khan.* Another wealthy secluded neighborhood, he drove past it yesterday, the neighborhood with huge houses built from drug money and corruption. His intuition told him: *turn south*. He started running again.

In a matter of five minutes, he approached the Saderat intersection, an overwhelmingly crowded area. He started scanning the faces in the crowd. But then he came to realize he didn't know what he was looking for. *Think.* He turned around and looked how far he had come. He covered a lot of ground, which could take an old woman double the time. That sounded right. Besides, he didn't see any woman on the street as he was running up this way.

She has to be here somewhere. He started scanning faces again. But, then very quickly he was reassured that he was looking at men's faces, because women's faces were covered under their *Burqa*. He saw a row of women sitting on the upper edge of the sidewalk, panhandling. And there were a lot more walking on the sidewalk, with their colorful burqas in green, blue, and turquoise. He had to resort to a strategy. He needed a plan. He could not pick her out in this vast crowd. He didn't know what she looked like; even if he did, her face was covered, behind the transparent holes of her burqa where it was purposefully not visible.

She has to come forward to me, but how? Again, his intuition told him to eliminate the veiled pedestrians. *She has to be among the ones who are sitting on the edge.* He fetched a bundle of local currency that he had exchanged at the airport the day before, from his pocket and held it in his hand. Then he approached the first woman that he saw on the edge of the sidewalk.

"I am the grandson of Agha Sahib, the former ambassador to Spain, during the king's era. Please pray for him." And he held out a twenty Afghani bill.

The woman fetched the bill from his hand and then raised her hands for a prayer. Omar eyed the woman's hands as she had them hoisted. Her hands didn't appear to belong to an old woman. She was young. And the name Agha Sahib didn't have any meaning to her. He moved on to the next, and repeated. Still nothing. She seemed younger too, and didn't recognize his grandfather. He kept on with that approach, until he had talked to all of those women sitting panhandling on that busy sidewalk. He had gotten no results.

He turned around and slowly made his way back. He started to believe that she somehow had evaded him by coincidence. He must have taken a wrong step somewhere, or what if she went north to Wazir Akbar Khan?

As he made his round back, his eyes fell on this woman who stood on the opposite side of the sidewalk and was looking his direction. She seemed a lot smaller around the shoulders from what he could see behind her old green burqa. As soon as she picked up on Omar's lingering gaze towards her, she swiftly turned and started walking towards a nearby alleyway, in direction of the chicken street. Omar followed his intuition one more time, hoping for luck.

As she made her way halfway down the deserted alley, Omar called out behind her.

"I am the grandson of Agha Sahib, the former ambassador to Spain, during the monarchy era!"

She ignored him, and kept on her pace.

"My name is Omar!"

Suddenly, her pace froze. She turned around and eyed him for the second time. Then she went down, sitting on edge of the sidewalk. Omar started running towards her, and as he neared, he realized he was looking at the old, wrinkled face of his grandfather's most faithful servant, Nakebakht. She lifted the burqa. Her weathered face was revealed.

He remembered her vividly. He remembered her songs that she sang to him when he was a little boy. Her soft voice harmonized the Hazara lyrics that still echoed in his mind at times. And above all, the stories that she told him.

For a moment he stood still, only looking at Nakebakht. Her face was dry to the extent where her skin had peeled off right underneath her eyes—the effect of salt filled tears running over the years—ultimately damaging the skin. Her lips were dry and nonapparent, the pale-yellowish color of her flesh. And the wrinkles caused by her unmoisturized dead skin stacked in layers upon layers on her face. He thought her face embodied the face of Afghanistan: how it used to be, and how it is now.

He sat next to her on the edge of the sidewalk.

"Nakebakht," he said, his voice just a tad louder than a whisper.

The old woman kept her gaze steady on him. She was eyeing him in the most curious way. He couldn't tell what went on in her mind.

"What has happened to you?" asked Omar.

She tried to say something, but then went quiet when she felt a shiver inside her.

"That house is no longer ours," said Omar, "but I was there this morning when you came, and that's how I came after you."

He noticed her tired old eyes turning from his to gaze into midair, as if she was recollecting her memory.

"They looted the house. I saw them do it!" she spoke.

Omar noticed the discomfort that his previous question had brought her, and thought that he should not ask her about what happened to them until she tells him, if she ever decided to. He was going to leave that up to her.

"Who?" he asked.

"The relatives."

"Did they take everything?" he asked.

"Yes… I couldn't stop them."

He fell silent. Wondering about what Nakebakht just told him. *So, she went back after we were gone.*

"Is that why you came back?" she asked. "You came for the house?"

Omar felt the inevitable sense of shame hovering over his consciousness when he heard that. This had become a common trend among Afghans who lived abroad. In the last four years, they only showed up in Kabul to sell their homes in the inflated real estate market fueled by drug money and corruption. That behavior on its own virtue drove the locals crazy, because from that standpoint, they just showed up and sold their real estate to take the money right out of the local economy abroad.

"No," he said, "the house is confiscated by a powerful commander now. No one can take it back."

Nakebakht didn't say anything. Her face was blank. He felt the urge to ask her what he needed.

"Did you remember the 'funny picture,' they used to call it?"

Her old, wrinkled eyes became stern suddenly when those words reached her ears. It was as if something deep inside her was stirred up.

"Yes, I remember it," she said nodding.

"I am here to find that," he said.

She eyed him intently and then moved herself a little closer.

"That's the only thing I was able to save from the looters," she declared in a hushed voice.

Omar was suddenly overjoyed, knowing what he was seeking to find so desperately actually did existed somewhere. *But where?*

"Would you be able to show me? Or tell me?" he asked, eagerly.

"Yes, I could, but you have to do something for me first."

"What?" he answered.

"I have a granddaughter…" she hesitated for a second, as she tried to articulate the words, "you have to find her for me first."

A granddaughter? That could only mean she was Rizwan's child. He had wondered if she ever had gotten married, and had children of her own, and how she lived in this country. But now he was reassured that after all she did bear a child. Then he was perplexed by the thought, *what has happened to Rizwan and her husband? And how was her daughter missing?*

He reckoned that soon he would learn everything about her, along with what really happened that afternoon when he came from school, and the treachery of Wali's actions, which resulted in their departure.

He solemnly looked at Nakebakht's battered eyes. He knew this was the moment when he had to commit to what he deemed essential for his own piece of mind.

"I promise," said Omar, "I will help you find her, Nakebakht!" he said eagerly.

Nakebakht kept her stern gaze on his face. She sensed reassurance that he will help her find that one person who she so desperately sought ever since she returned from her home land of Hazarajaat three years earlier. Hope had a dim appearance throughout her life, but right at that moment she knew, at last she too could hope.

Omar saw her eyes lighting up. The first formation of a toothless smile was forming around her old tired face, then suddenly Nakebakht's eyes widened. Her mouth opened, exclaiming in torment. Then he heard the sound of the snap and fell forward, face-first onto the dirt-filled concrete surface, perpetually losing consciousness.

Nakebakht wailed as she saw the large muscular man grabbing Omar's limp body and drag it to the backseat of a large vehicle, almost in a flash. She instantly covered her face under the burqa and started running. Behind her the man looked after her, as though he wanted to grab a hold of her as well. But she had already neared the busy chicken street and he could not follow her there. Beside, he was not instructed anything about her. Omar was the person he needed to get, and he had already secured him in the backseat of his Toyota Land Cruiser.

CHAPTER TWENTY-FIVE

THE OLD WOMAN, 1988: The cold winter air was sweeping across the old mud alleys of Wazierabad, a poor neighborhood in the northeast part of Kabul. On that cold dawn of December, the wind carried along a sound. It was the clatter of massive chains ripping through the ground as they were dragged by powerful diesel engines. Along with the sound of chains, there was also a deep hum of the engines sending waves of vibrations throughout the scattered muddy alleyways. It was the sound of Russian tanks marching their way down the nearby paved road, and they could be heard from miles away. It was like footsteps of the devil himself, echoing over mud-built houses of this poor neighborhood, getting closer and closer with each second.

Inside one of those mud huts rested a family of Hazara who found their peace on top of an old thin cotton mattress on this cold night. The old woman suddenly woke up when the rumbling noise made a loose part of clay fall from the ceiling of her mud house onto her abdomen. Luckily it was a small part, but it was still large enough to wake her up, as if a ghost had jumped on her in the midst of darkness. Her old, tired eyes were suddenly wide open, staring at the dark ceiling above and wondering about their fate. *God help us*, she whispered to herself. She lay still on the thin cotton mattress, eyes keen in the gloom, listening to the thundering sound of tanks passing on the road.

Slowly she managed to look to her left to see if her daughter and her infant granddaughter were okay. To her surprise, she was comforted when she saw them still in their sleep. Not too long after, she heard another sound—this time it was the morning prayer call coming from the loudspeakers of the nearby mosque. She felt a sense of rejuvenation streaming through her as she listened to the verses of Koran read by the Imam over the loudspeakers. The verses arrived in a crisp tone, overpowering the sound of tanks.

Everything will be all right. She told herself, *God is with us*. She thought of the prayer call as her family's savior—more like a metaphoric wall of a fort guarding them from the wrath of Russian tanks.

Her wrinkled and dry hand began to sweep the broken pieces of clay from her stomach. After clearing the debris, she managed to bring herself to an upright position. She had hoped for today to be better than the day before, but it didn't seem like it would be, not the way this morning had started.

Slowly she fetched a match out of its box and lit the kerosene lantern. There was no electricity in Kabul anymore, not for the past year. In so many ways, in the darkness of night that kerosene lantern had become the guiding light to her eyes—ushering her in the dark muddy alleys of Wazierabad.

For a brief moment she sat there and gazed at the burning flame as it danced inside the glass layer, and as her eyes honed on the little flame, her memory once again took her back to the glory days of her life. The glow from the lone flame transported her to the dancing flames that she saw in Agha Sahib's marble fireplace, at the house where she had lived most of her life, the house she thought she'd never leave, and the house that could never betray her. But just like the ending of every wonderful thing in her life, that house was gone, and now all that was there was a mud hut in this rundown neighborhood.

Whenever she thought of Agha Sahib's house, a dream reappeared, twirling in her mind in the same form every day.

"One day, Agha Sahib will come for me and take me back home."

It'd been a little over a year and half since she left his house, but so far, Agha Sahib hadn't returned for her.

A few moments later, the sound of tanks vanished. As it appeared, they just passed through her neighborhood. Sensing life come back to her, the old woman slowly rose to her feet. She gently opened the door with great caution; she was hesitant of the gushing cold air waking the baby while she stepped outside.

The neighborhood of Wazierabad had rows of mud-built houses side by side, each with a door that opened directly to the muddy alley in front of them. In her street, almost all the houses were like prison cells—one-bedroom settings side by side each other, and the only thing dividing them were the mud walls in between. The factor setting them apart from jail cells were windows overlooking the muddy alleys and the wooden door on the right. Unlike most jail cells, these houses did not have the luxury of a bathroom on the corner of the room. A commode used by the whole neighborhood was located at far end of the alley to the north. Instead of a toilet, a kerosene stove and a couple of pots and pans was present at the end of the room, and that was to be their kitchen—stationed in the same room where they slept.

There was no sewer or running water inside these mud houses. People brought drinking water from a nearby well in plastic buckets. Some families were even more than ten people, who all slept in the same room, but in her case, there were only three of them, the old woman and her daughter, and the infant granddaughter.

In that thick haze, she began to make her way around the potholes, carefully avoiding soft patches of mud, to the communal area. She was headed to make *Wudu,* the required ablution, before her morning prayer.

Kabul was not the same. At least not like how she remembered it. The peace she knew all her life had turned into turmoil by these blue-eyed, light-haired soldiers. Just like their gestures and language, their features were also foreign to her. They sat on top of their dark green tanks and ripped through the streets like an unwanted tornado.

"Why did they come here?" she often thought.

The only understanding she had about her life was the days when she lived in Agha Sahib's house. How it was then, and how it is now. Those were the days before the arrival of blue-eyed soldiers sitting high up on their tanks and pointing their machine guns whenever they saw a flock of people.

She remembers those days well; almost every day was a feast at his house. Chefs preparing entrées, guests arriving, music blasting, and people dancing in the entertainment room until the break of dawn. That was how life was in that house. A marathon of euphoria, even for the servants, for they, too, were dignified as part of his family.

The Shar-e-now Palace, as she called it, was known throughout the country as one of the most elegant estates of Kabul. Inside that mansion, she was the head maid—a very respected position among her fellow servants.

The residence sat in the heart of Kabul—directly in front of the Iranian embassy. Agha Sahib used to be a high member of the government during Afghanistan's monarchy. Along with his political power, he was a very successful businessman as well. He had started the first transportation company, which later became Afghanistan's very first corporation. In 1973, Afghanistan's king Zahir Shah was overthrown by his communist-influenced cousin, Daud Khan. Agha Sahib, who was known to be a friend of the king, gave up his political power to keep his family safe from communist wrath, because they started to massacre the ones who had closest ties to the monarch. That was the only way Agha Sahib could survive in Afghanistan: by being a businessman without any connection to the old kingdom. From 1973 until the current time, he mostly managed his wide variety of businesses. He didn't care about losing his political seat; for him, his family's well-being was much more important than an elite office in the government.

She arrived in Agha Sahib's house as a newlywed girl from Hazarajaat, the province of Hazara ethnicity. Her father accepted the dowry the gardener of a rich statesman of Kabul brought, despite him being thirty years older than her.

Ramazan was a servant of Agha Sahib for a long time. He had served as a gardener in his house for nearly twenty years. He was an older man who had never been married. Due to his profession, he did not have enough money to give for dowry to get himself a wife. One day, Agha Sahib saw that it was essential for his faithful gardener of twenty years to be married, so he gave him enough money to buy himself a wife. Upon receiving the money, Ramazan returned to his home village in Hazarajaat, where he purchased four cows to be given to his father-in-law in return for his daughter.

About a week later, he returned to Agha Sahib's house along with his young wife. That day marked her first arrival to civilization and into the ambience of Kabul, an infinitely different scene from her poor remote village.

After making Wudu, she stepped down from stairs of the communal area and made her way back to the hut. She was being extremely careful not to step on those water-filled potholes, because a drop of filthy water on her clothes would require her to change into a clean set for prayer. That was something she could not afford. The other set of clothing she had was still soaking wet, hanging from a wire in the corner of the room. Her other two sets were old and had holes in them—she could not use those for the *Namaz* prayer. Islam requires women not to have holes in their clothing during prayers; in essence, not to show any body parts, not even if it was presented from a small hole in the clothing.

As she maneuvered her way back through the alley, she heard another sound, the sound of an infant crying. She immediately recognized the cry; it was her granddaughter.

Why doesn't she feed her? She was angered by the carelessness of her daughter for not waking up to feed her baby. *Then again, she is a baby herself, what does she know of raising one,* she thought.

Her daughter had a baby at the age of fifteen—immensely younger than her when she had given birth.

From a distance, she spotted the dim light of the kerosene lamp burning inside her home. Her intuition told her that something was wrong, but she didn't want to believe it. She hurried through the door. Her attention fell to the crying infant lying on the floor. The space beside her, where her mother slept, was empty.

Where has she gone, leaving this child hungry like this? She kneeled down to pick up the baby, and as she stretched her arms forward, she heard squeaking of the wood behind her. She turned to the dark corner of the room, and as she focused her vision on the image, her stretched hands suddenly dropped. She was completely motionless, frozen and pale like a statue.

Her vision was fixed on a pair of dangling feet as they gently swayed in mid air. She was looking at her daughter, eyes shut and her chin down, as if she was gazing at the floor in her sleep. The only thing that kept her from falling to the ground was the thick wire, which was coiled around her neck.

The old woman brought herself back to reality. It appeared that this nightmare was real. She jumped up in terror and ran across the room. She put her arms around her daughter, still trying to save her. She tried lifting her, but she was too late. The noose had already done its job. Her body was limp and cold.

She stood there, still holding the lifeless body of her daughter, thinking that she would be soon awaken from this nightmare, but that didn't happened. The nightmare staggered until her ears started making out the sound of the infant crying again. And then, it all became true. *My sunflower is dead! My… sunflower is dead!* The phrase kept repeating in her mind.

The neighborhood woke up from the old woman's scream. Shortly after, women from the other houses stormed in. The men followed, but they didn't enter; they appropriately waited outside in the alley. A woman rushed outside the house and said to her husband, "Her daughter committed suicide! She hung herself!"

The news of her death stunned every man in that circle. All eyes were roaming across faces, searching for answers. But yet, no one dared to speak of why this had happened. One of the men who was proclaimed as the Peer, head of the neighborhood, spoke out.

"She probably didn't want to bear the upbringing of a bastard child, and maybe that's why she killed herself."

Other men nodded in agreement with the Peer. "Let's make sure she has a proper burial," and he started toward the nearby mosque.

According to the Peer, she deserved a proper burial because it was these people who contributed to her death. The burial was the least they could do for her.

After leaving Agha Sahib's house, the old woman had become a *Kallashoiy*, a launderer. Every day after her morning prayer, she set off to Wazir Akbar Khan, the upscale part of Kabul, and went door-to-door offering her services. She left at dawn and didn't return home until it was dark—especially on short winter days. Throughout the day, she sat on her knees and washed loads for one hundred Afghanis, which was equivalent to fifty U.S. cents.

After that dreadful day when she had to leave his house, washing clothes had become her main profession. Almost every day when her tired old back ached from washing load after load of dirty laundry, her dream reappeared.

Agha Sahib would see that the lady of the house was wrong, and he'd soon come to take us back.

On certain days, her pregnant daughter accompanied her, and with the two of them washing clothes, they managed to go through two houses. They earned enough money to pay the monthly rent to their mud hut, and the leftover money was spent on their nightly meals, which was a pot of vegetable soup and a long Afghan bread. If they had a good week, they'd manage to have lamb stew on Thursday nights. Soon after, her daughter stopped coming with her, because her baby was born and she had to stay home to nourish and take care of the child, so the old woman went alone—providing for her daughter and granddaughter.

They spent nine months roaming the poor neighborhoods of Kabul in search of a place where they would be accepted. The first place they resided was Shor Bazaar, a lower-class part of Kabul where hashish dealers and thugs anchored the streets. Then time came for them to move. It seemed like everywhere they went, they were not welcomed, and it was all for one reason: her daughter.

In an Islamic society, the biggest shame is to have a daughter pregnant without a husband—especially one who is barely fifteen years of age. It was because of that reason they were chased out of the neighborhoods. Sometimes, she forced her daughter to stay home, but then again, it wasn't long until a neighbor's wife or a kid saw her, and then it was the same harassment all over again. People referred to them as *Fiashas,* whores, a title cast upon them any place they set foot. On one of those nights in Shorbazaar, a man broke into their room and tried to rape her daughter. Luckily, the sound of their screams drove him away, but the next morning it was the same misfortune again: they were faced with people's vicious words and brutal demeanor, so they had to move to a different place.

Finally, after residing in four different neighborhoods, they found their relief in Wazierabad, a place populated by other Hazaras, people of their own descent. Even in Wazierabad people called them names, but the good thing was, their kids wouldn't throw stones at them when they walked through the alleys, as they often did in the previous neighborhoods.

In a closed Islamic society such as Kabul, where people were not accepting of young girls being pregnant without a husband, her daughter's fate was doomed. She couldn't live a normal life and be a part of the community. People saw her as an evil whore who was carrying a bastard child, something that was totally unholy and against their faith, and because of that, they showed no mercy.

The old woman didn't see it like that. According to her, her daughter was carrying the blood of the aristocrats inside her. She always thought that one day the truth would unfold, and these horrible days would be all behind them. Her unborn grandchild was heir to one of the prestigious families of Kabul.

One day, she thought, *the truth would unfold.*

Rays from the sun had begun to hit the rooftops. The old woman's cry was still echoing on the walls of the alleyways. It seemed like nothing mattered to her anymore. She had lost everything. Those thoughts she had for the last year and half would not make any difference now. Even if Agha Sahib showed up to take her, it still wouldn't matter. She had lost the most precious part of her life. Her daughter was dead.

The Peer's wife, Zarmina, a woman of middle age, showed up on her doorstep with a neatly folded white cloth. She had brought a *Kafan* for her daughter to be shrouded in after the Islamic bath. Three other women followed after her. The old woman didn't recognize any of them; they were *Mordashoiys,* women who washed dead bodie. The Peer himself had sent for them to come and bathe the young girl's body. Due to her being presumed a sinner, a proper burial would lift those sins and send her on a path to forgiveness.

One of the women sat above her head and started reading verses from Koran, while the other two begun preparing the body for a wash. The old woman was present in the corner of the room, but she didn't do anything. Her eyes were fixed on the lifeless body of her young daughter, still in disbelief that this had happened. On the other side of the room lay a six-month-old infant, crying for her mother's milk.

Zarmina slowly put her arm around the old woman and held her for a moment. She was still under shock and too disoriented to realize that someone had her arm around her. The last person who held her like this was her husband Ramazan, and that was over fifteen years ago. Zarmina slowly started whispering in her ear.

"We have to take her to a *Daiyee*." She was referring to the baby, who needed to be nursed.

She wrapped the crying infant in a swaddle, then brought her up and held her tight to her chest. She swiftly sat out to the only place she could think of. She was headed to the house of a woman who recently had given birth. She was hoping the young mother would be kind enough to feed this child, too. She reached the house in the next alley over, and started knocking on the wooden door. Shortly after, a man opened. He immediately recognized her as the Peer's wife.

"Salaam," he said.

"Is your wife home?" she asked.

The man's eyes were drawn to the crying infant; he already knew what she was there for.

"Yes… she is inside," his head was bowed as if he was holding something back.

"I want to go see your wife!" Zarmina demanded.

Before she could proceed inside, the man looked up and said, "We heard what happened." He then took a step to the right and blocked her way from entering the house.

That didn't come as a surprise; Zarmina had already anticipated that her husband might reject helping the bastard child. She looked deep into the young man's eyes and said firmly, "I need to take this baby to your wife. She has to feed her. This is God's will!"

Even the mentioning of God wasn't enough to make the young man give way. He held firm at his position.

"I speak for my wife. And I say that my wife is not giving milk to a bastard." And with his right hand, he shut the door.

That woman was the only one she could think who could provide for this baby, but then she thought maybe it wasn't the baby's fate, because a *Harami*, bastard, didn't have any leeway among people. Even if she was an infant—the doors automatically shut.

With the crying infant in her arms, Zarmina started making her way back to the house. She was running out of options.

Where am I going to find a Daiyee right now? She thought. The nearest neighborhood where she could possibly find a Daiyee was Shararrah, but the fierce fighting between Russian troops and the *Mujahideen,* Holy Warriors, has that road blocked.

She approached the old woman's mud hut, and then she held her breath and walked in. Not much had changed in her absence. The three women were doing their job preparing the body for the burial service, and the old woman was sitting still like a pale statue, her eyes keen on the corpus of her daughter.

Zarmina placed the crying baby in the cradle. Her face resembled the sign of defeat, not so much for herself, but for this infant that would soon meet her mother's fate with hunger.

The youngest of the three women rose to her feet. She walked to crib and kneeled down next to the baby. In a matter of a few seconds, the infant had stopped crying as she was sucking milk out of the young chubby woman's right breast.

"I have a three-month-old daughter, too," she said in her soothing voice.

Late in the afternoon on that short winter day, the sun had already sunk behind the Asmayi Mountain west of Wazierabad. As the heat of the sun vanished from the sky, the cold Kabul wind had already begun its charm. It hit flush like a wave of needles. The wind was pushing against the bodies of men who were returning from a hillside on Baymaro, after they had just buried a young Hazara girl who committed suicide earlier that day. The Peer paused from his pace; he then took a gaze towards the sky and thought to himself.

The cold winds are carrying her spirit. God have mercy on her. And he raised his hands to pray for her soul.

The old woman was in less of a shock now than she was earlier in the morning. The reality of her daughter's death had sunk in; she no longer was in disbelief. As she was becoming more coherent, the image of Agha Sahib loomed in her mind.

She started wrapping her granddaughter with colorful garments, and then her old shaking hands brought her up close to her chest.

"I'm taking you home now!" she whispered in the infant's ear. With the baby held close to her chest, she set pace towards the Shar-e-Now Palace. She was going to take her to where she belonged, because in her righteous mind, she had a right to be in that house. After all, she was the daughter of his son, Wali. That made her his own blood and righteous to live in his house.

After walking through the mud allies, through the dusty streets filled with dark clouds of smoke from the cars exhausts, she found herself stumbling to where rested her master's house. The big gray gate was wide open—something that had never occurred when she was there. *How could this be?* she thought.

She started making her way through the wide-open gate onto the big yard. She hadn't been there for more than a year and half; her memory was still crisp on how this place used to be. There were rows of rosebushes on each side of the cement pathway in the middle of the yard, but now, not a single one, except for the dirt in their place. The green house to the right side, where they kept flowerpots in the winter, also didn't look the same. There were no flowerpots to be seen inside, and some of the windows were shattered. Even the big walnut tree was no longer there. It appeared that it was chopped off and used for firewood, and the only thing left of its glory was a broken gray stump. She was stunned with what her eyes were presenting her; this was definitely not how she remembered this place.

She slowly began to make her way to the house, and once inside, she was shocked even more. The house was completely empty; it was like a ghost house with cold wind blowing through the broken windows. *Where is Agha Sahib?*

With her grandchild pressed against her chest, she started going through all the rooms. Still nothing, not even furniture. All the rooms were empty. Her master's house had been looted.

She made her way to the other side of the yard to the maid quarters where her room used to be. As she walked into her old room, the same thing reflected there. The room was empty, just like other rooms in the house. The only thing she could find was some old paper floating around the floor. As she walked across the room over piles of paper, she noticed something bumping her foot. She kneeled down and saw the plastic cylinder. She remembered her husband telling her that it was a gift from a foreign friend of Agha Sahib named Pappalo. It was something that Bebe jaan did not allow inside the big house. Agha Sahib had given it to him to keep as an Amanat, an obligatory safeguarding deed; otherwise his wife would have destroyed his friend's gift. Ramazan, the faithful servant, never even attempted to look what was inside, because an Amanat is something not belonging to him. It was his religious duty not to question what was hidden inside, or as to why the lady of the house was troubled by it. He just knew it was his obligation to fulfill his master's wish by simply keeping it without knowing the content.

After Ramazan's death, she had managed a few glimpses of it. She called it the *funny picture.*

It seemed like everywhere she went she came across an emptiness that robbed the life, the joy, and the warmth this place once had. It all had been abolished in its wake, and now all that was left were the high walls standing tall over the hardwood floors and the inevitable silence. The ground had opened and sucked up everything, along with the people—everything except for the plastic cylinder, which was worthless to the savage thieves.

As dutiful wife to her husband, she was obligated to protect the Amanat once trusted to her husband. She was not going to allow the thieves to disdain his word and his honor.

If this is the only thing that I can keep for Agha Sahib, then I must.

Back in the days when the mansion was full of life, the attic was used for restoring the food supply. Nobody went up there except for the servants who brought cooking materials down. The only two people other than the servants who went there frequently were her daughter and Agha Sahib's young grandson. It was her daughter's favorite place in the whole house. She thought in dedication to her dead daughter, it was essential to hide the last belonging of this house in a place she favored the most.

She started ascending the stairway to the attic. Once she was on top of the stairs, she noticed the big attic lock missing. *Why should this be any different than the rest of the house?*

She pushed open the double doors and made her way through. And again, just like the rest of the house, this place was empty, too. She remembered bringing milk and cookies for her daughter and Agha Sahib's grandson Omar, when they came here to play. She started making her way towards the back wall, to the place where they used to play hopscotch. The lines of chalk were still visible on the attic's floor, as if they were made the day before. For a moment her mind flashed back to how she'd come up and see the two of them hopping through the squares, then reality hit her as she sensed the silence.

The big wooden chest at the far end of the attic was also spared from the looters. Predominantly due to being nailed to the floor with castiron stakes, virtually impossible to steal. The chest was used to store walnuts, almonds, and other dry fruits, so it could prevent the rats from gaining access.

The chest was not completely attached to the ground; there were rows of two-by-fours nailed underneath it so it could stay above the attic floor, that way no moisture from the floor could affect the dry goods inside. She remembered one of those two-by-fours had not been nailed correctly and it was left loose.

She placed the baby down on the floor and then started pulling on the part where she thought it was not nailed down. A bit later she managed to bring out the loose piece of wood. She then stuck her hand in its place and felt around the hollow at the base of the chest for a correct estimation of space. She felt a gap between the top and the bottom two-by-fours, enough space to accomplish what she came there to do. The space was dry, and certainly undetectable, unless someone knew to move that particular piece. She put the plastic cylinder inside the hole and rolled it to the right. Then she grabbed the piece and placed it neatly back to where it was stationed earlier. It made it impossible for someone to think something was hidden there. She thought this was the least she could do for her master—hide the last belonging of his house from the thieves who robbed him. And at the same time, she could uphold her deceased husband's word and honor.

She picked the baby up and started heading to the door. As she circled her way down the stairs, she started hearing conversations outside on the yard. One of the voices seemed familiar to her, although she was hoping it wouldn't be that person.

Rashina was Bebe jaan's niece—Agha Sahib's wife. Rashina's father Ramat, Bebe jaan's older brother, died when Rashina was a young girl. Ever since his death, Bebe jaan has been taking care of her and her brother. Bebe jaan was kindhearted enough to share some of her husband's wealth with her niece and nephew. They were provided shelter in the family's farm on the outskirts of Kabul, and they received monthly allowances to cover their living expanses. Rashina and her brother did little work around the farm, merely a small gesture to convey their worthiness and fend off any revelation of them being scrounges. Neither of the two was educated nor had anything of their own. They practically lived off their aunt's charity.

The old woman made her way out of the house to the yard. She had hoped Rashina would be able to tell her the master's whereabouts. As she climbed down the stone staircase to the cement walkway, she didn't see anyone. She started looking around her, still nobody was found. *Maybe I'm imagining things,* she thought.

It was getting late, and the old woman was still clueless. She was drenched in the fog of uncertainty. Her only hope was Agha Sahib, but given the circumstances, his house was looted, and he was nowhere to be found. As she wandered around, thinking what she was going to do next, she heard someone calling from the other side of the yard.

"Hey! What are you doing here?" the voice asked in an ill tone.

She turned to see Rashina's short figure making her way towards her from the other side of the yard. Her big dark eyes were radiating anger as they held keen to the old servant's figure.

"Yeah… you! What are you doing here?" she barked again. Dazed by this young woman's demeanor, she stood silently with her head bowed, looking at Rashina's feet as they marched towards her.

Rashina stood about five feet tall. She had shoulder-length brown hair and a face full of acne. But what made her stand out was her voice, the loudest and most deafening when she was in a rage. People used to say, when Rashina shouts even the dead get disturbed. The old woman held her position, head bowed and eyes keen towards the ground. And with her broken voice she answered, "I'm here to see Agha Sahib."

"Agha Sahib?" Rashina burst into laughter. "He's long gone…"

"Where?" the old woman demanded.

Rashina's laughter started to evaporate, and once again she began glaring at her with those devilish eyes.

"Your master is no longer here, can't you see? This is my house now, so get out and never come here again."

The old woman could not believe what her ears were hearing. *My master is gone?* She felt her knees going weak. This house was the only thing she knew in her life. It seemed like everything she based her life on was stripped away from her in one day.

Her tired eyes were searching for tears to shed, but the tears had gone dead along with her daughter. Instead, they just closed. Her arms had also gone weak, they were about to give way, but then her mind subconsciously kept them steady for the sake of the infant she was holding.

Across from her stood a woman whose eyes were filled with hate. There was no way she was going to be allowed to reside in a place she once knew as home.

"Oh God, why didn't you have mercy on me?" she exclaimed.

"Because you are a damn liar. That's why!" Rashina's voice stung her like a scorpion.

The old woman stood there motionless waiting for the echoes of Rashina's words to settle in. *I'm a liar?* She thought. *No. I'm not a liar. I've never lied.*

"Are you here for money?" Rashina demanded. "If you are, there is no money! Your master is no longer here to give you money. Now get out of my house before I throw you out!"

She was suddenly awakened from her thoughts. With her left hand, she slowly pulled the green scarf over her head to cover her hair—a gesture showing readiness to leave. There wasn't much she could do, so she turned around and started heading for the big gate. She didn't know where she was going, other than knowing that she was going out of this house. This house where she served most of her life was not here anymore—not now, when she needed it most.

Rashina didn't feel sorry for her, nor did she really care why she was there. Since Agha Sahib and his family were no longer there, she gained the automatic right to his abandoned house because she was the nearest relative.

"Oh, and don't you dare think that bastard child of yours is heir to this house," Rashina barked, "Everyone knows you sold your daughter, and that's how she got the baby."

Upon hearing those words, the old woman let out a loud moan. It sounded as if she was stabbed in the heart. It was the sound of sheer weakness without any power to retaliate.

She knew that she could no longer live like this. She remembered her master's words. "When hope dies, then the person dies with it." *I know. I know where I'm gonna go.*

She started making her way past the big gray gate. Her body showed no sign of life, other than her eyes fixed in a straight line without a destination. She was in the midst of two worlds, this one, and the other one where her daughter was—also the place where she was ordained.

The old woman had set pace for nearly an hour; she was occupied in her own madness. Nothing seemed to capture her eyes, except for the patterns of the sidewalk on the dusty street. The whole world was passing her by and she wasn't noticing—not even the excessive cry of her granddaughter was making her snap out of the insanity. Due to such a tremendous amount of emotional pain, she had lost coherence. The worst day of her life was taking its toll, and nothing mattered to her anymore.

Far off on a dusty street, a young woman was on her way home. She had just finished her third job for the day, and she was in the hurry to get back to her three-month-old baby, whom she had left with her sister while out working. As dusk approached, her hands lifted the hem of her burqa from the inside to accommodate her strides. After another ten minutes of walking, from the small holes of her burqa screen she saw the hem of a woman's burqa dragging over the dirt road in a distance. She had seen this woman before, the same burqa, dragging behind her as she walked the muddy streets of Wazierabad mourning her daughter's death earlier that day. She remembered bathing and preparing her daughter's body for the burial, and most of all, she remembered breast-feeding the infant while her mother lay dead a few feet away.

She picked up her pace and hurried to the old woman. As she got closer, she started hearing the infant's cry again, the same agonizing cry that she heard earlier in the day—the cry of hunger. She tapped the old woman on her left arm.

"Is everything okay?" the chunky young woman asked.

The old woman could not make out the words that the white-complexioned girl was saying. All she could make out was the young woman's voice, the most soothing voice she had heard that day, perhaps in months. Drowned in her deep daze without the spark of a thorough understanding, the old woman handed the baby to the young girl. As fate granted again, the young woman kneeled and took the crying baby underneath her burqa. And a few seconds later, the crying stopped. As the baby was being fed, the old woman's insanity was temporarily distracted for a brief moment. She reached under her neck and pulled out a pouch from the undergarment. She then untied the knots and pulled out an old golden watch.

"This belongs to her father. Make sure she knows that," she said.

The watch belong to her master's youngest son. He wore it on his wrist for the longest time. After seducing her fifteen-year-old daughter, he had given it to her as a token of his good gesture.

The old woman placed the watch on top of the baby over the young woman's burqa. Then insanity returned. She started taking steps backwards, her dazed eyes still fixed on the young girl, and with few more steps she disappeared into the crowd.

CHAPTER TWENTY-SIX

PRESENT DAY: The cool breeze was blowing through the Zimarai Valley in southeast Afghanistan. The valley sat beneath the two dark mountains that stood face to face. It was as if the two mountains had fought a battle with one another a long time ago and left remnants of broken rocks on the floor before them. Or there could have been a river here at one point, which now it seemed had gone dry for millennia. The only thing evident was the view of black and gray stones that covered the floor of the valley like an endless bed of rocks. The valley sat solely in its own despair, away from any civilization or sign of life for that matter, but it still received its fair share of punishment from the agonizing Afghan sun, which stayed in the sky only to burn anything that moved in this godforsaken place. Travelers between Afghanistan and Pakistan deliberately avoided Zimarai Valley, which was in the no-man's land between the two countries, for its rough terrain and harsh conditions, but mostly due to the lack of water.

There, on the hem of the east mountain, someone had managed to build a shack from rocks stacked on top of one another and a metal roof, which lay uneven on top of the rock walls. The presence of metal and how it got to this remote place was an enigma in itself.

The sound of wind passing underneath the metal roof and the gaps of empty space created by the supporting uneven rocks made a synchronized whistling sound. Only this wasn't a harmonized whistle, but rather an awakening sound serving the misery of this place. Upon hearing the sound of the wind, Omar lurched awake from sleep. His mind still kept alert.

Although he wished that it didn't. Every bit of consciousness reminded him of his current situation. *I am left out here to die.*

He was brought here when it was dark the night before. He could only reconcile the memory of what happened the day before from the pain in the back of his head. That and the dim light shimmering from the kerosene lantern slung from a wood stick pierced in one of the gaps of the left rock wall. His wrists were tied to the armrest of the wooden chair with yarn rope as he sat upright. The same process was followed down to his ankles, which were tied to the chair's wooden legs. He did try to free himself, but no movement was allowed. The rope was tight. It made the armrest and front legs of the chair bind to his limbs as if it was all one piece. Even death wouldn't be the worst thing- he thought it would free him at last. The most unbearable element was the truth of not knowing what would happen to him next.

His abductor had not spoken a word. He was well versed in the psychological game. He wanted to bring him to this remote area to obtain what he wanted to gain. He thought the best way to produce the accurate result was to leave him isolated for a period of time to reconsider what he wanted to do, given the harsh conditions. Then he would reappear again after Omar was mentally broken to collect the information. In his experience, the information obtained from a person after isolation was closer to the truth than otherwise.

Omar sat still, tied down to the wooden chair, bracing the agonizing pain in the back of his head. He was absent of choice, other than considering the possible answers to explain his current state that resided in his own mind in an obscured puzzle. He started contemplating when this whole journey began, two weeks earlier.

CHAPTER TWENTY-SEVEN

TWO WEEKS EARLIER: The elegant estate of Chateau de Vauvenargues was located in the Mediterranean region of southeastern France. The Chateau sat on the edge of Ste. Victoire Mountain and included most of the northern slopes, which were intricately decorated by urbane French gardens. On the south side, the wrought-iron gate with the whirling bars was supported by two pillars made out of Santini Italian marble, and behind it, the spiral driveway was filled with white Brazilian pebbles—ones that illuminated under blacklight in the night—spanned around three acres of more gardens and ended beneath fifteen steps of crystal marble, which led to the grand entrance of the mansion. The rock-embedded house rested on a high foundation to capture the picturesque views of its indulgent gardens. Above the marble staircase, two lion statues chiseled from whole granite appeared on each side, and behind them the pre-Napoleon chestnut door, which revealed the date of the architecture as the seventeenth century.

On this early morning, the tranquility of the estate was disturbed by the consistent ringing of the telephone. Pierre Renoir angrily stretched his arm over to the nightstand and picked up the receiver.

"C'est Pierre Renoir," he answered with irritation.

"Monsieur Renoir, planindre quelqu'un prep ce telephone. J'ai quelque chose a vous dire," said a man's voice in broken French.

Renoir could instantly pick up from his accent that he was an Englishman, but what made him wonder the most was, as to why this Englishman was calling him at 3:26 a.m.?

"Monsieur… there better be a good explanation to my disturbance this morning."

"Oh indeed there is, sir," the man answered. "My name is Peter Wilson, and I am very sure that you would be interested in what I have to offer."

Renoir who happened to be one of the wealthiest Europeans had his share of encounters with people who were trying to get him to make donations. Generous by nature, in the past he had contributed obscene amounts of money to various charities. *But a phone call at this hour?*

He brought himself to an upright position as he was getting ready to hang up the phone, but before hanging up he said, "Look, whatever it is, I'm sure I'm not interested."

And as he took the receiver away from his ear, the voice replied, "So you are not interested in the Peasant?"

Renoir already had the receiver away from his ear, on the verge of hanging up, and then he thought he had heard a word that he had been hoping to hear for the longest time.

"What did you say?" he asked eagerly.

"I said the Peasant, sir… are you interested?"

By now Renoir was wide awake, sitting on the edge of his bed, ready to capture what he had longed for all these years.

"So I take it that you are interested," the man said abruptly.

"What is the price?"

The man chortled for a brief moment. "You have to bid on it."

"Is it in Christie's?" Renoir asked.

"No… not that kind of an auction… I mean, not yet, but it will be there if your price isn't satisfying."

Renoir's thoughts were whirling around his mind like a warm, promising summer wind from the Mediterranean coast. He could feel the adrenaline streaming through his pulse; his yearning had arrived, at last.

"What is the price?" Renoir asked again.

"Well, whatever price you and the owner settle upon… and my ten percent on top, of course."

"Then I must speak to the owner at once," Renoir pressed.

The Englishman hesitated, "My dear sir, that is not possible. I'll speak with you on his behalf."

Renoir was quite used to this type of a salesman, presumably a middleman searching to make a commission on the transaction.

"What about the authenticity?" he asked. "I mean, how do I know that I'll be getting the real one, and also the history? Where has it been all these years?"

The other end of the line went quiet for a second; it appeared that the man was contemplating the right answer. Apparently Renoir's enthusiasm about the matter wasn't going to seal the deal; there remained some legitimate questions.

"You'd be provided with a certificated of authenticity," he spoke. "Would that satisfy you?"

"Perhaps," said Renoir, "but what about the history? You know the Peasant without its history would be…"

That was a long harpoon that Renoir threw at the Englishman. He was trying to ascertain his knowledge about this matter from a value standpoint. But evidently the English knew the game too well.

"Monsieur Renoir, let's not dance around. You know as well as I that the value of the Peasant is based on its mystery rather than history. And to be frank with you, my client would prefer the history of it to remain unknown."

Renoir was in a vague state of mind; the English had been keener than he had anticipated.

"How much?" he asked for the third time.

"The bidding starts at sixty million dollars."

"When would you deliver it?"

"Sir, that part is unclear to me as well, but once I see it, I would most urgently let you know," the English's voice echoed uncertainty.

"You mean to tell me that you don't even have it? And yet, you are trying to sell it," Renoir pressed with irritation.

"Monsieur, the purpose of this phone call is to let you be the first bidder. If you are not interested, then we'll gladly auction it. Perhaps then you can come and bid on it there."

Renoir knew bidding in an auction would be the perilous way of capturing it; in essence, he had to outbid all the other people.

"When would you have it?" Renoir asked.

"Soon," the English replied, "but Monsieur, my client is very serious about keeping the history of it safe, meaning he does not want a soul to know about its whereabouts, and certainly you would not have any knowledge of such information. In fact, I don't even know, and I don't expect him to tell me."

Renoir was puzzled, but he still didn't show any sign of losing interest on the matter. "Okay, where would we go from here?" he asked in agitation.

"I would call you once I hear from him."

"And how long would that be?"

"I don't know. Could be this month, or next, or the month after, but be patient Monsieur, like you have been for all these years." And he was gone.

Renoir took a stroll down the hall, then down the circular stairway to the grand lobby on the first floor. The custom Priscilla chandelier hung above the black granite lobby where it revealed Renoir's exquisite, elegant taste. The chandelier, which was also known as "la dama de la luz," the lady of light, happened to be Carlos Priscilla's masterpiece. The famous Spanish chandelier builder was approached by Renoir when he was well into his seventies and was asked to build his life's masterpiece before his death, and that would be his last work. Priscilla agreed to the hefty price of one million dollars, and built the lady of light for Chateau de Vauvenargues in just under ten years. The project was complete two years before his passing. Five thousand pieces of crystal were intricately handcrafted and carefully tied to each other with chains of white gold. When the five hundred white bulbs were at full blast, it appeared like a crystal mountain hanging upside down, illuminating the world beneath it—a marvelous introduction of Pierre Renoir at first glance when his guests stepped inside the mansion.

He started making his way through the main marble hallway to the mansion's grand gallery; once he arrived there, he started fixing his vision on what hung from the walls. Even under the dim light coming from the lobby, the gallery seemed full. He already had a location for the Peasant; he had picked out the place long before he had acquired anything else. It was like a dream of having the perfect woman—one whose beauty radiated like rays of light from the sun, and making love to her was the longing of all men, only this was better. At last, he would get the admiration of the European aristocrats. *The Peasant,* he thought, *my true long lost love, you'll come to me at last, and when you do, the light will shine on me from heaven.*

CHAPTER TWENTY-EIGHT

Peter Wilson had dedicated his life to arts and artists. He studied art history in Oxford under the renowned professor and Nobel prizewinner Sir Edward Thomas. For the last twenty-five years, Wilson has made a career as an art dealer who specializes in lost art—a terminology given to undiscovered works of the famous artists.

Over the years, Wilson has climbed to fame in the art community by discovering lost works of artists that people had not imagined existed. His discoveries began with extensive research on an artist's life. Then having done that, he backtracked on the artist's footprints, from the city he was born, the cities he lived in during his life, the friends he made, and his children, and his children's children. It was commonly known that at one point in their lives, the struggling artists that the world knows today were exchanging their work for food, which gave birth to the category "starving artist."

At times, those early unknown works sat inconspicuous in the basement of a house, or hung on a wall in someone's barn without them knowing its true value or what it really was.

Six years ago, a French pub owner was cleaning the basement. He came across an old black and white picture of Paris taken possibly by the early Kodak Brownie camera. The picture had a residue of beer and other patches of spattered grime on the surface from all those battered years when it hung on the pub's wall. A time had come when someone, most likely the previous owner, put the old photograph with some other items into storage in the basement. Some years later, the new owner had ventured to the same basement to clear out some of the junk. As fate had it, the new owner liked the frame of the old Paris picture, and he decided that he'd tear out the picture and keep the frame. Upon detaching the edge of the picture, he noticed a colorful canvas lurking in the back. After making a few phone calls, he was referred to Peter Wilson, who went and studied the obscured painting. The painting was declared a Monet—one of his earlier works. It was auctioned for twelve million dollars in London, a winning lottery ticket for the new pub owner.

Two days ago, Wilson received a phone call from someone who had knowledge about a Vallecillo painting from the mid-fifties called the Peasant. It was a portrait of an old man done in oil-based paint. He remembered coming across it a couple of years ago when he was doing research on the famous Spanish artist Pablo Vallecillo. The portrait revealed a man in analytic cubism. It was said that it captured the suffering of the object, while it illustrated a colorful background. The depiction of the portrait was about an unprivileged man surrounded by a privileged world. The portrait was declared one of Vallecillo's most controversial works. Throughout his research, Wilson had discovered that this painting exhibited in the Madrid Museum only for one day, and then it was pulled out by Vallecillo himself and vanished, without a trace of its whereabouts.

He sat in his dim office wondering about the nature of the work. He knew about the painting's existence and its controversial message. Some speculated that it was created in a time before Vallecillo was declared a communist, and this painting validated his political stand.

Maybe that's why he pulled the portrait out of the museum—because he didn't want to be label as a commy, thought Wilson.

"It's in Afghanistan?" the caller had said.

"How did you come about finding it?" Wilson asked the caller, Omar, who had only given his first name.

"My grandfather... he was a friend of Vallecillo," he said. "They met when he was Afghanistan's ambassador to Spain in the early fifties."

That didn't come as a surprise to Wilson. He knew that Vallecillo's fame had earned him favor among dignitaries. But the only information he had about the Peasant portrait was the fact that it was exhibited only once, and then it disappeared.

"I need to know a little more to see if I can authenticate what you are telling me is true," Wilson had said.

"I could tell you what I know, but it has to remain concealed and off the record."

"Sure. That's fine," Wilson agreed.

"My grandfather met Vallecillo a few times in Spain in the span of his three-year tenure. He invited Vallecillo to visit Afghanistan, which he described as, 'One of the mystic places in the world.' And to his surprise, Vallecillo spontaneously agreed. So, two months later he arrived in Kabul, and that's where he painted the Peasant."

"Wait a minute," Wilson countered, "you mean to tell me that he painted the Peasant in Kabul?"

"Yes, in my grandfather's house."

The caller could tell that Wilson was flabbergasted with what he heard. He felt an urge to hear more.

"Kabul, Afghanistan did not have a suitable hotel that could host someone of that stature. Besides, it is not part of the Afghan custom to stick an invited guest into a hotel. And for that reason, he was housed within my grandfather's mansion. Of course, this was all before I was born."

"Oh I see," said Wilson, "And he decided to paint there? From what the world know about Vallecillo, he was very meticulous about his work."

"Actually, my grandfather said it was spontaneous of Vallecillo. He never intended to paint. He was simply there for a vacation. But on the third day of his visit, he had woken up early. He was strolling around the mansion's gardens when he came across my grandfather's gardener, a thin Hazara man name Ramazan, who was hunched over making irrigation channels with his bare hands. Upon seeing him, Vallecillo demanded to paint him. My grandfather sent someone to the city to bring some painting materials for his guest. That person returned with some oil paints and brushes, but failed to find a canvas. He did not want to disappoint his guest with the fact that they couldn't find a canvas for him, so he went and fetched an existing canvas already in the house and gave it to Vallecillo to paint on the back."

"Wow, that's an intriguing story," Wilson said, "but what was in the front of the canvas?"

"I think it was a map of some sort that my grandfather had inherited from his father."

"Did you say a map of some sort?"

"Yeah. My grandfather's father encountered a sudden death fighting against the British in the Third Anglo-Afghan war in 1919. So, he never was able to tell my grandfather, who at the time was a very young boy, what the map was for. It was just a souvenir passed down to my grandfather."

"Do you have the painting now?"

"No, it's still in Kabul."

"I see," Wilson said.

"But there is a problem," the caller had said. "My grandfather's house was looted after our sudden evacuation of Kabul in 1988."

"Then how would you know that it's still there?" Wilson shot back.

"I know because such a thing would have no monetary value to the savages who looted the house."

"How can you be so sure?" Wilson asked.

"Well for one, the portrait was not allowed inside the house. You have to think from an Afghan's standpoint: my illiterate grandmother lived a very superstitious lifestyle. She would not have a portrait of her servant hung in a wall of her house. Also, the other factor that led to her dismay was the fact that she thought the houseguest was a demon."

"A demon?" the startled Wilson asked.

"Well, yeah… according to her. My grandfather had prepared a feast in honor of Vallecillo's arrival on the first night when he arrived. After dinner, when the music blasted, Vallecillo gave in to his European ways and started dancing as other guests sat and watched. The biggest cultural shock happened when he grabbed my grandmother and pulled her to the dance floor. He dipped her a couple of times, and then spun her around a few times until she managed to get away from him. Now imagine if someone did such a thing to the Queen of England. How would the queen feel afterwards? That's exactly how she felt; not only that, but she had become the laughingstock of all dignified, conservative women around the city."

"I see," Wilson echoed his sentiment.

"A couple of months later, my grandfather returned to Kabul from his last ambassadorship trip to Spain. He had brought along a gift to my grandmother from Vallecillo, illustrating the gesture of his appreciation for their hospitality during his visit to Kabul. The gift was the portrait of her servant Ramazan."

"Oh wow," Wilson, exclaimed, "how did she take that?"

"Not too well," he chuckled. "She was on the verge of throwing it in the burning fireplace when my grandfather grabbed it from her."

"You mean to tell me that your grandmother was going to throw a Vallecillo in the fireplace?" Wilson asked, shocked.

"Yes!" He continued. "You have to understand that she only saw Vallecillo as a rowdy houseguest who shamed her in front of her peers. That's all she knew about him. We have to look at this from the perspective of a woman who had never left the conservative cultural environment, and at the same time she was illiterate, which prevented her from accessing a window to the outside via reading about the world. So, in essence, to her, Vallecillo was a loudmouth buffoon. And that's all he was."

"I think I can see that," said Wilson. "So, what happened then?"

"Well, my grandfather could never trust his hysterical wife to not destroy the portrait, so he gave it to the gardener Ramazan to safekeep it for him in a room across the yard where he lived, also a place where my grandmother would never go, due to it being the servant's house."

"That is quite a story," Wilson said.

"Yeah, it shows how twisted things were in Afghanistan. The complete opposite of Europe."

"So, do you think it still sits in that room?" Wilson asked.

"Well, it is logical to believe that the looters would not be interested in what they could find in the gardener's house. They naturally would have gone after the main house."

Wilson contemplated this for a second and sighed in disbelief.

"Tell me something," the caller said, "if it were to have been already sold, would you have known about it?"

"Yes, I'm quite certain, I would have..." Wilson responded. "I know that because for the last ten years, whenever a Vallecillo has sold, it has made a headline in the press. So with respect to that, I can say that it hasn't been sold."

Those words were very promising to the caller. *So it means, it hasn't been discovered yet.*

"I'm going to find it," he said, "and I trust that you'll keep this story discreet?"

"Of course," Wilson reassured him.

CHAPTER TWENTY-NINE

Jamal had enjoyed the past couple years of his life in his native country of Egypt, but now his path has brought him back to the place that made him who he become. He rolled up the driver's side window to prevent the dust from coming inside the vehicle as it sat idle in this crowded bazaar. Soon, he will drive eastwards on the lone dirt road, which will lead him to Zimarai Valley. He knew about not driving on the vacant country roads during the daylight. The Americans had technological equipment that could spot a car driving solely in a desert, which frequently grew their suspicion of carrying explosives. It was safer to drive at nights. His mentor had managed to give him a pair of night goggles, which were made for the French military. He could see the road and the surroundings without having the headlights on.

He had called his mentor earlier, before he boarded his flight in Islamabad. He was pleased to hear his mentor expressing gratitude and praising him for the extraordinary work he had done. He never disappointed him and had always executed his tasks. His mentor had said that he was the pinnacle of their cause—the same cause that his father believed, and the cause that he died for.

Jamal vividly remembers the day when the news of his father's death came. He could still see the image of his sobbing mother as if it was a film projected in his memory. He wanted to avenge his death at all costs necessary. But then he was deterred by his mentor, who taught the virtues of patience.

Peshawar Pakistan, September 2, 1998

"This is not the eternal life. That life begins when we reopen our eyes on the Day of Judgment. As the sinners await the wrath of Allah, a Shaheed will have a straight passage to heaven. Allah never forgets those who have given their lives to serve his cause."

The fifteen-year-old Jamal fixed his gaze upward towards the teacher, a man wearing a black turban and black *Perahan Tunban*.

"Take a look at your brother sitting next to you. Each of you will have the honor to carry out Allah's will! And when you do, you shall wake to find yourself on the steps of heaven. That is only if you perform Allah's task courageously."

Jamal could not find too many things to be grateful for. A month ago, on that hot August day, on the outskirts of Cairo, he found himself sitting on the floor leaning against the cement wall of their two-bedroom flat. His elbows resting on top of his knees, and his eyes unfocused, filled with tears, looking across the room to the sobbing image of his mother. She was mourning his father's death. The man who called from Pakistan did not give his name, but said that his body was disintegrated when the American missiles hit Khost, Afghanistan.

His mother had begged him not follow his mentor, Ayman al-Zawahiri, to Afghanistan. But he refused. He had said that he was only following the will of Allah, and Ayman had only shown him the path to reach his will. He had said, "It will be a great honor as a doctor to be healing those who would be striking against America, the biggest enemy of Islam." To him, that was a cause far greater than his life.

Hours later, the sun had receded behind the rooftops. A cool breeze had broken the blaze of that scorching day. Jamal's eyes were still keen in the same direction. He was now looking at the silhouette of his mother under the dim light peering in from the wood-frame window. Her mournful wail had turned into short gasps of breath. Her eyes were fixed to the corner of the room. And the thought of raising a boy without a father was smeared all over her mind as she sat there in silence.

The evening call to prayer came to life from the nearby mosque's loudspeakers. Jamal found himself rising up and setting pace towards the door, then down the stairs through the dirt-filled alley in the direction of the mosque. Every step brought memories of his father as he walked him to the mosque in the evenings for prayer. He thought about his words of wisdom, encouragement, and above all the presence of his confidence hovering over him in times of hardship. And now, with him gone, all of that had evaporated. What remained was a void, his direction unknown. A while later, he found himself passing the mosque at the hem of the nearby hill in the dark.

"Your father was a brave man!" A man's voice came from behind, one he had never heard before. Jamal turned to see who it was, but on this moonless night everything was pitch black.

"You knew my father?" he asked. A few seconds later, he began to hear footsteps grinding over pebbles and sand as they got closer.

"Yes. I knew him as a brother," the man replied.

Jamal saw the figure of a tall man appearing from the dark. He was standing right in front of him now.

"I know you have questions about your father. I am prepared to answer them for you," the tall man said as he lifted his arm and placed his hand on top of Jamal's shoulder.

"Are you surprised at how I found you?" the man asked. "Well, don't be. I follow the stars… and they always lead me to a warrior."

He pointed his index finger to the night sky.

"You see that?"

Jamal shook his head.

"There is his belt, his shield, and his right arm stretched up high, his sword drawn."

Jamal was looking at the Orion constellation.

"That's what I do. I teach of the stars."

Jamal recalls his fascination with the stars ever since he was a little boy. On hot summer nights, his family slept on the rooftop of their building to evade the heat. And as his mother and father slept, he remained awake, gazing upwards in pursuit of his curiosity.

"Your father told me that you are a bright young man."

Jamal stayed quiet, still startled by this man's presence.

"I am here because your father and I swore a vow to each other to look after the other's son, and to make sure that they take our place in God's duties if one of us fell martyr. Had it been me who had fallen, your father would have been seeing my son right now."

"Am I to be a Jihadi?" Jamal asked.

"Never. You will be implementing God's orders. Not as a mere soldier, but as a scholar further enlightening God's will."

The man's name was Hamza. He had left his native country of Egypt for Afghanistan. He had met Yasser, Jamal's father, a year earlier in Kandahar as he tended to the wounded Taliban while they were battling to gain the control of the country. Bonded by their Egyptian background in the same cause, the two men had become close friends over the year. Yasser's life work was in medicine. He thought of himself as the doctor who healed and preserved the flesh that thrived to restore the laws of Islam. Hamza had the same beliefs when it came to restoring the Sharia law, but his mythologies differed from his friend.

Hamza spent most of his adult life studying at Al-Azhar University in Cairo, Egypt. The university stands as the second oldest in the world, founded in year 970 as a madrasa with emphasis on Islamic Studies and Arabic Literature. The *Ulamas*, Legal Muslim Scholars, are held in a prominent position by the Muslim community. They also possess the authority to issue Fatwa, should there be any dispute that negated the perceived ways of Islam in the modern world.

"Now that your father is no longer here, his calling is yours."

The boy remained motionless, standing under the star-filled sky. This man's timing couldn't have been any better.

"Would I be able to take revenge on those who killed my father?" the boy asked.

"That would be a definite… if you follow Allah's will. But first, patience should be in order."

Jamal stood still, looking at the man's face under the dark sky. He thought about his father. He was honored to take on a cause that his father had given his life to. In a flash, the agony of the day was transformed with eagerness of vengeance. Jamal felt proud and ready.

"I will take on my father's cause."

The man was comforted when he realized the boy was brave and faithful as his father had described him.

"We will leave the day after tomorrow," the man said.

The madrasa had students from various Arabic states. They were ages from the teens to adults. The madrasa was moved from Khost, Afghanistan to Peshawar a little over a month after the U.S. missiles attacked its previous location. Seven people died in that attack, among them Jamal's father, who was the camp's doctor, a man who had earned the utmost respects of the Islamic militants. Because of his high standing, fifteen-year-old Jamal received special attention from the teachers and fellow students due to being the late Dr. Yasser's son.

In the span of seven years, Hamza took the boy under his wing. He had made arrangements for him to be trained by the elitest of the militants in weaponry as well as explosives. Once the boy had become proficient in those, he was sent back to Egypt to study psychology. After seven-years time, the twenty-five-year-old Jamal was a fierce warrior, with skills and intelligence. He had become the go-to guy for Hamza whenever he wanted something done with perfection.

֍

Dusk had started to set on the busy bazaar. Jamal reached the ignition and turned the key. In a millisecond, the engine of the Toyota Land Cruiser came to life. He canvassed the bazaar for any sign of irregularity. Clearly he did not want to be followed. Paranoia was a natural attribute of his profession. He was taught to always search before executing, even if it's as simple as driving a vehicle. *Never have the guard down.* He glanced to the vehicle's passenger seat to see if he had everything that he needed. Food, water, and a spare fully charged car battery with extra copper wiring, which he hoped he didn't need to use. *This will do for now.*

CHAPTER THIRTY

Omar opened his eyes from a doze. For second he thought this was all a dream, but then he suddenly was reminded by the pain in the back of his head, again. He lifted his head from the slouching position. He thought his eyes were still closed, but then he started blinking rapidly, only to realize that this place was pitch black, dark enough that it didn't matter whether his eyes were open or shut. Once again he thought that his assailant had left him out here to die, *but why?* Nothing was clear. He had no enemies in Afghanistan or anywhere else he could think of, for that matter.

From a distance, he heard a sound outside. His first impression was the wind, but then he reminded himself of the whistling sound, which was now silent. This sounded like a car, like the one he remembered from the night before as he went in and out of consciousness in the backseat. In the most irrational way, he was happy to hear the sound of that car, even if it meant it was his own assailant.

Shortly after, a light from a flashlight appeared inside the hut. Then it rose from the floor and stopped on his face, blinding him. He turned his face and wailed in agony. He tried to look at the man's face, but as he tried to focus his vision, the man shifted the lightbeam directly to his eyes, hazing his vision.

"What is it that you want?" Omar called out.

The man ignored him. He put the flashlight down and then untied his left hand from the armrest of the chair. Then he placed bottled water and a loaf of bread in front of him.

"Eat!" he said in a growling voice.

"Who are you?" Omar asked, "and what do you want from me?"

The man took a few seconds to consider his answer, and then spoke.

"I want the Vallecillo."

"The what?" Omar asked, shocked. "I don't know what you're talking about!"

He studied Omar's face some more and turned around and started his pace towards the car. It appeared that what he had hoped would not happen was inevitable. *The sooner the better,* he thought. *I don't have a lot of time.* He knew that this location was not going to be safe forever. It wouldn't be long until an American surveillance drone would spot them. After all, he was holding an American hostage, and the U.S. embassy had most likely been alerted about this missing American, and presumably they already notified the U.S. military. He needed information, and he needed it now. He fetched the car battery along with the wires from the car and started making his way back to the hut.

Inside the hut, the terrified Omar watched the dim image of his assailant enter with an object in both of his hands. He placed it in front of him and instantly began tying his left arm around the armrest again.

"Looks like we are going to do this the hard way," the man spoke in a hushed tone.

"Doing what?" the horrified Omar asked quizzically. "What are you doing? I told you… I don't know!"

The man purposefully ignored him. He tied the two ends of the copper wire to the two terminals of the battery. Then he grabbed the two end wires and connected them together for a second. Omar saw sparks fly violently when the two ends met.

"No!" he screamed in horror. "I told you I don't know!"

Jamal was well-versed in the art of interrogation. There was a psychological aspect to the process, which proved to be more efficient. The threat factor of the torture created more impetus towards getting the truth than the actual physical pain. Jamal knew the body would naturally build a tolerance to the physical pain upon inflection, and once that's obtained, then the information could be hazy; even so, it maybe dwindled. He knew his timeframe was short. It was between now and the time that he forcefully had to electrocute him.

He took the wires and brought it closer to Omar's face, and then he made contact with the two tips. Sparks flew again, hitting Omar in the face.

"Is it worth losing your eyesight for?" he barked. "You are going to tell me now, or when you are blind. Either way, you will tell!"

"Okay! Okay… I will tell you what I know."

Jamal had a good hunch about him not having possession of the Vallecillo yet. He had been watching the house closely for the last week. And he was there watching the day before, when Omar just arrived. His mentor phoned him from Pakistan a week earlier, telling him that he had confirmed information from a great source stating that Omar was coming to Kabul to retrieve the Vallecillo. Jamal needed to hear a cue in Omar's story to determine if he was lying or not. His mentor had said that an art dealer was looking for a buyer. And if that art dealer was mentioned by Omar, then he could move to the next phase of this mission by confirming the information obtained was solid.

At this instant, he needed to allocate the time to his captive, so he could tell his whole story. *This was far too important*, as his mentor had said. He needed to be crisp.

"You have five minutes to tell me everything you know," he commanded, "and if I even suspect you are lying to me, I will press these two wires in one of your eyes. You tell me which one."

Omar watched his assailant stepping away from him. It didn't seem too promising, but enough where he could buy some time. At least he was not going to lose one of his eyes in that moment. He started to put together the words he hoped to buy his freedom.

⁂

The great Ulama Hamza—his mentor, had started this quest thirteen years earlier. He had forecasted the advancement of the Internet to be a crucial part of their communication to link their scattered Islamic army around the world. But their enemy was much more advanced in technology. They would've intercepted their communications and unveiled all their planning. Hamza needed a system that they couldn't trace.

The first computer versus the modern-day computer, the first codes going over the latest. Hamza had thought.

He had learned about the astrolabe—a system of coding that Afghans used in a war against the British in 1919. He became convinced that such coding would give them a clear path to communication.

He knew of the module existing at some point in the history, that part was confirmed throughout his research, even by the British, but the question remained: how was he going to find it? His conquest started with following the leads he had acquired from the local Afghans. The leads were sketchy, but that's all he could find. There was no official data on the whereabouts of the module. In essence, it was lost to history; however, there were stories that could eventually lead him to it, he had to be more creative. He started inquiring with some Afghan scholars about the war stories their grandfathers' fought against the British. The focus of the stories was a wise general who sent his troops messages in the form of astrology—ones in quatrains that the British could not decipher.

He followed a path on the history of that general, who happened to die towards the end of the war. The stories' said that he hid the module in one of the shafts in the Bamyian Statues to protect it from the British, who were looking for the source of the codes that they were receiving from Kabul in that war.

In 2001, Sheikh Hamza, who also happened to be one of the key advisers of the Taliban regime as a respectable Ulama, advised Mullah Omar, the supreme leader of the Taliban, to destroy the anti-Islamic Buddha statues for the matter of religious purposes. The content of the astrolabe and its discovery was kept obscured from the imbecile Taliban altogether, as he deemed them to be.

The demolition of the statues came as a disappointment to Hamza. The astrolabe was not hidden in the shafts. He had to follow the second lead, which placed the book in the Kabul Museum. Then came the other verdict of Mullah Omar, where he called for the destruction of the Kabul Museum—not only the artifacts, but the demolition of the walls as well.

And that was the second set of disappointments for Hamza—when it turned out empty.

The third piece of the legend said that the general left the map of the hidden treasure to his son, who grew up to be a prominent diplomat during the monarch Zahir Shah's time. It spoke of the map hidden in the back of a Vallecillo portrait. That was one avenue Hamza hadn't explored. The Hafizi house had been looted prior to the arrival of the Taliban into Kabul. Even afterwards, he had sent a search team to the old Hafizi residence, but they came up empty-handed. Hamza had realized there would eventually come a time when someone would arrive looking for the Vallecillo. And that's when he would make his next move.

Now, the time had come. The person was more credible than he had imagined. It was Hafizi's grandson who arrived to Kabul looking to retrieve the Vallecillo. Hamza had pondered the idea that he maybe was looking to find the astrolabe, but then had rejected that notion. His sources convinced him that Omar Hafizi is only interested in the Vallecillo and not the map.

Upon receiving the awaited news, he dispatched his most reliable soldier to go about fetching Omar Hafizi before he makes news of the discovery of a Vallecillo from Afghanistan. His soldier would retrieve the Vallecillo and dispose of Hafizi's body.

※

There in the rocky valley, fortified by two barren mountains, the dim flame of the kerosene lamp kept glowing in the dark night. On the other side of the hut, the looming figure of a villain stood glaring at its prey.

Jamal turned his left arm and glanced at his wristwatch. He had given his captive enough time. Now the time had come for him to make his next move. As he stood in this hut in the middle of this desolated place, staring at his captive, he is reminded of the great Ulama's words: *This is an important piece of our cause.*

"This old woman you speak of, does anyone know where she lives?" Jamal asked.

Omar tried to fix his vision in the direction of his voice, but all he saw was a tall figure's silhouette in the dark. He had contemplated his own faith in the midst of telling him his story. It came as a shock to him that his assailant knew about the Vallecillo.

I didn't tell anyone. How could this thief know about it?

"No… the boy didn't know." Omar answered, "She is a beggar that wanders around."

"Is that what she told you?" asked Jamal.

"No." *She would have told me if you hadn't showed up, you bastard*, thought Omar, as he tried to keep his anger contained.

Jamal didn't get a good look at the old woman's face. He was concerned with striking a perfect knockout and had his eyes focused on the back of Omar's head the whole time as he neared them. The only thing that he remembered was the sound of the old woman's wail after he struck. Then he just saw the image of her back, covered by a burqa, frantically running from the scene. He wished he could've picked up both of them, especially now that she played a crucial role in being the only one knowing the hidden place of Vallecillo. Now he rested in a difficult predicament. He had to find a way to fetch the old woman, too. The problem was, he didn't see her face. And even if he did, her face would be veiled behind a burqa, just like any other woman in the city. The other factor remained: she had seen him abduct the American. There was a chance that she had alerted the authorities, and they could be on the lookout for him. He needed a plan. He stood there weighing the possibilities.

Omar had pleaded, but the thief didn't make any sign of being interested in bargaining. He had caught a glimpse of his eyes, which didn't come as a surprise to him; they resemble the rest of his demeanor: cold and unyielding to human regard. He was determined to rob him, which Omar knew he would do so at all costs. Except the irony remained that he didn't have what the villain was seeking in his hands, and that's why he still kept on breathing. But that could all change very soon.

He did fantasize about an escape, making a run to the nearest unknown place. He had not seen nor heard anything other than the whistling wind and the villain for the past two nights. *Where would I run to?* Then came the other daunting reality: his hands and feet tied to a wooden chair, a sharp pain emerging in his back from being upright on a rigid chair for more than twenty-four hours—he also couldn't feel his legs.

On the other side, standing tall in the dark, his assailant had already come up with his plan. He needed the night to pass. He would put his plan in motion just before the break of dawn. If all went as he envisioned, he would have what he was after. And for that, his cause would be immensely stronger—the same cause where his father was martyred trying to carry. *He shall smile down on me from the heaven.*

A few hours passed. Jamal fixed his vision on his captive's body as it slung sideways on the chair.

The time has come, he said to himself.

He moved his muscular body directly behind the chair. Then with the full force of his right leg, he kicked the chair forward, sending the sleeping body of Omar face-first to the ground, along with the chair that strung above him.

Omar saw his captor standing over him as the left side of his head laid on the ground. He saw the barrel of a handgun nearing his face, and then heard a clunk as the chamber revolved. Past the gun barrel, he saw the figure, now squatted down next to him. His hands stretched forward, holding the revolver where the tip touched his right eyebrow. The metal felt cold pressing against his face.

This is it, he thought. Omar fixed his vision on his assailant's face for a better read—a natural tendency for a victim to try to recognize their killer before dying—he saw what he needed to see. Then he closed his eyes and waited. *Soon this pain will be gone!* He waited, but the anticipated loud sound never came. He heard another click. He opened his eyes to discover the hammer back in its original place.

"If you disobey me, I will shoot you!" roared the voice.

He tucked the revolver onto his back behind his belt. He pulled out an army knife from the knife-holster strapped around his right hip and cut the ropes loose, releasing Omar's hands and feet.

"It's time to go!" he commanded.

Omar stretched out his hands and feet from the position that they were held for the last couple of nights. A moment later, he was able to feel his legs again. He lay on the bare dirt floor contemplating about what didn't happen. He was wrong about earlier when he thought that he was about to die. As it turned out, that was not part of his plan yet.

Jamal squatted in front of him again. This time with a new set of ropes, which he used to tie his hands, his palms facing each other.

"Let's go!" he said, as he grabbed his right arm with his burly grip and forcefully hoisted him up on his feet.

Omar felt his knees go weak—almost not bearing his own weight, but he pushed hard and managed to keep himself standing.

Jamal fetched a dark yarn bag and placed it over his head. He used another rope to tie the draping edges around his neck.

"Where are you taking me?" he cried.

He ignored him and gave him a shove in the back.

"Walk!"

Omar started to move his feet forward. After a couple of steps, his foot caught the edge of a pothole on the uneven surface of the hut. He felt himself falling forward, face down. His tied hands jolted forward, preventing his face from hitting the ground, then he felt the masculine grip of his assailant's hand around his arm again, pulling him up. And once on his feet, he felt a hand yanking his arm forward with immense force. He perpetually kept his numb feet moving at his assailant's pace as he was being tugged. A few steps later, he met the wind that he had been hearing in the last couple of days. It was cool and crisp, with no whiff of a scent or fragrance. Omar's feet were now wobbling over a bed of uneven rocks. His assailant had tightened the grip around his arm for extra precaution.

Soon his nose picked up the strong smell of gasoline, one that he recognized from the beginning of this anguish. He heard a door open, then Jamal's hand around the back of his neck thrusting him forward on the backseat.

"Stay down!" he commanded as he slammed the door shut.

Jamal circled around the back and climbed into the driver's seat. He turned to see that his prisoner had obeyed his command and rested sideways in the backseat. He turned the ignition and the vehicle came to life. He then put it in gear, and the car advanced forward, wobbling over the rocks and down the potholes, clawing its way to the nearby dirt road.

Jamal could see the first rays of sun glittering on the high peak of the east mountain. He knew that he had to hurry to get off this deserted road before daylight. He was aiming to reach the Shingdan Bazaar, the place where yesterday he made the call to his mentor. From Shingdan to Kabul, the road would be more crowded with cars, where the Land Cruiser could blend in for the rest of the two-hour drive.

Lying in the backseat of the SUV, Omar was feeling every bump of the dirt road. He hadn't brought himself to the point where he could coherently assess the discomfort of his current moment. He was still baffled by the idea of what was going to happen next. He lay there with his eyes open behind the dark hood that covered his face and was strapped tight by rope around his neck like a dog collar. He tried to move his hands, but the rope once again was coiled tight, preventing any wiggle room. He was reluctant to attempt to free himself because he knew his assailant had a line of sight on him, and could easily see him before he freed himself. He decided to be patient; perhaps an opportunity could be presented later. He was grateful for one thing so far: being alive.

CHAPTER THIRTY-ONE

The Gulfstream V started its descent over the city of Kabul, Afghanistan. Suzanne peered out the aircraft's window for a better look at what was beneath them. Her eyes were met with the pollution that hovered in a cloud of light-brown smoke. *This is far worse than LA,* she thought.

She hadn't been to LA in a while. Not since she broke up with David Moose. She thought of him as the epitome of a flamboyant California boy: good natured, with a slender, fit body, which he took immense time tending to in a gym. She had met him five years ago at Yale when she was working on her dissertation. He told her that she was a late bloomer, referencing her reserved personality, a notion that she attested to, knowing that he was somewhat right. She hadn't had many boyfriends growing up. Because ever since she could remember, she was occupied with her main task in life, and that was her schooling. Although she had met a few guys at Yale, none were able to intrigue her in the manner that David could. At times she wondered why, and found herself not quite attracted to his good looks, but rather his goofy personality, which made her laugh effortlessly. But what captivated her most was the way she could not predict what he would do, which always took her by surprise. She vividly remembered the time when she landed in LAX to spend a quiet weekend with him at his house, but he had shown up at the airport with two first-class tickets for a flight departing to Playa del Carmen, Mexico forty-five minutes after she landed. She was frantically chasing him throughout the airport as he was dashing towards the departure counter to check them in before missing their flight.

All her life she had been a planner, ever since she could remember, but David flipped that to the other extreme: breaking her monotony and instilling a sense of adventure that she never thought she had.

"I will bring out the fire you never knew existed in you." He had told her one night before making love.

David, who was an IT architect, had landed himself a job in Orange County, California, where he grew up. Around the same time, the NSA recruited Suzanne. They kept up the long-distance relationship for a couple of years, but that didn't go too well. She wanted to be with him more, but he was not going to leave his California lifestyle to settle in Georgetown alongside all her boring intellectual friends. And she, too, was not ready to leave behind her job in the NSA to move in with him in Southern California. After a period of disgruntled arguments over his relocation and her career, they both mutually agreed to move forward without one another. At times in the quiet nights as she lay in her empty bed, she thought about him, and the inevitable thought of living a dull life in Southern California outside the NSA, had she agreed to his terms, but then she jolted herself out of it, recognizing that she had worked hard to be where she had gotten. Most importantly, she believed that she could make a difference in her job, but in an unfair way, it had to be done without him.

As she gathered her thoughts back to the moment, she closed her eyes and exhaled. *The time of difference-making is now.*

The plane touched down on Bagram Airbase, fifteen miles north of Kabul. Jack was unsure about his new partner in this mission. It was rare that a field agent such as he, who had experience in danger-zone territories, was paired up with someone who had no combat experience. It was exceptionally normal for these types of missions to take a turn where they had to resort to combat, whether firing at enemies or even hand to hand, with one objective: do everything necessary to complete the mission. What really came as a baffling surprise to Jack was that NSA agents were not allowed to conduct any field operation outside the U.S., which in this instance, Suzanne's departure to Afghanistan was granted inside the airplane in London as the mission took a top-secret turn.

Jack knew where they were headed once the intel was gathered in regards to the possible location of Omar Hafizi. He had seen the barren and desolated mountains of Afghanistan a few times. He also knew the people of Afghanistan, men with traditional tunics and trousers and turbans, women covered from head to toe under a burqa, and children bearing weathered faces from the harsh elements. He'd felt their quizzical glares upon seeing foreign military pass through their dirt-filled streets. But the daunting part came to be the Taliban. They sat among the people and watched the coalition military as civilians, but then when the opportunity presented, they had taken their rifles and fired abruptly, taking everyone by a surprise, and if they were out numbered or placed in a disadvantage, they ran back and vanished among those same people. There was no military code of ethics that the Taliban followed. And for that, Jack and his team always had to be on an intensive lookout, because they could be attacked by the same civilians who approached to greet them. In Afghanistan, being attacked was not only possible, but inevitable once they left the perimeters of Kabul. His mind was swirling around one question when it came to Suzanne.

How the hell is she going to perform if that happened?

"You ever shot a gun?" he asked, as they were getting ready to deplane.

Suzanne eyed him, bearing a smile. She knew he hadn't read her file, because he still remained ignorant of her capabilities.

"What's your best on a twenty-five yard with that G-23?" she said, eyeing his sidearm.

"On a twenty-five yard?" he said in an astounded tone, "around two."

"Two out of thirteen?" she said in a sarcastic tone. "Hopefully they were two bullseyes."

"No, just the target."

"Oh…" she tapped him in the back as she was about to walk off the plane. "Thirteen out of thirteen at target. Oh, and five of them were bullseyes. My best round, so don't worry, you'll be very safe with me!" and she shot him a wink.

Thirteen out of thirteen and five bullseyes. And she hit that with a handgun? That's seventy-five feet. Wow.

CHAPTER THIRTY-TWO

Suzanne got her first whiff of the dust-filled air when she stepped on the tarmac at Bagram Airbase. She fixed her gaze on a man in a full army combat uniform who was walking towards the plane.

"There he is," said Jack as he came and stood right next to her.

"One of your buddies?" she asked.

"Oh yeah," he answered as he looked in the man's direction. "Poor guy has been stuck here for three months now."

"So how was the director's plane?" the man said as he neared them.

"Not bad at all, you should try it sometime," said Jack.

"Nice," the man said as he came face to face with them. "Maybe I can ride it home."

"Yeah right," said Jack. "It's not like they're going to allow you to go home anytime soon."

"Yeah I figured that much," he said as he eyed Suzanne with a mildly surprised expression.

"Special agent Sam Whitman, this is Dr. Suzanne Bernard with the NSA."

"Nice to meet you, Dr. Bernard." And he brought his hand forward for Suzanne to shake.

"So, who is this guy?" said Whitman. "We've got all the bigwigs calling with a laundry list of commands, mostly telling us to keep this top secret."

"We are not too sure as of yet," said Jack.

"Well, they sure are treating this as if a big-time U.S. diplomat had been kidnapped."

"Well, he is an American citizen, Agent Whitman," said Suzanne.

Whitman looked at Jack in an astounding way, and received Jack's signature inward smile, and then shifted his eyes back to Suzanne.

"We have American citizens getting kidnapped all over the world pretty much everyday, but none receives the same level of a royal treatment as this security guard guy here."

"Yup, I know," said Jack. "I'm going to leave you two here for a second to talk it over." And he started walking away.

"Where are you going?" he heard Suzanne's voice from the back.

"To my locker. I'll meet you in the study hall."

"Study hall?" Suzanne repeated and then noticed Sam Whitman laughing. On noticing her stern look, he stopped abruptly.

"So is this always what you FBI guys do? Crack jokes from your high school days?"

"No, ma'am. High school was too mind-boggling."

She shot him a quizzical look.

"We actually crack jokes about elementary school, most of the time," he said smiling.

She stood there silently, exuding distaste for the subject of laughter. It occurred to her that this was the first time Jack was in the presence of another one of his Tech-Ops team members. She wondered if the two of them would continue this type of humor like a couple of quirky fratboys. But her thought was interrupted when Whitman spoke.

"Sorry, Agent Bernard. When you spend three months in this place, away from home, you'll get a good laugh over just about anything."

"It's okay," she cordially nodded.

"We gotta go this way," Whitman pointed.

As they set out on their walk, Suzanne's eyes started canvassing the base. From the far end she recognized the portable buildings stacked right next to one another, like rows of containers in a shipyard. But unlike the setting of a place near an ocean, this place was extremely dry, with a dense dust floating in the air. She felt her eyes watering and her nose getting congested.

"It's dusty here," she said.

"Oh, it's always like this here," he said, "but don't worry. You'll get used to it in a couple of weeks."

A couple of weeks…

The thought of being there a couple of weeks brought Suzanne a sense of unease. She hoped she wouldn't be here that long. That was something that she had not pondered yet: the length of time that it would take for them to complete this mission successfully. A couple of weeks sounded steep to her.

From a distance, she noticed the appearance of two military Humvees straight in front of them. There were four soldiers casually standing around, with their assault rifles slinging down from their shoulders. Upon noticing their presence nearing them, their postures became militarily firm—the position of awaiting command.

"What is our plan?" she asked.

"Well, we have a command center set up in the ISAF building outside this base."

Suzanne arched her eyebrows.

"Oh, it's too busy here in the base. Giving the secrecy of this thing, we have to operate from there. We have the whole side of a building there."

"How far is that place?" she asked.

"It's inside the city of Kabul, about fifteen miles."

The soldiers saluted them as they neared the Humvees.

"You guys don't need to solute us. We are not military, we just barrowed ACUs."

"Yes, sir," said the staff sergeant.

"We always travel in two vehicles wherever we go in the city, two drivers and two guys on the machine guns on top of the vehicles," said Whitman.

Suzanne saw the two M2HB-QCB machine guns mounted on top of each vehicle. Two of the army PFC got inside the vehicles and took their position behind the machine guns that sat between armored plates.

"You'll ride in the rear vehicle, following us," said Whitman.

Suzanne fought the urge to call out, *"Where is Jack?"* she thought it might taint her credibility in front of these men. She climbed in the backseat of the rear vehicle, as Whitman told her. Soon after, the Army Staff

Sergeant climbed into the driver's seat. She watched Whitman and the other two PFCs get into the front vehicle.

The Humvees made a turn around the tarmac and came to a halt in front of a row of those portable houses. As she peered out the window, she noticed the large crowd of people that were scattered all over the base, as if it was an outdoors concert on top of the dirt desert. Except for being obstreperous and drunk, people were very sober here.

Her eyes fell on Jack, who now had a full ACU on. She was impressed with how fast he was able to get out of his FBI black suit and change to the Army Combat Uniform, in a matter of five minutes.

"Here, these are your two best friends in this place." He handed her a Kevlar-vest and a G23. "I want this one back," he said about the Glock.

Suzanne took the two items from him.

"Well?" said Jack.

Suzanne looked at him in confusion, wondering if she is missing something.

"Ma'am," said the staff sergeant, "it is strict procedure for all personnel to have their Kevlar body-armor before we leave the base."

"Oh, I'm sorry." She witnessed Jack's inward smile again as he shook his head. She swiftly undid the buttons on her ACU and put on the Kevlar, then strapped it tight around her waist and wore the ACU jacket over it.

The two vehicles moved past the armed gate of the base on to the lone road heading south towards Kabul. The evidence of the thirty-three years of war in this country was present at each side of this road. Suzanne saw the carcasses of old Russian tanks scattered throughout the landscape. They were mostly shells of bare metal, as any removable parts appeared to have been extracted by the scavengers and looters for scrap metal.

In the distance loomed the image of the city where a cloud of dust hovered densely. She saw the PFC shifting his body in an alert mode, intently placing his hand around the machine gun—waiting to return fire. She saw the right hand of the sergeant move over the horn of the vehicle as they approached a congested area on the road near Kabul. Another two hundred feet later, the consistent sound of the Humvees' horns started resounding through cluster of traffic. She saw the cars, motorcycle, and people all moving away from the path of the two American Humvees that drove in the middle of the a two-way street, like a knife cutting through butter.

From the backseat, for the first time she saw the face of an impoverished world. It was bearable to see these types of images on TV or the Internet, but being in the midst of it brought a sense of excruciating reality to her.

"They replace the horns in these vehicles four times a year here." said Jack from the front seat.

Her gaze was taken by a group of children, barefoot, dressed in tattered clothes curiously looking as their vehicles moved through the crowded section.

And they wonder why we don't win too many friends in these parts of the world.

She thought that as she watched the PFC on the front vehicle circling the mounted machine gun on top of the Humvee, pointing it directly at the crowd, and the sergeant holding his palm on the horn with a slight periodic removal just so he can accent the sound.

"I am sorry for the discomfort, ma'am," said the sergeant, "but this is how we've got to travel. We don't know who is in crowds."

Yeah, but you don't have to be such a bully.

"It's okay, Sergeant," she said, as she was not in the mood to spoil his southern hospitality, which he carried well in his southern accent.

The military vehicles entered the ISAF compound in the *Shash-darak* neighborhood of Kabul. Once the vehicles came to a stop, Whitman got out and led the path towards their command center, which was on the right wing of the two-story building.

CHAPTER THIRTY-THREE

THE OLD WOMAN: On that cold December evening in 1988, the night when she parted from her granddaughter, she wandered the streets of Kabul until late, a madwoman absent of cognition. Eventually, the communist patrol guards who roamed around the city enforcing the government-mandated curfew, discovered her.

The guards pitied the disoriented Hazara woman. She was picked up from the street and was taken to a homeless shelter. The day after, she was put on a bus and sent to Hazarajaat. Upon arriving in Hazarajaat, the dazed woman had wandered her way to her village, the place of her birth, explicitly guided by her childhood memory. In a miracle upshot, she was discovered by her two sisters who still lived in that village.

There on the scattered dry hills of Hazarajaat, within the straw and mud houses, she had found her sanctuary amongst her sisters and their family. At last she was accepted. That was a present Rizwan wanted to give her. She didn't receive the indignities of having a pregnant daughter without a husband anymore. Rizwan had taken care of that. The old woman hated her for what she had done.

Ultimately, time elapsed on the hate, and then changed to guilt. But time is elusive and evasive of the past. After flashes of despair, time had flourished the sight of hope. Even as it appeared to be on a small scale, it was enough to have her strive forward. Despite all of her prolonged anguish, the mere hope of possibly being reunited with her granddaughter gave her purpose in life once more.

The news of the Taliban's collapse had reached the Hazarajaat providence in the early 2002. In the spring of that year, for the second time in her life, the old woman left the mud walls of her Hazarajaat village for Kabul on a quest. She arrived to search for a face that she dimly remembered from fourteen years earlier in that dreadful day.

For the next three years, she spent her days looking for the chunky young woman who had a white complexion. It may have been very unreasonable realistically, but in her reality, it made perfect sense. Finding her had given her a hope perpendicular to defining her life as meaningful, and above all, the redemption of guilt that echoed in her consciousness without ever fading.

Every day she set off on the streets, bazaars, and other places only imaginable in her uncompromising search. She endured hunger, sickness, and weather, all based on a mere hope of finding that woman.

That leap of faith was granted on a summer afternoon in 2005, when the old woman was taking a rest on the side of a bakery among some other poverty-stricken woman who sat in her vicinity—all awaiting those who were generous enough to share part of their purchase.

In the midst of the crowded street with the bustle of vehicles and tumult coming from all directions, she was jolted by one voice coming from the steps of the bakery. In a miracle pulse, her intuition awakened her like a sixth sense—commanding her to follow.

She abruptly rose to her feet and followed her intuition. As she came around the corner, looking dead-ahead to the short steps of the bakery, her eyes came in contact with the pair of eyes she was searching for over the last several years.

The young woman that she remembered from seventeen years ago had aged to her midthirties now. She recalled her eyes, the faded color of emerald, exactly as she saw them on that day. Her round face had gone thinner, with apparent wrinkles seen in the corners of her eyes. Her light skin wasn't weathered or sunburned; it was well moisturized and almost flawless.

Upon seeing the figure of the old woman in front of her, the young woman drew back in apprehension as if she had reservations of her own.

"My granddaughter… where is she?" the old woman said in an eager tone.

Without speaking, the young woman dropped the hood of her burqa and tucked the bag under her right arm and started walking away.

She followed her, trying to keep pace with her young feet. She called out behind her a couple of times, but her words were only met by her turning around once, and she kept on striding. She picked up speed in hopes of losing the old woman in the crowd. But the old woman hobbled on, despite all her physical pain. She was relentless and was not going to lose the sight of her. She had been searching for her the last three years and had thought about her the last seventeen years. Whatever stamina was left in her, she was going to use it today.

The young woman took a right turn off the busy street into a dark alley, but before making the turn she looked behind her to check for the old woman. Her eyes could not see the old green burqa that had been tailing her for the last ten minutes. Now she had the alley to herself, and she had to make it to the end where it forked to two opposite directions. She hurried through the potholes of the muddy ground that went straight between the rows of mud-built walls in this old neighborhood of *Shore-bazaar*.

The old woman caught a glimpse of the young woman taking a right in the alley. She was well-versed in these old alleys from her endless search of the last three years. She knew that there was not going to be any doors that would led her to a house until she reached the fork at the end. She also knew the left side of the fork was a dead-end. The young woman had taken the long route in hopes of evading her in the long alley, which ultimately circled back to the right side.

She will be coming back this way, thought the old woman.

She took a right on another alleyway leading to the same path after she had taken a right turn at the fork. She kept on her pace, her rubber *Kalauches* simultaneously avoiding the broken scattered glass and garbage in the filthy alley as if she was playing hopscotch from her younger days in the village.

Once she had gone past the waste-alley shortcut, she emerged on the path of the young woman. She could see another dark alley kitty-corner from where she was. She scanned the long alley and there were no signs of a blue burqa, so she hobbled into the other dark alley. Once she emerged, she saw the hem of the blue burqa going up a straw-mud staircase.

"Hey!" she called out.

The other woman did not budge, but instead picked up her pace, going faster up the stairs. Then she heard a wooden door bang shut fast on the second floor.

In a country absent of a justice system and all other decency afforded to people in the other parts of the world, the old woman resorted to the only justice she knew. She sat on the first step of the staircase and began wailing.

Soon after, a mob of people had gathered around her, like a scene resurrected from seventeen years before—when people responded to her cries on the day her daughter had hung herself. In the midst of the agony, she heard voices asking her to remain calm, but to their dismay, they were ignored. She was dedicated to get what she was after.

One of the neighborhood women started ascending the stairs to the second floor. Upon reaching the top, she started banging on the wooden door with her fist, calling for the occupants to come out as the people of neighborhood witnessed the cries of an old woman.

Soon after, the image of the young woman appeared on top of the staircase. She was accompanied with her husband—a man wearing light-colored blouse-trousers. They started their descent down the stairs past where the old woman had been sitting. She noticed the light-complexioned woman's faded emerald eyes welled up with tears—not a sight she was hoping to see. She turned her head towards the stairs in hope of seeing her granddaughter, who'd now be well into her teens, but the staircase remained empty.

"They took her!" said the young woman in a stuffed voice.

She gazed astonished at the young woman's face as she tried to make sense of what happened.

"Who?" she asked baffled.

"Taliban," said the husband.

The old woman's tired old eyes fell from the young woman's face onto the ground, sporadically searching the patterns of the clay near their feet.

"They came one evening and took her," said the husband.

The old woman lifted her gaze up to his face, and then shook her head in disbelief.

"She was grown, a beautiful young girl," said the young woman. "Her beauty was her curse."

The old woman sat in a daze, trying to understand what she was hearing.

"Just like other beautiful girls Taliban snatched from other parts of the city. They took her, too," said the young woman in a mournful voice.

"Where did they take her?" the old woman cried. She skeptically gazed on the faces that had gathered around her, but all she could find was haunting silence and blank expressions.

"They're telling you the truth," a woman's voice rang from the back. "The Taliban do that regularly. I know of a girl who jumped to her death from a Mekorayan flat, because two Taliban had entered their flat, demanding to take her with them. Instead of obeying their demands, she jumped off the third-story balcony to the concrete ground. She too was beautiful."

"And she wasn't the only one," another woman chimed in. "There were more… and even more they did manage to take."

Where could she be? I would've been satisfied with one glimpse of her.

"Please come inside." The husband said and gestured for his wife to help her.

The young woman helped her up the stairs to their house. She then ushered her into a room where three cushion mattresses lay on the outer perimeter.

"Please have a seat. I will bring tea." The young woman left for the kitchen.

She sat there in silence, envisioning her granddaughter as an outcome of a long dream that she had yearned for the last seventeen years. But that dream had now evaporated from her clouded mind. She was faced with the daunting reality of her granddaughter gone missing. It wasn't quite the agony of the seventeen-year wait, nor was it the pain of looking for her through hunger and cold, but it was the most heartbreaking of all—the loss of hope. For the second time in her life she was experiencing this. The hope died once with her daughter, and now it died again with the loss of her granddaughter.

The young woman reappeared in the room holding a tray, and on top of it two glasses and a pot of tea. She knelt on the floor and placed the tray in front of the old woman.

"I never forgot the day when you placed her on my lap," she said as she poured the glass. "I thought I was blessed with another daughter. One that God had commanded me to look after and raise like my own. And that's exactly what I did."

"Then why did you allow them to take her?" the old woman asked with her wrinkled eyes tightened in anger.

"I didn't," said the young woman.

The old woman's facial expression changed from stern to baffled.

"You didn't?"

"No," the young woman said, as tears streamed down her cheek. "They pointed their guns at me and my husband, demanding for her to go with them. And upon seeing that, she volunteered to go, because she didn't want them to shoot us."

"Have you heard anything from her?"

"No." She shook her head. "No one really hears from or sees any of the girls who've been snatched." She passed her hand across her face and wiped the trail of tears off her cheek.

Across from her the old woman sat motionless. It appeared this had become a new agony for her. Her resilient mind was not ready to give up. Through thick and thin, she conjured a way to seek the help that she needed. She had decided on her next path, to a place where all her misery began. She was going to seek out Agha Sahib's help. She had seen the wealthy once-residents of Kabul returning from abroad to reclaim their properties after the fall of the Taliban. She had no doubt that soon Agha Sahib would follow to reclaim his Shar-e-now mansion from those who occupied it. The ringing sentiment played in her head again.

She is his heir.

"You know, she did know about you…" said the young woman. "I told her the story."

"Why?" the old woman asked, and then noticed that she shamefully lowered her eyes in search of the right words.

"I had to…" she said, "no one was going to believe that we had a half

Hazara child. She even asked why she looked different from us. I had to tell her the truth."

The old woman had been conceived by the plague of discrimination all her life, which she had accepted a long time ago as a fabric of her life, but the thought of her granddaughter sharing the same fate hadn't hit her before. Not until she heard from the young woman that she too had shared the same misfortune.

"I told her that this was passed down to her from her father." The young woman said as she fetched the black pouch from an old aluminum chest in the corner of the room and handed it to her. "At times, I'd see her sitting and looking at it for long periods of time."

The old woman untied the thread on top, and shifted the pouch upside down, and then the old gold-plated watch fell on her palm. She ran her old weathered hands over the faded leather band. Once again her memory had fallen to the time when the watch was worn by the devil, Wali. She placed the watch back inside the pouch, as she was in no mood to reminisce to Wali's treachery once more.

So, she knows about this, which means she knows about her father, too.

"Can I take this with me?" she asked.

"Yes, of course. It's yours now."

Her eyes revealed a sense of relief. In an afterthought, the old woman pondered why she didn't say all this to her when she saw her in the bazaar. She couldn't grasp her first reaction as she tried to evade her through the city. Whatever her reasoning, the old woman decided not to question it. There was only one thing evident: her granddaughter was snatched by the Taliban, and the only person who could help her was someone of wealth and power. She rose to her feet and left on her next endeavor.

Her feet set pace in the direction of Shar-e-now. It may have been a long shot that she would find her master after seventeen years, but that didn't stop her. In her madness she needed only the sliver of hope to keep her going through her days. She had been possessed by the obsession of finding her ever since the day when she gave her up. It was truly the thought of her granddaughter that kept her living, and for that reason she needed to continue without giving up.

The sun had sank behind the Asmayee mountain when her eyes fell on the frame of the big wooden gate that after all these years sat purposefully still, obscuring the lifestyle of the rich from the prying eyes of the poor. As she neared, her nose picked up the fresh smell of paint. That on its own gave her hope that perhaps Agha Sahib had returned and freshly painted his gate.

She stretched her old hand and grabbed the heavy doorknocker and started tapping it at the metal plate of the gate. Shortly after, a man opened the passageway within the gate.

"What can I do for you?" he asked in a brute voice.

She eyed the man intently but could not make out his face as having any resemblance to anyone she had ever seen before. He was tall, with a thick mustache that made his upper lip look invisible. His most daunting aspect was slung on a strap from his right shoulder—one that has brought the utmost misery to this country.

"I am looking for Agha Sahib," she said in a broken voice.

"Who…?" The man's eyes grew stern.

"He lives here," she declared.

"There is no one here by that name," the man said in a firm voice.

"Yes, he does. This is his house," she pressed.

"Let me tell you one more time," the man placed his hand on top of his slung Kalashnikov in a gesture of holding his ground. "There is no one here by that name!"

She obediently took a step back from the gate. She fixed her eyes on the man's face for a second time and realized that this man had a northern accent from the Panjshir Valley.

She turned away from the gate and headed back south towards the old city. She was baffled by the idea of someone from the Panjshir providence living in her master's house. Her mind recalled Rashina's words on that day when she set foot into this place the last time. *He's long gone!* But still, despite all of that, she wasn't going to give up. She would continue to come to this door until she found him. He was the only one who could recover her granddaughter. And above all, she thought he was the only one who could amend the truth. The same truth that she believed was hidden from him on that afternoon when her and the three-months-pregnant daughter were thrown out of this house, in which he was not present at that time. She had pondered that endlessly: *what would have happened had he been there?* He was a fair man, a man that afforded her all rights to dignity. And she believed he was not going to sell her short in the time when she needed him the most. Her path had done a complete circle and had landed her back at the place where everything had started.

Sooner or later, he will return. And at last he will see that the lady of the house was wrong.

CHAPTER THIRTY-FOUR

For the first time in two days, Omar was hearing the sound of other life. He tried to concentrate on where the sounds were coming from as his face pressed against the old cushion of the backseat while the black hood over his head blocked his vision to a pitch black. It had been about four hours since they had set off from the hut. The only indication of time was the consistent pain in his neck from absorbing the harsh terrain and then a rough road.

The dust was hovering over the congested city of Kabul like a thick fog. But unlike the fog, the color was a faded yellow. On this morning, the sun appeared like a dim yellow circle over a city that housed more than five-million people, most of whom were returning refugees from the neighboring countries among villagers who streamed into Kabul in hopes of finding an economic uplift.

There, in the shadows of a row of oak trees, a white Toyota Land Cruiser with dark-tinted windows was parked facing the crowded Sedarat intersection. The only thing apparent to the naked eye was the driver's features presented only from the windshield of the vehicle, as the rest of the interior remained completely dark behind the thick black tint.

Jamal extended his right hand to the backseat and grabbed the rim of the hood around Omar's neck. He pulled on the rope with force.

"Sit up!" he commanded, as he pulled to the upper left, hoisting him suddenly upright.

He then canvassed his surroundings for anything suspicious. Nothing unusual came to his view. He turned his body and untied the rope around

Omar's neck, and then with another slide of the hand, he pulled the hood off his head.

It took Omar well over a minute to adjust his eyesight after being in the dark for forty-eight hours. Once he gained his focus, he fixed his eyes around his abductor's right arm toward the steering wheel. He saw hands screwing a silencer on the barrel of another gun, not the revolver he had seen and felt on his face from earlier, but one with a magazine.

Omar thought about attacking him in this moment, but then he realized his hands were still tied. Also, his eyes fell on the revolver where it sat on the console of the car with the hammer drawn back in a ready-to-shoot mode.

"You see these bullets?" asked Jamal. "They're subsonic ammunition. Meaning no one would hear the sonic boom of the bullet. So it means it would be very quiet! It also means I can shoot you at any time without drawing a crowd."

"You speak English very well. I didn't expect a thief to be so skillful around here," said Omar.

Jamal eyed him in the rearview mirror. Almost as an afterthought he thought back to his mentor saying that he might not even know about the astrolabe and could only be interested in the Vallecillo.

"The Vallecillo is worth a lot of money, my friend," said Jamal, but deep down he was pleased to know that he seemed oblivious. "You are going to find that old woman, now."

Omar saw the reflection of his brown eyes growing sharper in the rearview mirror when they locked eyes. He then fixed his eyes on the crowd outside, which was moving through the street like ants around a nest.

He's got to be out of his mind, thought Omar.

"How the hell would I be able to do that?" said Omar in an irritated voice, disregarding his current situation.

"Let's hope for your sake she comes here again." He revealed the barrel of the gun with the attached suppressor.

"I want you to go ahead and try to open the door." He said as he eyed Omar.

"You want me to open the…"

"Yes, try it!"

Omar eyed him skeptically wondering why he would command him to open the door. He hesitated.

"Open it!" he barked.

Omar stretched both of his tied palms to the side panel of the right-rear door and with his two fingers he pulled on the lever. Nothing happened. The door did not budge.

"Child safety," Jamal called out. "Now, if you did that without my permission, you'd be shot!" he pointed the gun at his chest now. "You know that both of these doors are not going to open from the inside."

He turned his head towards the windshield and started the car.

"What happens to me once you find the Vallecillo?"

"I take Vallecillo, you go home."

For a brief moment, Omar almost believed what he just told him, but his intuition told him the opposite. Omar wanted to have the portrait, but he wasn't willing to lose his life over it. There had been a few times when he was tied up in that hut where he thought about a way to forget about this whole thing. All he wanted, more than anything in those moments, was to go back to Seattle to his simple life and his simple job. But then there was the shrewd analysis that made him disposable once this man got what he wanted. This man was a killer. Omar could see it in his eyes, as they remained like two brown stones, cold without a shard of emotion. His slender, tall body, which appeared to be well trained, like a military man, his tone of voice and the way he carried himself, all described a man who would stop at nothing. He was not going to risk letting him go once he had the Vallecillo. Not in this lawless place. All his moves were methodical to the full extent without a slip.

I need to find a way to get out of this car.

The car lurched forward when he popped the clutch. He slowly started driving towards the crowded street.

"Keep looking for her!" he commanded.

Omar saw his razor-sharp eyes looking at him in the rearview mirror, emitting distrust.

The Land Cruiser started crawling at a slow speed once it entered the cluster of traffic.

"Don't try to make any sudden moves," he said, "no one can see you inside this car." And he wrapped his hand around the gun and held it steady on his lap.

The vehicle took a right at the Sedarat intersection. Slowly it kept crawling with the traffic jam, which served a convenient purpose to Jamal, because the slow speed maximized visualization.

"Keep your eyes on the sidewalk!" said Jamal.

Omar kept his gaze out of the backseat toward the crowd on the sidewalk, as he was told. This was clearly the place when he saw Nakebakht for the first time two days earlier. He began contemplating whether he should point her out if he did see her.

How would he know that I'd be lying to him?

"Do you see her?"

Omar saw Jamal's eyes quizzically looking at him as if he was studying his response.

"No," he said, keeping a straight face.

The vehicle kept on rolling for a few more minutes in the crowded street. Then he took a right on the Chicken Street.

"Keep your eyes on both sides of the street!" he demanded.

The Chicken Street was notorious for tourists roaming up and down to buy embroidery and handcrafted clothing along with all sorts of other souvenirs that would entice the foreign tourists to come and spend their money. The other aspect was where there were tourists, there were more beggars and panhandlers, waiting for the rich and compassionate foreigners to open their wallets.

Jamal saw Omar's eyes in the rearview mirror looking into the crowd on both sides of the street in search of the old woman. He was reassured that his story about the old woman knowing the location of the Vallecillo had proved to be correct. He had meticulously played this as a psychological game by having Omar totally unaware of his complete plan. He had grown skeptical about his story and his doubts had to be tested in a different manner. This was his way of refining fiction from fact, by gauging his ability to tell the truth in a different form. Jamal knew who they were looking for and knew exactly where he would find her. But what didn't seem credible was whether Omar's tale about the old woman had any connections to the Vallecillo, as he claimed it did.

"Do you see her?" he asked again.

"No," Omar answered, his face bearing a blank expression. "I haven't seen her yet."

Jamal shifted his eyes from the rearview mirror back to the windshield. *He is telling the truth.* Had the old woman been on the street and had not been picked out by Omar, then his fate would have taken another turn—one that would have required Jamal's expertise in the art of interrogation—which he often thought of as being very messy, especially in a place like the hut where he didn't have access to flowing hot water to wash the human blood off his own body and clothes.

In that instant, he truly felt happy for Omar. But that's all he could spare him. In the end, he didn't feel any remorse for treating him this way. In Jamal's eyes, Omar, too, was an infidel, living in the U.S., a country that brought a despicable trauma to the land of Islam, and above all, the country that fired the missiles from thousands of miles away that killed his father.

Jamal steered the Land Cruiser right at the end of the Chicken Street. Now that Omar had proven that he was telling the truth, it was time for him to start the second phase of his plan. He had been watching the Hafizi compound from a distance for the last week, anticipating Omar's arrival. He needed to collect as much intel as he could about his mission. So in the span of a week, he sat in his car while keeping his focus on the house, mentally observing and recording all the activities there. He had seen the old beggar woman who ritualistically showed up every morning knocking on the door. He wondered about her and her business there. But then he had seen the passageway of the gate opening and shutting. Sometimes he heard shouts demanding her to leave resounding throughout the street. But one thing that he was sure about was the fact that it happened every morning. The other part that he was certain of was that she was talking to Omar when he snatched him two days ago. It was the same woman, and the circumstances of going to the Hafizi residence everyday and talking to his grandson had a certain correlation.

From the backseat, Omar saw the gray frame of his grandfather's gate. Then the car rolled slowly on the outer edge of the street and came to a stop about two hundred feet before approaching the gate. He began to wonder if he had told Jamal the exact location of his grandfather's house. But then he realized that he hadn't. He tried again to remember, but his memory didn't recall telling him.

How the hell does he know…?

"What are we doing here?" he asked.

Jamal calmly looked in the rearview mirror to his reflection.

"She'll be here soon."

Omar felt a surge streaming through his body as he recalled Abdullah's words.

"She comes here every day asking for some people."

He took a deep breath and closed his eyes for a brief second, again reciting Abdullah's words. But he still remained bewildered as to how the thief would know that. If Abdullah was correct, then she would be coming here very soon. He was bogged down by one question: *what am I going to do?* He needed a plan of his own.

CHAPTER THIRTY-FIVE

Suzanne trailed Jack and Whitman into the command center within the ISAF building. The large room, thirty by thirty, was divided with a Plexiglas in the center. On the left side of the glass was high-tech communication equipment along with three other FBI agents presiding over the devices. One of them waved at Jack as they entered the room.

"Dr. Bernard," said Whitman, "welcome to the FBI Attaché office in Kabul."

"Thanks." She smiled cordially.

One of the agents started tapping on the Plexiglas from the other side. "Jack, did you bring my bottle of scotch?"

"Sorry Phil," Jack replied, "You are not allowed to drink when you are in the war zone."

"Oh, how convenient for you, huh?" he said in a sarcastic tone.

Jack looked at Suzanne and gestured towards the agent behind the Plexiglas.

"That's my Skip."

"Your what…?" she seemed confused for a second, and then it hit her. "Oh, I see… well, my Skip doesn't drink."

"It's because your Skip hasn't hit puberty yet."

Suzanne shook her head in disbelief of the resentment that he was feeling towards her younger NSA counterpart.

"I can see that you're still tickled by that mission in Cairo. Well, you shouldn't only blame Skip for that. You can blame me, too." She said, raising her eyebrows, claiming a part for the time when the NSA irritated Jack in Cairo as he sat in a flat over the bakery on a hot day.

One of the black phones on top of a desk buzzed. Whitman hit the speaker button.

"Yes."

"The Interior Minister is here with his son," a woman's voice came over the speaker.

"Okay, we'll be right down," said Whitman.

Whitman hit the "End" button on the phone and then shifted towards Jack and Suzanne.

"So, I summoned the Interior Minister and his son here. I figured that's where you two wanted to start."

"Yeah, of course," said Jack. "They are the only two people who were in contact with Omar Hafizi here. Right?"

"I'm not sure," said Whitman.

"Well, let's go and find out then," said Jack.

Only a select few local Afghans were allowed to enter the ISAF building in Kabul. Even then, a designated place on the first floor of the building was set up where they could tend to their business with the ISAF staff. It was done so to take extra precaution, to prohibit Afghans from seeing the equipment, which could result in a leak to Taliban and Al-Qaeda gaining intel on the ISAF's counterterrorism tactics. Based on those strict guidelines, no local Afghan was to be trusted.

The trio made their way down the staircase to the first floor, and then arrived behind a brown wooden door. Before entering the room, Whitman turned to Jack and Suzanne and gave them a nod. He then turned the knob and the door opened. They made their way inside the room to the waiting Interior Minister and his son as well as their local translator.

Suzanne noticed the Minister's gaze as she entered the room. He seemed a little shocked upon noticing her presence. He nervously tried to pull his shirt down where the collar seemed to be gripping tight around his short, wide neck. Then he stood and beamed a wide smile like a schoolboy.

"Mr. Minister: this is Jack Rivers and that's Dr. Bernard. They're here to take your testimony in regards to the American citizen, Omar Hafizi." Whitman made the introduction.

Jack extended his hand for the Minister to shake. After shaking hands with Jack, the Minister took a few steps closer and firmly shook Suzanne's hand, and said in his broken English, "Bery nice to meet you!"

Jack wondered if Suzanne knew that her good looks just bought her an instant admiration from the Interior Minister of Afghanistan.

"Please, let's all take a seat." Whitman motioned Jack and Suzanne to the seats around the conference table, across from where the Minister, his son, and his translator were sitting.

Suzanne looked at the boy who sat next to the Minister; he didn't seem to be more than twelve to thirteen years of age. She instantly registered that he was their true witness, because he was the one who actually saw Omar Hafizi getting abducted, or at least that's what the report said. On the left side of the Minister sat his translator, a man in his midtwenties, slim-figured, with a long narrow face.

"Mr. Minister, thank you for coming to see us this morning. My colleagues and I have a few questions in order for us to find Omar Hafizi," said Whitman.

The young man with the narrow face started speaking Dari to the Minister, translating what Whitman just said.

The Minister only introduced himself as Commander Khaled to the Afghans. He knew that the Americans would not give him the title of a commander, because prior to their arrival into Afghanistan, they did not deem any previous Afghan military as credible, therefore their titles were disregarded. Luckily, the warlord Commander Khaled had turned into the Interior Minister of Afghanistan after the American raid, so among the American personnel he went by the new title that had been bestowed upon him—Mr. Minister.

After the translator was done speaking, the Minister nodded in agreement.

"Mr. Minister," said Jack, "Did Omar say or mention anything to you that would probably get him in trouble? I mean, can you think of anything like that?"

The translator started speaking in Dari as the Minister kept his eyes towards Jack.

"No, nothing that I can think of," said the translator. "He wasn't there that long. He came and he was taken the next day."

"Did he tell you why he came to Afghanistan?"

"He came here to work for me, as a translator."

Jack glanced at Suzanne for a second.

"A translator?" said Jack, "I mean, it seems like you already have one." He gestured towards the thin man who was speaking to him in Dari.

"Yes," the translator spoke, "the Minister says it's better to have an American translator because it will make him more trusted."

Jack revealed a cordial smile and noticed that his expression was mimicked by the Minister, as if they both were pondering the array of complaints that Afghan officials had made because the Americans posed them as untrustworthy.

Jack lifted his eyes up higher, revealing a curious expression. "How did he apply for the job? I mean… did he know you?"

"No," said the Minister's translator, "he called his office a lot of times for job."

Suzanne could see that the Minister's current translator was not very proficient in English, so she thought that could be a reason, too. Perhaps he wouldn't want to say it in the presence of this guy next to him.

Jack studied the Minister's blank expression. He pondered if there was something else here that he was missing or something that the Minister didn't tell him in his opening questions. If there was more, he thought it most likely would surface later. His experience guided him through the first phase of an investigation. *Eliminate the potential suspects.* After all, it was the Minister who reported him missing to the Embassy and had used his position of power to advocate for an escalated investigation.

That makes him clean, for now, thought Jack.

"And you mentioned that this young man saw Omar hauled into the car?"

Jack looked at the young boy as he sat on the edge of the chair, which was too big for his size. He had his elbows anchored on top of the conference table, so he could keep himself from sinking. His small face was glazed as his overly large, light-brown eyes were fixed at Jack.

"Yes," the translator echoed his word in English.

"Can you ask him to tell us exactly what he saw?"

The translator started speaking to the boy, who now had his full attention on the thin man.

"He says he ran after Omar, then followed him to the small street, and that's where he saw a man hit him in the head with some kind of a stick and then put him in the back seat of white car," the translator narrated as he fumbled some of the words.

"Did he say he ran after him?" asked Jack.

"Yes."

"Ask him why he ran after him."

He said, "Omar ran and then I ran."

"Why was Omar running?" asked Jack.

The boy shrugged after the translator asked him. But then in an afterthought, he started to speak—his voice carrying a bit of childlike excitement.

"He ran to talk to a beggar," said the translator; "he says he saw him talking to her before he was hit."

Jack glanced at Suzanne to get her take on this, but she sat still, wearing a deadpan expression as her eyes remained fixed on the boy.

"A beggar? You mean like a homeless person?"

The Minister shook his head, radiating a bleak look.

"The city is full of beggars," said the Minister.

Then the boy started speaking to his father. The three agents saw the Minister asking his son something with a keen expression. Then he motioned to the translator.

"Abdullah says that he was talking to the crazy woman."

The crazy woman? thought Jack.

Jack glanced at Suzanne again, and this time she was looking right back at him, as if she was concurring his thoughts.

"Can you ask Abdullah to tell us everything from the beginning?"

"This old woman," the scrawny man narrated, "she is…" he pointed his index finger next to his right ear and made a couple of circles. "Comes to the house every day. Omar ran after her. And then Abdullah run after Omar. Then he saw in the little street, Omar get hit."

Suzanne looked at Jack in anticipation of wanting to ask the next question. He nodded.

"Ask him if he knows that woman," Suzanne asked the translator.

Before the boy could find his words, the Minister had already started speaking, with a look of appeal.

"The Minister says he takes care of the beggars, he truly feels sorry for them when they come to his house, because he is a very nice man…" and the translator went on as the Minister kept speaking.

Suzanne noticed Jack wearing his habitual inward smile as he had his head down, scribbling on the peace of paper. She was peeved by the Minister exuding his likeability, and even more so by Jack's pursed-lip smile, which radiated: *Look who has a crush on you!*

Jack quickly picked up on Suzanne's bilious demeanor, so he cleared his throat, drawing the Minister's attention to himself. He fixed his gaze on the translator and said, "Please let them know that it's important for us to know if Omar knew the old woman that they speak of."

The Minister shook his head, "I don't think so," said the translator.

"Ask them if there is anything more they can tell us about this old woman," said Jack.

The Minister turned to his son in a disoriented manner and then turned back to his translator.

"She comes to our door every day asking for someone by the name of Agha Sahib. We don't know anything else about her," said the translator.

"This person, Agha Sahib, do you know who he is?" asked Jack, and then he glanced at Suzanne.

"That could be many people, says the Minister."

That could be many people? Didn't he just say that she asks for someone?

Jack cocked his head. "I thought he said that she was looking for someone by that name?"

The translator and Minister continued in a dialogue for a moment.

"Yes, but Agha Sahib is not a person's name. Minister says a lot of families have Agha Sahib," said the translator.

Jack turned to Suzanne, presenting his baffled look. His gaze was met with her slight shrug.

"It is not a name, but a lot of families have that? What does that mean?" Jack pressed.

The Minister shared a dumbfounded look with his translator and then they exchanged a few more words.

"It is a name, but not a real name. It is a family name. Only," said the translator, "a lot of families have someone called Agha Sahib, but that's not that person's real name."

"So is it more like a title for a person within a family?" asked Suzanne.

"Yes," the translator blurted out, "a title for someone in family. Especially old man."

"And there is nobody by that name in his family?" she asked

After hearing the translation, the Minister wore his eager smile once more and said to Suzanne a couple of English phrases he knew, "No, me, not old."

Jack controlled himself not to laugh, but on the other hand, he noticed Whitman sitting sideways and resting his elbow on the conference table as he has his palm pressed against his mouth, squeezing his cheeks—hiding what he just discovered—the Minister's admiration for the NSA's bombshell.

Jack decided to say something quickly, even if it may not be relevant, just so he could change the air in the room.

"What type of a white car did he put Omar into?"

The boy said, "Toyota," in a loud and proud voice.

Jack turned to Whitman and Suzanne, seeking if they had anything further, but they both gently shook their heads. He knew that there was definitely more to the story that he was not going to get from the Minister. If he wanted to get more info, then he had to give out Omar Hafizi's true identity and their belief as to why he came to work for the Minister. And he wasn't ready to give out that information yet.

"Mr. Minister," Said Jack, "thank you so much for coming to see us this morning. I think that's all we have for now. We will let you know if we have any further updates."

The Minister cordially nodded. They got up to leave. As Suzanne was exiting the room, her gaze fell on the Minister's face, which radiated fondness of her.

A very awkward man, she thought.

CHAPTER THIRTY-SIX

They ascended back up the stairs to the control office. Jack walked towards the window and took a peek outside over the compound's courtyard, eyeing the rows of almond trees that sat on dry ground. He put his arms around his hips and arched his back in a long stretch. Then he gasped for a long breath and exhaled.

"Alright, what did we learn today?" he said as he turned to look at Suzanne and Whitman. "Any thoughts?"

"Looks like we have two new players now," said Suzanne.

Jack pursed his lips and lowered his gaze to the ground for a second.

"Yes… the old woman and Agasaeib."

"I believe its spelled AGHA space SAHIB," said Whitman.

"Thank you for correcting me," Jack said as he rolled his eyes in sarcasm.

"So, why would Omar Hafizi go to this guy's house, as a houseguest, and then chase a beggar the next day?" asked Suzanne. "What do we have on other Afghan-Americans' behavior patterns when they come back to Afghanistan?"

"Well, we could generalize it and go by the CIA intel on them," said Whitman.

"And what does that intel say?" she asked.

"Well, it's a generalization. I don't think it'll be relevant here."

"Sam, this whole thing is a big cluster from the get-go, so we've got to look at it from a whole bunch of lenses," said Jack. "So, what is the general intel on these U.S.-citizen Afghans?"

"Nothing illegal. Those who generally show up here in Kabul are the ones that own properties, and now that we've inflated the real estate market by our presence and our dollar, they show up here and sell those properties, and wire the money back home in the States."

"And that's exactly what I think Omar is doing," offered Suzanne. "He tried to find the Vallecillo for that exact reason."

Jack walked over to one of the desks and rolled a chair back and sat on it.

"So we have three entities here. That title name, the old woman, and the Minister's residence," said Jack as he reclined in the chair. "What are the relationships with those three? And why would he want to be a translator working for the Afghan Minister, if he could sell a Vallecillo for sixty million dollars?"

"Oh, wait…" Suzanne said as her eyes widened. "What did Wilson say? He said something about Omar telling him that his grandfather was friends with Vallecillo, right?"

Suddenly Jack's face grew dour, as if a lightswitch inside his head just turned on. He turned to Whitman.

"This Minister. The house he lives in. When did he buy it?"

Whitman shrugged. "I don't know. Prior to becoming the Interior Minister, this guy was a warlord. And rumor has it that after the Taliban fell, the warlords that we supported who fought against the Taliban went and claimed some of the nice houses of Kabul as their own. Generally those were houses that the Taliban officials had seized before them."

"They could do that?" asked Suzanne in a naive voice.

"Of course they could. We were the only ones who could stop that, but we didn't," said Whitman.

"Well, we are here for two reasons: Al-Qaeda and the Taliban. Any economical or moral dispute among Afghans should be done in their own courts. That's not our job," said Jack.

"So, it is within reason to believe that Omar planned this whole translation job thing, just so he could get access to the Minister's house, which we assume was his grandfather's at one point?" said Suzanne.

"It makes sense. And that could very well be the place where he would look for the Vallecillo as well," offered Jack.

"Still, even if that was true, why would he run after the beggar?" said Whitman, "and where the hell would this assailant come from who would hit him over the head and then haul him limp into a car?"

"Good point," said Jack. "The beggar, we don't know about. But I have an idea about the assailant." He pressed a button on the black phone in front of him. A voice came on the speaker.

"What do you want?" he asked.

"Can you get in here? I got something for you," said Jack.

The other side of the Plexiglas swung open and Phil emerged into the room.

"Can you backtrack the city's surveillance data from the last five days?" asked Jack.

Phil glanced at Suzanne for a second in hopes of an introduction, but none was made, so he swiftly fixed his gaze back to Jack.

"Okay," he said, arching his eyebrows. "What section, and what am I looking for?"

"You are looking for a white Toyota in the vicinity of the Interior Minister's residence. Most likely the vehicle was stationary in one place for long periods of time."

"And what section is his residence in?" Phil asked.

"I don't know. Look it up," and he shot him a nod.

Since Kabul did not have proper addressing system, the U.S. military had divided the city into eight different sections in which they could recognize and pinpoint activity.

As Phil turned to leave, Jack said, "By the way, this is Dr. Bernard with the NSA. Now, they have some seriously smart people there, so don't let me down."

Phil turned and eyed Jack's toying face and then turned to Suzanne and nodded. "This might take a few minutes. Do you want me to run the thermal automatically if I find the car?"

"Yeah, go for it. And let's hope the vehicle is newer than 2002," said Jack.

Suzanne revealed a puzzled look. "What's a thermal?"

"Oh, it's the technology that enables us to recognize a VIN, the vehicle's identification number. That way we can track down where it's been and it's current location," said Whitman.

"Yeah, but there is one catch," said Jack. "The vehicle has to be newer than 2002, because that's when we mandated car companies to put the Synthetic Diamonds CVD inside the engine-blocks of vehicles exported to central Asia, the Middle East, and north Africa."

"The CVD is cut mimicking a car's VIN number, and when the engine starts to heat up, the CVD glows brighter through the thermal conductivity process, because the car's engine is thermal resistant, therefore, those engraved CVDs would be readable in the thermal imaging cameras. That technology enables the military to have a readout on every vehicle made past 2002. The other ingenious factor is the CVD was mixed with the engine block's steel compound in the melting phase; therefore, it could not be extracted or destroyed," said Whitman as he revealed a proud expression. "Sorry, I'm a total car guy."

"That's very impressive," said Suzanne.

"Yeah, and you guys think you have all the cool stuff in the NSA," said Jack.

A few moments later, the black phone buzzed again. "Yeah," Jack answered.

"You better get in here, Jack," Phil's voice resounded over the speaker.

The three of them walked inside the Plexiglas room and stood behind Phil, who had a few satellite images broadcast on the fifty-inch LCD monitor in the center of the room.

"You see this?" he pointed to the screen. "There is the satellite image of the house," then he clicked a few more keys for a close-up, and the monitor revealed the street with a lone SUV sitting within eyesight of the house. "And this car had been camped here for six days."

"How long did you roll back the data?" asked Jack.

"Eight days… but he wasn't there on the first two days, so the first sighting was… six days ago."

"Is this a live feed?" asked Suzanne.

"No, the satellite passed an hour ago, and given its altitude of 660 miles and its orbit velocity of 1,638 Miles Per Hour, it will come around in sixty-six minutes."

"Roll back to the last couple of days," said Jack.

Phil hit a few more keys and the image of the street reappeared on the monitor.

"That's the car," said Jack.

"What do you mean? The car was not there for the last couple of days," said Phil, and they all looked intently to the monitor which revealed the street in front of the Minister's house without the presence of the Toyota Land Cruiser as it sat there in the previous snapshots.

Jack turned to Suzanne with a reassuring gaze.

"I told you that someone was waiting for him. And here it is. We don't see him here in the last couple of days because he had already snatched Omar two days ago."

She looked at him wryly and then fixed her eyes back on the monitor.

"If the car was sitting there for that long, hopefully it shows up in our routine thermal checkup," said Jack.

Phil opened a new screen on one of the monitors in front of him. After striking a few more keys, he eagerly shouted, "Yes! Finally this thermal monitoring has produced results. We have the parked SUV's VIN!"

"Alright, good," said Jack. "Register that VIN with all surveillance and make the call for the UAVs to start an aerial thermal search for that vehicle, immediately."

"Are you out of your mind?" barked Whitman. "You do realize that search has to be done at the altitude of no more than 2,000 feet because that's the range on those heat-seeking cameras."

"Yes, I know," confirmed Jack as he revealed a puzzle look.

"So, you want to fly drones at a very low altitude over the city of Kabul?"

"Yeah…" said Jack, dumbfounded.

"Do you realize that Karzai would shit his pants?"

"Let him," said Jack. "This is only surveillance. We are not going to be shooting anyone."

Whitman let out a sarcastic laugh. "And who would authorize that?

Do you think the Bagram Base Commander would allow those drones to take off?"

"Yes, he will," he turned to Suzanne. "Can you call your friend, Steven Williams?"

Suzanne brought her phone out and started dialing.

"I don't know, Jack," Whitman's wary voice rang again, "Karzai could cry about this for a long time."

"He can cry," said Jack. "Oh, and he could go fuck himself, too, while he's at it."

CHAPTER THIRTY-SEVEN

On a frigid day, the old woman returned to her ritualistic wandering. Her feet kept marching through the cluttered streets of Kabul as they had over the last three years, one reason illuminating her disoriented mind. Her thoughts, impaired to her surroundings, were focused on the dim image of hope that only she could see. *My prayers have been answered.*

Two days ago, she had seen hope. It may have been a long shot to a sane mind, with only glints, but in her mind, it stood as a beacon on top of the high mountain, far above but close enough to where her feet kept on treading.

Omar. She recalled him from her undistorted long-term memory. She remembered his unyielding generosity as a boy—one who from a young age did not ascribe to the metaphorical brick wall that stopped everyone else from reaching her. He eased through it blindly, without his eyes defining her as the untouchable servant. He didn't seem to care about that stamp inked on her brow. To him she was simply Nakebakht. The affable Hazara lady who took care of him, to whom he revealed his gratefulness by welcoming her daughter, her sunflower *Aftowgoo*, as a solemn playmate and friend. She could still recall the dim image of Omar, a teenage boy, sitting cross-legged on the grass by the trunk of the walnut tree in his crisp blue jeans and navy-blue button-up sleeveless shirt, looking straight at Rizwan. And Rizwan, indulged by that moment, attentively sat and relished his company.

One day, Rizwan brought a notebook with her. And when she asked the purpose, Rizwan gloatingly answered that Omar had given it to her so she could write down the homework that he assigned her.

She didn't see the value of education for her and never thought it would elevate Rizwan to a place above her current standing. But then, she was overcome with Rizwan's eagerness of wanting to be more than what she wanted her to be. And to see Rizwan soothed in hopes of being someone more than a servant brought her life a new meaning, an optimism. Omar was the matter behind Rizwan's tenacity. He was her inspiration.

The boy with the narrow face and a pointy chin had grown up to be a man. She saw that he still carried that generous sparkle in his dark-brown eyes when she saw him last, two days ago. But she doesn't remember him saying that they no longer have the house. Then the trauma happened. Omar was struck over the head and was hauled off to a large car.

Who was that man? She had never seen him. *And why did he attack him?* Her steps took a path in the only direction that her boggled mind commenced. She walked through the alleys to the Maiwand intersection, then passed the dried-up fountains, which surrendered its blue paint and glory to thirty-two years of war. Then on to Istiqilal High School, and ultimately she made her way past the wool shops that surrounded Sedarat intersection.

In the side pocket of her long cotton blouse remained a pouch, one that she had heard was kept close to her granddaughter, but other than that, dementia had washed away the prize it carried or why she had it in her pocket.

She made the right turn; she could see the sight of the gray gate. She kept walking forward. She was propelled by her long-term memory of this place, yet forgetting the part that she comes to this door every day. To her, every day is a new search when she comes to this door looking for her master, but in reality, she was met with the same disappointment everyday. Yet when the sun rises on the next day, her dementia replaces yesterday's disappointment with the same hope for a new day that brings her back to this door without any recollection that she was there the day before, and every day for the last three years.

CHAPTER THIRTY-EIGHT

Omar squinted through the windshield over the hood of the car. He was looking at a figure he hoped not to see. In a flash, he thought that his assailant would not see what he was looking at, but he was wrong. He saw his head move straight on, with his piercing eyes fixed, looking over the steering wheel in the same direction as Omar.

Goddamn it! Why did you come here today? he cursed.

For a moment he wanted to cling to the hope of her seeing the car and abruptly running away, but that hope remained a fantasy in that moment. Her wobbling feet kept pace forward towards the car. He fixed his eyes to the rearview mirror and saw his assailant's eyes widen where he could see his black pupils, staring at him in the rearview mirror with mistrust.

Omar didn't make a move. He sat still, waiting to see what he was going to do. In a glimpse, he could see her nearing the car. She was about a hundred feet away. From the backseat he saw his assailant took out that metal pipe, one that he could instantly remember feeling in the back of his own skull.

He thought about wrapping his tied hands around his neck and slinging him against the driver's seat, like the scene from the *Godfather* movie where Michael executes the betraying Connie's husband, Carlo. But then he saw the gun with the suppressor touching his assailant's knee in the center console. The assailant would have his hands free and could easily pick up the weapon and shoot him backwards over his shoulder as Omar has his tied hands around his neck. After all, Omar realized that he no longer had any use for him. His plan would be the usual. He'd pick up

Nakebakht and torture her until she told him the whereabouts of the Vallecillo. In that second, Omar realized that he has to make a run for it. The assailant had no reason to kill the old woman instantly. She'd stay alive until he got what he needed, and then they'd both be dead.

Jamal reached forward and wrapped his right hand around the grip of the gun. He then turned to the backseat and eyed Omar fiercely.

"Don't make a move!" he said in a stern voice.

He was pleased to know that his captive was soft, obeying every command thus far. His plan would play out in a couple of minutes, once he has apprehended this old woman. He saw her now, wobbling, almost to the right side of the car, and he had a feeling that she'd be an easy fetch. He wanted her to pass the car, so he could sneak up behind her. By the time she realized it, he would have his arms around her shoulders and already have her hoisted and ready to throw in the backseat next to him.

From the backseat, Omar saw the old wrinkled face of his grandfather's most loyal servant passing through the dark tint of the rear window. Then, he heard the driver's side door lever click as it released the door from its latch. He caught a glimpse of his assailant's eyes again in the rearview mirror, giving him a last look before exiting the car. He remained calm, yet his mind echoed his thought from earlier.

Now is the time.

He heard the door swing shut. Shortly after, he saw him walking around the front of the car and as he made his way to the sidewalk, he turned his head and looked at Omar through the windshield, assessing and making sure that he was sitting still. Then his face turned to the old woman and his eyes focused on her.

The long-awaited courage hit Omar at once. He lunged his body forward onto the driver's seat. He then grabbed the door lever with his loose fingers and yanked it backwards. The sound of the door pop came as the door moved outwards.

He heard a scream on the right side of the SUV. Down deep he felt his instincts telling him to go around the car and attack the man who had his hands on an old woman, but instinct was overshadowed by his reasoning. And reasoning prompted him to run the opposite direction. So he did.

He didn't turn around, for he already knew the outcome. As his legs kept on striding forward, his ears heard the sound of the struggling old woman, frantically screaming at the top of her lungs. A few more feet and he was close to the Naswaan intersection to the north. His ears still heard the wail of an old woman. And then he heard a door slam. Then her voice disappeared from the street, muffled inside the enclosed cabin of the SUV.

He heard a hiss sound on his right, then in a millisecond a loud ding on the wrought-iron fence of the Iranian embassy a few feet in front of him. His cramped muscles suddenly thundered with more energy. His strides picked up faster. Then, the hiss sound again. This time it passed him on the left. He saw debris fly from the trunk of a tree on the sidewalk ten feet in front of him. He didn't stop. Another three seconds later, he banked right, following the path of the sidewalk on the perimeter of the intersection. As he made the right turn, he mustered his last courage to turn to see what he left behind. Somewhere in the back of his mind, he subconsciously wanted to see how he was going to get shot. His gaze followed kitty-corner through the hollow spaces in the iron fence. He saw the long figure of his assailant standing on the left side of the SUV, pointing the gun in his direction from a hundred and fifty feet. He heard the sound of bullets hitting the fence again and then ricocheting to another metal part, making a bang sound. It repeated four more times, but Omar kept on running. He thought about checking his body to see if he had been hit, but then convinced himself as long as he could run, then that's exactly what he'd do.

Now almost three hundred feet away, he heard the familiar sound of the bulky engine revving up. He knew what was coming next. He wished his hands were free, for his speed could have been twice as fast if he had the luxury of his arms balancing his strides. He had both of his tied palms raised in front of him—away from his body—maximizing his speed, as he tried to keep his legs striding straight.

He saw the end of the Iranian embassy's fence and with it, the start of the Turkish embassy's fence. His mind hypnotically took him back to his childhood days for a tad. This was the same road where he traveled as a young teenage boy going to Lasee Amani, his school in Kabul. It dawned on him that this was not the first time he was running this same road; he did it almost every day, coming from school. Then in a flash, everything cleared up. All of a sudden his running had a purpose now—a destination.

His mind recited the words that he answered in front of a naturalization officer in the year 1995. Raising his hand and swearing to obey all the laws as he became an American citizen, in that moment, when he frantically kept running for his life, he was uplifted by a jolt of patriotism. Proudly, for the first time, he saw the value of an American citizenship. Adrenaline surged through his body and his expression turned purposeful as he felt the might of the U.S. military and its duty to protect him at all costs.

You fuckin' Arab, mah boys will fuck you up now! That's right!

His mind twirled on the TV images of GTMO detainees wearing orange jumpsuits as their faces proclaimed defeat. Then to the images of the Al-Qaeda corps blown to pieces at the beginning of this war. As an afterthought, he wanted to stop and fight in a courageous way that he fantasized. He heard the sound of the tires screeching behind him as it spun out of control in his direction.

To the left side!

His mind told him to cross the street, so he did. As he ran across, he heard another screeching sound. He fixed his eyes on a yellow taxi hitting the breaks and stopping a couple of meters away from his body. He saw a panicked look on the driver's long, bony face when he locked eyes with him. He kept on, now on the left side of the street.

He heard the sound of the SUV's engine again, that loud sturdy inline six-cylinder revving at a high RPM, now on his right side. It passed him. Then in the approaching intersection it banked left, stopping dead ahead on his path, twenty feet away. He saw the driver's door opening and the image of the gun with the attached suppresser looming from the window. Shortly after, he saw the driver's left foot hovering over the paved road, and then the door swung outward when his foot touched the ground. Instinct propelled him forward, faster than ever now. And as he neared the SUV, he felt both of his feet leaving the ground and his body taking the shape of a spear thrusting forward. His feet came to a solid halt when they hit the SUV's door. He fell to the ground on his left side.

To his astonishment, he saw the assailant's head trap between the roof of the car and the upper metal edge of the door above the window. The tall man's head was burdened by an excess of force as it got caught between the two metals. His large figure went limp in an aftershock and then fell on the ground next to him.

Omar hurried back to his feet; amazingly, he had not broken a bone, although there was a new set of sharp pains around his neck and left shoulder from hitting the ground. He stood up, wobbling to his feet. Then he saw the assailant's body on the ground, blood gushing out the side of his head where the two metals had caught it like a vise from each side. He took a step back, then swung with the full force of his right foot and kicked the man in the head. To his own surprise, the man's eyes opened. He regretted doing that. Now he was fully awake from the previous shock.

Omar saw the man flip his body facedown in swift motion, like a cat turning to its feet in midair. He kicked him again, leveling him back to the ground. The man suddenly rotated his body on the ground, like a relentless large reptile. He kicked him one more time, but this time the man didn't budge after receiving his kick in the back of his head. He kept hoisting himself up in a pushup position. Now he was at the edge of the SUV's door and he was working his hands towards the gun, which had fallen inside the vehicle by the control pedals.

Omar's senses alerted him to this man's strength. He was too strong to take down, especially by a weaker man with tied hands. As his hand lunged inside the vehicle, Omar kicked the door one more time. This time the man's upper torso was caught between the lower part of the door and the panel. The assailant let out an agonizing sound. His yowl was the most harmonizing sound that Omar had craved to hear, but it wasn't the end. He was still moving for the gun. Soon he would have it.

With a glimpse around, Omar brought himself back to his surroundings. He caught the image of Nakebakht. She was pale in the backseat while the commotion was going on outside. He wanted to free her, but she could never run like he could. Her freedome would confirm a death sentence for both of them.

He hastily moved around the vehicle and continued to run. It wouldn't be long until the relentless man would regain his energy and come chasing after him again. He needed to get out of there fast. He noticed a flock of cars, now stopped on both sides of the street, and their drivers and passengers as spectactators—all looking at Omar as he dashed away from the scene. He heard some voices in the background calling for him to stop and face justice for what he had done. Abruptly, their voices changed to a chorus of hysterical screams. *This could only mean…* shortly after, he heard gunfire. This time it was the revolver without the suppressor.

He fell face first. His arms lunged forward, preventing his face from hitting the ground.

I'm shot.

He lay there on his stomach. His eyes went to the thick layer of dust on top of the concrete sidewalk. His mind started analyzing his body; the only pain he felt was in his left toes. He turned to see the uneven surface on one of the cement blocks disproportionately with its edge sticking up. That's where his left foot got caught and tripped him face first.

He clambered back to his feet and started running again. Another fifty feet, and then he took a right on the next street and kept on. He heard the honking of the SUV behind him as it weaved its way around traffic in pursuit. To his fortune, this area was more congested than earlier, giving him advantages to beat the car by foot. Another two more minutes of running gained him the image that he longed to see ever since he had found himself strapped to that wooden chair inside that hut.

He proceeded forward on the barricaded street—passing the concrete barriers placed horizontally in the middle. As he passed the fourth one, he stopped and turned around. He saw the SUV, now slowly rolling in his direction, and then taking a left turn on the cross street before the first barrier. The driver eyed him intently as he stood behind the barricades.

"Come on, you motherfuckin' coward!" Omar yelled frantically like a madman, "I'm right here, come on… come and get me!"

Then suddenly the SUV's tires screeched and the vehicle thrust forward on the cross street, now out of his view.

"Come on! You bastard!" Omar yelled again.

A minute later, after the Land Cruiser disappeared, he felt exhilarated, a feeling known only to those who've been captive and then got their first whiff of freedom. He dropped to his knees. There, in the middle of that street, he hysterically started to scream.

"Keep your hands where I can see 'em."

A voice came over his shoulder—one he was relieved to hear in perfect American English. He arched his tied hands over his head.

"My hands are tied!" he called out.

"What's going on here?" said the Marine. He came around his left, pointing his rifle at Omar's chest.

"I'm an American citizen and I was kidnapped! My name is Omar Hafizi!"

He saw the Marine take a couple of steps backwards and then lowered his rifle. He then pressed against his hip over his jacket and started speaking. In a matter of ten seconds, his facial expression changed from stern to pity when he heard something in his earpiece.

"Sir, I'm instructed to take you inside the embassy. Can you walk?"

A minute later, another guard arrived at the site, and the two of them each placed a hand under Omar's arms and hoisted him up.

As he was being escorted inside the U.S. embassy in Kabul, he was taken into a nostalgic moment of his own when the building's white structure appeared behind the wrought-iron gate. He vividly remembered as a teenage boy when the Afghan communist government yanked all the students from his school and brought them in front of this building to denounce American involvement in fueling the rebels. There he stood and watched an American flag burned in front of this building, yet he felt jovial—no one knew he had a miniature American flag of his own behind the emblem of his American-made backpack, which no one could ever burn.

CHAPTER THIRTY-NINE

Omar sat in the room behind a gray-composite desk. He had received a bottle of water along with a turkey sandwich. The yarn rope was removed from his hands, too. But it left dark bruises around his wrists in circling rings. A few minutes earlier, he had given a statement as to why he was there and what had happened to him in the last forty-eight hours. The officer who took the statement said that there were two agents who were on their way to speak to him.

About an hour later, Jack walked in the room and Suzanne trailed after him.

"Are you alright?" said Jack as he fixed his eyes on his pale face.

"Yes," Omar answered in a weak whisper.

"We are going to take you to Bagram Airbase to be thoroughly checked out by a doctor. Do you have any pain?"

"My head. It was hurting a lot, but the pain is gone now."

"We'll have it checked out for you. They have an MRI machine there. In the meantime, we have a few questions that we were hoping you could answer for us," said Jack, then he turned and connected eyes with Suzanne.

Omar nodded.

"Anyhow, I'm agent Jack Rivers with the FBI, and this is Dr. Suzanne Bernard with the NSA. You can call me Jack, if you like," and he motioned towards Suzanne.

"That's only if you are up for it," said Suzanne, "and if you can't talk now, then maybe later…" She gave him a reassuring smile.

Omar eyed the two agents who wore the ACU. He contemplated what they wanted to hear, but most importantly, he wanted to tell them what he thought was the most essential factor.

"He took her," he said.

Suzanne and Jack shared a look.

"Who are you referring to?" asked Jack.

"Nakebakht, this woman who worked for my grandfather as a maid."

Suzanne's mind had already registered the authenticity of their earlier theory, which now seemed to unfold.

So, the old woman was someone he knew.

Jack slightly tilted his head and gave Suzanne a nod, indicating *go ahead.*

"Omar," said Suzanne, "ever since the news of your kidnapping, we've been checking every direction, trying to understand this. Our main interest was making sure you were not harmed, and the other thing was, we were trying to understand why you were kidnapped in the first place."

Omar rolled his eyes from side to side, almost in a flabbergasted expression.

"Well, I think it's obvious. That thief wanted the Vallecillo…"

"Did he tell you that?" asked Suzanne.

"Yes, that's the only reason he abducted me."

"Omar," Jack chimed in, "these people are radicals. They don't care about money."

"We have spoken to Wilson," said Suzanne. "He told us the story about the portrait. We are trying to understand a few things… can you help us?"

"Yeah, sure…" said Omar, as he looked at her in a surprised way.

"Wilson said that you had told him vaguely that the portrait had a map of some sort behind it… and it was passed down to your grandfather by your great-grandfather… can you tell us about that?"

"Yeah, but actually there is a bit more history here… it wasn't really passed down to my grandfather by his father. It was passed down to him by the exiled King, Amanullah Khan. What you've heard is the short version, more like the cover-up one…"

Jack observed Suzanne taking a keen interest in what Omar just said. He wasn't really in the mood to take an Afghan history lesson today, but he held himself back from interjecting because he knew that a big part of Suzanne's theory relied on the Afghan history.

"Go ahead please, tell me what you know," she said as she straightened her posture on the chair.

Omar eyed them both for a second with a dazed look. In the back of his mind, he was questioning the relevance of why the NSA agent wanted to hear about his family's eighty-year history.

"My great-grandfather was a general and a devoted follower of King Amanullah during the Third Anglo-Afghan war, a war commenced by King Amanullah, trying to proclaim Afghanistan's independence from the British at that time. My great-grandfather died in that war. Ultimately, the war resulted in an armistice in the year 1919 between Afghanistan and the British India. After the war, the King took my grandfather, who was the orphaned boy of his top general and dear friend, into his own custody as a token of returning loyalty to his fallen father. Then another revolution arose in 1929, where King Amanullah had to abdicate and go to British India in exile. After the revolution had settled, some of the King's followers and loyalists had inquired regarding his return to his rightful throne. But his return and the will of his followers were not granted by Mohammed Nadir, one of his other generals who had taken over the country and had proclaimed himself as King. To make it more concise for you guys: later on, my grandfather became the ambassador to Spain. And apparently he went to see the old King Amanullah, who by now was living in Italy. On one of his visitations with his father-figure, the old king had given him the map, merely as a relic. And that's how he got possession of it."

Jack shifted his weight from the right side of the chair to the left.

"And when Vallecillo needed a canvas, he gave him that because they couldn't find one in the Kabul market," said Jack.

Omar was astounded by Wilson's memory in relaying what he had said to him over two weeks ago on the phone.

"Omar," Suzanne's voice came to life again, "did your grandfather ever talk about the map?"

He lifted his eyes higher in an act of accessing his memory.

"No… not really," he said, shaking his head lightly.

"Well, I think the guy who kidnapped you… he is looking for the map. Not the portrait."

Omar's eyes widened as he studied Suzanne across the table.

"Have you ever heard of a language based on astrology?" asked Suzanne.

"Yeah…" he quizzically narrowed his eyes. "Vaguely, in an Afghan history class, a long time ago. I think it was affiliated with the British war… something like that."

He was puzzled by why would he want a map. Clearly, Omar was under the impression that all the man wanted was the Vallecillo for his own personal gain.

"What is this map for? And what does he intend to do with it?"

"I'm sorry, we can't disclosed that, Omar," said Jack. "That's classified stuff. But we do need to find it."

"The only person who knows where it's at is in the back of his car now," said Omar.

"Is that why he has taken her?" asked Suzanne.

"Yes," then in an afterthought he cocked his head. "The guy… there was something off about him."

"What you mean?" asked Jack.

"I don't really know. It was his determination… he kind of lacked the human aspect. No signs of emotions whatsoever."

"Well, some of these guys get brainwash really bad. Trust me, I've seen quite a few of them," said Jack.

Suzanne took out a cell phone from her ACU's front pocket. Her eyes went to the screen as she started typing.

Send me everything you can find on Afghan King, Amanullah Khan.

Suzanne had reservations of her own about some of the matters she had learned about since arriving in Kabul. She tried grasping it freely, in a nonliteral manner, but there were still doubts that had arisen inside her. One of them was the evaluation of the old woman as crazy by the minister and his son. She was hoping to receive a different understanding from

Omar, something that would make more logical sense, but it appeared the trail was still hazy, and it followed the old woman.

"How can you be so sure that this old woman actually knows the location of the Vallecillo?" she asked.

He looked at her with an assuring gaze. "She told me that was the only thing she could save from the looters. Meaning, she was the one who hid it."

"She didn't tell you where?" asked Suzanne.

"No. She wants me to find her granddaughter first. And then she will tell me."

"Her granddaughter…" said Suzanne in a puzzled look.

"Yeah… and I was hit right after that and didn't get the chance to ask her anything further."

Jack's phone buzzed to life. He pulled it out from his pocket and fixed his eyes on the screen. As he read the text, his eyes grew wide.

"Okay… looks like we have the SUV on the tracker. We need to go to Bagram now! You need to tell me about this assailant on the way," he said to Omar.

CHAPTER FORTY

The Humvee went pass the security gate, entering the compound. Omar told Jack everything he could remember about the assailant in the forty-five-minute drive to the base. As they neared a few portable housing units, Jack turned to Omar.

"There is a medical examiner waiting to check you out. We'll come and get you if we need you." When the vehicle came to a halt, military personnel was there to escort Omar to the examiner. As he exited the vehicle, Jack turned from the front seat towards Suzanne who sat directly behind him.

"We need to set a plan in motion immediately to go after this guy."

Suzanne contemplated joining in, but thought that she'd never be allowed to go on the field with the military guys. This was not her forte, and the military was not going to have her on the field, for she could be another liability that they would have to protect, or worse, she could be taken hostage.

The Humvee kept on driving past the general area of the base, away from the crowded area to the east. There, under a lone hangar, Whitman had already assembled a few of the special-ops soldiers. The vehicle came to a stop. Jack stepped outside and made his way towards the group standing around a table where a few maps of Afghan terrain lay flat.

"So, what do we have here?" said Jack as he approached the assembled group.

"Kunar province," said Whitman. "That's where we tracked the white SUV."

"Is it still moving?"

"No, it stopped about three minutes ago."

"Okay, where?" said Jack as he hunkered down over one of the maps.

"Right in this area," Whitman pointed to a mountainous region photographed from above.

"These are photographs taken from a UAV two minutes ago," said one of the special-ops guys.

The photographs showed a tall man with his hand around a much smaller female. The next slide held the same image, but closer to the mountain, and it just kept on until the two human images disappeared from the UAV's sight.

"Alright, so he has taken her into a cave," said Jack.

"How do you know it's a cave?" asked Whitman.

"I've seen a lot of these damn pictures around here," he pointed to a lighter area within the satellite map the size of a pencil tip. "You see this, the light didn't return to the camera, so it means it went into something hollow."

Whitman closed in and squinted to where he was pointing. "Alright. Well, that makes sense."

"Alright guys," said Jack, "we have a hostage situation. The abductor is a skilled man, and he is not a Taliban. And we are not sure whether he is Al-Qaeda."

He noticed a perplexed look on the men's faces. He felt he needed to explain more.

"All we know is that he is of Arab descent, which eliminates the Taliban. But we're not sure who he is. He's taken a woman who has information that this guy desperately needs, and we can't let this guy get that from her, because that would be a major threat to our national security. We need him taken out and the woman alive. Let me say it again, we need her alive at all costs!"

"Sir, what kind of a raid are we talking here?" asked Sparks, the special-ops team leader.

"I want a team of six. Also, I want UAV's air support once we have entered this cave. Their job would be to shoot any vehicles or personnel approaching that remote area. Last thing: I want this to be an ambush. We don't want anyone entering that cave after us!"

"Do we have any specs on this guy?" asked Sparks.

"So far the only thing we know is this guy operates alone. That's the intel we have from a pervious hostage."

Sparks' expression revealed skepticism, but he quickly changed his demeanor to a stern, determined military look to exude confidence for the morale of his team.

"We will be ready to deploy in less than ten minutes, sir." Then he faced his team and gave the command. "Let's go gentlemen!"

"I'm going too, Jack," said Whitman.

"No you are not!"

"Hey, I was with the Army Rangers doing this stuff back when you were trying to bang the prom queen in your high school."

For a second Suzanne was taken back to her high school days, when she was the prom queen. She always thought she was voted in because she was a brainiac, but hearing what Whitman just said made her tilt away from the *brainiac* perception.

Is that what every guy wanted to do in high school?

Jack let out a chuckle. "Yeah, that's what I'm afraid of, Sam. You were doing this shit *that* long ago."

"Hey, who was the person that saved your ass in Gardez two years ago?" said Whitman in a loud macho voice.

"You did, Sam. But this is not really an FBI thing," implying that this was really a NSA operation.

"Well, there is a kidnapping going on here, which makes it an FBI operation," countered Whitman.

"Am I going to be able to stop you?"

"Hell no! I'm going with you, and that's final."

Jack shook his head. "Alright, looks like you are going."

CHAPTER FORTY-ONE

The blades on the MH-60L Black Hawk slowly started to rotate. From inside the hangar, Suzanne saw a cloud of dust kick up in the air as the helicopter's rotor picked up speed.

"Alright, off we go," said Jack, who was about to make his way to the Black Hawk. He had full combat gear along with a FN SCAR machinegun fitted with a grenade launcher mounted on the lower rail of the rifle, the magazines of ammunition buckled around his waist.

"Good luck," said Suzanne, sounding a bit reticent because she really wanted to say: *be careful.*

"Thanks," he shot her a cordial smile, then turned around and started walking towards the awaiting helicopter.

She stood there and watched Jack, Whitman, and the four special-ops enter the Black Hawk. *God, this is real now.* She was bewildered by the notion of this whole operation being propelled based on her theory, one that only she could attest to being real, but then, there was still doubts that arose in her mind, which made her wonder about being wrong. *Someone could die here today.*

She watched the Black Hawk blades kick up a thick, blinding cloud of dust as the sound of its twin engines grew louder, then a few seconds later, the aircraft was hovering over the ground, and by the tilt of its nose it started moving through the air. She turned around and started walking towards the control room where the ground support personnel were monitoring the operation.

"Base to Pelican One." The controller called on the radio.

"Pelican One. Go ahead."

"We have air support backup ready to launch," said the controller.

The special-ops air command center was isolated from the main command centers, which rested in the tower of the Bagram Airbase. This facility was located in the remote part of the base because some of the special-ops missions were highly confidential where the content of the mission had to be kept obscured from other military personnel.

"How long is the flight there?" asked Suzanne.

"About twenty-five minutes," said the controller.

She checked her phone to see if she had heard from Skip regarding what she had asked earlier. As she turned on the screen, sure enough, there was an email from Skip containing literature on King Amanullah. She saw an empty station twenty feet away on the left side of the control room. She went and sat in front of the monitor and logged into her account via the military's secure network and opened the content.

Inside the Black Hawk, Jack remained in anticipation. There had been a couple of other times where he went on a mission with the Special Forces. He thought those times were a little easier. The challenge of this mission was that cave. There had been frequent occasions of these types of caves being booby traps. He thought about the possibility of Omar's assailant trying to lure them purposefully into an ambush.

"Six more minutes," said the pilot.

The men started putting on their helmets and then closely checked their weapons—making sure that they had everything they needed.

Jack fixed his eyes on Whitman, who sat directly in front of him. He was relieved to see Whitman not having any reservation about going down today. In a muse, he thought maybe Whitman wanted this because he had been stuck in the attaché office far too long, and this could be something that would take him back to his days as an Army Ranger—more like reconciling with his past and bringing it back to life.

When the Black Hawk banked right, Jack could see from a distance the white SUV sitting in the middle of a dry, desolate foothill that lead to a dark, barren mountain.

It's on now. He could hear us…

The Black Hawk flew over the SUV from a thousand feet. Then the pilot scattered around the mountain to better assess the mission from the line of sight. As it appeared, there were no other vehicles or any signs of other insurgents from his view.

The cave—the one that Jack pointed out on the surveillance photo—was in the lower part of the black mountain, a hundred feet above where the SUV was parked.

"Major, put it down away from the vehicle," said Whitman.

That was to take an extra precaution. Whitman had been called to investigate quite a few car bombs in his eleven-month tenure here in Afghanistan. His instincts always sway him away from all unattended vehicles in this country, especially one driven by a possible Al-Qaeda.

Within the next minute, the Black Hawk touched the ground two hundred feet away from the SUV.

"Let's move out," called Sparks.

The four special ops jumped out of the helicopter, followed by Jack and Whitman. Jack fixed his eyes on the mouth of the cave, which was about a hundred feet up in the mountain. The team assembled in a two-man formation. Two special ops led the pack, then Jack and Whitman, followed by Sparks and the two other special-force guys.

As they made their hike up the mountain, the Black Hawk lifted. It hovered about two hundred feet in midair, facing the cave in a ready-to-shoot mode if the team came under fire from the elevated position.

The team precariously made its ascent of the mountain in the direction of the cave, but then stopped fifty feet short before entering. To their good fortune, this mountain was extremely dry. It appeared it hadn't rained in this region for a while. That in it's own virtue gave them the advantage of visibility.

Jack took out his binoculars and started canvassing the area. He was intently looking for any sign of dust kicked up on the mountain. That was one of the best giveaways of the Taliban hiding from plain view behind the rocks.

"Do you guys see anything?" said Jack as he lowered his binoculars. "Any movements?"

"I don't see any," said Whitman.

Jack gave a sigh of relief that there could only be one perpetrator here, exactly as it was when Omar was taken hostage. But he wasn't prepare to announce that sentiment with the team because of the chance of there being more people in the cave.

"Alright!" said Sparks. "Gregorini, Buchman: you two tail Rivers and Whitman. Sayre, you and I are going in first.

Jack saw Sparks and Sayre approach the cave. They eyed the surroundings around the mouth. It was clear. They both turned on the LED lights above their helmets and proceeded inside. Jack followed with Whitman. A few feet in, the cave walls closed in to a small passage where only one man could go through at a time. Sparks climbed on top of a boulder where from this elevated position his light could beam further past the narrow area.

After a few more seconds of scanning beyond the narrow passageway, he motioned to Sayre, "Go." He held his rifle pointing over Sayre's head, in case the enemy approached, so he could shoot as Sayre ducked down.

"Clear," Sayre called out from the other side of the passageway.

Sparks made the hand gesture for the rest of the team to go through as he held his high position covering them. When Jack approached the other side of the passageway, he started canvassing the cavern, which was an area the size of a train car in the same long shape going deep into the mountain.

Sparks lift his left hand and gestured at the stop sign. For the next thirty seconds everyone stood frozen like a statue, listening intently for any kind of sound coming from the other side of the cave, which was pitch black from their view.

"Okay, crack em," said Sparks.

The team fetched a series of LED light sticks from their pockets and began cracking them in half.

"Turn off the helmet lights!" called Sparks.

The helmet lights could give the enemy an advantage of shooting directly towards the light, which could definitely hit them in the head. Sparks wanted to eliminate that advantage by simply illuminating the cave with lights that did not point to his team, given that they were at a disadvantage already, because the enemy could see in the dark towards the lights and would know exactly where to fire.

They pitched the light sticks inward. This was a far better strategy, as each of those high-powered light sticks was the equivalent of a forty-watt bulb.

As the cave illuminated, they could see the rock wall at the far end. Jack grabbed another light stick and threw it to the right corner. The light stick fell without sending any light back.

"Okay, there is a huge drop on the far right," said Jack, "seems deep, so watch your step!"

Sayre prowled forward with his rifle pointing in front of him to the back wall, then he turned. "This place is empty."

"Check the right," called Sparks in a hushed voice.

He turned to the right side; he couldn't see anything beyond the ledge. It was too dark.

"I need some more sticks," he called back.

Buchman rushed from the end of the file towards him. Then the two of them cracked four more light sticks and threw them over the ledge on the other side. The sticks landed in various spots, lighting a few large boulders and trace of water on the wall.

"It's empty," Sayre called again.

Jack made his way further up where the two men were standing, looking over the dark sinkhole ten feet over to the other side of the cave. After intently looking in the same direction, he came to share their conclusion.

It's empty. He turned back towards the rest of the team who all stood there baffled. This was the only cave apparent from the chopper when it made its way around the mountain.

This can't be, mused Jack.

He shifted his eyes higher and noticed there was another layer to the cave right above where the rest of the team were standing, like a subfloor of a house, but this one was made of solid flat rock. He stepped a few feet back—touching the back wall—and threw a light stick on the upper dark hollow above. Nothing. The light shimmered around the edge, but still nothing was evident. Also, logic suggested that it would be much more difficult to have an old woman elevated to a surface fifteen feet high without an access point.

He turned to the right side again. He was looking at an area past the ledge from a different angle, given his position by the inner wall now. Something caught his eye behind the very last boulder. It had a distinct color that did not naturally blend with colors in the cave.

Fuck! That's it!

He signaled the team with a hand gesture. It appeared they had already taken down their guard as they had come to think the cave was empty, but it was not. It seemed his biggest fear had came into play now.

This is a fuckin' ambush! he thought. *We need to counter this. Now! Think…*

"This place is empty. Let's move out!" Jack called in an unusually louder voice—louder than their earlier decibels of communication.

He saw the team quickly picking up on his portrayal. They shifted their demeanor. They redrew their weapons and carefully started scanning around. Jack fixed his eyes over the dark ledge and noticed a narrow walkway on the edge of rock wall leading to the boulders. He signaled Sayre to follow him. They made their way over the walkway leaning backwards from the dark drop where they could not see the bottom. After a few more hellish steps, they made it to the other side. Jack pointed his rifle to the boulder and swiftly went around it—ready to shoot. In that dark space behind the boulder, his eyes made out the silhouette of a human body subdued in the dark without any movement. He flicked the light in front of his rifle. In an instant, he saw an old woman staring back at him over the barrel of his machinegun. He aimed the light downward and saw her hands were tied with the palms facing one another, the same with her ankles, tied together. She also had duct tape slapped across her face, covering her mouth.

Where the hell is he, now?

He turned to see Sayre was right behind him.

"Help me with her," said Jack

As Sayre kneeled down beside him to help the woman, Jack's view of what stood behind them became clear. His eyes suddenly fixed on the ghostly image of a tall man in a white Taliban like outfit standing on the flat rock above Buchman.

"Get your hands up!" called Jack, pointing his rifle towards the man.

In a sudden move, Bachman turned to point his rifle upwards towards the man's chest.

"Hands up!" called Buchman in Pashto.

The man just stood there, very calmly looking at Jack and then fixing his gaze back on Buchman who stood right underneath him.

"Put your hands up!" called Buchman the second time.

"Just shoot the motherfucker!" yelled Sayre.

"He's unarmed!" said Buchman, who could see the man's empty hands.

Jack fixed the spotlight on the man's face. After noticing the light directly hitting his face, he turned to look in his direction. From the distance of twenty-five feet, Jack could see the man's large brown eyes. They reflected a purpose, that's what he read when he saw the calm in the man's face. Then as the man brought his gaze lower, Jack saw the man's clothing pressing outwards, as if he was wearing a thick coat under his tunic.

Oh God, no…

"Shoot him!" Jack called out to Buchman, "Now!"

Buchman started firing, but he had been a second late. The man had already taken the leap to drop in front of Buchman by the sound of Jack's voice. As he came down, a blast shook the cave.

Jack found himself behind the boulder on top of the old woman, weathering out the fire and heat.

"Clint!" called out Sayre through the cloud of smoke, which was now in the place where Buchman stood. But no one could hear him. All ears were deafened from the shock.

When the smoke thinned, the only thing that remained of Buchman was his rifle, a few pieces of dislocated metal lying on the side of the cave's wall.

Jack's survival instinct took over. He started to untie the rope from the old woman's limbs. He knew all of them had to get out of here in a matter of a few seconds. They couldn't breathe, as the fire from the blast had sucked in all the oxygen. Every time he took a breath, he felt his lungs burn from the smoke that still laid heavily over the entirety of the cave. He saw Sayre still down on the ground, shocked and disoriented by the sudden loss of a team member. Jack knew that the sad reality dictated survival in their current situation, and survival was a must.

"Sayre!" he called to the disoriented soldier, "we have to go! Now!"

Through the thick smoke, Jack saw the image of Sayre standing back on his feet. He rushed and helped Jack pick up the old woman and the two of them walked her over the narrow walkway to the other side.

"Get her out of here!" called Jack to Sayre, who was a few feet in front of him tugging the woman. And with that, Sayre started dashing towards the opening—hauling the woman behind him.

In the midst of the smoke, Jack stepped on the platform just a few feet away from where Buchman was earlier. Suddenly he felt himself going down towards the ground. He landed half a foot away from the edge and on top of him was another man who had tackled him from above. His instincts alerted him of what this was; he saw what happened a few seconds earlier with Buchman. He swiftly gripped the man's hands, which were much smaller than his and not as strong. He tightened his grip with all his force. He felt the tip of a tube over the man's fist, and the man's frantic struggle to free his thumb, which was held motionless beneath Jack's strong grip. The man kept fighting chaotically, trying to free his hand from under his grip. Jack already knew the outcome; the man was struggling to push that button on top of the cylinder, where the battery would then send a surge through the wires around his arm to the explosives that he carried in a vest under his tunic. Jack knew sooner or later his thumb would free up through the struggle, and he would hit that switch, like the one in a propane barbeque. He had to do something fast.

He pulled his knee upward, positioning it on the man's ribcage, and then with a great amount of force he turned his body to the left, sending the man over the edge. Jack's grip came loose as gravity pulled the man towards the pit of the sinkhole. He then rolled to his right, turning his back to the rim. A few milliseconds later, the second blast happened inside the sinkhole as the falling man had managed to push the detonating switch with his thumb. This blast wasn't as effective as the first. The rock walls of the sinkhole absorbed most of the shockwaves.

"Jack!" he felt someone fiercely shaking him. Then as the smoke thinned, he saw Whitman kneeled to his side. "Get up!" Whitman yelled.

He could feel Whitman shaking him, but his voice came in dim audio, as if it was coming from afar over the reverberating buzz. He felt hard pain in his head and ears.

In another second, he felt another hand under his right arm. For a second he thought it was another suicide bomber, but then felt himself being lifted up, and as he rose higher, he noticed Sparks' face through the smoke.

"I got him," Sparks yelled to Whitman.

Jack had been lying for more than a minute after the blast without oxygen. His feet could not move. He was dizzy and coughing excessively. Sparks managed to carry him through the narrow opening near the mouth of the cave. From there, Jack could see the light from the narrow crack between the two rock walls.

"Go!" Sparks called as he thrust him forward through the passage. Halfway between, he saw another hand gripping his arm and pulling him outward. It was the other special force member, Gregorini. A few seconds later, Jack found himself stumbling into the open and gasping for air. Gregorini and Sayre helped him down from the mouth of the cave onto a flat surface on the mountain about twenty feet lower. There he went face forward, hunching over a big rock, catching his breath. About a minute later, his ears started to make out the sounds outside. He started hearing the chopper hovering in the air and Sayre's voice calling on the radio.

"Do not shoot the cave!" he called to the UAV pilots who sat stationary in Bagram Airbase and had the whole situation lit up on their screens. "We still have friendlies inside!" He was saying in a panicked voice. "Hold your fire!"

The two drones made a turn over their heads and retreated back.

As Jack regained some of his strength, his mind went back to the cave. He looked upwards towards its mouth and saw nobody insight.

Whitman and Sparks are still in there.

"How long until backup is here?" yelled Sayre on the radio. "That's not enough! We need them here now!"

I need to go back in there, Jack mused. He tried to clear his lungs with excessive breathing. In a flash, Sam Whitman's wife and daughter appeared in his mind on that sunny afternoon when they invited him to their family picnic in Great Falls Park. The afternoon had become pretty eventful after Sam had poured barbeque sauce in the potato salad and became the subject of the family chortle. The affable Sam, as Jack knows him, was still in that cave. He had risked his own life for him earlier after the blast.

He grabbed his weapon from the side of the rock and slung it over his shoulder. He looked up to the twenty-feet hike, which went around the ledge to the cave. As he was getting ready for it, he heard Gregorini's voice, "They are coming out!"

Gregorini had taken position halfway between Jack and the cave, and from his elevated position he had a clear view of the mouth's inner perimeter. A few seconds later, Jack saw Gregorini tightening his weapon's aim. Right at that moment, Jack knew that something was not right. He took a few more steps back to have a better look over the ledge, which stood in front of him like a fifteen-foot wall. From there he shared the same view with Gregorini. His eyes made the image of Sparks backing out from the cave. He had his weapon directly pointed as he took steps backwards—careless of the fifteen-feet drop behind him.

"Give it up! You're surrounded!" said Sparks. His voice bounced back out of the cave mouth. He then veered to his left and took a few steps down on the narrow ridge.

Jack looked upwards and saw the image of Whitman appearing at the mouth. He was walking slowly outwards. Then he noticed a left arm strapped around his chest from the back, and the other holding a handgun at the back of his head. As he moved outwards he could see the villain's white garment hidden behind Whitman. A few more feet and Jack could see the man's face. His tall figure towered over Whitman, who was a foot shorter than him.

So, this is the bastard, thought Jack, as his memory recalled Omar's description.

"I go with the woman!" the man commanded.

"You are surrounded!" yelled Sparks. "Let him go. We will not shoot you!"

The man started canvassing the vicinity and saw that he was overpowered. He saw four rifles pointing at him as well as a hovering chopper and two UAVs that circled directly in front of him at a lower altitude.

"Get down there!" he yelled to Sparks and Gregorini, pointing them to the lower platform where Jack was. "I will kill him!" he prodded the back of Whitman's head with the gun. It made his head jerk forward.

Sparks saw that he didn't have a clear shot. There was no way that he could take the villain out without hitting Whitman. The man had glued his body tight behind him.

"I shoot him now!" he yelled.

"We will move down," said Sparks in an unsettled voice. "Don't shoot!"

Jack saw Sparks and Gregorini slowly make their way down the ridge to his position.

Why is he herding us all to one place? he thought.

He assessed the surroundings and saw the man was all by himself. He would have a strategic advantage to have the team assembled in one area where the fire would come to him from one direction.

But what did he really intend to do here? Is he trying to run back into the cave? That cave would be a definite death trap for him. We don't have anyone in the cave now, and we'll just blow it up if he is in there. No… there's got to be something else.

Sparks and Gregorini watchfully made their way down, with their rifles still aiming over the ledge.

"They will take you out like Buchman," Whitman yelled.

"They?" Jack was startled by the earlier image of Buchman.

"Call the air support and tell them that we have another suicide bomber in the higher position. Tell 'em to shoot on sight!" said Jack to Sayre.

As Sayre finished calling in the command, Jack saw the man's left hand move away from Whitman's chest and went up.

Goddamn it. We are sitting ducks here. Nobody has eyes on the cave now, thought Jack.

In the background he heard the buzzing sound of the UAVs getting closer, directly behind them as they were approaching the face of the mountain—a hundred and fifty feet above ground—where they were standing.

Then in a sudden move, the man's left hand dropped from its raised position and pointed in their direction.

"No!" Jack yelled as he pointed his rifle upward, to the right side of where Whitman and the assailant were standing.

In that instant, everyone's quizzical gazes fell on Jack, as he was aiming his rifle in a direction that only indicated an empty space. And then to their astonishment a figure of a man emerged on top of the ledge. He was running towards the edge to a fifteen-foot drop where they all stood underneath. They watched the man's tunic and trousers pressed by the wind of his velocity against his body, revealing the formation of the explosives strapped around his torso under his tunic. The man ran with keen determination—careless of the fact that he was jumping to his own death. On his last stride over the edge, he leaped and jumped high—giving himself maximum leeway to land on top of them.

The shots had already been fired. But no one had heard them in that fraction of a second because of the fact of a bullet traveling faster than the speed of sound. On that rare instance, the law of gravity was defied. The man's elevated body started changing direction in midair. The momentum, which had propelled him forward, was now pushing him backwards. The sound arrived. And it was not the sound of explosives that they had heard earlier in the cave. The man's body was intact, still. The sound came from XM296 machineguns—attached on the side of the OH-58 Kiowa helicopter—a hundred-fifty feet away. The array of fifty caliber bullets threw the man backwards over the ledge, pushing his body another ten feet into the cave mouth. The ammunition designed to pierce armor had dismembered the man's right arm before he was able to push the detonator. His lifeless body lay on the front of the narrow passage into the cave.

In the midst of the shots being fired on the suicide bomber, Whitman had seized the opportunity when the assailant's attention was drawn to the firing helicopter. He made the jump over the fifteen-foot cliff, leaving the gunman exposed in front of the team. A couple of seconds later, the exposed gunman started firing his handgun as a last alternative before his failure. The team immediately returned fire. Soon after, they saw his figure collapse on top of the rock.

"Sam!" Jack called, as he saw him lying on his side. As he neared, he saw Whitman rolling from his side to his back. Then he pinned his elbows on top of shredded rocks and hoisted himself up.

"Goddamn it!" he cursed as he saw his broken leg, and his knee which had turned sideways.

"You'll be alright," said Jack. "We'll get you out of here, just hang in there!"

"The cave!" yelled Sparks. "We need to see if there's more bombers!"

"She's been shot!" yelled Sayre as he stood near the old Afghan woman.

Jack turned to the old woman lying on her back. He could see the red soaked in her blue tunic.

"She's alive, but losing blood fast!" yelled Sayre.

"Put pressure on it and call for airlift, now!" said Sparks.

Jack started tailing Sparks and Gregorini up the ridge towards the cave. They had to take precautions to make sure there wouldn't be another bomber emerging from there. As they made their way on top of the flat rock, Sparks and Gregorini took position, aiming their rifles at the mouth of the cave, awaiting any other insurgents. Another ten feet to the right, Jack saw the body of the man who was holding Whitman earlier—lying on the rock, without any movement.

"I'll check him out!" Jack called to Sparks.

He walked warily, with the anticipation of the man carrying explosives, which he could detonate if he was still alive. But as he neared, he saw a glimpse of the red bullet holes on the man's chest and part of his tunic ripped on the left side, revealing his bare flesh.

"No explosives on this one," he called to Sparks.

He continued his walk around the corpse to double-check his description based on what Omar had provided earlier, to make sure he was the same person. And as he focused his eyes on the man's face, he was reassured that this was the man who had taken Omar Hafizi hostage. A few seconds later, as Jack continued his examination of the man's body, he was jolted by a sudden surprise when the man opened his eyes. Jack quickly pointed his rifle at the lying man's chest.

I will shoot you! He thought as he saw him still alive. Then his eyes fell on the man's hands, which rested empty, lying motionless at the sides of his body. *Killing an unarmed man would still be murder, even if I could get away with it.* His conscience was not going to have that.

"I'll get you some help," said Jack.

The man let out a broken whisper, "Shoot me!"

"No… we don't do murder. We are not like you," said Jack as he lowered his weapon.

The man's lips tightened as he fought a surge of pain, and then spoke again in his weak, hushed voice. "He lied to me. I just saw it. He lied."

Jack's instincts took him back to his training, which prompted him to extract as much information as he could. He wondered who this man was talking about, but first he needed to preserve the safety of his team.

"Are there any more suicide bombers in the cave?" he asked.

The man started shifting his eyes side to side under the light of the bright sun, as if he was contemplating his own loyalty.

"No," he answered. "But they're everywhere."

Jack fixed his eyes on the man's face. He felt that he wanted to tell him something more, but then he coughed and blood gushed out of his mouth. His pierced lungs were not able to hold any oxygen, he was going to pass out and die at any second. Jack knelt down and desperately placed both of his palms over the three bulletholes on the man's chest, hoping to save his life. The man tried to lift his head to say something, but he couldn't; only his lips started to move.

"It's in their blood!" he said, fixing his eyes intently on Jack's. Then he was hit with another shock, and his eyes went dazed.

CHAPTER FORTY-TWO

Jamal lay on that rock, his eyes fixed to the sun that hit his face. He was oblivious to the commotion around him. He didn't hear the sound of the helicopter hovering, or the screaming voices of American soldiers commanding the rescue mission. He wanted to see the sun. The bullets piercing his chest had sent him into a sudden shock right after he had received them. His mind had shut down for a minute, sending him into a dark blank phase. Then he had gained consciousness and had come back to the pain. That glimpse of darkness defied everything that he was told about being a martyr. There he was, experiencing death, but it did not come parallel to what he had been preached for years. He didn't see any white-paved passage to heaven, nor did he lie there absent of pain—one he was told to be nonexistent. It was there to the extent where it had paralyzed his body. He could not escape from it; he felt like time had warped just to prolong it. He had seen the abyss that was upon him.

I don't want to go there.

He tried to ignore the pain, straying his mind to something else in hope of waking up and finding himself in a different place. He became saturated in the thoughts of his younger days: an agile boy running over the fields that rested nearby their house. Then the times of bouncing the soccer ball off his head, unaware of the shaded ideals that had brought him in this place—the times when he wish he could relive that moment. Then his memory perched over the faint image of his father, his tall figure looming by the door, wearing all white, his long black beard giving his white attire a contrast, and then his eyes—ones that radiated a determined purpose. Jamal, a boy, who had just returned from a soccer match; his team had won that day. He didn't want his father to go. He advocated his departure in his own thoughts as his lingering gaze read the face of his father—a man in pursuit of a cause, a man possessed. Then came the news of his death. And then came the demon—one that had taken his father— one that passed the curse onto him and made him share his father's fate.

There was no light! he reminded himself again. He wanted to absorb the sun as much as he could. He didn't want to go. It was pitch black.

I was taken by lies and deceit. I was weak.

He wanted a second chance. A new beginning, away from those who plagued his mind with lies—ones that had promised him eternal light, fulfilling a cause for Allah.

This was not a cause for Allah. It is a cause for him. His thoughts faded in the dark, and then remerged, reminding him of the destined darkness that he was bound to. He begged not to go, promising to make good. Then, another darkness emerged. It faded the thought of a second chance, along with the hope of living again. His mouth opened wider, gasping for more air, but that didn't work. He had lost too much blood, and oxygen was not getting into his brain. As he was fading away, the utmost disappointment lurked in his mind. He wept. He cursed the man who had brought him to this point. *Liar.* At last, he closed his eyes and prepared himself for his distorted destiny.

⚜

Jack saw the image of the Black Hawk helicopter disappear from his view. It was carrying the wounded special agent Sam Whitman and the old Afghan woman, who had taken a bullet in her chest from a man who he just saw die on the rock next to him.

The backup team had arrived a while earlier. They did a second raid into the cave, and as they went in, they found no other suicide bombers or insurgents.

The man was telling the truth, thought Jack, recalling his question to the dying terrorist, asking him whether if there were more suicide bombers in the cave. And the man had said *no*. What puzzled Jack was what the man said afterwards, *"But they're everywhere. It's in their blood."*

The terrorist had also said something about someone lying to him. He tried to wrap his head around those phrases, but nothing was clear about them. He didn't have any names or any other thing substantial enough to really make a case for an investigation. He tried approaching the information from another perspective, but still, nothing remained tangible that he could submit as a lead.

He saw Sparks, Gregorini, and Sayre respectfully carrying the stretcher that bore remains of their fallen comrade, Buchman. He removed his hard hat and bowed his head, honoring the brave Buchman, who was struck by the first suicide bomber. In a memory flash, that whole scene started playing in his head.

He recalled the instant when he was looking in Buchman's direction over the sinkhole. Then the appearance of the ghostly man's image in a Taliban white outfit. He wondered if he had missed something there.

Think! He played it out over and over in his head. He started recollecting the video images of other suicide bombers—ones gathered by video surveillance before they blew themselves up. Almost all those instances shared one commonality among them. The videos showed those bombers as extremely nervous before detonating themselves. But when he merged those images from his memory of the cave, he was left perplexed by the lack of correlation.

This is very odd.

He was puzzled by the pattern of behavior. The ones in the videos undoubtedly matched each other, but the ones in the cave, as he saw, were completely different. He recalled the man as he stood on top of the flat rock, above where Buchman was standing. He remembered shining his rifle's spotlight on the man's face. He did not react, as he had three rifles pointed at him. The man purposefully took his time looking at Buchman and towards him and Sayre, which made him wonder why.

Did he stand up there and watched us? He mused, considering that the bomber could have acted suddenly. Then it dawned on him. *He was measuring his distance between his two targets. We were too far; he could've not made a twenty-five-foot leap. That's why he chose Buchman. He was standing underneath him.*

As Jack kept on contemplating, his memory became more photographic. He recalled the man's face. It was expressionless. That's what puzzled him.

A man jumping to his own death, yet not showing any expression! Now that's very odd.

Also, he recalled his own encounter as he was fighting the second bomber, where the man's mission was only to blow himself up, along with Jack. He couldn't really see the man's face through the thick smoke, but he did feel him relentlessly trying to free his thumb just so he could blow himself up, and the instance outside, where the third bomber ran to his death. It was almost inconceivable to have three people determined to blow themselves up with the uttermost determination where they lack the ability to show any kind of a natural human tendency.

Something doesn't make sense here; I know I'm missing something.

His mind retreated from the cave back to the man outside, again, to the words he spoke before he died. As he pressed his thoughts onto the man's words and then linked those words to the images that he saw, suddenly he felt a cool breeze hitting his face and goosebumps on his flesh.

They were not regular people. They were fucking human weapons! Literally human weapons!

He frantically started scattering his gaze around that mountainous region. This was something that was hard to fathom. His mind fell to the dying man's last phrase, and those words kept echoing in his mind.

"It's in their blood."

CHAPTER FORTY-THREE

From inside the hangar, Suzanne watched Jack stepped down from the helicopter. She was happy to see him alive. Sadly, that wasn't the case for Buchman, who she had heard about while she was in the control room. Now it was mid-afternoon; they had been gone for more than two hours.

Jack made his way from the thick dust cloud created by the helicopter's blades, and emerged into the hangar. He came and stood in front of her. She noticed his face; it showed a mystified uneasiness, almost like a daze. She wanted to ask him, but then she hesitated. In a glimpse, she thought his odd demeanor could be the effect of various things that happened while they were out there. She had never been in combat, so she thought she'd be ignorant to ask. She waited to hear what he would tell her.

"The Afghan woman…" he said, "do you know her condition?"

"I'm afraid she didn't make it," answered Suzanne, revealing a sincere look. "She lost too much blood. They tried to stabilize her, but she went into cardiac arrest."

Jack closed his eyes and sighed. Then he lifted his gaze upwards and stared at the old rusted beams.

"She was talking when they landed," said Suzanne, "so I sent Omar with the medical team to translate."

"Where is he now?" asked Jack.

"On the other side. He's pretty shaken up about her passing. He said that she used to take care of him when he was a boy."

Jack shifted his gaze from Suzanne to the right; he was following a new trail of thought now.

"Alright… let's go see him."

They went out of the hangar's rear door. Outside, on a shade, directly behind the hangar, Omar sat on the ground with his back resting against the wall. His eyes remained keen on the light brown hills that loomed more than a mile away from the base. He was in his own world, somewhere in his mind. He turned his head to the approaching footsteps that ground the pebbles on the ground.

"I'm sorry about your loss," he heard Jack's voice.

He did a slight nod, and then shifted his gaze back outwards to the hills.

"The man who brought this grief on you is dead," said Jack.

Omar still didn't budge. He just sat there and kept his silence. Suzanne looked to Jack, bearing a compassionate look, indicating, *let's give him some time.*

"Take all the time you need," said Jack, "we'll be inside," and nodded to Suzanne. They both turned to walk away.

As they neared the door, they heard Omar's voice ringing behind them.

"She told me the whereabouts of Vallecillo."

Jack and Suzanne shared a quick look.

"It was the deed of her loyalty to my grandfather. And she made the pledged in her last breath."

They offered him a moment of pause to see what he would say next. They chose not to rush him as he sat there unburdening his grief. But then the time had prolonged, and Suzanne felt like Omar wanted them to say something next.

"You know, that map behind the portrait is very important to us," said Suzanne.

"Yes… I know," said Omar.

"You know," said Jack, "as an American citizen, you are under no legal obligation to show us the map if you don't want to. But it is for the best of our national security if you did let us see the content. Will you let us?"

Omar hoisted himself to his feet and then turned towards them.

"We need to go to my grandfather's house, then."

"You mean the place where the interior minister lives now," said Jack.

"Yes."

They set pace towards the vehicle.

CHAPTER FORTY-FOUR

They waited by the gray wooden gate inside the compound, as Abdullah had gone to fetch his father. The Minister was phoned about their arrival to his house. The presence of American agents invoked a wary feeling, but yet he still remained heedful and accepted their company.

The Minister's round figure appeared on the walkway. They had already consulted amongst themselves that Omar was going to lead the next phase of the conversation with the Minister. Jack had already advised Omar in explaining his and Suzanne's presence there for his support. The Minister had to understand that the two American agents were there to support the endeavor of an American citizen who had been abducted and was in need of support. Other than that, the U.S. government had no legal merit to be in the Afghan government official's house.

As the Minister neared, his eyes fell to Omar, whose clothes had dirt and wrinkles all over them like an old used-up rag.

"I am glad to see you're alright," said the Minister, as he suspiciously scrutinized Omar's face for a better reading, perhaps why he came back with the American agents.

"General Sahib," said Omar speaking in Dari. "I wanted to wait awhile before telling you my true intent of why I came here in the first place. But, due to circumstances, such prolonged time wasn't granted. Without further ado, I must be candid now."

The Minister eyed him quizzically as he waited to hear what he'd say next. "Alright," he said, and presented an attentive expression.

"This house belonged to my grandfather at one point. Also, this is the house where I grew up as a boy."

The Minister's eyes widened as he anticipated the thought of the trend where Afghans came back from abroad to claim the properties that they left behind years ago. And Omar could see that in his face.

"I have no quarrels with you claiming this house as your own," he said as he fixed his eyes directly on the Minister's.

"Okay then," said the Minister as he wondered why he was being told of all this.

"However, there is something that was left in this house that belongs to me. I would like to have it."

"Oh… in this house?" the Minister sounded surprised. "I took over this house after the fleeing Taliban who possessed it before me. And I had heard that before the Taliban's arrival, this house was looted."

"Yeah, I've heard that, too. But the item was concealed by one of my grandfather's faithful servants."

"I see," said the Minister as his eyes narrowed. "What is it?"

Omar tried to choose his words carefully, as he was advised by Jack to not reveal what he was trying to extract from this house.

"It's just something that my grandfather had for a long time, more like a heirloom."

"In that case… of course. You are entitled to all your belongings here," said the Minister, revealing a dignified look. "And Abdullah will give you access to anywhere you need to look."

"Thank you," said Omar, bowing his head in obedience.

Omar turned to Jack and Suzanne and gave them a slight nod. Then he turned to follow Abdullah towards the main house. Shortly after, he had found himself on the steps of the wooden staircase leading to the attic. He started hearing the wood crack beneath his feet, a thing he had not experienced in the past as he climbed these stairs, the reason being he didn't weigh as much last time when he went up. Once he reached the attic floor, he found himself living in his childhood memories. His eyes fell to the short clay walls and the slanted metal roof that rested on top of them in the shape of a long triangle. He saw the wooden posts in the center, supporting the beams that held the metal roof—on one of them, he could still see a part of an old worn-out yarn rope hanging from a swing that he built for him and Rizwan. And then, he saw the floor, where he saw himself hopping relentlessly inside the chalk-drawn squares. That's when for the first time the feeling of her loss settled.

She is not alive. What happened to her?

His thoughts roamed as his footsteps circled around the attic, hypnotically taken by her memory. The questions he had he knew he could never find the answers to. Both Rizwan and Nakebakht were dead now.

"Are you alright?"

He heard Abdullah's voice. It served as an instant reminder that he was not there by himself. He gathered his thoughts to the main task of why he was there in the first place. He turned towards the far left wall. To his amazement, he saw the old wooden chest still sitting on the attic floor beneath a thick layer of dust and cobwebs.

He sat on the floor and reached underneath the chest. He remembered her telling him about the loose two-by-four, but he did not know which one. He started yanking the nailed pieces of woods. The first four from the right did not budge. He kept working to the left, and as his fingers touched a piece in the center, he felt a seam on the tips of his fingers, and as he pulled, the two-by-four extracted from its place and fell onto the attic floor. *This is the spot.*

He extended his right hand inside the hollow space underneath the wooden chest. The space seemed empty. As he moved his arm to the right, his hand hit another piece of wood in the shape of another two-by-four laying flat on the attic floor under the chest. Above it, he felt something moving with the back of his hand. When he fixed his grip around it, he felt the shape of a cylinder. Nakebakht had come through on her promise. He wondered about his promise to her.

❦

The crush-stricken Minister and his scrawny translator stood in front of Jack and Suzanne. The Minister had engaged in the stories of his heroism from the times he fought against the Taliban in an invigorating attempt to gain the approval of the two Americans, especially Suzanne, who he had hope to see again where he could impress her more. His moment of triumphal talk ended when he noticed his American audience looking over his shoulder towards Omar, who had emerged with a black plastic carrying tube in his right hand.

"Did you find what you were looking for?" said the Minister upon greeting him.

"Yes, I did," said Omar, "thank you for allowing me, General Sahib."

The Minister offered him a mild grin, and then eyed his clean beige khakis and the new shirt he had freshly worn.

Upon noticing his gaze, Omar said, "If it's okay, I will be back for the rest of my stuff later."

"Of course," said the Minister.

The Minister watched the trio get inside a U.S. military Humvee. He wondered about the contents inside the carrying case that Omar uncovered from the house. Whatever it was, he thought it must've been valuable, but then, he still couldn't get his head wrapped around why the American agents would accompany him.

CHAPTER FORTY-FIVE

The FBI offices inside the Kabul Embassy were located on the east side of the building. The trio made their way through the long marble corridor that led to the east side of the building, where the majority of the seventy-five bureau personnel were stationed in Afghanistan. Their mission was to examine the content of the portrait, but it had to be done in the most secure location. Also, due to the portrait's value, Omar asked to be present during the examination period. As a token of Omar's generosity, which allowed the U.S government access to information, the government had offered safeguarding of the item in the U.S. embassy for him, which is technically the United States. It was to be stored in the embassy vault and could only be extracted by Omar himself or could be shipped as diplomatic cargo to anywhere Omar pleased.

After passing a room that housed a vast amount of cubicles, they came to a door at the far end. Inside the enclosed room, an oval shape conference table sat in the middle.

"Okay," said Jack, "moment of truth. Let's see what this is." The three of them were standing around the conference table.

"Can you open it for us?" Suzanne asked Omar. "You can use these. You don't want the grease from your hands to touch the canvas." She handed him a pair of latex gloves.

Omar took the cap off from the end of the tube. Then he gently brought the canvas out and placed it on top of the table. He then placed one hand on the bottom and started to unroll it flat on the table.

"Wow," said Jack. "Now this is what a real Vallecillo looks like."

They spent a few seconds admiring the abstract image of what seemed to be a man's face in a blue triangular shape within an array of straight black lines.

"This must be the smallest Vallecillo portrait I've ever seen," said Suzanne as she gazed on the perimeters of the canvas, which appeared to be two by four feet. This was far smaller than those oil paintings by Vallecillo that she had seen at the Met.

"Yeah," said Jack, "according to the legend, this was the only canvas they could find for him in Kabul."

"Well, let's see what's behind it," said Suzanne as she turned to Omar.

He gently lifted the canvas and flipped it. Once the canvas laid flat on its backside, Suzanne's eyes fixed on the faded image that sat behind the portrait. She was looking at a clocklike image that had the Afghan numbers all around it, as well as text on the outer perimeter. The image appeared to be drawn in a simple manner, possibly with a quill pen using blue ink. It sat in the middle of the canvas, six inches in diameter surrounded by words above and underneath.

"I know that this is… a sundial," she pointed to the larger image, "but these writings…" She hovered her finger over some wording under the image.

"They're in Dari," said Omar.

"Can you read them?"

"I can try."

He started studying the text above the image. Halfway through it, his expression changed; he was not seeing what they were looking for.

"This actually is not a map." He lifted his eyes off the canvas and looked at Suzanne. "This is a blueprint."

"A blueprint?" she repeated after him.

"So, we don't even know if this was ever completed," said Jack.

Omar took his gaze down to the canvas and started reading the rest of the text.

"It's talking about the latitude and longitude and how this device should be constructed."

"Does it give the numbers for the latitude and longitude? Cause we could find the location," asked Jack.

"No… no numbers. The text only gives instruction."

Suzanne noticed Jack's stolid expression revealing disappointment that they may have came to a deadend. "These wordings here," she pointed to the letters outside the perimeter of the blueprint. "What are they?"

"They're the names of the zodiac signs in Dari," responded Omar.

"Okay, so this sundial is based on the Solar Hijri calendar. Meaning: it begins on the vernal equinox, which is thought to be the most accurate calculation, but in order for it to work properly, there're a lot of mathematics that go along with it, like the orbit of the earth, the longitude of the position and elevation, etc., numbers which we don't have on this blueprint." Said Suzanne.

"In other words, we don't know where this thing is at then," said Jack in a somber tone.

"There is this phrase in the middle of the command construction that really doesn't correspond to the two sentences that comes before and after it," said Omar. "It says, 'You follow the arrow until you stop.'"

Suzanne started scanning the canvas, but she could not see any symbol in the shape of an arrow.

"Okay, that appears to be a code from the way it's placed, looks like it's a simple one. We need to do some more digging here."

She pulled out her smartphone and started tapping on the LCD. "Did you say this canvas was handed to your grandfather by the King Amanullah himself?"

"Yes," he answered.

"According to what I found, King Amanullah was fascinated by astrology. Most likely this could be his own handwriting." She pointed to the canvas. "But this seems very simple to be a treasure map. There is definitely something missing here."

Jack felt the sudden urge to speak and say that there were a lot of things that were missing, but he fought that urge. He was taken by a new disappointment adhering to the fact that after all this time they had come to a map, which actually was the blueprint to an ancient clock that people hadn't used for nearly two hundred years.

"So, what's the plan now?" asked Jack.

Suzanne shot him a quick glance, then fixed her eyes back to the LCD screen.

"We will do more research," she said. "So, according to the British General Molesworth, those astrological codes started appearing in British India's press prior to the Third Anglo-Afghan War of 1919, which started two and half months after King Amanullah had became the ruler of Afghanistan."

"So, what does that mean?" asked Jack.

"It means," she revealed a perplexed look, "that those encrypted messages were sent by the king himself. So, he did have the possession of the astrolabe."

"Okay," said Jack, who wasn't quite intrigued by Suzanne's fascination of history.

"The question is: what did he do with it?"

"Well, King Amanullah's reign ended in early 1929 when he abdicated and went on to exile. The Afghan pseudohistory claims the British had a hand in the 1929 revolt against the king, but of course the Brits' history denies that. Also, from what I had gathered earlier, the Brits knew about the astrolabe and had made attempts to recover the module while King Amanullah was at his thorn in the 1920s."

She took a step away from the table and paced around the room. Her big brown eyes gazed in midair without a purpose as her mind kept contemplating what was within reason for the Afghan king to do at that time.

"So," she said as she turned to face Jack and Omar, who now stood a few paces behind her, "it was prudent for the king to obscure such modules that would give his enemies a great military advantage."

"Okay…" said Jack, "but the question still remains: where would he hide it?"

Omar lowered his gaze to the blueprint. Then in a flash, his eyes grew focused on the names of the zodiac signs that sat around the image. There were resemblances between this image and the one he had seen at the Gasworks Park in Seattle. He was a frequent visitor in the park on summer days where he went for an evening stroll. He would climb the thirty-foot hill that offered the perfect view of downtown Seattle over Lake Union, and there on top of the hill rested a twenty-five-foot concrete sundial, inlaid with contrasting cast bronze, ceramics, shells, and other ornaments. He recalled the time when he helped a little girl stand in the proper place, where her shadow fell on the spot that told the time. He knew exactly how to guide her to the proper place where her shadow could fall on the correct time. He had learned from his grandfather how to read a sundial. And then the memory came of his grandfather and the scent of his cigar on his clothes, as he stood behind him pointing to the sundial.

"I know where this is," said Omar. "I've seen one just like it here."

Suzanne and Jack looked at him in a skeptical way as he revealed a sudden eager look.

"Where?" Suzanne asked.

"In Paghman. But that does not really look like this blueprint."

Jack revealed a dumbfounded look. "Can you elaborate a little more?"

"Paghman is a place where my family went for holidays in the summertime. I remember on one of those trips when my grandfather took me to one of the gardens to see a sundial."

"And you said that you recall that particular one being different from this blueprint?" asked Suzanne.

"Yes… from what I remember, the actual one was much more elaborate than what's drawn here."

Jack remembered one of his missions, when their convoy had traveled through Paghman, which stood to be a popular summer destination for the residents of Kabul at one time. He recalled their older Afghan translator saying that this place had had an array of manicured gardens at one point, where the architects were summoned from Europe by a visionary king to build the elegant landscape.

"I had heard of an Afghan king who had summoned European architects to lay the foundation of the gardens in this town," said Jack.

He noticed Suzanne's eyes speedreading the content on the screen of her smartphone.

"It was him," she said, "King Amanullah."

They shared a confident look between each other, knowing that they were on to something here.

"According to these facts," said Suzanne, motioning to the content of what she just read, "King Amanullah was one of the most modernized figures of this country, and building these gardens was one of his first testaments to bringing the European culture into Afghanistan. Also, Paghman happened to be his own birthplace."

"Well then, let's go there to see if we can find this module for you," said Jack.

Suzanne abruptly turned to Omar. "Did you say the actual sundial was different from this blueprint?"

Omar's eyes beamed high in the attempt to recall his childhood memory. "There were stone figures laid flat on the ground around the outer perimeter. It didn't have written text on it."

"Okay," said Suzanne, "do you think it was the zodiac signs? Because Afghanistan uses both signs and texts to define the months in the year."

"I'm not sure what they were," said Omar.

"Well, looks like we'll find out very soon here," said Jack. He then fetched a tablet computer and took a few snapshots of the blueprint. "We will leave your Vallecillo secure here and take this with us," he hoisted the tablet and showed it to Omar.

The trio exited the conference room on their way to the next phase of the quest to find what Suzanne Bernard deemed the most threatening module to U.S. counter-terrorism. She was the only one who she thought felt the importance of this module if it had fallen in the wrong hands.

As Omar checked in his valued possession at the embassy vault, Jack had already radioed a convoy of special forces to arrive in Paghman from the Bagram Airbase with ground extraction equipment.

CHAPTER FORTY-SIX

The Black Hawk helicopter landed on a grass field at the hem of the Hindu Kush range. The patches of the green grass appeared to be the only thing that had survived the thirty-two years of war. The field seemed like an island surrounded by the piles of concrete rubble, which were the remnants of the structures that once stood in the Paghman gardens.

Paghman, a summer retreat for the residence of Kabul, was known for its rows of fruit trees and fields of flowers along with mosaic-tiled pools in its gardens. And above all, the ornament of beauty was the nearby Paghman River, which flourished up on the Hindu Kush and brought the glacier water from the mountains. It was the perfect marriage of craftsmanship and nature.

Omar stepped out of the helicopter and made his way onto the field. He fixed his eyes on his surroundings. Nothing in this place echoed any of his childhood memories. This land appeared foreign to him, and his childhood memories were buried somewhere under the piles of rubble that stretched two football fields in front of him. He started canvassing the area to see if he could recall anything from those long summer days they spent in their summer home here, but none came to his mind. This land was desolated. It looked like the ruins of an ancient city that had decayed over thousands of years, except for the process was expedited here by thousands of RPGs and bombs. He could still see the empty shells on certain part of the collected debris. This was another reality of today's Afghanistan that gloomed in his mind.

Afghanistan: a true "war-torn country," he thought.

The sound of the Black Hawk engines inevitably went quiet as the helicopter sat on the ground, awaiting their return. On the south side, the military convoy that Jack had summoned appeared to be waiting and ready to go on their mission, which in this case, was a possible digging.

"This land," said Omar, "it's nothing like I remembered."

Suzanne followed his sad gaze over the landscape that revealed only the misery of this once glorious place. She too, offered him a dishearten look that echoed his sentiment.

"This whole place is upside down, I wouldn't even know where to begin," said Omar, as his gaze lingered towards the piles of dry gray rubble made out of shards of concrete and stones.

"It is buried here somewhere, but I'm not really sure where exactly," he eyed the field some more. "This place used to have tons of trees, and there were rows of shade that covered the ground."

"Omar," said Suzanne, her voice still soft and tender, "the sundial has to be in an area where there is no shade in order for it to work."

"Yes, you are right," he said as he started pacing forward.

Shortly after, he found himself on a ledge that stretched fifty feet diagonal. There were parts of it that had been broken off, but for the most part, he could see the straight line, which was formed by packed stones and concrete.

"This was the outer edge of a reflection pool," said Omar, and then he fixed his eyes on the far end of the ledge.

As he intently looked at the broken ledge, a portion of his childhood memory loomed in his mind. He was reminded of a day when the air was crisp and fragrance from the flowers was hovering in the air like an invisible fog. He stood where his grandfather told him to stand, on top of a stone designated for early morning reading, so his body could act as a gnomon, casting his shadow to the appropriate time.

He followed the long ledge. And as his feet continued to set pace on top of the broken concrete and stone, his mind was reflecting his childhood. In a flash he was running around the long pool without a sole purpose. Suddenly, he had found himself in a time thirty years before. He could see where everything was in this garden. His pace turned to strides again, as they often did when he was a boy.

"What the hell is he doing?" said Jack as they were walking behind him. They just witnessed a grown man frantically running over mounds of ravage debris.

"I don't know," she said. "He could be on to something."

"He's running over these ruins like a mad man," said Jack.

They watched as Omar ran over a few more piles of rubble and finally came to a stop on a section forty feet away from the ledge.

"Right here!" he shouted. "This is where we need to dig!"

"Are you sure?" Jack called out to him.

"Yes!"

Jack radioed the special forces unit who had shown up with a military HMEV loader.

"It's underneath this pile," Omar said to Suzanne, who by now had made her way to where he stood.

"Okay, we'll move this stuff and see what's underneath," she said.

A few minutes later, their attention was drawn to the loader as it made its way over the piles of rubble to their direction. "I'm going to have him shovel this stuff off the ground," said Jack.

"Yeah, hopefully they won't be scraping the sundial that sits under all this stuff," said Omar.

"Well, hopefully it's still there and has not already blown up, like everything else around here," Jack remarked.

The three of them stood and watched the heavy machine shovel the debris over the spot that Omar had suggested. About five minutes later, the loader had managed to move all the large pieces that sat on top of the area, revealing only earth underneath. Clearly this was not something that they wanted to see. There was no concrete structure beneath the rubble here.

"This is not looking good," said Jack. "I don't see any concrete sundial here."

Omar took a few steps forward and squatted down on the cleared area. He scraped some dirt from the ground and started examining it.

This dirt is like powder, he thought. Then his mind rested on an article that he had read about fifteen years earlier.

"This whole field was flooded about fifteen years ago. We need to dig deeper."

"Omar, these ruins are not the result of a flood. They were blown up," said Jack.

"I know," countered Omar. "The flood came afterwards. Look, this is powder-like dirt that gets carried out with the flood water." He held out the dirt on his palm for Jack to see.

"Okay, if you say so." Jack called on his radio to the loader's operator, "Keep going until you hit something hard."

They stood and watched the machine shovel away the compacted dirt on the ground. A few minutes later, they heard the metal shovel of the equipment scrape against concrete.

"Looks like we found it!" said Suzanne in eager voice.

The machine operator hoisted the shovel a little higher, where the blade hovered over the concrete. He then lightly started moving the dirt without touching the hard surface beneath.

"That's enough," said Jack in his radio. "We need the water."

The loader moved backwards to give way to the Navistar water truck that started making its way on the field.

Omar kneeled on a corner of the surface. He clawed his fingers into the hardened brown mud and started extracting until he reached the concrete a couple inches underneath. "What's the PSI on that thing?" he asked.

"Not really sure." Jack shrugged. "It's pretty powerful. It'll clear this up very quick."

"No." said Omar, "this ground was frozen many times over and over, that concrete is very fragile, and that thing could ruin the surface. Could they tone down the PSI?"

"Yeah, they have a small utility hose that they could use instead of the fire hose," said Jack, referring to the garden-size hose that was mounted on the water truck to provide water on a small scale, mostly for the radiators of other military vehicles.

"Okay, even with that, the water has to fall straight down like rain. I think that's the best way to preserve the surface."

"Alright," said Jack, "I'll tell them to be gentle."

The images of the concrete patterns started to loom as the water washed the layer of mud that had sat on the sundial for more than a decade. Suzanne's keen eyes started to follow the trace of water as it rolled off the cement surface. After a lingering gaze, it became clear to her that Omar was right. This wet image was not like the one they had seen behind the Vallecillo. This was more elaborate. There were blue, green, and sapphire tiles mixed with colorful glass in the outer perimeter. On the inner perimeter rested pieces of bronze within the concrete that resembled the shapes of the zodiac signs. She took a few paces forward, bringing herself in the center of the sundial.

"Do we know what we're looking for here?" she heard Jack's voice behind her.

"There was something on the text," she said.

"Follow the arrow," called Omar.

"Well, the only arrow I see is on that figure right there," said Jack.

"The Sagittarius," Suzanne called out. "Generally the Sagittarius points its arrow at the heart of the Scorpion, but not here."

Suzanne turned to Omar, bearing a skeptical look. "Are you sure you didn't read anything else possibly affiliated with that phrase?"

"No, as far as I remember it said, 'follow the arrow.'"

Suzanne looked across the ruined field over to the other side, where she saw the image of a white structure in the distance.

"What's that?" she asked, pointing her finger to the structure.

"Its called Taq-e-Zafar. It means Arch of Victory. It was built after the Third Anglo War to commemorate Afghanistan's victory over the British by King Amanullah," said Omar.

Suzanne gazed at the image of the Sagittarius, a Centaur, holding a bow and an arrow.

The Archer's arrow is pointing to the arch instead of the scorpion. She lifted her gaze and followed the direction of the arrow to the Arch of Victory.

"We need to go this way," she pointed the direction.

They begin walking over the field of ravaged concrete towards the arch structure that sat three hundred yards in front of them. This arch resembled the Arc de Triomphe in Paris, but at the fraction of the size. The European architecture inspired King Aamanullah to built the triumphal arch after defeating the Brits. The arch echoed his vision to move Afghanistan towards a more European society.

They walked on the pathway made from shards of white limestone leading to the main arch. The structure was supported by two Greek concrete pillars and sat above a cement platform. The top part of this structure was made of two layers hoisting a solid curve. Underneath the arch, a mosaic of white marble and limestone with wording inked in black was plastered on the curvature.

Suzanne's eyes fell on the plaque that hung horizontally by two metal chains in the center of the two pillars.

1919.

Suzanne wasn't astound when she saw the numbers 1919 hanging down from this plaque in Paghman, Afghanistan. She remembered vividly the occasional appearance of that number throughout her research over the last two years regarding this ancient astrological module. What puzzled her most was that the year 1919 commemorated the Gregorian calendar, while the whole country used the Solar Hijri calendar. She eyed the foundation of the arch for any writing that resembled astrology.

"This part was destroyed during the war," said Omar. "They recently rebuilt this."

Suzanne gazed at the columns only to discover the freshly laid plaster with the bright white color that deflected the sunlight. "I can see that."

"What are we looking for?" asked Jack.

"I'm not sure yet. Something maybe out of pattern… or something that has to do with a sign."

As they approached the Taq-e-Zafar, Suzanne fixed her eyes on the writings on the curvature that hovered twenty feet above them.

"Can you read these?" she asked Omar.

"They're only names," he said, "probably the names of those who died in the war."

Suzanne stood there for a few moments and scanned the arc. She wasn't exactly sure what they were looking for, but she knew that something was out of the ordinary or out of context. She took a few steps forward and went outside the structure. Then she turned back and looked at it from the outside.

Nothing.

She then walked around the left side. As she made her way around the ten-foot concrete support, she saw a wooden panel sitting above the cement base of the structure ten feet above the ground.

"This wooden board does not have a structural purpose," she said.

"It could be a ventilation shaft or something," said Jack, who was standing behind her now.

"Let me take a look," said Omar. And he put his right foot on a ledge—halfway in the middle of the base—and hoisted himself up to the surface of the concrete base. He then tiptoed to the front. He pushed on the panel, but it didn't move. Something was holding it. He then placed his fingers around the seam and pulled. The panel opened.

"It's dark here," he called out after peering inside the shaft.

"Here," Jack produced a LED flashlight from the side pocket of his ACU and tossed it to him.

Omar pointed the flashlight in the hollow space that measured three feet wide and six feet in height. He did not see any vents leading to the top. The LED reflected from the side walls without showing any type of texture. But as the light hit the back wall, he caught something.

"I think you might want to see this," he called out from inside the shaft.

Suzanne climbed on top of the concrete base and then squeezed her way into the shaft. Once inside, she squatted in front of the rear wall where she saw writings engraved on the concrete.

"I need more light," she handed Omar another LED to shine on the back wall.

She cleared the cobwebs with a swipe of her hand, which made the engraved writings conspicuous. Then her eyes sharpened on the image before her.

"This is a calendar," she said. "I've seen engraved Mayan calendars that looks pretty similar to this, but not quite the same."

The three-foot circular image was meticulously carved into a stone slab within the cement wall. It had a clock shape, but instead of the twelve numbers, the zodiac signs were carved on the outer perimeter. And in the inner circle, there were numbers depicted days to the corresponding months that the signs represented. In the center of the engraved slab, there were two brass arms in the shape of arrows. She touched one of those brass arms and felt it rotate clockwise.

"I think this is a combination lock," she said, looking at the two arrows that extended out from a center like the hands of a clock, except the two arrows were of equal length. The base in the center had a slight play when she pulled on it. She eyed the surroundings of the stone for more clues, but all she saw was the zodiac signs and the numbers below it. But then her eyes fell on some faint text at the bottom of the surface, which was carved in Dari.

"Omar, what does this say?"

Omar moved to get a closer look at the letters on the bottom of the slab.

"It's a riddle," he said. "It says: 'find the perfect match between two fires.'"

Suzanne took a moment to ponder what she just heard. *Find the perfect match between two fires. Fire… the three fire signs. Aries, Leo, and Sagittarius.*

She remembered from earlier that it was the disproportionate arrow of the Sagittarius in the sundial that pointed them to this place.

Sagittarius has to be one of those fire signs.

She took a close look at the numbers inside the inner perimeter below the Sagittarius sign.

These numbers are written in English. Afghanistan uses an Arabic numbers system, so why are these numbers engraved in English?

She recalled the previous English number that she had seen on the blueprint and the plaque outside. *1919.*

The year of the Third Anglo War, when King Amanullah claimed Afghanistan's victory from the British, a date plastered in English number system.

If the number system is in English, then the months should be in English, too.

She looked at the zodiac signs outside the circle. *They mimic the western months.* Her mind swirled to the basic principles of algorithms. *Use the numbers at hand first.*

She split *1919* in her mind; she converted the first apparent zodiac fire sign, Sagittarius, to the English calendar.

December 19.

She moved the lower hand on the slab over to the number *19* under the Sagittarius sign. Then she started to move the other arrow to Aries, the second fire sign that the riddle suggested.

April 19.

As the second arm came hovering on top of the proper place, she heard a click. When she looked down to the right, she saw a brass lever that had popped out on the bottom right of the slab. She pulled the lever and heard a rumbling sound in the background as the balancing weight, tied with metal cables, moved the slab inwards like an opening of a door. Behind it was a space the size of a five-foot cube. And in the center of it sat a chest—three feet in length, two feet tall, and two feet deep. Suzanne unlocked the leather straps and opened the lid. She was looking at the leather cover of a large book that sat well-preserved inside. She lifted the cover on the eight hundred-page binding, and on the first page she saw the image of an astrolabe, meticulously handdrawn.

CHAPTER FORTY-SEVEN

Omar found himself on the narrow pathway of his grandfather's house once again. He had come to grab his belongings. Tomorrow he was going to leave Afghanistan with the American agents. The U.S. government had offered to take him to London, where he prompted a deal to sell his Vallecillo portrait. After this agonizing time in Afghanistan, he should be grateful for it to be over. Now he could go back to his hometown of Seattle as a very rich man. But he was reluctant to feel that way. There was something else eating him up: the promise he made to an old dying woman, one who stayed loyal to him, more than anyone he knew.

"Promise me that you will find my granddaughter and look after her," she had said in her last few breaths after telling him the whereabouts of the Vallecillo.

"I promise," he reassured her.

He made his way on the path to the maid quarters while his mind kept repeating his own voice making that promise. He swung the door open and entered the room. His gaze fell on his clothing, no longer left scattered throughout the room as he had left them. Instead, they were all nicely folded and placed on top of the wooden table.

Somebody has been here, he thought. He might have been angered by someone touching his personal belongings, but then he remembered he was in Kabul. Hospitality is offered on a whole different scale here.

"I was told to wash your clothes. I hope I didn't ruin them." He turned to see a young girl standing outside, peering into the room from the doorstep.

He remembered her from the first night when he returned to this house. Even more so, he remembered Commander Khaled's triumphal, heroic story of rescuing her from the human trafficker. She stood still in the doorway, her green headscarf curled at the bottom, covering her face, only revealing her eyes, a pair of radiant emeralds contrasting her light brown complexion. Her long tunic, green and blue, had handcrafted miniature mirrors in the shape of a V that covered the front. She was an average height, around five foot four inches tall, but her persona carried her larger than her size. She seemed far too mature for her age, which could've been a testament to the endurance of hardship, one that had robbed many young Afghan girls of their naïve phase.

"It's Hawa… right? That's your name?"

The girl nodded but remained motionless, with her eyes quizzically fixed on Omar as if she wanted to hear something else.

"I don't think you have ruined my clothes," he said. "I'm quite grateful that they are clean now."

Omar fetched his duffle bag from the corner of the room and placed it on the table. He then grabbed a stack of the neatly folded items and placed them inside the bag.

"You go back to America?" she asked.

"Yes."

For a second he choked up on that word. His conscience gave him a solid reminder of his promise to the old woman. But then, he knew he couldn't stay longer this time. The agents had made the deal with him to leave Kabul ASAP. He had to come back again after he made the transaction. That way he would have a lot of bribe money to spend. He needed a plan on how to go about that, which he hadn't pondered yet.

"The commander told me the tale of your bravery," he said.

He noticed her eyes were downcast; he clearly broached a sensitive subject. He instantly regretted the statement.

"I'm very sorry. I forget my manners sometimes."

"It's alright," she said. He caught the faint image of her lips moving behind the green nylon scarf.

"It's very sad that the Taliban would abduct young girls to sell to that Arab man."

Her eyes grew keen as she shook her head.

"I was not abducted…"

"You were not?"

"No. I was sold."

A layer of moisture instantly formed in her eyes. He wanted to say something, other than being sorry. He needed something uplifting to attest to her self-worth.

"Now I understand why you chose not to go back to your own house. It's hard to go back to parents who would do such thing."

The girl's eyes closed and then reopened.

"Sorry, the commander told me the story."

"They were not my parents."

Omar grew curious about what she just told him. For a second, he stood quiet, wondering whether she was going to tell him anything further. He had pondered her presence here. He couldn't really get his head wrapped around why she stood there and had a conversation with him, considering that they did not know each other. It definitely wasn't a trait of young Afghan women to go and start a conversation with random men, in her case, a houseguest who was just about to leave.

"I came here to ask you something," she said, and with that she relieved him of his awkward feelings about her presence.

"Sure, please do."

"I emptied your pockets when I was about to wash your clothes. I found this in the pocket of your pants." She held out her hand, and on her palm sat the old wristwatch that was given to him by the medics after Nakebakht had died.

He took a few paces towards her and then reached and picked up the watch from her extended hand. He eyed the plate. The color had faded through years of oxidation to a gray, except for the outer seams of the circle where he could still see the original gold-plate in a fainted yellow. The band had also changed color from what used to be brown to now black with creases in the leather.

He lifted his eyes from the watch and connected with hers.

"Have you seen this before?" he asked, following his intuition.

"It belonged to my mother."

It came clear to him. He had seen those set of eyes before, that distinct emerald color that could change from dark to bright under the sunlight. Once again, he had found himself in the same room, in the presence of Rizwan. The two of them were together again, seventeen years later. He felt his eyes welling up. He lifted his chin and looked up to the ceiling, gasping for a deep breath. Suddenly he felt his knees giving in. He found himself slumping on the ground. Everything had gone dark in an instant.

From far away, he heard a faint sound repeatedly calling for him to wakeup. Then there was movement. He could feel the constant shaking of his body propelled by two hands gripping around his right arm, rocking him back and forth as he lay sideways on the ground.

"Wake up!" He heard her voice again.

He opened his eyes and found himself collapsed on the room's floor. He was okay. It may have been fatigue, which had brought him down, but no… he hoisted himself up and sat.

As he turned towards her, he noticed her scarf absent and her face unveiled as she kneeled by his side. Without any hesitation, he wrapped his arms around her and pulled her tight against his chest in an embrace that he would not release her from anytime soon. He had already seen what he needed to see. Her narrow face and pointy chin were a mirror reflection of his. It became clear to him at last. It wasn't the deeds of his uncle Wali that drove Nakebakht and Rizwan out of this house on the fall of 1987. It was what he had done with Rizwan on that summer night when he was provoked by Wali. Rizwan allowed him to please himself when she lay next to him. It was his action and her silence. He recalled one morning, a few days before their departure, when Rizwan was sick. He asked her if she was okay. She said: "I think I've got the jaundice." Now, it all made sense. She didn't have the jaundice. She was pregnant. All the years he wondered about what his uncle Wali did that resulted in them losing their home, and today, Wali was exonerated. This was all his deed. He was never going to find out what was said on that day. The inevitable silence would carry on: everyone involved was now dead. The only truth he knows now is the one staring him in the face. His daughter.

CHAPTER FORTY-EIGHT

Suzanne had the book opened on top of a table inside the FBI's attaché office within Kabul's embassy. On the right side of the room, she had a laptop that transmitted the information via a secure VPN to the NSA database back in Fort Meade, Maryland. She held a laser scanner in her hand and was running the one-foot diagonal device over every page of the large book. After each page was scanned, she checked the computer screen to make sure that all contents were shown exactly as they appeared in the module. Other than the zodiac signs that she could recognize, there were a lot of other signs that she had not seen before. Some of them seemed to be constellations and star clusters, which she thought would give a good run to the agency's astronomers. By far, this was one of the most sophisticated, if not *the* sophisticated piece of fifteenth-century artifact that was ever discovered.

When she was halfway through her scanning process, she heard the buzzing of her phone.

"Yes," she answered.

"Is the process complete?" said Steve Williams's baritone voice.

"It's getting there. Maybe another twenty minutes."

"Okay, good," he said, followed by a pause. "There is someone else on the line who has further instruction for you."

Suzanne anticipated the *"someone else,"* who remained anonymous. Generally, Steve Williams makes the introduction, but not this time. She had a good idea about the identity of those people who worked behind a layer of anonymity.

"Dr. Bernard," the voice rang. "It appears you've been proven right. I congratulate you on the discovery."

"Thank you, sir," Suzanne answered, but remained skeptical about the true intent of this person.

"Dr. Bernard," the man's voice rang again, "there will be two men arriving within the next hour to take that module off your hands."

"Sir, that was not part of the plan!" she said in an agitated tone.

"It is now," the man's voice corrected in a firm tone. "Please give precise direction on how to place the module in the same place where it was retrieved, so there will remain no trace of its discovery."

"I beg your pardon sir, but I don't really get it," said Suzanne.

"Suzanne," she heard Steve Williams's voice again, "there have been some new developments, and a new plan has been put in place."

Suzanne took a second to absorb what she just heard, and as she dove into contemplation, the man's voice appeared again.

"Dr. Bernard, we were watching your whole operation. Remember, the NSA is only the ears, but we are the eyes!"

Suzanne wanted to resist their plan. This discovery was part of her extensive research over the last couple of years. Then she thought it through and eased up her personal sentiments.

"Okay," she said. "I will do everything necessary."

"Thank you, Dr. Bernard," the man's voice said. "The NSA will have an exact copy of the module, therefore, the actual hardcopy is no longer needed. Isn't that correct?"

"Yes… that's correct," she answered.

"Good. Now we need to make sure the Vallecillo gets sold to the same people who signaled the Marks to go radio silent. We are confident that it will through that British art dealer."

"Okay," she agreed and hung up the phone.

Jack entered the room holding two cups of coffee in his hands.

"Here. Not exactly Startbucks, but not bad, either. Didn't know if you took cream with yours."

He placed the cups on the table.

"Looks like the CIA wants the module now," said Suzanne.

Jack revealed an ironic smile. "Well, that's nothing new. But don't worry, they'll screw it up and send it back to the FBI."

"Huh," she sighed, "they're going to put it back in the same place, exactly as we found it," she said, eyeing Jack intently.

"And let me guess…" he said. "They are going to follow the money, hoping to find the next person who comes after it."

"Yes, something like that."

"Okay… you've got what you needed, so let them have it." He shrugged.

༄

Two hours earlier, The national security advisor had called a meeting with the directors of the FBI and the CIA. The director of the FBI initiated the urgent meeting after the bureau's chief forensic scientist stormed into his office about the latest discovery.

An hour prior to that meeting, the forensic team had received the scans of tissue sample from the Bagram Airbase in Afghanistan. The tissue was taken from the corpse of an enemy combative who had died earlier in an operation conducted by a team of special forces. Unlike the previous tissue samples from the Taliban insurgents, these tissues showed a trace of porcine growth hormone, where the properties of the hormone did not show the same content that is used in the U.S. This hormone had different properties that affected the human brain, as opposed to the common porcine, which enhanced muscle and bone growth. The FBI forensic team could definitively say that this hormone was meticulously engineered for a purpose, which they did not know as of yet.

CHAPTER FORTY-NINE

The sun had set behind the Asmayee Mountain. There was a red cast of the sun's rays glowing in the Kabul sky as the evening approached. Suzanne had finished the scanning process and given over possession of the module to the two CIA agents who showed up in the embassy a few moments earlier.

"Ready to go home?" she heard Jack's voice behind her as they stood in the embassy's courtyard awaiting Omar's arrival.

"I'm ready to go to sleep," she answered, giving him a mild smile.

"Well, from the way things look, we might have to be in London for a couple of days."

She pondered the idea. "Maybe I could finally walk around that city as a tourist," she said.

"Maybe I could even show you a few places there," Jack remarked.

She turned and made eye contact with him, but then coyly turned away.

"I meant… maybe I'd take you some place where you could see those signs that you like," he chuckled.

She let out a slight laugh. "I'm sure you will."

The Humvee that was dispatched to bring Omar made its way through the embassy's gate into the compound. Suzanne and Jack shared a perplexed look as they saw Omar emerge from the vehicle making his way towards them. On his right side there was an Afghan girl, wearing the traditional Afghan woman's clothes. He motioned to her to stay by the vehicle.

"Ready to go home?" asked Jack as he neared, but then his eyes fell over his shoulder to the girl who was waiting by the vehicle.

Suzanne noticed a shade of somberness on Omar's face, one that wasn't there a couple of hours ago when they parted. It appeared he had been emotionally distressed. She could see the redness in his eyes.

"Omar," she softened her tone, "who is she?"

His gaze fell to the ground. "She is my daughter." He answered in a choked up voice. "And she goes where I go."

Suzanne and Jack shared a glance. They knew this was not something in which they could intervene. The only thing was the logistics of the matter that they had to see about.

"You know there will be red tape around this," said Jack as he looked at Omar, who by now revealed a sudden disappointment. "But, I think we can cut that red tape."

Omar took notice of the grinning faces of Suzanne and Jack, which gave him the assurance he needed of Hawa going with him. Tears of joy welled up in his eyes. He used his sleeve to wipe them away.

"Let's get your Vallecillo and then go about seeing the ambassador," said Jack. "We'll be flying out tonight, and you'll meet your friend Peter Wilson tomorrow in London."

They started walking towards the building. "You need to bring her along with you," said Jack.

"What's her name?" asked Suzanne.

"Hawa," he answered in a joyous tone.

An hour later, the four of them were boarded the Gulfstream jet on their way to London. Omar looked to his right and noticed his daughter anxiously trying to strap herself in with the seatbelt. He closed his eyes and reconciled himself to his fate. He pondered all the things unknown to him prior to coming to Afghanistan. And as he took another glimpse of his daughter by his side, a feeling of contentment soothed him in knowing that a part of himself had been alive for all these years and now was sitting next to him.

To be continued on the next sequel.

www.ingramcontent.com/pod-product-compliance
Ingram Content Group UK Ltd.
Pitfield, Milton Keynes, MK11 3LW, UK
UKHW041256160325
5017UKWH00016B/58/J